Bureau of Medicine and Surgery, Joseph Wilson

Naval Hygiene

Human health and the means of preventing disease, with illustrative incidents

principally derived from naval experience

Bureau of Medicine and Surgery, Joseph Wilson

Naval Hygiene
Human health and the means of preventing disease, with illustrative incidents principally derived from naval experience

ISBN/EAN: 9783337368678

Printed in Europe, USA, Canada, Australia, Japan

Cover: Foto ©Andreas Hilbeck / pixelio.de

More available books at **www.hansebooks.com**

NAVAL HYGIENE.

HUMAN HEALTH

AND THE

MEANS OF PREVENTING DISEASE,

WITH

ILLUSTRATIVE INCIDENTS PRINCIPALLY DERIVED FROM
NAVAL EXPERIENCE.

Y

JOSEPH WILSON, M.D.,

MEDICAL DIRECTOR U. S. NAVY.

SECOND EDITION.

WITH COLORED LITHOGRAPHS, ETC.

PHILADELPHIA:
LINDSAY & BLAKISTON.
1879.

PREFACE.

THE plan and object of this work have not materially changed.

Not intended exclusively for the use of medical officers, it has been found very useful in imparting information to others, to whom, in many contingencies, questions of vital importance must eventually be referred. Thus the business of the medical officer is greatly facilitated. "A little knowledge" is found to be a very good thing, the more of it the better; it is so very much better than mere ignorance.

A few botanical illustrations have been added, selected partly from Pereira, some of the poisonous plants from Fonssagrives; and their elegant appearance is principally due to the good taste of Mr. Hugo Siebold.

Some important reforms, previously insisted on, have been so far accomplished, that it is thought convenient at present to be very brief in their discussion. This affords an opportunity to introduce important new matter, without too much increasing the size of the volume.

HOLMESBURG, PHILADELPHIA,
    January, 1879.

PREFACE TO THE FIRST EDITION.

THE present work was prepared for publication, with the hope of being useful to some of those who are so situated, that their conduct may have great influence in the preservation of human health.

Such are the captains of ships on long voyages, who, without such information as we have attempted to give, are liable to destroy the health and consequent efficiency of their ship's company, by ignorance or inattention to some apparently insignificant circumstance, which they may easily understand.

As the work is not intended exclusively for the professional reader, it was necessary to keep within the compass of a moderate sized volume, and to avoid subjects too abstruse or too technical for the general reader. I have tried to discuss intelligibly, and as fully as consistent with the general plan, the leading principles of hygienic management.

CONTENTS.

ILLUSTRATIONS.

LITHOGRAPHS.

INTRODUCTORY.

HYGIENE treats of the means of preserving human health.

Health is the regular action of the bodily organism, under the influence of the forces of the universe upon the material world, by which we are surrounded.

Heat, light, and electricity are the principal forces constantly present to our thoughts. These are probably modes of motion in a material that pervades the universe, as far as the most distant visible star, as incompressible as water, and many thousands of times lighter than hydrogen. We must wait for some future Newton or Ampere, to demonstrate and reduce to more simple formulæ, more of the characters of these forces—the properties of this all-pervading form of matter. Besides their controlling influence on climate, we are familiar with their controlling power over health and life in many ways. We may be injured or killed by lightning; we may be burned or frozen, besides suffering other injuries from variations of temperature. In regard to the influence of light, our information is not so precise. People living in dark places are pale, and are supposed to be sickly and weak, as potatoes growing in the cellar are pale and weak; but workmen in coal mines are not always weak, and if they are short-lived, there are other circumstances to account for it. We are greatly in want of more precise information on the physiological action of light.

The atmosphere is a very important and complicated subject of study. It is composed of mixed gases in nearly uniform proportions, and an infinity of minute particles of almost every substance in nature. Variations in the proportions of gaseous constituents are important, and when excessive, occasionally fatal to life ; but slight variations, such as frequently occur, seem to be without serious influence on health. The chemical examination of the leading constituents is easily enough made; but the minute quantity of almost unknown matter, sometimes causing disease and death, is, for the most part, beyond the reach of chemical research. The contagion of variola may be smelled, but chemical analysis does not reveal its presence. The same may be said of typhus. Other infectious matter is known to be present in the atmosphere, not by the smell, not by chemical analysis, but by the fact that persons inhaling the air of a certain locality, at a certain time, are subsequently affected by a specific disease; as in cases of scarlatina and rubeola, typhoid and cholera, yellow fever and the malarial fevers. Chemical analysis, however, is of essential importance, for contamination with dangerous infectious material, under certain circumstances, goes on in proportion to the change in leading constituents. In ordinary respiration the air is deprived of oxygen, and contaminated by excess of *carbon-dioxyde*, very nearly if not exactly in the same proportion as it is contaminated by *pulmonary* and *cutaneous* exhalations.

We are hoping for more information from the microscope. The air everywhere is full of floating particles, some of them, in the sunbeam, visible to the naked eye. They vary in size from the thousandth of a centimeter (M .00001) to objects infinitessimally minute. Some are mineral particles; some, fragments of all kinds of organic material, of wool and feathers and hair, of silk and grass and flax—the species and amount depending principally on the locality. But, besides these, there are an infinity of distinct organic forms,—the pollen of flowers, the spores of fungi and other cryptogams, even entire plants, the grains of starch, and other objects much more minute, which have never been specifically recognized. It is suspected that some of these minute objects are the poison germs of *variola, scarlatina, typhoid, typhus, malaria, yellow fever,* and nearly all the other infectious diseases received through the atmosphere. It has been objected that these poison germs have not been recognized, perhaps never seen; but the objection should not discourage hopeful inquiry, when we consider the vast amount of evidence pointing in this direction. For it is a constant miracle of our race, that stout men and women, by proper nourishment and proper surroundings, are developed from an organism so minute as not to be seen by the most powerful microscope. This particle of minuteness after some growth, is seen by a microscope magnifying a thousand diameters, as a mere speck. In a few days more it is big enough to show definite size and form under the microscope; and yet this minuteness is the potential man or woman of determined features, even to the color of the hair and size of the nose, the predisposition to drunkenness or epilepsy, phthisis or insanity. Who then shall say that specific poisons in the air are not definite organisms, merely because no one as yet has detected them? The spread of infectious diseases is in accordance with the theory of definite organisms, floating like thistle-down through the air. Such movement would capriciously plant them on the individual, the danger increasing very rapidly with the nearness of the source (inversely as the cube of the distance). If it were a case of the diffusion of poisonous gases, or other matter soluble in the atmosphere, all should be poisoned, the severity of the disease being in proportion to the amount of the poison inhaled. It is thus with known poisons, as the fumes of arsenic and phosphorus, lead and mercury, hydrogen-sulphide and zinc. Our most reliable test at the present time, of the presence of poisons in the atmosphere, is the fact that persons visiting the suspected locality suffer from the specific disease. How else do we know that certain marshes are malarious? How else do we know that variola and rubeola and typhus are contagious? Sometimes we know that the atmosphere is impure, and even judge of the kind of impurity by the sense of smell. Sometimes we judge by chemical analysis. Sometimes we know that poisons are being thrown into the air from certain manufactories.

Water comes next in physiological importance; it is a principal constituent of the human body, so that we constantly need it for nourishment. When water for domestic use is grossly bad, we are likely to be informed by the color, smell, or taste; and our powers of discrimination in this respect, may be greatly increased by the careful cultivation of our senses, so that they often give us very precise information.

The microscopic examination of water is fruitful in important results, not often of itself, but in connection with other circumstances. The presence of a fibre of cotton or linen, silk or wool, is of itself unimportant, but it indicates, with great probability, that human filth from a leaky drain is mingled with the water. But nearly all water, good and bad, contains a multiplicity of visible objects—some unimportant, as the earthy particles constituting mud. Many living things are nearly always present and cannot indicate harm, but only that the water is not quite bad enough to kill them. Two or three species are present only in good water, as almost any kind of impure water destroys them. Some species are much more common in dirty or marsh water; some are positively dangerous, such as the joints and eggs of tapeworm and other entozoa. Many are so small and so regularly rounded in form, as not to be easily distinguished from each other. Some, doubtlessly, are so minute as to escape observation altogether.

The chemical examination of water is, perhaps, still more important, and so far as possible, should always be quantitive. Chlorine is always present in small quantities without much significance, but any considerable increase of the quantity in water from any particular source, indicates probable contamination by sewage. The mineral constituents always present in varying minute quantities, are doubtless useful as nutriment; but varying proportions of these, so far as we know, are of no account. The greater or less proportion of organic matter in solution, is an important matter to determine, though the importance is not always in proportion to the amount present, for water contaminated by peat is generally wholesome, while much less contamination by sewage is very dangerous. Thus in order to determine the character of water, it is necessary to consider all these circumstances—source, sensible characters, chemistry, and microscopy. The really bad character of water, sometimes, can only be determined by having persons drink of it. Such is water contaminated by typhoid infection. Of course we do not propose this method of testing suspected water; but people will perform this experiment on themselves, in spite of us, and we may have an opportunity to observe the result and to record it. The facts we possess, demonstrate that very small quantities of organic matter in water may produce terrifically fatal epidemics, while very much larger quantities of other organic material may do no appreciable harm.

Food and clothing likewise require chemical and microscopic examinations,—sometimes with reference to crime, such as suspected poisoning, or more frequently mere swindling. Every board of health has employment for an expert chemist, with the conveniences of a small laboratory.

Naval Hygiene is popularly considered as the art of preserving health on board ship, and thus we might have naval hygiene and city hygiene, a special hygiene of farmers and of merchants, of weavers and of tailors, of carpenters and of masons, of millers and of lapidaries. Popular treatises on this plan and on these several subjects have been found exceedingly useful. But human health is so nearly the same everywhere, that to the student of science there is no special hygiene. The hygiene of the weaver is merely a chapter of general hygiene, illustrated by the study of the effect of inhaling dust and working in a confined atmosphere. The hygiene of the carpenter supplies opportunities to observe the effect of varied out-door exercise, with occasional exposure to dust in close apartments. The house-painter's hygiene is similar, with the addition that he handles and inhales more or less of his poisonous paints. But what condition of life is free from the occasional inhalation of dust, of poisonous fumes, of confined or otherwise impure atmosphere. And so of Naval Hygiene. It is but a contribution to general hygiene, with some of its illustrations drawn from incidents of naval experience.

Since this work has been in press, I have visited some parts of the State of Colorado, and have had some curious experience in illustration of the above view of the case, and reminding me that the prophylaxis of hydrophobia belongs to naval hygiene. In the City of Pueblo, in the forenoon, I was walking on

* *

the east side of the principal avenue, looking at objects in the shop windows, when suddenly I felt something at my elbow, and there was a great black dog which had seized me from behind. He pinched pretty hard and tore through three thicknesses of cloth. The dog evidently belonged to a wagon, the horses of which were tied to an awning post, and he had probably been trained to defend his master's wagon in this manner, for in the course of a minute or two that I remained in the nearest store, he attacked several other persons in the same manner, always retreating under his wagon. The dog and his owner were taken care of by the witnesses and the bitten.

The arm, on first examination, was thought not to be wounded at all, the only apparent harm being a little pinching and tearing of clothes. This, however, did not quite satisfy me, especially as I felt a smarting point on the surface, and by a closer inspection with a pocket lens, it was evident that the cuticle was slightly abraded. Here are the characteristic particulars of the causation in the majority of the cases of hydrophobia; if I should suffer, the dog is evidently mad; if I should escape, the dog, of course, is a healthy dog—an uncommonly good dog zealously defending his master's property. To avoid needlessly alarming friends I sought a tinsmith, in order that with a white-hot soldering-iron, this little speck of skin might be converted into smoke and ashes; but, so far as I could learn, there is no tin worker in the city, and a friend did me the favor to burn the spot with a cigar, which he puffed vigorously to make a glowing end, and he applied it several times. The part was deeply burned, hardened, and blackened, but not removed. The next morning at Colorado Springs, the sight of a blacksmith shop reminded me that hot iron may be found even in Colorado; and as fire insurance is considered reasonable prudence against a minor misfortune, I made up my mind to be reasonably prudent in regard to the hydrophobia risk. But the hot-iron in the smith's shop seemed a little too dramatic, the smith might refuse, and I found a physician who did me the favor to dissolve the injured tissue by means of strong nitric acid. If the others were not otherwise wounded than through several thicknesses of clothing, and if they were as cautious—we shall probably hear no more of this dog's doings.

After this long digression, it may be well to continue the subject a little longer. Does the prevention of hydrophobia belong to the subject of naval hygiene? Yes, or at any rate the emergency has occurred in naval experience. In 1846, in California, by command of Commodore Robert Stockton, there was formed a regiment of mounted riflemen—an amphibious little army on horseback. While encamped with this naval force at the Mission of San Juan Batisto, about midnight, I was aroused from sleep by my companion, who informed me that he had been bitten in the foot by a mad dog. Luckily he slept with his boots on, and the fangs did not penetrate the leather. But, notwithstanding a pretty general alarm of the camp, three men were actually wounded; two in the face and one through the hand. I have to reproach myself with inefficiency in the care of these cases. I knew of the terrific death to be apprehended, and was aware of good authority for amputating the hand, but this seemed too strong a measure, and besides it left two cases unprovided for. The good spirit did not remind me of the hot-iron, which, with the help of the horse-shoer, I might readily have applied. The remedies actually used were so much like nothing in this serious emergency, that they need not be mentioned at all. No further serious result occurred to the men, who remained under observation for nearly a year. An account of these cases exists in the medical history of a cruise of the U. S. Frigate Savannah, on file in the Bureau of Medicine and Surgery. To complete the history of my experience on this subject:—In 1840, Charles Baker, of Philadelphia, teased a pet dog till after much snapping it finally bit his finger. He gave it a cuff for its crossness, and thought no more of the matter. It afterwards bit two children that had been accustomed to play with it. Baker became my unhappy patient and died of hydrophobia. *Am. Jour. Med. Sci.* In 1851, in the same neighborhood, Henry Bender found his pet dog in the stable, very cross with his horse. It bit the horse and himself too, before he succeeded in driving it away. It likewise bit a child before he was able to give the alarm. Mr. B. soon after died of hydrophobia. The child escaped, and is now a healthy woman more than thirty years old.

Here we have a record of (9) nine persons wounded by the bites of dogs; (5) five of these were bitten by mad dogs, and one of the five died of hydrophobia; (4) four, including myself, were bitten by dogs supposed to be healthy until the subsequent development of disease, and one of the four died of hydrophobia. These few numbers thus placed, suggest the possible fallacy of some of our statistical tables constructed without a proper analysis of the records from which the numbers are taken. Some of them are constructed without any record whatever of important incidents necessary to any useful analysis. This valuable modern method of study, from want of due consideration, has already imposed some fallacies upon the world.

NAVAL HYGIENE.

CHAPTER I.

THE OUTFIT—THE SHIP.

(1.) In the summer of 1860, I reported at the Philadelphia navy yard for sea-service. The first duty is to obtain a suitable outfit of medicines, surgical instruments, disinfectants and deodorizers, and other needful appliances; and this having been properly attended to, we leisurely survey the ship which is to be our home for a year or two or more.

(2.) The form of the ship is controlled by the circumstance that it must be propelled through the water with the greatest facility. Every other consideration gives way to this; and hence the form is the same in all ages and in all countries. There is less variety of internal arrangements than would readily be imagined. Thus, in a very small vessel we have simply the hold, with a single deck over it. When the vessel is larger there are added one, two or more decks, like the stories of a house; the hold is divided into several parts by transverse partitions, and the space between decks into store-rooms, sleeping-rooms, and cabins. These we examine in detail.

(3.) Beginning above, we have first the *spar-deck*, which in our ship carries the battery. This is the only place where we can be in the open air at sea. It is, hence, the place of a little daily exercise for the whole ship's company. The seamen get their exercise by their regular work, and the officers by walking back and forth as they find it convenient.

(4.) The after part of the spar-deck, partitioned off, is the cabin—the appropriate residence of the commanding officer. This

2

apartment being well ventilated, lighted by good-sized windows, and neatly kept, is all that can be desired in healthful arrangements, and being occupied by a single person, is relatively large. The forward part of the spar-deck, in most ships, is protected by the forecastle—a small triangular deck, which is exceedingly useful in stormy weather, affording shelter to the men employed in this part of the ship. Our ship has no forecastle, but the hurricane-deck, over the engine and between the wheel-house, answers the same purpose.

(5.) Next below the spar-deck, in a frigate or larger vessel, is the main *gun-deck*, appropriated to the accommodation of the battery. It is the sleeping-place of a great part of the crew; and having the large gun-ports at the sides, and hatches in the deck above, it is perfectly ventilated. The after part of this deck is partitioned off to afford apartments for a commanding officer—for the admiral, if there is one on board. This apartment is similar to the spar-deck cabin in regard to light and ventilation. The line-of-battle ship has another gun-deck below the first, but it is so near the water-line that the side-ports must generally be closed at sea; and having two decks above, the deficiency of air and light begins to be seriously felt. It is a region of poor air and comparative darkness. The after part of this deck is partitioned off to form the ward-room—the apartment of most of the commissioned officers. But the ship that now interests us has no gun-decks.

(6.) Next below the spar-deck of the smaller vessels is the *berth-deck*. This is occupied by the crew. The arrangements for ventilation are good, much better than formerly. Instead of the large square gun-ports of the frigates, there are circular air-ports about seven inches in diameter, and so high from the water that they can generally be kept open, except in stormy weather. The after part is the ward-room. This apartment is quite neat, and has a range of small rooms on each side; each room, about six feet square, is appropriated to an individual officer. These are the officers' staterooms, where each one, according to his individual taste or fancy, accumulates a wonderful amount of conveniences and comforts.

(7.) Below the berth-deck is *the orlop*, below the water-line, so dark and so poorly ventilated as not to be habitable. It is used

for store-rooms, which are arranged on the sides of a narrow
central passage. The forward part of this deck is the yeoman's
store-room, used to store various small things frequently called
for. It is occupied much of the time by the yeoman. No light
penetrates here, even at noonday, except the light of lamps and
candles. It has one small hatch, generally covered by a grating
to prevent accident, and even by a tarpauling; and there is no
corresponding hatch in the spar-deck, lest rain should get down.
The door is in part of open work, but this is mostly obstructed
by a curtain—the curious inhabitant of the place holding ventilation in such contempt that he thus cuts off the very deficient supply. This room is always neatly arranged, and with such attention to ornament that it is one of the places of chief attraction to
visitors; but it cannot be otherwise than unhealthy, and its strange
occupant is conspicuous for his pale, sickly look. He has so much
attachment to his submarine abode that he is generally compelled
to close it at a certain hour, and to pass a portion of his time on
the spar-deck. We think it would be advantageous to have the
hatch gratings of this apartment, and indeed all the gratings of
the ship, except on the spar-deck, made of metal instead of wood,
so that they might possess the necessary strength with the least
possible obstruction to the circulation of air.

(8.) There are likewise narrow passages—the *wings of the orlop*—
leading back of the store-room on each side, so as to separate the
stores from the damp sides of the ship. The wings might be well
ventilated by flues in the heated bulkhead, which separates them
from the engine-room. Such an arrangement would give pretty
good ventilation to the whole orlop forward, and would greatly
contribute to the preservation of the stores.

(9.) *The hold* is the lower part of the ship. It is damp, poorly
ventilated, and it is used for general storage. It is divided by
transverse partitions to suit various requirements. Commencing
aft, there is first the powder-magazine. This is kept dry and neat
for the preservation of powder, and calls for no special attention
from us. The sail-room comes next, and to it the same remark
is applicable. There are in many ships of war, in all large ones,
an additional sail-room and magazine forward. Forward of the
sail-room is the *spirit-room*, the most dangerous part of the whole
ship. It is used for the storage of molasses, vinegar, cheese, and

various other articles of provisions. Heterogeneous fragments and leakage are likely to form an offensive mass of putrid mud at the bottom; and this division of the hold being rather small, has but one hatch, which is generally closed, so that it is not much more ventilated than the interior of a well-corked bottle. It always has a peculiar offensive odor, which can only be corrected by ventilation and good order in all the arrangements.

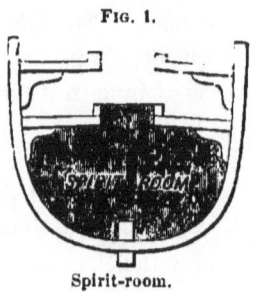

Fig. 1.

Spirit-room.

(10.) The *engine-room* occupies a middle section of the ship from the floor upwards. A leading peculiarity of this part is its high temperature. The engineers are doing whatever can be done to obviate this inconvenience, by abundant ventilation, and by covering the boilers and other heated parts of the engines with thick masses of felt and wood. A serious mistake has sometimes been made, by securing the machinery to the floor in such a way that the drainage was not sufficient, and there were spots which it was impossible to clean. Under these circumstances, pools of mud and grease from the engine have accumulated, and have been the cause of disease, especially of yellow fever, whenever the vessel has been a few weeks in a warm climate (*La Roche*). The diffi-

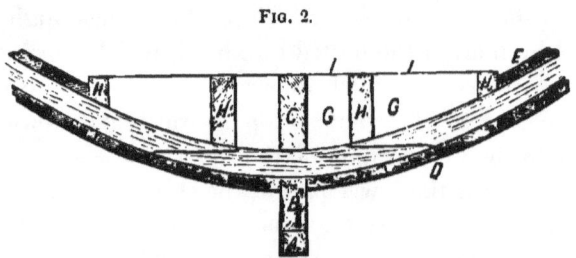

Fig. 2.

Floor of Steamships.

culty has been remedied only by removing the machinery and rearranging it in such a way that every spot underneath could be reached for the purpose of cleaning.

(11.) The main-hold, forward of the spirit-room and the engine-room, is the great storehouse of the ship; and the storage and care of it are of the first importance to health. Constant attention is required to prevent fragments of packages, chips, barrel hoops, and miscellaneous dirt from getting beneath and out of reach. The iron water-tanks are very advantageous in this respect, as they can be so arranged as to form a nearly level floor, and the joints between them can be calked in such a way that dirt cannot possibly settle between them. With barrels and casks it is otherwise, for with them the dirt cannot be kept out. The hold is provided with two hatches, near the ends, for convenience of storage and access; and the arrangement is really of great advantage for ventilation. The hold should always be stowed, with a passage on each side, reaching from the main to the fore-hatch, large enough for a man to pass through. With both hatches uncovered, there is then sure to be a little more pressure of the atmosphere at one hatch than at the other, and thus a good ventilation current is established without further attention.

(12.) The chain-lockers are sometimes so constructed that mud brought up by the chains, reaches the bottom of the ship, to be a nuisance and to obstruct the pumps. These lockers should be made of plank, well fitted and calked, so that if the chains introduce any mud, it may be cleaned out and thrown overboard.

(13.) We see nothing of prison or hospital, because, in fact, there are no such apartments on board. If it should be attempted to allot space to prisoners, such as is deemed necessary for the preservation of health elsewhere, they would be at least five times better off in this respect than the rest of the crew. The prison is an allotted place for the prisoner to sit, generally between two guns, in charge of a sentry.

(14.) The sick on board ship, commonly occupy the same sleeping-place as when they are well. When they are unable to do this, a cot is provided and swung in the best place, the man displaced by the arrangement changing places with the sick man. In frigates and the larger vessels, there is a triangular space from the foremast forward, called the sick-bay or hospital, large enough to contain four or five cots. This answers a good purpose, as the worst cases are thus withdrawn from the noise and confusion of the berth-deck. But the place is poorly ventilated, and in cases of serious illness, it is usual, as a matter of necessity, to appropriate a portion of the gun-deck, screened off for the purpose.

In cases of severe epidemics, the ship becomes a floating hospital altogether.

In merchant ships there is a three-cornered place in the bows, forward, partitioned off for the crew, and a cabin aft for the officers and passengers. The remainder of the ship is the hold, for the storage of cargo.

The cabin, from its convenience with reference to air and light, is sometimes superior to the corresponding apartment of the ship-of-war. But those little sleeping-shelves, which we sometimes see in very fine ships, are none too good. The triangular place forward which the crew inhabit, the forecastle, is for the most part really shocking. It is seldom visited by the officers, and is generally filled with disgusting emanations from the untidy persons of those who occupy it. It may sometimes be difficult to assign more space to the crew, but the sleeping arrangements might be much improved by removing the shelves on which they lie, one above another, with the usual nuisance in the shape of vermin. The hammock, such as is used in men-of-war, costs little more, and is readily removed to the deck, aired and dried. The clothes, kept in canvas bags, would be much cleaner and in better order than with the present arrangement of chests. The partitions, especially in vessels that carry offensive cargoes, as guano or hides, should be calked air-tight. But above all, there should be frequent attention to this part of the ship to keep it clean and neat, and there should be no sparing of whitewash. We sometimes hear complaints of the scarcity of sailors, but under present circumstances we might as well complain that there are few suitable candidates for the penitentiary. Though such laborers may be profitably used, it is to be hoped that the number of men who reach this degree of misery may not be increased.

CHAPTER II

(15.) ONE of the most important things influencing health on board, is certainly the free circulation towards the pumps of the water which collects in the lower parts of the ship. This water, driblets of which are constantly flowing from various points, certainly putrefies unless it flows freely to the pumps and is removed. Epidemics of dysentery, yellow fever, and typhus, have appeared to owe their existence on board to stagnant pools of muddy water. It is hence of the greatest importance in all the details of construction and outfit that this should be kept in mind. The pump, to be a good one, must reach the very lowest part, in order that it may remove nearly all the water. It should have the lower end guarded by a sieve, coarse enough to admit muddy water, and fine enough to exclude fragments of clothing and cotton waste; for articles of this kind sometimes get into the pump-well, and their presence might seriously interfere with the working of the pump. The arrangements in our public vessels are commonly quite sufficient.

(16.) The principal defect that I have noticed is that the pumps are sometimes too short, especially if the vessel is very dry. In these cases a small pool is formed about the pump-well, and the leakage being small, it may take a number of days for the pool to enlarge so as to make it appear necessary to work the pumps. It hence becomes stagnant, and small as it is, very offensive, and injurious to health as well as to white paint. Seamen have a maxim, in some degree true, that a leaky ship is free from bilge-water, and I have had the misfortune to be on board a vessel in which it was attempted to imitate the leaky ship in this particular. Sea-water was introduced every day for about a week and pumped out again, and the evil was horribly aggravated, so that the nuisance was hardly removed afterwards during a cruise of four years. On board two other vessels, the only other vessels on which I have sailed with perceptible bilge-water, it was readily removed by a small copper pump, a bilge pump, extemporized for the occasion. This was made to reach the very bottom by withdrawing the valves from a large pump, and passing the bilge-pump down through its centre. We confidently recommend this expedient where there is bilge-water in a dry ship. Of course, if dirt is allowed to obstruct the limbers no pump can remove the nuisance. In steamers the pumps worked by the engine are most efficient.

(17.) The pumps are inclosed in a small space called the pump-well, which is accessible for the purpose of cleaning and introducing disinfectants. To this place various drains bring the water that leaks into the ship. The principal of these drains are *the limbers*, channel-ways each side of the kelson, and extending the whole length of the ship. From negligence or poor management, they are liable to be stopped up by chips, mud, tar, oakum, rags, and fragments of all sorts. The consequences of such an accident are annoying and dangerous. Formerly it was the custom to have a chain or a rope—the limber rope—passing from end

FIG. 3.

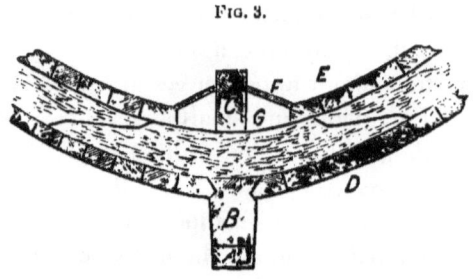

Floor of Ship.

to end through the limbers, and so arranged that by acting on the ends it might be moved backward and forward, thus stirring up mud and moving obstructions. The better way is to omit the limber rope, which is itself an obstruction, and to take care of the hold in such a way that no mud or dirt shall ever enter the limbers.

(18.) Naval constructors occasionally try the experiment of building the floor of a ship very flat, so that the water cannot readily flow from the wings—from the sides of the ship to the limbers. Fortunately for health, all vessels of this form have proved utterly deficient in sailing qualities.

FIG. 4.

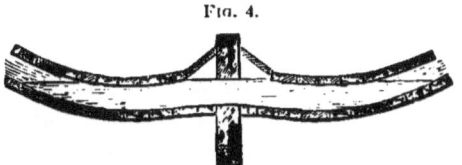

Floor of Badly-formed Ship.

(19.) Ships are now built somewhat longer than was formerly the fashion. This form has such advantages in the way of speed, that we must do the best we can with it. The keel being straight, and the pump near the centre of the length, when the ship is on even keel, the water has but little fall from either end, and must flow very slowly to the pumps. When the ship is not on even keel—either by the head or by the stern—there is necessarily a pool of stagnant water at one end or the other. The remedy is simple enough,—a bilge-pump at each end in addition to the main pumps.

(20.) Vegetable matter decaying in a pool of fresh water, gives off a large quantity of light carburetted hydrogen gas. This may be collected from almost any half-stagnant pool in a meadow, by inverting a tumbler in the pool and stirring the mud with a stick, and when set on fire it goes off with a light explosion. In a pool of sea-water the same process of decay takes place; but, on account of the presence of sulphate of magnesia and other sulphates, by interchange of elements, the carbon of the gaseous product is replaced by sulphur, forming (H_2S) hydrogen sulphide, sulphuretted hydrogen gas, a most deadly poison—the offensive material to which bilge-water owes all its important peculiarities. Possibly the poisonous properties of this substance may have been exaggerated. We know that it is nearly always present in the intestines without apparent harm; and it may exist on board ship, to a very offensive amount, without our being able to point out any resulting injury to health. But, on the other hand, we read of one man falling dead, and others made very ill, by un-bunging a cask of sea-water which had been used as ballast. We have likewise the evidence of the chemists who have occasionally inhaled it in experimenting. The identity of (H₂S) hydrogen sulphide and the offensive matter of bilge-water is not doubted by any person at all acquainted with it. It is easily obtained by keeping sea-water a few days in a bottle with a few bits of cork, or other vegetable matter. It may be made in dangerous quantities by allowing some sea-water to remain for some time in a wooden cask with the bung closed, as in the case above mentioned. On the whole, we infer that there is not much danger from hydrogen sulphide, when sufficiently diluted to be tolerated by the senses.

(21.) The only *remedy* for bilge-water is to keep the ship dry and clean. This is accomplished by frequent pumping, thorough cleaning, and constant care, to prevent dirt and fragments from getting into the lower parts of the ship and out of sight. The scouring of decks is of less importance, and does not make a clean ship in a sanitary point of view. The means of mitigating the nuisance of bilge-water, are the frequent use of hypochlorites, such as chlorinated lime or chlorinated soda (Labarraque solution), antiseptic salts, iron chloride, zinc chloride, iron sulphate, etc.; and certain salts which have the property of decomposing (H₂S) hydrogen sulphide, and leaving nothing but inoffensive material in its stead, such as lead nitrate.

(22.) The commonly recommended way of using *chlorinated lime,* is to place it in saucers, or to sprinkle it about in places where it seems likely to be useful. It parts freely with its chlorine under these circumstances, which being diffused in contact with the hydrogen sulphide, perfect decomposition takes place promptly. A better way is to mix it with water, or put it in the common whitewash mixture, and apply it with a brush to the lower parts of the ship, and more particularly about the pumps. It thus presents a large surface for evaporation, and is very effective. The chlorinated soda, Labarraque solution, may be used in the same way; but, on the whole, is not, perhaps, quite so convenient. It has the advantage, however, that when thrown into the limbers or pump-well, it leaves no residuum likely to interfere in any way with the working of the pumps.

(23.) Zinc chloride, Burnett solution, is probably the most effective, and the most generally applicable of all chemical agents for mitigating the effects of bilge-water. It is best applied by placing it directly in contact with the organic matters which, by their decay, are giving offence. This is done by pouring it, properly diluted, into the stagnant pools from which the offending emanations come. It is likewise useful sprinkled about in any place where the smell is perceived. The iron sulphate, and various other substances, have similar properties, but in an inferior degree. In steamers, the coal-ashes wetted to prevent its blowing about, affords a large quantity of iron sulphate; and if it be made very wet and allowed to drain into the limbers, it is a very important and a very convenient means of disinfection for this class of vessels.

(24.) These applications give very satisfactory results for the time; but, as the accumulation of sea-water goes on, any store of them which could be carried, would be speedily exhausted if they alone were depended upon. They are to be considered only as occasional means of mitigating the evil. The black color of bilge-water, generally observed in pumping out, seems to be of little importance; the water, having lain in contact with oak wood and iron ballast, has merely brought together the constituents of writing ink. This color constantly belongs to offensive bilge-water, as the stagnation of sea-water in contact with these things must necessarily produce both hydrogen sulphide and the black color.

(25.) The metals used in ship-building are in many ways beneficial to health. They are mostly innocent in themselves, and their great tenacity gives them great advantage in tightening joints. Every year they are used more extensively, and we may congratulate ourselves that health is constantly improving through their influence. Iron is taking the place of wood in many parts of the ship, and some vessels are built almost exclusively of iron. Its gradual oxidation seems to be the only way in which it decays, and this has been prevented, in boats, and some parts of larger vessels, by coating the plates with zinc-galvanizing, as well as by painting. The general use of iron water-tanks, instead of wooden casks, has been of very great benefit to health and comfort. Good spring water generally contains enough sulphates from the soil through which it has filtered to become exceedingly offensive when confined a short time in a wooden cask. But in iron tanks, if it contains a portion of vegetable matter, this soon decomposes, and as the iron contains no new material for decomposition, the water quickly becomes good, and remains so ever afterwards. The iron likewise, by its oxidation, decomposes the salts of brackish water—the best obtainable at some places, so that the water is greatly improved in quality by being kept for a time. An incidental disadvantage of iron ships, is the rapidity with which the external temperature is communicated through the thin sides. A tropical sun shining on the side of a ship, especially if painted black, will sometimes make it hot enough to burn the hand. The metal, conducting heat perhaps a hundred times faster than wood, must become nearly as hot inside as externally ; and if there be a broad surface thus heated, the vessel can scarcely be inhabited for the heat. In cold weather, it is not quite so bad, but in the navy, I once had occasion to make a report and recommendation to the following effect :

U. S. STEAMER M——, Nov. 25th, ——.

SIR : I have to report a long sick list, about five times the average, caused by the discomforts of the ship as at present situated. The hull being of iron, there are large surfaces of bare metal in the walls which inclose the berth-deck and hold. These surfaces of iron in mild weather trickle with condensed water, and in cold weather they become more or less thickly coated with ice. At present they become coated with ice during the night, and are wet with dribbling streams at all other times. In my opinion it will be found impossible to keep the crew on board in tolerable health without some additional provisions for their comfort. I would therefore recommend that such surfaces below deck of bare metal, as are accessible, be ceiled with wood without any delay, except such as may be rendered unavoidable by the exigencies of more urgent duty.

Very respectfully, etc.,

COMMANDER —— ——.

(26.) *Copper* is much less used than iron. The sheathing which protects the bottom of the ship from various sea animals is its principal use. It is occasionally used where iron would be better, being both stronger and cheaper. Copper was formerly much used for cooking utensils, and occasional carelessness may have allowed its poisonous oxide to adhere to its surface, and thus it may have been the cause of accidental poisoning. It is used for many other purposes, especially alloyed as brass, for mere ornament. There is no great injury to health from this source ; but too much of it involves useless labor and some annoyance from the greasy rags used in polishing.

Lead is not much used in ship-building. Its easy malleability causes it to be used to a limited extent, but its cost and its poisonous properties are so well understood, that there appears to be no disposition among constructors to use it where it is capable of doing harm.

(27.) The paint employed in various parts of the ship is an important subject for consideration. Designed principally for the preservation of the wood, we desire that as much of it may be used, at proper times, as is likely to contribute to this object. In so far as it is used for mere ornament, it should give way to certain considerations of health. Of this the medical officer may consider himself the best judge. Fashion has established great uniformity in the manner of painting the outside. This is always black, with a white, red, or gold streak; and some variety in width, color, and situation of this streak is left to individual fancy. There is no material inconvenience in this fashion except in warm climates. The rays of the sun striking the side of a ship increases its temperature, the degree of increase depending much on the color. This increased temperature is communicated to the interior, and may seriously incommode those on board. In iron ships especially, the disadvantages of black paint are very great. There are many vessels, particularly small coasters, in which the interests of health and the preservation of the ship, should control the color, rather than any idea of taste or fashion. Any fancy color, or even varnish, is certainly better than black. Our river steamboats are generally painted white, the very best color; and there are many good reasons to be pleased with it. Our public vessels, when laid up, are generally painted a dull yellow color, much better than black, where the only object is the preservation of the ship.

(28.) There may be some military advantage in the black color of ships-of-war; but probably various shades of lead color, in the form of zebra stripes, or leopard spots, would, under certain circumstances, be better. We will, however, leave this for the discussion of others. Black, we think, should not be used for other parts of the ship. The interior of bulwarks, the combings of hatches, and other parts about deck, are better in reality, and neater and in better taste, of the natural color of clean wood, produced by scraping and scrubbing, or by painted imitations of the proper color. The best arrangement of colors—best for the preservation of the wood and for avoiding bad effects on the eyesight—is to paint the broad surfaces white or nearly white, with occasional stripes or mouldings of wood color, buff, or green. There is so little green on the broad ocean, that it always produces a pleasant impression. The ship below deck should be painted white, and the only important consideration connected with it occurs when it becomes necessary to renew the paint in the course of a cruise.

(29.) The effects of *tar and pitch* on the salubrity of the vessel are in every way advantageous. The vapor is sometimes offensive, but custom reconciles us to it, and under ordinary circumstances it can do no harm. When pitch is cold and hard it gives off very little vapor. An important incidental advantage is that the vapor is very offensive to most insects, and it thus has much influence in limiting their numbers.

CHAPTER III.

(30.) AUGUST 25th.—The marines march on board from their barracks, the rest of the crew come from the receiving ship, the flag is hoisted, and the ship is regularly in commission. We have to study the character and condition of this crew—these sailors and these marines—so as to become somewhat acquainted with our shipmates. The employment of the sailor, or rather his surroundings, have usually been such, so wretched and degrading, that not many, except the most miserable, could be induced to accept this occupation knowingly. The best recruits are the sons of fishermen, who live in sight of the ocean, and are accustomed to it from their infancy. Such recruits are furnished by the islands and coasts of New England, and still more by the countries bordering on the Baltic. There are a few recruits brought forward by the reading of Robinson Crusoe; but these, and all others brought into the service by the romance of the ocean, are very glad to escape after a short experience. But not a few are outcasts from their families on account of worthlessness and crime, some of them escaping the hot pursuit of the officers of justice through the shipping rendezvous. There are many young men in every community, excellent in all other respects, who, from want of force of character, or even of opportunity, fail to establish themselves in any employment, until they are willing to accept almost anything which affords a fair prospect of a constant means of livelihood. They often possess excellent abilities, and succeed well in whatever they happen ultimately to adopt as their vocation; of these the navy gets a share.

(31.) The number of good and reliable seamen for the purposes of modern commerce, and to supply recruits for the navy, is utterly insufficient. Hence it is necessary to do the best we can with such men as are to be obtained. With the discomforts

which necessarily belong to sea life, and the additional wretchedness occasionally added by caprice and cupidity and indifference,
it is generally the case that the better sort of men, unless they receive promotion, or very good treatment, are apt to make an
effort to escape the service at the end of the first cruise, or even
sooner. Some of the best of them succeed; but others, failing to
establish themselves, get into the sailor boarding-houses. They
are soon hopelessly in debt, without any resource but to
ship again. They receive an advance of pay to discharge old
debts, and if they find an opportunity are pretty sure to desert
without caring to return the money thus advanced. They are
kept by placing them on board after the ship is removed from the
wharf, and by guarding them to prevent the possibility of escape.
The unhappy men thus detained, and without sufficient force of
character to keep out of the situation, form the typical sailor;
they are subjected to such discipline as is necessary to obtain from
them a fair amount of useful labor. But the worst of it is that
the whole crew are subjected to nearly the same discipline, though
they do not all need it.

(32.) Much is now being done to improve the character of the
sailor, and with very encouraging success. But the time is perhaps distant when young men will choose the sailor's profession
as they do almost any other laborious employment. In the navy
men have such inducements to re-enter that a large proportion
come back before they are so reduced in money and reputation as
to have no choice. The abolition of flogging has brought more
thought and more common sense into the investigation and punishment of various petty offences; and there have thus been introduced into the service many comforts and indulgences of which
men may occasionally be deprived by way of punishment. The
entire crew is no longer kept continuously on board by the year,
not permitted to visit shore at all, merely because some of them
would get drunk. There is evidently great improvement in this
business, so that men have less repugnance to the employment on
this account. The system of honorable discharges has conferred
a very great benefit, as the drunkard and the escaped convict no
longer hold as good a character at the naval rendezvous as the
correct and well-behaved. They often find this resource closed
against them, while the owner of the honorable discharge enters

as soon as he pleases, with the advantage of a gratuity equal to three months' pay, and a very much better chance of promotion. Nearly every sailor, with these advantages before his eyes, makes some effort to gain this honorable discharge. Drunkenness, with its consequent disorders, and some others formerly in fashion, has ceased to be admired and imitated as heroism. Correct conduct has become the rule. The system of honorable discharges is gradually being extended so as to embrace marines, firemen and coalheavers; it should include every enlisted man.

(33.) The crew of our ship are mostly honorably discharged men, the rendezvous having for some months been closed against all others. The deficiency of landsmen required to make up the complement, was promptly made up after the arrival of the order to place the ship in commission.

August 29th.—Some of our crew have already been to sea in other vessels since their enlistment, and among them are a number of invalids returned from the station to which we are probably destined. On the recommendation of a medical survey these invalids are returned to the receiving ship, to be sent to the naval hospital.

·(34.) The physical fitness of recruits is determined by an inspection which has reference to health, form, size, age, and muscular power. The qualifications of naval recruits differ somewhat from those of the military service on land. Deficient strength of the foot, as exhibited in the deformity called "splay feet," may disqualify a soldier on a march, but it is no serious disqualification in a seaman, who has very little marching to do. Extreme youth is not so objectionable, as there are no fatiguing marches, in which fatigued and lame boys have to be left to perish by the roadsides; but if the ordinary labors are too severe for them, they can be relieved from any excessive labor. In fact youthfulness is rather an advantage in a new recruit, as life at sea is of such a character that an adult accommodates himself to it with extreme difficulty. Hence the limit in regard to age for naval recruits is (13) thirteen years, height (56) fifty-six inches. The limit of age in the other direction is, for landsmen, (33) thirty-three years, over which age they are not received except for special duties.

Many important things in this connection are stated in numbers, so as to admit of tabular arrangement for easy reference and comparison. The ages and heights are so expressed in the descriptive lists. Some officers have a fancy for very tall men; but when the men are not otherwise well developed this is not an advantage. This height is often made up of a pair of long legs, which produces an awkward weakness, somewhat like marching on a pair of stilts. Any casual inspection gives sufficient evidence of the existence of this conformation when excessive; but perhaps it would be useful to determine tendencies in this direction in inches. The recruit might be made to sit on a level bench with a straight back sufficiently high, graduated to inches and fractions. This would measure the length from the ischia to the vertex, which deducted from the height would give the lower extremities with sufficient precision. In studying the development of children, this would be a very useful measurement, and very convenient. The measurements of the chest are very valuable, as evidence of the healthy working of lungs. The muscular power might be measured by acting on a spiral spring and stating the result in the number of pounds lifted.

The following table embraces too small a number of subjects, perhaps, to afford any general conclusion of value. The average height of seamen is probably somewhat less than that of men of the same age in laborious occupations elsewhere. This, however, is not certain, the average of this table, which includes youths of about (16) sixteen, being (67) sixty-seven inches, not much less than the average of adults elsewhere. The firemen and coalheavers are physically the best men. The marines show nearly the same average height; but none are enlisted for this service who are less than (64) sixty-four inches.

Average Age and Height, according to Rates of Various Groups of Enlisted Men.

| RATES. | Whole number. | AGE. | | | HEIGHT. | | |
		Oldest.	Youngest.	Average age.	Tallest.	Shortest.	Average height.
		Years.	Years.	Yr. Mo.	Inches.	Inches.	Inches.
Petty officers, seamen,	31	60	26	37 3	74	63	66.23
Petty officers, not seamen,	11	48	22	31 2	72	$64\frac{3}{4}$	66.34
Seamen, ...	23	42	23	30 7	70	$61\frac{1}{2}$	65.62
Ordinary seamen, . . .	50	42	20	25 5	72	61	66.23
Landsmen, ...	34	31	21	23 1	$70\frac{1}{2}$	$60\frac{3}{4}$	66.50
Boys, under 20 years, .	3	20	16	17 7	$67\frac{1}{2}$	60	64.47
Servants, negroes, . . .	4	30	19	25 0	$68\frac{3}{4}$	62	66.63
Servants, mulattoes, . .	10	50	17	25 9	$67\frac{1}{2}$	58	63.03
Firemen, ...	23	40	23	29 5	$70\frac{1}{2}$	$63\frac{1}{2}$	67.61
Coal-heavers, ...	21	28	19	23 7	$72\frac{1}{2}$	$63\frac{1}{2}$	67.29
Marines, ...	43	46	21	26 0	73	64	67.50
Aggregate and general average, ...	253	60	16	27 6	74	58	67.05

(35.) *August 31st.*—We steam down the river to the powder magazine, and we have a startling incident—*a man overboard.* The ship moving under steam, is obliged to move too fast for the safety of two boats towing astern ; and the consequence is that they are both filled with water, one of them passing so far beneath the surface that the men in her are left swimming in the current. Others follow their impulses, and pursue the proper measures to rescue the men from the water, while we try to remember and arrange the proper means to restore life, in case one of them should be brought on board in a state of suspended animation. We are greatly in want of evidence of the special efficacy of the measures usually adopted for this purpose. We know that a person withdrawn from the water within a minute, generally recovers without any particular assistance. If he should remain a little longer in the water, his chances of recovery are greatly diminished; and if he should remain three or four minutes wholly immersed, the chances are that he will not survive, with all the assistance which we may be able to give. But cases do occur of recovery after intervals of nearly an hour, without our being able to say which of the means adopted produce the result, or indeed whether they had anything to do with it. Our choice of remedies is, therefore, guided more by our ideas of physiological fitness than by any of the results of experience.

(36.) The first, the only object is to re-establish respiration; so we remove promptly whatever we perceive to interfere with that process, and adopt measures to produce respiration artificially. As soon as the drowned man is removed from the water he should be placed on his side, and preferably on the right side. One person should support the head, opening a little the jaws, removing anything which may be found to oppose the entrance of air, emptying water or mucus from the mouth by turning the face downwards, even holding the head lower than the rest of the body a moment for this purpose. Another person acts on the chest and abdomen in such a way as to imitate, as nearly as possible, the natural movements of respiration by pressing the lower part of the chest and stomach toward the spine, and allowing them to return by natural elasticity at the rate of twelve or fifteen times a minute, as rapidly as a person would count five deliberately. During the minute occupied by these operations, others should provide, if possible, dry flannel clothing, or if nothing better can be had, dry hay or straw. The wet clothing is to be promptly and gently removed, and the body wrapped in dry, and if convenient, warm flannel blankets. But it is not desirable to warm the body materially until there is some evidence of re-established respiration.

(37.) The clearing of the mouth and the artificial respiration may perhaps be accomplished by one person, as effectually by Dr. Marshall Hall's ready method as by any other means. The body is placed on the side as before, one hand of the patient against or partly under the forehead to prevent the face from coming too rudely in contact with the floor, the other hand is placed under the stomach with the arm across the body, the body is then rolled forward on the stomach and back to the side alternately, about fifteen times in a minute.

Nearly all who are to recover at all, will show some sign of returning life during the minute or two occupied by these first cares. The patient should now be carried gently on a board—not picked up by the feet and shoulders with the head hanging down—to a place of more convenience for any further measures that may be deemed advisable. The body should be wiped dry, clothed in flannel, placed on a mattress between two blankets. The movements of artificial respiration should be continued perseveringly, whatever else may appear necessary. The body should occasionally be placed on the side, and the head so inclined as to favor the discharge of water or mucus. If the discharge be tenacious, it may be assisted by the finger or other convenient instrument. If the teeth close, they may be kept apart by a piece of soft wood. If the tongue fall back into the throat, as it is pretty sure to do with the patient on his back, it must be seized, pulled forward and between the jaw teeth on one side or the other, and kept there; even a piece of wire or a stout thread might be passed through the tongue to hold it from falling back and stopping up the fauces.

Artificial respiration has been recommended by inflating the lungs by the use of a pipe or a bellows, or from mouth to mouth. But this is, perhaps, a more difficult operation than is generally imagined. It results sometimes, in inflating the stomach instead of the lungs; which may be prevented by pressing the larynx down and back against the spine, so as to close the gullet.

(38.) The Royal Medical and Chirurgical Society recommend the method of Dr. Sylvester, which, instead of compressing, expands the chest, thus imitating deep inspiration, as follows: In cases of drowning the following plan may, in the first instance, be practiced: Place the body with the face downward and hanging a little over the edge of the table, shutter, or board, raised to an angle of thirty degrees, so that the head may be lower than the feet. Open the mouth and draw the tongue forward. Keep the body in this posture a few seconds longer if fluid escapes. The escape of fluid may be assisted by pressing once or twice upon the back. All obstruction to the passage of air to and from the lungs should be at once, so far as practicable, removed: the mouth and nostrils, for example, should be cleaned from all foreign matters or adhering mucus. In the absence of natural respiration, artificial respiration, by Dr. Sylvester's plan, should be forthwith employed in the following manner: The body being laid on its back, either on a flat surface, or better, on a plane inclined a little from the feet upwards, a firm cushion or some similar support should be placed under the shoulders, the head being kept in a line with the trunk. The tongue should be drawn forward so as to project a little from the side of the mouth; then the arms should be drawn upward till they nearly meet over the head, and at once lowered and replaced at the side. This should be followed immediately by moderate pressure with both hands on the lower part of the sternum. This process is to be repeated twelve or fourteen times in a minute. If no natural respiratory efforts supervene, a dash of hot water (120° F.) or cold water may excite respiratory efforts. The temperature of the body should be maintained by friction, warm blankets, dry clothing, etc. (*Am. Journ. Med. Sc.*, xliv, 516).

As soon as there is any appearance of re-established respiration, —gasping, sobbing, or catching breath—we may relinquish all measures in this direction. During the operations already described, preparations should be made for warming the body. Hot water, even boiling, may be poured into any convenient vessel—a bottle or tin cup would answer—and we should pass it gradually over the flannel clothing, about the stomach, chest, and back, keeping it more particularly about the pit of the stomach. Other bottles, not too hot, may be applied to the feet. Many other means have been recommended with more or less confidence, among them an enema of tobacco-smoke, with complicated apparatus, not likely to be on hand when wanted. This enema may be administered if required, with a common clay pipe, which, when well charged with tobacco and lighted, may be introduced, and the smoke blown through by a common bellows, or by blowing through a second pipe inverted over the first.

(39.) When animation is restored, the patient should be kept comfortable in his bed, and not disturbed by useless visits or conversation. If he has been long in the water he will probably require further medical care.

But happily our men returned on board pretty well exhausted by swimming. We had no occasion for the various appliances of which we had been thinking.

CHAPTER IV.

THE SEA—ROLLING AND PITCHING.

(40.) SEPTEMBER 1st.—Having received powder from the magazine near Fort Mifflin, we move slowly down the river and proceed to sea. We might be a little sentimental, we certainly feel so, over the tramping around with the capstan, the clinking of chains as link by link comes in, the departure of friends, the movement of the vessel on the smooth surface of the river, passing the Breakwater, the departure of the pilot, and our perfect isolation from all but our small floating community. Entering the domains of the broad ocean, we are instantly conscious of a great change in the physical influences that surround us. The most characteristic of these is the oscillating movement in obedience to the various impulses of the waves. This movement is in three directions, vertical, rolling, and pitching. The vertical movement is felt principally near the ends of the ship. Each end is alternately raised to the top of a wave and falls into the trough of the sea. It is not uncommon for waves six or eight feet high to succeed each other at intervals of about five seconds; and a ship frequently receives nearly this amount of vertical motion, with this degree of frequency, in fine weather. It is not rare for this movement up and down to be so sudden as to make us feel that we are about to be tossed into the air, the ship subsiding so rapidly that the feet can scarcely be kept in contact with the deck. There is no doubt that occasionally in rough weather, there is actually vertical motion enough near the ends of the ship, to toss an object some distance into the air. But the feeling of discomfort and insecurity from the sudden sinking of the floor on which we stand, is sufficient to keep everybody from these parts of the ship, when there is much motion of this kind.

The motion called *rolling*, is the rotation laterally of the ship, back and forth on its axis. This movement is very considerable, even in large ships, sometimes amounting to (20°) twenty degrees on each side. A considerable amount of muscular exertion is necessary to keep the body in anything like a vertical position under this constant change of inclination of the surface. Standing on deck is a laborious occupation.

Pitching is mainly due to irregularity of speed, as affected by the waves. The oscillations are not nearly so rapid as those of rolling. The ship gradually ascends the slope of a wave, reaches the summit, balances like a scale-beam, the forward end preponderates, and we descend an inclined plane to the trough of the sea, attaining great speed as we descend; we strike, perhaps, with great force, the next coming wave, slowly ascend to its crest, and thus we go on repeating the motion. The rapid descent to the trough of the sea, with the plunge of the forward part of the ship into the coming wave, suggests the expressive name of this motion. It goes on pretty smoothly with the sea aft and the wind on the quarter; but with a head sea, the waves and the bows of the ship come into such violent collision, that it is necessary to reduce sail in order to prevent the ship from being destroyed by the prodigious force of the concussion.

(41.) It requires some little muscular exertion to stand on the substantial earth, but the case is very different on board ship, where the surface is rapidly inclined first to the one side and then to the other, and is gliding rapidly forward and stopping with a sudden concussion, or is oscillating vertically with velocity nearly sufficient to toss us into the air. We think it not difficult to comprehend, that when all these motions are combined in an exaggerated degree, as in great storms, it is exceedingly laborious exertion merely to stand up, and walking is quite out of the question. In ordinary states of weather, men do walk, more or less; but at first there is some difficulty in accommodating the movements of the body to the disadvantageous circumstances. This is overcome somewhat by time and practice, and then we have our sea-legs on. Being once practiced in these movements, we practice them instinctively, even on shore, where there is no need of them. Hence the sailor is known by his walk, his wide straddling feet, the swaying to-and-fro of his body, and the balancing with his arms.

(42.) Even lying in bed, these irregular oscillations give us trouble.   In the ordinary *sleeping-berth,* the rolling is, at times, sufficient to throw us out of bed, if it were not for the boards at the sides, converting the berth into a sort of trough.   As it is, we are rolled about in a most uncomfortable way, till we learn to grasp these boards in our hands and hold on during sleep.   The rougher the weather, the more firmly we grasp—as the bird in windy weather grasps more firmly to the branch of the tree on which he is perched.   Lying in a *hammock* or cot hung to the beams, so as to swing about and accommodate itself to the move- ments of the ship, is much less subject to these inconveniences. There are, no doubt, real modifications effected in all our organic functions by these peculiar movements, both directly and by the constant need of muscular exertion to maintain the equilibrium. But these, so far, have only been suspected, not distinctly indi- cated, except the singular violent perturbation known under the name of sea-sickness.

CHAPTER V.

SEA-SICKNESS.

(43.) As soon as we meet the swell of the ocean, most of those who have not sailed before, and some of those who have, begin to feel unable to keep on their feet; they feel unaccountably helpless; soon they have vertigo and nausea; and it is not very long before the impulse to empty the stomach becomes irresistible. This is the miserable beginning of the sailor's rough profession. The characteristic symptoms are headache, vertigo, nausea, pale, cool, moist skin, muscular relaxation, increased flow of saliva, sunken features, and disagreeable hallucinations of the senses of taste and smell. In fact, the symptoms are nearly the same that are caused by the operation of an ordinary emetic. In bad cases the vomitings are frequently repeated, and the muscular prostration and the general feeling of wretchedness, are such as to render the sufferer utterly indifferent to everything around him.

(44.) Individual susceptibilities in this disease vary exceedingly. The relaxation of the œsophagus is sometimes incomplete, and then the spasmodic action of the stomach and diaphragm is very painful. Occasionally the nausea and vertigo are distressing and persistent, lasting several weeks without any vomiting. Sometimes the vomiting comes on suddenly, without much antecedent distress. Sometimes obstinate constipation is the only symptom; and some of the captains between New York and Liverpool, are said never to have an alvine motion between the two ports. There are some rare cases of individuals who appear not to suffer at all. Most persons obtain comparative exemption from suffering after a week or two. There are very few, however, who do not suffer more or less from vertigo and headache, and a feeling of discomfort at the epigastrium, if not nausea. Sometimes this feeling is compared to the sensation of hunger; and I have known a commander, who had experienced this feeling very often, say that rough weather always made him feel hungry, even immediately after his meals. He always feels hungry while the storm lasts. All that is distressing about this disease subsides soon after landing or getting into harbor. The hallucinations of sight and touch continue, in a degree, for some time; the trees and houses seem to swing about, and our senses fail to assure us of the steadiness of the earth.

(45.) The cause of this singular disease is certainly the irregular motion of the ship; but we are unable to say with any certainty how this cause produces such effects. One of the oldest theories is that it is caused by fear; but probably no one who has felt it refers it to this cause; and besides we have never heard of anything like it caused by fear merely elsewhere. The reign of terror in France, and the Inquisition in Spain, afford no account of such a disease. Another explanation refers it to the muscular exertion necessary to maintain the body in equilibrium; but we do not observe that anything like sea-sickness is ordinarily produced by mere muscular exertion, however severe or long continued. A third theory refers the disease to the agitation of the abdominal viscera, with the constant friction among themselves; but running, and especially riding a hard-trotting horse, would shake the viscera quite as much without causing the least nausea. The disease has been attributed to the agitation of the brain itself against its bony case; and this theory has great plausibility. The symptoms are analogous to those caused by simple concussion of the brain. Of course, as the violence of agitation is not sufficient to break down the tissue of the brain, such symptoms as belong exclusively to the most violent cases of cerebral concussion are absent; but the symptoms which belong to the milder forms of concussion are present, exaggerated in degree, as should be expected from the continuance of the cause. But this theory will not stand the test of the trotting horse, which would agitate the brain quite as roughly against its bony case. And finally, sea-sickness has been attributed to nervous derangement produced through the senses by the irregular oscillatory movements of neighboring objects (Darwin). To this it can only be objected that the proof is not quite conclusive. Blind persons, it has been suggested, may be sea-sick, but they have the senses, except sight, active enough, and are certainly very conscious of some of the movements about them. Swinging, walking, and riding backward in a carriage, have been observed to produce similar disturbance in a milder form. This last theory explains the fact that riding backward is much more likely to produce vertigo and nausea than riding with the face forward. I have known the symptoms in a mild degree to be produced by sitting on an elevated seat near the sea, and watching the rollers breaking over a bank at some distance from the beach. Merely closing the eyes sometimes produces considerable relief. Lying in a horizontal position with the eyes closed, in a well-balanced cot, renders the affection quite bearable in nearly all cases. Sitting on deck near the side of the ship, so that no swinging object interferes with a steady view of the horizon, is known to produce great relief, the horizon and the clouds near it being the only steady objects in sight. Altogether we must be nearly right in adopting this last theory.

(46.) From what has already been said it may be inferred that there is no effectual remedy for sea-sickness, except to get on land. It, however, admits of some mitigations. Freely circulating air is a great advantage. It is important to keep as far as possible from either end of the ship, so as to avoid the excessive vertical motion. It seems generally best to remain on deck as long as possible, avoiding much observation of the spars and rigging, but in preference directing the view to the distant land or horizon. The young, and those who are to be sailors by profession, should continue this course, partaking moderately of food and continuing their exercises, if possible, in the intervals of vomiting. Some of the boys promptly find places in the tops, where the exaggerated motion soon excites vomiting, and by remaining there a day or two they obtain immunity from suffering in other parts of the ship. For passengers it is useless to struggle much in this way. When there is much motion and they find themselves unable to keep up, they may as well seek the most comfortable place to lie down, until a smooth sea enables them to get on their feet again. It is worse than useless to swallow drugs. It is disadvantageous to eat full meals in anticipation, and it is still worse to keep the stomach quite empty. Persons who have suffered much and are recovering, with some nausea and a disgusting flavor of soap about the mouth, derive great comfort from the use of certain articles of food of very decided flavor, such as smoked herring or other salt fish, broiled ham, ginger cakes, preserved ginger, etc. Stimulating and aromatic drinks have their use here, such as tea, coffee, wine, rum, brandy, but excess even of tea or coffee may do harm. These things are likewise useful in preventing the disease when the predisposition is not very strong. Any aromatic or stimulant may be occasionally useful in this way, as well as any common article of food of very decided flavor, and not distasteful to the patient.

If from excessive severity of the disease or peculiarity in the condition of the patient, serious accident be apprehended, some additional remedies may be used, as ice-water, lumps of ice, acidulated drinks, chloroform, chloral hydrate, opiates, endermically if they cannot be retained in the stomach; and also the remedies for any accident, as abortion, which may be particularly apprehended.

(47.) Sea-voyages have always been more or less recommended as a remedy for diseases, and like other perturbations of the system and changes of habit, they may have occasionally broken up chronic diseases. We should, however, always prefer some more manageable remedy. The motion of a ship increases the difficulties of treating fractures, and thus sometimes renders amputation necessary to save life.

CHAPTER VI.

SOCIAL INFLUENCES—NOSTALGIA.

> " When o'er the silent seas alone,
>   For days and nights we've cheerless gone,
>   Oh they who've felt it know how sweet,
>   Some sunny morn, a sail to meet;
>   Sparkling at once is every eye;
>   Ship, ahoy! ship, ahoy! the joyful cry.
>   Then sails are backed, we nearer come,
>   Kind words are said of friends and home,
>   And soon, too soon, we part with pain,
>   To sail o'er silent seas again."
>
> THOMAS MOORE.

(48.) In the last two chapters we have considered some of the material ups and downs of sea life, with their consequences. Let us now examine the *social relations* and moral influences. The crew have just collected from various parts of the world, and the great majority of them have no personal acquaintance, except such as they have formed during the past week or two, on board the receiving ship. Each one has separated from his home, his relations, his associates, his friends, from every object of his affections on earth. The desolation of his affections appears complete, but hope gilds somewhat the future. Some of the men may have met previously, but the whole business of forming friendships and antipathies, and selecting companions, is, for the most part, among entire strangers, to be accomplished without any previous knowledge of each other. We wonder and find that human nature is capable of this. The officers even, for the most part, meet the first time in their lives, at the navy yard where the ship is fitting out, without any other introduction than the order which each one has received to report for duty, on board the same ship. Conventionalities veil the awkwardness of this introduction, and a good understanding is established in the beginning. This we may reasonably hope will not be interrupted;

and some friendships and some agreeable social relations may eventually spring from it.

(49.) This breaking up of old social relations and the establishment of new, is accomplished under a forced intimacy, which is far from pleasant to a person of any refinement of feeling. The crowding together of so many and such diverse characters, and the life in common, which admits of no privacy, day or night, would seem perfectly intolerable; sailors, however, are not very conscious of the social or moral hardship of this crowding. Of its physical inconveniences, the want of space for exercise or sleep, and the contamination of the atmosphere, they are well aware. The officers, whose sensibilities from education and association, are more refined, are relieved in some degree from this annoyance. They have each, for the most part, a small room, about six feet square, to which the proprietor may retire when he will, to commune with his own thoughts and enjoy his individual tastes; it is the place for his bed, his bureau, his library, his museum of curiosities. Prying curiosity and discipline very rarely interfere with his comfort in this little room.

(50.) The first few days pass with some degree of constraint, but we converse, we form social circles, we cease to be strangers. The associations thus hastily formed have not always that congeniality of tastes which perpetuates friendship, or those disparities which render friendly social relations impossible. There is, hence, some variation from time to time in the various circles, and soon something like social order grows up. This vagabondism, this breaking up of all social relations, every two or three years, is the great annoyance, the great hardship of naval life.

(51.) Another peculiar influence, is the monotonous solitude of the ocean. The land with its dim outline being left behind, there is nothing in sight outside of the ship, except sky and sea; none of the objects which ordinarily induce us to approach a window. A bird, a fish, or a bit of sea-weed is enough to excite a general commotion. A sail in sight, even so distant as to require a telescope to see it at all, is an object of universal interest. If it comes near enough to be plainly seen, it is thought of and talked of for days. But should it approach near enough for the few usual inquiries—what ship? where from? whither bound?--it creates a scene of enthusiasm, of which any amount of poetic exaggera-

tion of incident fails to convey a full impression. The increase
of distance and the final disappearance of the stranger behind
the horizon is watched with the same interest, and some occasional
damage to the eyesight. This breaking in on the monotony has
a singularly beneficial influence in promoting cheerful conversation, cheerful thoughts of home, and confidence in the future. It
is full of cheerful and healthful influences.

(52.) *Nostalgia.*—The confusion of moral and social relations,
as just described, does not, of itself, cause any specific disease,
but greatly complicates various diseases; and we may, hence,
have occasion to allude to it again. We here design to treat only
of home-sickness, nostalgia, a disease caused by this kind of influence, though by no means peculiar to the ocean. This distressing disease has its origin in affection for the mere locality of
our childhood. It has been considered peculiar to the Swiss, and
a celebrated national air has been found to awaken such mournful
recollections in the young Swiss soldier or sailor, as to cause this
pitiable disease. The playing of this tune has hence been prohibited, even under penalty of death. But there are abundant
instances of nostalgia in all countries, so that it has its origin in
the very constitution of human nature. There is no country in
the world so wild or so savage as not to interest thus the affections of the natives.

> " Dear is the shed to which his soul conforms,
>   And dear the hill which lifts him to the storm."
>   GOLDSMITH.

The Laplander becomes despondent and enervated and dies, if
kept from his snowy mountains and frozen lakes. Our American Indians, after becoming accustomed to the comforts and conveniences of civilized life, sigh for their native wilds, and eventually escape to their bark wigwams and endless deserts. Many
recently imported slaves in the West Indies, though changed
from savage owners to others of comparatively gentle deportment,
have become despondent and committed suicide or died of the
sulks. The greatest amount of suffering from this disease of
which we have any account, was probably among the young con-
scripts of the French army in the beginning of the present century. The disease originates in the feeling of attachment for
home which we all feel, and we all deeply sympathize with the

sufferer. With most of us the feeling of depression and even perhaps the thoughts of home are occasionally replaced by other thoughts, studies, or amusements—cheerful influences. But with some this thought of home becomes a *fixed idea*—the absorbing thought that occupies the whole soul to the exclusion of all other thoughts. They are shy, the countenance becomes stupid, sad, and pale, with dark shades about the lustreless eyes. There are palpitations of the heart, with constant tendency to syncope—fainting. The patient conceals, however, the cause of his distress, or more probably is not really aware of it. There is frequently a presentiment of death without any consciousness of its cause, and this presentiment is sometimes realized.

The disease is easily discovered by a question or suggestion about home. The rapid pulse, the blushing, and the fainting tell it all. Nostalgia, with these symptoms, is a serious disease, likely to end in death. Examinations after death have disclosed large quantities of purulent matter about the surface of the brain. (*Larrey.*)

(54.) The prevention of this disease and the cure of the milder cases is accomplished by the application of all available cheerful influences, pleasing occupation in accordance with the taste of the individual, visits to the shore, plays, music, and the whole catalogue of amusements. If we can gently withdraw the sufferer from his isolation and interest him in some object, either amusement or employment, for an hour or two each day, he is already nearly cured. Harshness and rough language only aggravate the evil. Among the slave-dealers on the coast of Africa, where the ravages of this disease were enormous, the remedy in vogue was music and dancing, in which all, but more particularly the quiet ones, were forced to take part by the use of a scourge in the hands of a leader of ceremonies. If the slaves made much noise of themselves, the dealers were happy, and had no fear of losing their property by the sulks.

When nostalgia is really established there is but one remedy,— the patient must be sent home. Where delay is unavoidable, we must do the best we can with the influences above indicated, and we may use tonics and such other remedies as appear appropriate for the symptoms. In serious cases they are only temporary means of mitigation.

CHAPTER VII

CLOTHING—SMALL STORES.

(55.) At length we are fairly afloat on the ocean and have leisure to examine the every-day life, the dress, the food, and the occupation of the sailor.

The dress of seamen is regulated with reference to convenience and comfort in their peculiar situation without much reference to absurd mutations of fashion. In the navy the articles of clothing and small stores named in the following tables are usually kept on board every ship in suitable quantities. They are supplied at a very moderate cost and charged against the pay account of each man. Recruits must be supplied before coming on board with a complete suit, and enough additional articles to enable them to make the changes required by cleanliness.

Clothing.

NAMES OF ARTICLES.	Outfit for each recruit.	Price.	Cost of outfit.	Annual allowance for 100 men.	Average annual cost for each man.
Blue cloth pea jackets, ...	1	$9 90	$9 90	50	$4 95
Blue flannel jumpers, ...		1 40		50	70
Blue cloth round jackets, . . .	1	7 04	7 04	50	3 75
Blue cloth trowsers, ...	1	3 80	3 80	88	3 12
Blue satinet trowsers, ...	1	2 57	2 57	88	2 13
Flannel overshirts, ...	2	1 60	3 20	150	2 40
Flannel undershirts, ...	2	1 23	2 46	133	1 64
Flannel drawers, ...	2	1 13	2 26	133	1 50
Linen frocks, ...	2	1 18	2 36	133	1 57
Linen trowsers, ...	2	1 19	2 38	133	1 58
Blue satinet, yards, ...		76		100	76
Blue flannel, yards, ...		42		600	2 52
Canvas-duck, yards, ...		50		100	50
Sheeting, yards, ...		64		133	85
Blue nankeen, yards, ...		10		67	7
Calf-skin shoes, ...	1	1 65	1 65	83	1 37
Kip-skin shoes, ...		1 56		50	78
Yarn socks, ...	2	32	64	167	53
Caps, ...	1	1 00	1 00	100	1 00
Mattresses, ...	1	5 15	5 15	100	5 15
Blankets, ...	1	2 00	2 00	100	2 00
Black silk handkerchiefs, ...	1	1 03	1 03	130	1 32
Total, ...			$47 44		$40 19

Small Stores.

Names of Articles.	Annual allowance for 100 men.	Average price.	Average annual expense for each man.
Tobacco, pounds, ...	2400	$0 31	$7 50
Soap, pounds, ...	2520	6	1 51
Beeswax, in small cakes, pounds,	8	64	6
White thread, pounds, ...	13	96	12
Blue or black thread, pounds, .	13	96	12
Ribbon, pieces, ...	100	67	67
Tape, pieces, ...	80	3	3
Cotton, spools, ...	40	5	3
Sewing silk, pounds, ...	1		
Pocket handkerchiefs, ...	96	13	13
Needles, papers, ...	27	2	1
Thimbles, ...	48	1	1
Scissors, ...	32	19	7
Razors, ...	8	22	2
Razor strops, ...	8	13	2
Shaving boxes, ...	8	13	2
Shaving soap, cakes, ...	33	3	1
Shaving brushes, ...	8	13	1
Scrub brushes, ...	32	19	7
Blacking brushes, ...	24	20	5
Clothes brushes, ...	8	16	1
Eagle buttons, large, dozen, . .	10	30	3
Eagle buttons, small, dozen, . .	40	17	7
Eagle buttons, medium, dozen, .	10	30	3
Pearl buttons, dozen, ...	48	2	1
Fine comb, ...	100	16	16
Coarse comb, ...	100	22	22
Blacking, boxes, ...	20	4	1
Grass, hands, ...	500	3	15
Tobacco, pounds, ...	800	31	2 48
Jack-knives, ...	100	25	25
Mustard, bottles, ...	216	13	28
Pepper, bottles, ...	216	10	24
Total, ...			$14 40

(56.) This supply of clothing enables the sailor to dress comfortably, with a little occasional dandyism. The blue cloth round jacket is only used in dressing up for exhibition on shore. The flannel undershirt is essential to comfort and health. It is merely a plain garment without collar or sleeves, worn under the linen frock or flannel overshirt, according to the weather. It is really important that this, or something equivalent, be constantly on hand to meet the sudden changes of weather.

In very warm weather, where even this amount of flannel is sometimes excessive, great benefit results from the use of a flannel belt. This is a strip of fine flannel worn under the clothes, about four inches wide and forty inches long, with two or three buttons at one end, shortened a little at the upper side by two or three tucks to make it fit the better.

FIG 5.

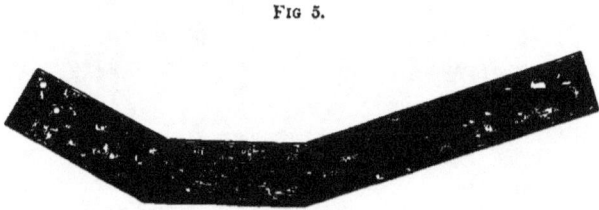

Flannel Bandage.

The idea of this belt appears to have come from India. Perhaps some sufferers from dysentery at Calcutta noticed that the natives generally wear a sash—the cummerbund—and thus escape the dysentery that destroys the foreigners by scores and hundreds. At any rate, we are fully convinced of the great value of this article in the prevention and cure of the dysentery of warm climates; and we think there is no exaggeration in the statement that it has saved many thousands of lives. It appears to act by affording a gentle support to the walls of the abdomen at a time when they need such support on account of the exhausting effects of climate, and by keeping up a zone of perspiration around the body through all the variations of temperature, and thus preventing the evils of suppressed perspiration. [" I have known this article, worn in temperate climates, to relieve effectually a dysentery contracted in the tropics." (T.)]

(57.) If so disposed we may possibly find some fault with the sailor's dress. We occasionally notice some little embroidery in red, yellow, or brown silk, a childish taste for finery, not perhaps quite in keeping with coarse, sunburnt features. What a prodigious improvement there will be when no worse fault than this can be found in the fashions of dress elsewhere! The hands of grass among the small stores are palm leaves for the fabrication of hats. These hats are commonly made much too heavy for comfort, the object being to make them preserve the precise form deemed most elegant by the nautical milliners. There is no necessity for this; the preservation of the precise form of a hat is of no such importance as to render it necessary to sacrifice comfort and health for this object. There is so little comfort in the straw hat at present in use that it is never worn except on dress occasions, the light cloth cap being universally preferred for common use in all climates. There was formerly in use a black hat, made of the straw one by covering with linen and saturating with beeswax and black paint. It weighed about two pounds, and was polished to shine like varnish. This absurdity is probably quite obsolete, though a few specimens, like mummies, may be preserved in the cabinets of the curious.

(58.) The officers of a ship are generally able to dress themselves comfortably, with few restrictions other than those imposed by the conventional usages of society; the regulations scarcely interfering, except in matters of color and lace. The undress cap is very convenient covering for the head, except in warm weather, when the straw hat may be substituted.

(59.) The small stores are principally such small articles as are required in repairing the clothes and keeping them in good order. This repairing is useful not only as a matter of economy, but the employment is one of the most valuable of the moral and social influences, apparently of small account, but which in the aggregate make existence at sea tolerable. We should never object to see a sailor's working clothes patched to any extent, but no raggedness or other want of neatness should be permitted. There is generally one afternoon of the week allowed for mending clothes; and probably the happiest moment of an old sailor's life is when he succeeds in threading a needle to sew the patch on his trowsers; having spent about half an hour in selecting a proper patch, arranging things around him, and adjusting his spectacles. It must carry him back in memory to the innocent days of childhood, when he probably contemplated the features of his grandmother similarly occupied. The sailor should never be deprived of his mending day without a very good and very urgent reason.

(60.) But the leading article of small stores is tobacco—that solace of wretchedness, that exalter of happiness, that stultifying luxury of indolence! It is even introduced twice into the allowance table for fear it might be forgotten—"don't forget pigtail." If there is any condition in life in which the use of tobacco should not be discouraged, it is certainly that of the sailor, whose life is nothing but labor and wretchedness, mitigated principally by contrast, and variety, and tobacco. Whatever of consolation or comfort is to be had from it fairly belongs to him.

CHAPTER VIII.

FOOD—THE RATION.

(61.) The food of the sailor is much restricted in variety and deteriorated in quality by his situation at sea. It must consist necessarily of such articles as can be preserved for a long time in various climates. The ration as regulated by Act of Congress is abundant in quantity and of excellent quality. The laws have been changed from time to time so as to conform to improving intelligence. Experimental improvements not greatly increasing the cost and not objected to by the men are constantly being introduced. The weekly allowance is exhibited in the following table arranged to correspond with the usual issue at sea:

Exhibit of Navy Ration for Each Day of the Week.

Articles.		Sunday.	Monday.	Tuesday.	Wednesday.	Thursday.	Friday.	Saturday.	Weekly quantity.	Commutation price.	
										Rate per lb.	Price.
Biscuit, ...	ounces,	14	14	14	14	14	14	14	98	$0 04	$0 $24\frac{1}{2}$
Beef, ...	pounds,			1			1		2	8	16
Pork, ...	pounds,		1		1			1	3	10	30
Preserved meat, .	pounds,	$\frac{3}{4}$				$\frac{3}{4}$			$1\frac{1}{2}$	20	30
Flour, ...	pounds,			$\frac{1}{2}$			$\frac{1}{2}$		1	5	5
Rice, ...	pounds,	$\frac{1}{2}$							$\frac{1}{2}$	6	3
Dried fruit, . .	ounces,			2			2		4	12	3
Pickles, ...	ounces,				4			4	8	8	4
Sugar, ...	ounces,	2	2	2	2	2	2	2	14	16	14
Tea, or, ...	ounces,	$\frac{1}{4}$	$\frac{1}{4}$	$\frac{1}{4}$	$\frac{1}{4}$	$\frac{1}{4}$	$\frac{1}{4}$	$\frac{1}{4}$	$1\frac{3}{4}$	90	$10\frac{1}{2}$
Coffee, or, . . .	ounces,	1	1	1	1	1	1	1	7	24	
Cocoa, ...	ounces,	1	1	1	1	1	1	1	7	24	
Butter, ...	ounces,	2				2			4	30	$7\frac{1}{2}$
Desiccated potato,	ounces,					2			2	20	$2\frac{1}{2}$
Desiccated vegetab's,	ounces,								1	28	$1\frac{3}{4}$
Beans, ...	pints,		$\frac{1}{2}$		$\frac{1}{2}$			$\frac{1}{2}$	$1\frac{1}{2}$	36	$6\frac{3}{4}$
Molasses, . . .	pints,					$\frac{1}{2}$			$\frac{1}{2}$	48	3
Vinegar, ...	pints,							$\frac{1}{2}$	$\frac{1}{2}$	20	$1\frac{3}{4}$

Average (25), twenty-five cents per day.

(62.) This table allows important variation. For instance, the article dried fruit is usually raisins; on other stations it is dried apples, and occasionally prunes, dates, and figs are issued. Tea, coffee, and chocolate are supplied, sometimes the one, sometimes another, according to convenience, but not generally at the option of the men. The amount of the ration is so abundant that messes of fifteen men commonly draw but twelve or thirteen rations. The value of the undrawn portion is received in money at the end of the month, and forms a small mess fund, which supplies mustard, pepper, and other condiments, besides fruit and fresh vegetables in port.

(63.) With our present knowledge of the subject we are not able to suggest much improvement in the ration. But without new legislation it would not seem difficult for the proper bureaus, with the concurrence of the officers of the navy, to introduce very great improvement in the issue and manner of preparing some of the articles. Fourteen ounces of hard biscuit is a very poor substitute for bread. It is so hard that the teeth are soon worn out in chewing it, and the older seamen can only manage it by soaking it in their tea or water. It is nearly impossible to preserve it in tropical climates free from insects and mouldiness. The bread rooms are lined with tin and kept scrupulously clean and dry, but large quantities of biscuit are necessarily condemned and thrown overboard, spoiled. This might perhaps be obviated in a degree by having most of the biscuit put up in air-tight tin packages. But the law allows the substitution of soft bread when convenient for the hard biscuit. This substitution is commonly made when the ship is in port, so that fresh bread can be purchased. But as it will conduce greatly to health, and probably to economy in other respects, we hope the time is not distant when it will be found convenient to bake on board at sea, and issue to each man a loaf of fresh bread nearly every morning. There is no real difficulty on board the larger ships in having a good baker and a good oven for the purpose. In sailing ships, and perhaps steamers, the oven for this purpose should be associated with a distilling apparatus of sufficient capacity to supply every man on board with an abundance of drinking-water. A number of objections, which are still occasionally urged against these proposed innovations, have been answered again and again by those who

have studied the subject during the past half century. First, it
is objected that it would be difficult to carry the requisite amount
of fuel. This is answered by the fact that one pound of fuel,
economically used, is more than sufficient to evaporate a gallon of
water, and probably a pound of fuel can be as easily carried as
eight pounds of water. Secondly, there is supposed to be some
difficulty in carrying so much flour. But the barrel which holds
nearly two hundred pounds of flour can be made to hold but one
hundred pounds of bread, and it certainly takes no more space to
carry one barrel of flour than two barrels of biscuit. Thirdly,
it is objected that no place can be found on board for the oven;
it would be in the way. There is something in this objection;
but in small vessels the oven and distilling apparatus may be associated with the cooking galley, a moderate increase of size and
a little mechanical ingenuity being sufficient to accomplish the
object. I inspected a contrivance of this kind in 1846, drank
some of the water, and found it very good. The navy moves
slow, very slow in some directions. Even if it be desirable to separate the oven from the distilling apparatus and the cooking galley in larger vessels, the difficulty we conceive to be by no means
insurmountable, for we have seen a place found for a commodore's
galley—a matter of some importance, certainly, as it saves vexation in settling quarrels between the cooks, but we think it quite
as important to supply the ship's company with wholesome and
palatable bread. Another objection is, that the sailor hates innovations and innovators of all sorts, and if the hard biscuit should
be altogether replaced by soft bread, he would suspect it to be
some new and cunning trick to cheat him out of his rights, and
the grumbling complaints would be altogether intolerable. This
may be true, and probably on other accounts a sudden change of
this kind is not desirable. The change should be brought about
gradually. By way of experiment, an oven of sufficient capacity
to bake a hundred pounds of bread each day might be placed on
board a ship with four or five hundred men, so as to supply a loaf
of fresh bread once or twice a week to each man preferring it.
Each man will be ready for his fresh bread as often as he can get
it under this arrangement. The ovens can afterwards be gradually enlarged and adapted to every description of vessels, and
thus the desired change will be made without the confusion and

trouble which usually attend the sudden introduction of radical reforms.

(64.) Beef that has been long salted becomes so hard and tough that the teeth and other digestive apparatus can hardly convert it into nutriment. On this account, freshly packed beef is very much better than that which has been packed two or three years. Salt pork is much better preserved, probably, because of the greater proportion of fat and its more thorough blending with the muscular tissue. This may prevent its so thorough saturation with salt, and consequent hardening. Both deteriorate by keeping, and so far as possible, it is best that meat should be used before it has been too long salted.

(65.) Flour is used in comparatively small quantities, principally for plum puddings, but we expect to see it used in much larger quantities, so as to supersede the necessity for so much hard biscuit.

It is not always so well prepared and packed as it should be. To keep well in all climates it should be made of wheat at least one year old, or thoroughly kiln dried, and packed in tight casks, with four iron hoops in addition to the common wooden ones. Much flour for want of this cure is spoiled and thrown overboard. Flour, as commonly prepared for the market in temperate climates, of new wheat and packed in loose casks, is quite worthless when transported to the tropics.

(66.) Rice keeps well in all climates when properly packed. Sailors formerly had a great prejudice against it, and fed most of their small allowance to the fishes. They said it contained no nourishment, had no more taste or substance than sawdust, and caused blindness. These nonsensical notions are giving way, and the small quantity of rice now allowed is properly used. Various small luxuries, by way of experiment, were occasionally offered as a substitute for the rice, till the men have come to think better of it. Most of them are now unwilling to do without the rice; and they are disposed to keep the substitutes. Rice is probably the most useful of the smaller articles of the ration.

(67.) The raisins or other dried fruit are of great advantage. On the Mediterranean and some other distant stations raisins are commonly supplied, being more convenient and more easily preserved than other dried fruits. They are commonly cooked with the small quantity of flour issued to make plum pudding, a mass of not very good-looking material dotted with fruit. It is commonly covered with molasses, and custom has made it attractive. It certainly possesses important good qualities not found in any other article of sea diet. On the home station, and occasionally elsewhere, dried apples are issued instead of raisins. They are made into pies and dumplings with flour, and seasoned with molasses, so that they answer about the same purpose as the raisins; some of the men even prefer them. They are not generally so well liked as the raisins and are more difficult of preservation. Prunes, pears, and peaches are occasionally substituted, the regulations wisely permitting such substitution when convenient. We confess to a very strong partiality, which may be only a strong prejudice, in favor of dried fruits as a part of the seaman's ration. It seems to us that various fruits and vegetables, and even flesh, lose less of the peculiar properties which belong to each of them as fresh food by simple desiccation than by any other process of preservation yet imagined, not even excepting the use of air-tight cans.

(68.) The *pickles* are various tender vegetables and fruits simply cured in vinegar, or with salt and vinegar; but usually they are half-grown cucumbers prepared according to the domestic process, with occasional variation of the spices for the sake of variety of flavor. They were introduced with a view to the continuous use of a small quantity of varied vegetable material, as little changed as possible from the fresh state, for the purpose of affording protection against scorbutus—sea scurvy. They form a pleasant condiment to the substantial meal, and are probably quite as useful as the preserved lime-juice so much lauded for the same purpose. They are more pleasant and more convenient.

(69.) *Cranberries*, which were formerly indicated as the substitute for pickles, I have never seen issued as a part of the ration. This elegant little fruit, though highly appreciated and used in many ways, has not yet received among us anything like the attention to which it is entitled, or found half the applications to which it is destined. A few years ago it was an unimportant wild fruit, growing on land despised because it would produce nothing else. But the fruit picked from this wasted land was sold at a good price per quart. The price increased with the comparative scarcity of the fruit, till cranberry swamps came to

be valuable property ; and the growth of the fruit has been encouraged on contiguous land till the cultivation of cranberries has
become a regular branch of agriculture.   In cool weather, this
fruit is easily kept perfectly fresh for several months by merely
keeping it immersed in clear water.   We are not aware of any
real attempt to preserve it for sailors' use on long voyages.   The

FIG. 6.

Cranberries.

constantly increasing demand for it keeps up the price, so that it
is only an article of occasional luxury, except among the wealthy,
and so long as this continues to be the case it cannot be extensively used in the ration of seamen.   For occasional use on long
voyages, it might be slightly cooked with a little sugar in small
air-tight tin cans.   If extensive cultivation should ever make
the fruit sufficiently abundant and cheap, it would probably be
worth more dried than all the rest of our dried fruits put together.
At present the cranberry crop is probably worth as much as any
fruit crop in the United States, except only apples and peaches.

(70.) Tea, coffee, and chocolate form by their aromatic infusions delicious beverages of great advantage to health and comfort.   The sugar is used mainly to soften the flavor of the tea
and coffee, which without such addition are too pungent or bitter
for our palates ; but the brown sugar commonly issued doubtlessly contains in its coloring matter substances of much importance to nutrition.   Refined sugar, though more pleasant generally
to the taste, is on this account probably much less advantageous
as an article of diet in the absence of fresh food.

(71.) *Tea* and *coffee* are found, by appropriate chemical treatment, to contain a curious alkaloid, which bears a relation to the
plant from which derived, similar to that of quinine to cinchona,

or morphine to opium. When procured from tea it is called theine ; when from coffee, caffeine ; but it is now generally agreed to consider these two preparations as identical, no sort of difference in properties being observable. Several other plants, though of very different botanical characters, *Ilex paraguayensis*, *Paulinia sorbilis*, etc., whose infusions have come to be extensively used as beverages, are found to contain this same theine, which is hence supposed to possess the insinuating qualities which have brought most of them into use. Chocolate, too, has its theabromine, which is very like, if not identical with, theine.

Tea is usually *prepared* by simple infusion in boiling water, and is used almost immediately. The aroma is so delicate that it is quickly lost by standing or boiling, and the infusion is then bitter and it is thought to be spoiled. The fresh infusion with its aroma is certainly the most pleasant, and the Chinese are in the habit of adding fragrant flowers to some varieties of tea in order to increase and vary the aroma. But this fragrance is not the only or probably the most important property of the tea, and hence the tea is probably at least half wasted in our common process. The Chinese and the Japanese use tea much more economically. After the first fragrant infusion, which they fully appreciate, they add an equal quantity of boiling water for a second infusion, which is considered nearly equal to the first. They do not always stop at the second infusion, but have been seen every time a cup of tea was poured out to add a cup of boiling water, till everything soluble about the leaves must have been removed ; the last drawing being nearly tasteless and colorless. We are able to state that even this last is a refreshing drink under some circumstances. The *teapot* should always be provided with a strainer in the upper part, as in the pharmaceutist's infusion cup. This arrangement, besides preventing the leaves from entering the spout, very much promotes the rapid and perfect drawing of the tea.

FIG. 7.

Teapot with strainer.

(72.) *Coffee*, though probably no better than tea hygienically, or as an article of ordinary diet, is certainly much more highly esteemed by the portion of mankind with whom we more particularly concern ourselves. This high appreciation of coffee is probably due to its more decided and more characteristic flavor, which is not so easily destroyed or lost as that of tea. But this preference actually existing must be taken into the account in adapting diet to the wants of the individual. The late Prof. Chapman, of the University of Pennsylvania, has been heard to express himself after this fashion : "The Yankee likes pork and molasses ; the Virginian is fond of bacon and turnip tops, and the Pennsylvanian likes sourcrout and goose ; and these are good and wholesome food for those who like them, and greatly appreciated by convalescents sometimes, though the very thought of them be really nauseating to nine-tenths of mankind." Another ounce of coffee has been added to the ration, May 23d, 1872, "An additional ration of coffee and sugar, to be provided at his first turning out." Coffee is the dried seed from the berry of a small tree which grows abundantly everywhere in the tropics, having probably been introduced into most of its present localities from Arabia. The seeds are parched and crushed so as to be more readily acted on by boiling water. The aroma of coffee is not so easily dissipated as that of tea, and it requires a more protracted application of hot water to extract the virtues of the seed. Coffee is, therefore, prepared by a short boiling instead of simple infusion. The roasting of the coffee seems necessary to develop the peculiar flavor which we require, and which is perhaps necessary to its wholesomeness ; but this process is often carried too far by our cooks, who appropriately enough call the process "burning" the coffee. It should be rapidly roasted over a good fire, and constantly stirred, and the operation should be continued till it attains a chestnut-brown color, or a little darker. If the roasting be continued much longer than this nearly everything that distinguishes coffee from other vegetable matter is decomposed, and there remains little but charcoal, creasote, and the like, which acorns, beans, or chiccory would supply just as well. Coffee-grains which have been spoiled in this way have their black surfaces slightly tinged with iridescent purple. If it be desired to prepare a substitute for coffee, of beans or acorns, it may be well to continue the roasting to nearly this point, and the decoction will have very nearly the flavor of the best Mocha prepared in the same way.

(73.) *Chocolate*, though very similar to coffee and tea in nutritive properties, is very inferior in fragrance, is full of fatty and starchy matters, and is not much esteemed. It seems necessary to mix it with spices in order to give it sufficient flavor to render it digestible among men who think so little of it as our seamen generally do. It is very liable to adulteration, and is sometimes made up of spices, starch, suet, and coloring matter. These frauds can only be detected by the microscope and the flavor; and as the flavor depends mainly on the spices properly introduced, there is much annoyance in purchasing it, except in the entire seeds. On the whole, there is so much annoyance and so little advantage from the use of this article that it might without harm be omitted from the ration altogether.

(74.) *Butter* is such a common article of diet that it is very disagreeable to attempt to do without it at sea. Its preservation is very difficult in tropical climates, and the navy is very fortunate in having it packed in such a way that it keeps with comparatively little deterioration or loss. It is valuable in helping to keep up the variety of customary articles of diet which habits and constitution seem to make necessary. It is probably of great importance as an antiscorbutic. Its nitrogen compounds being blended with fat, probably undergo less change from their fresh condition than similar material in most other kinds of preserved food. There is no sort of use in taking it to sea unless specially prepared and packed for the purpose, as it would soon decay and be worthless.

(75.) The regular *bean* of the navy ration is the small white kidney bean, which seems to be universally preferred. Other varieties and even horsebeans have been sometimes used where the white bean could not be procured fresh. On foreign stations this substitution is often made advantageously, but where the regular bean is procurable in good condition, no other is comparable to it. Beans are, in every situation, good food; but their great excellence at sea is referable to the fact that they are seeds still possessing the germinating property. They hence contain the nitrogen compounds in the same state in which they exist in living plants, and therefore, probably, they possess the antiscorbutic virtues which appear to belong to all fresh vegetables, even grass and weeds. Beans are prepared for cooking by a preliminary soaking in fresh water for nearly twenty-four hours.

During this time, if of good quality, they imbibe moisture; the process of germination commences, and they swell to about four times their previous bulk. This is a genuine process of vegetable growth, and hence we understand that good beans, properly prepared, have valuable properties, which are to be found only in freshly grown vegetables. Beans which have been kept more than one season lose in some degree the germinating property, and though in good condition otherwise they should be rejected on the mere fact of age. The only real test of good beans is to have a cook who understands his business to cook some of them. When the beans of the ship's stores, either by age or decay, have in great degree lost the germinating property, any kind of blue or black beans procurable on the spot, in fresh condition, may be substituted very advantageously. Several varieties, occasionally used in this way, have gained temporary popularity on account of their advantageous comparison with white beans that were old or spoiled.

(76.) *Molasses*, used principally with plum-pudding, is important, as it renders this article more palatable and wholesome. It is probably valuable also, from containing a large proportion of the nitrogen compounds (nitrogenous organic principles) of the cane, but little altered from their fresh condition. It is, perhaps, more rich in this respect than brown sugar. On this account, molasses should be preferred which is derived most directly from the cane. The best is made by merely evaporating the juice of the cane to a proper consistence; the next best is the drainage from the crystallization of brown sugar; the worst in this respect, is sugar-house syrup, however excellent it may be in other respects.

(77.) *The vinegar* of the rations is not all taken by the men; the small quantity allowed is more than the seamen finds use for, in seasoning his food, mixing his mustard, and curing his pickles. Vinegar prepared from the juice of apples, is that contemplated by the law; and inspectors should particularly guard against deception in this article. The more gross adulterations, with sulphuric acid, etc., are easily enough detected by chemical re-agents. But much of the vinegar of commerce is prepared from other material than the juice of fruits,—from whisky, rum, and molasses; from malt, sugar, and starch; and however good in other respects, it is not suitable for the use of seamen on long voyages. There can be no reasonable doubt that good vinegar, from fresh fruits, contains much of the nitrogenous principles of the fruit from which it is derived, besides acetic acid, and malic, tartaric, or citric acid. It is probably not inferior as an anti-scorbutic to lime-juice, except when this latter is but recently expressed from the fresh fruit. The most reliable test of good vinegar is the aroma, when carefully examined by an experienced person.

Preserved meats, desiccated potato, and desiccated mixed vege-tables, have recently been added to the ration. The value of these additions have not yet been determined. The quantity of pre-served meat is probably too great, as officers' messes are not often willing to have a dinner of such meat oftener than once a week. The desiccated potato is not much liked by the men, and as a substitute for fresh potatoes in preventing scorbutic troubles, we apprehend it will prove a failure. The desiccated mixed vege-tables have long been in use experimentally, and have been of great benefit in long voyages; but with steamships, and short voyages, and abundance of fresh vegetables, they are not much used.

CHAPTER IX.

ARRANGEMENT OF MEALS—NUTRITION IN GENERAL.

(78.) The common arrangement of meals, on shipboard, is to have breakfast at eight o'clock, or immediately after the morning work; dinner at noon; and supper at about five, varying a little for occasional convenience. Each meal occupies an hour, which is not interfered with or disturbed, unless by a call for very urgent duty. This supplies food at proper intervals, without unnecessary interruption. The only apparent objection to the arrangement is the long fast, from six o'clock in the evening till eight o'clock next morning—fourteen hours. Much of this time is occupied by sleep, and on that account the want of food is not so severely felt as otherwise it would be. But seamen are required to keep their watches, and they are thus employed on deck nearly half the night; and they are commonly called at daylight for the morning work. This involves two or three hours of labor, which is performed in the morning before breakfast. Many men suffer greatly during this labor for want of a biscuit and a cup of coffee. Their sufferings are relieved, in some degree, by a traffic in coffee with various cooks at the galley. But there are times, particularly in the beginning of the cruise, when the men have no money to spend in this way; and it sometimes happens that the cooks dishonestly appropriate coffee for this business. It would be much better to supply the cup of coffee constantly by regulation than to continue the present practice, which, though it meets a real want, by relieving the protracted fast at the right moment, still does it ineffectually, and leads to many annoying abuses.

It may be objected that it would be inconvenient to light the galley-fires early enough to make this cup of coffee. This would sometimes be the case, but we see no more inconvenience in doing it regularly than in permitting it to be done for the private sale of coffee. The morning work is sometimes postponed till after a somewhat earlier breakfast, with great advantage. In times of extraordinary labor in cold weather, as in approaching our coast in a winter storm, it is customary to continue the galley-fire all night, with the privilege to the night watches of making coffee. There is great comfort and convenience in this arrangement. We should very much like to see the sailor regularly supplied with his cup of hot coffee in the morning watch, and in night watches of excessive fatigue and labor.

(79.) The subject of food and nutrition is of such paramount importance, that we are not nearly done with it. The object of food is to supply, in a state capable of assimilation, the material needed for the growth of the body, and to supply the place of that which may be removed by the wear and tear of the system. We say capable of assimilation, because the proper elements may exist in such shape that we cannot use them as food. For instance, woody fibre has about the same ultimate chemical composition as starch and sugar. The sugar and starch are available food; but our teeth and our stomachs are unable to digest chips of wood. And again, the atmosphere by which we are surrounded contains in sufficient abundance nearly, if not quite, all the elementary substances which enter into the constitution of living beings; but these cannot all be appropriated directly from the atmosphere by the animal organism in sufficient quantity to supply the wants of the system. Of about sixty-four elementary substances recognized in nature, more than one-fourth have been obtained from the human body by chemical analysis. These are oxygen, hydrogen, nitrogen, carbon, sulphur, phosphorus, silicon, chlorine, fluorine, potassium, sodium, calcium, magnesium, iron, manganese, aluminium, and copper. The first four, forming the bulk of the tissues, are called essential elements. The others, being in much smaller proportions, and not entering universally into the constitution of all the tissues, are called incidental elements, though their presence, in due proportion, is quite essential—necessary to the existence of the tissues.

(80.) These elements must all be supplied by the atmosphere, and by our food and drink. Let us examine in succession each of these sources of nutriment. The atmosphere is composed of about twenty-one per cent. of oxygen and seventy-nine per cent. of nitrogen, with three or four parts in ten thousand of carbonic anhydride (carbonic acid gas), and a large but very irregular proportion of watery vapor. The other constituents of the atmosphere are in very minute proportion, and their presence is sometimes apparently due to local circumstances. The air acts through the lungs and the skin. In the process of respiration it is warmed to about 37° Centigrade (99° F.); loses about five parts in one hundred of its volume of oxygen, gains about four parts of carbonic anhydride, and is nearly saturated with watery vapor (Dalton). Thus four-fifths of the oxygen which disappears goes to form the carbonic anhydride eliminated, and one-fifth must enter into the constitution of our tissues to be eliminated by other channels. It is not known in what way nitrogen is affected in ordinary respiration. In some experiments a small portion has appeared to be absorbed, in others the opposite result has been reported. It would seem that in cases of long fasting a small quantity of nitrogen always disappears from the respired air. In the case of herbivorous animals, it is difficult to imagine that the nitrogen of the grass and other food equals in quantity that eliminated by the kidneys, the intestines, and the skin; and, hence, we may expect to see it definitely announced that these animals receive large quantities of nitrogen directly from the atmosphere. We hence infer that the office of the lungs is to receive oxygen for the use of the system, and occasionally nitrogen, and to eliminate carbonic anhydride, water, and effete material, useless and noxious, from the system. Some substances incapable of assimilation when taken into the system, promptly find their way to the lungs for elimination, as alcohol, turpentine, etc.

(81.) The skin, under ordinary circumstances, seems not to absorb anything from the atmosphere. It is capable, however, of absorbing many substances, medicinal and others, and much more readily when the cuticle is abraded or removed by a blister, or by friction. It is probable that water may be absorbed by this surface from a bath, or from a moist atmosphere, in cases where there is much need of this fluid, but it is difficult to determine the point by any direct experiment. Sailors, when unable to procure drinking-water, have been able in some degree to assuage their thirst by wetting their flannel clothing with sea-water, but this is not conclusive evidence of absorption, as the damp clothing by checking evaporation must somewhat relieve thirst, whether there is absorption or not.

The exhalations from the skin are constant and appreciable. The only substances exhaled in considerable bulk are water and carbonic anhydride, which under ordinary circumstances pass off at insensible perspiration. But when the quantity is greatly increased by warm weather or exercise, and the evaporation is restrained by a moist atmosphere, the perspiration collects in drops on the surface of the body. Still more important, probably, than the carbonic anhydride and the water are other materials exhaled in comparatively small quantities. We have the report of a boy who was varnished and gilded for the purpose of exhibition in a parade; the perspiration from a large portion of his body being arrested, he promptly gave symptoms of suffocation, and he died before it was possible to remove his unfortunate finery. Now, it is impossible to refer this and similar results to the retention of the carbonic anhydride and the water of the perspiration, for the elimination of the carbonic anhydride would impose on the lungs only two per cent. additional labor (Reignault and Reiset), and surely the water could be eliminated by the kidneys. The case of this celebrated boy has lately been the subject of some doubt, as the varnish might have been composed of poisonous material, but the experiment has been often enough repeated on horses and rabbits, and it kills them—the more complete the coat the more quickly they die. It is to be hoped that no one will have the foolhardiness to try the experiment on himself; accident may some time repeat the experiment. The character, and especially the amount of this additional matter of perspiration, can only be guessed at. Thénard, in the perspiration from a well-worn flannel shirt, discovered the following substances: Chloride of sodium, acetic acid, phosphate of soda, phosphate of lime, oxide of iron, and *animal substance*. Berzelius, in sweat which had run from the forehead, found lactic acid, chloride of sodium, and muriate of ammonia. It is difficult for us to conceive why all these substances cannot be eliminated by the lungs and by the kidneys and the other eliminating organs, but the evidence is sufficiently conclusive that they cannot. The offensive character of cutaneous perspiration is often very appreciable by the sense of smell. We have had occasion to experience this on visiting the crowded berth-deck of a man-of-war when it was necessary to close hatches in a storm, and the wearers of patent leather boots may have had such experience without going so far from home.

(82.) So far as we know, the atmosphere containing nearly, perhaps quite all the elements of our bodies, supplies directly for nourishment oxygen only. But it is one of the great avenues by which worn-out, effete, useless, and poisonous materials are removed. These, when not freely diluted and removed by ventilation, are sometimes very poisonous, capable of exciting dangerous disease in those who inhale them, and they always become poisonous by some process of decay if kept thus concentrated for any considerable time. In this way, by the decaying exhalations from the skin and the lungs, typhus fever was formerly caused very often in jails, emigrant ships, crowded tenements, etc. Terribly destructive epidemics have originated in this way.

CHAPTER X.

(83.) Though neither air nor water comes under the ordinary designation of food, they are quite as important as solid food for the maintenance of the body. Human life can be continued but a minute or two without a renewed supply of air, perhaps a day or two without water, and a week or two, possibly a month, without any nutriment except air and water. While on this subject we shall conclude what we have to say of water as nutritive material and hygienic agent.

Water, with oxygen and hydrogen in the proportion necessary to form water, constitutes the bulk of the human organism. If the body be desiccated, the tissues, except the bones, fat, and skin, are reduced to a small fraction of what they were. This loss in size and weight is principally due to the removal of water, which partly existed as water in the system, and partly as oxygen and hydrogen in the constitution of the tissues. The desiccated remains are still composed, in large proportion, of oxygen and hydrogen. Much of this water, and of these elements of water is derived from the water we drink, and, hence, it is scarcely possible to overestimate the hygienic and therapeutic value of water.

(84.) Besides forming more than two-thirds of the whole body (Blumenbach), water gives its necessary fluidity to the blood, without which it could not be distributed to the tissues and organs. The atmosphere, if deprived of its water, would be wholly unfit for respiration, as it would carry off the vapor from the lungs and air-passages so rapidly as to cause exhaustion and death. Water forms a large proportion of all the organic substances used as food. The common potato, for instance, is about three-fourths composed of water, which can be separated by mere drying; and the starch particles remaining are still largely composed of oxygen and hydrogen in the proportion to form water. Animal matter, such as muscular flesh (ordinary meat), is composed of water in much larger proportion. Digestion in the stomach cannot be carried on without a due proportion of water, and that is to say a very large proportion. Thirst can be relieved only by water, or by food or drink composed mainly of water. Water abounds in all habitable regions of the globe; only the ocean and the desert are without abundant supplies of drinking-water. This universal beverage is placed by a bountiful Providence nearly everywhere.

(85.) The most eminent physicians of all times have had a high appreciation of the great value of water. Pliny thought it a great absurdity for men to be at so much trouble and expense to make a variety of drinks, when nature has supplied them so abundantly with one of such excellence as water. Hoffman says that "no remedy can more effectually secure health and prevent disease than pure water." "Water proves agreeable to persons of all ages." He points out what we are sure are facts, that water-drinkers are more healthy and longer lived, have whiter and sounder teeth, and are more brisk and alert than those who habitually drink wine and malt liquors. Haller, the eminent physiologist, drank nothing but water. The classical Gregory, who lived in an age and country where alcoholic compotations were general, declares spring and river water to be the most wholesome drink, and the most grateful to those who are thirsty, whether sick or well. We might increase to any extent the catalogue of the praisers and drinkers of water without coming down to the times when people separated themselves into parties on this subject, and commenced calling each other fanatics and sots.. Dr. Miller, of New York, long before the temperance movement, pointed out the instructive fact that " in all the frequent attempts to sustain the intense cold of winter in the Arctic regions, particularly in Hudson's Bay, Greenland, and Spitzbergen, those crews who had been well supplied with provisions and liquors have generally perished, while, at the same time, the greatest number of survivors have been uniformly found among those who were accidentally thrown on inhospitable shores, destitute of food and liquors, and compelled to maintain an incessant struggle against the rigors of the climate in procuring food, and obliged to use water alone for drinking." But the end of the gigantic breweries is not yet. (*Bell.*)

(86.) There is much importance properly attached to the different varieties of water. Ships, on leaving home ports and on most foreign stations, obtain a supply of good water, the quality being ascertained by abundant experiment and traditional use. Under such circumstances there is no difficulty in making the proper selection; but this is not always the case, and we may be called upon to determine the comparative salubrity of water from various sources. *Rain-water* is the purest water found in nature. It is, indeed, water distilled principally by evaporation from the surface of the ocean and condensed by varying changes of atmospheric temperature. The small quantity of iodine which it contains may be evaporated from the ocean, and in the act of precipitation it takes up atmospheric air with an additional portion of oxygen, carbonic anhydride, ammonium nitrate and carbonate, undetermined nitrogenous matter, and various impurities from dust and other sources of local contamination. Liebig tells us: " It is worthy of observation that the ammonia contained in rain and snow water has an offensive smell of perspiration and animal excrements; a fact which leaves no doubt respecting its origin." The first rain of a shower is much more charged with this nitrogenous matter and dust, especially after a protracted period of dry weather, and, therefore, it should be allowed to run to waste in collecting rain-water for domestic uses. It has been suggested that the nitrates are formed by the discharge of electricity in thunderstorms. This, however, can hardly be the case exclusively, for there are places, in Peru, for instance, where rain and thunderstorms are unknown, and where the nitrates are constantly precipitating and incrusting the earth, so as to be profitably extracted by lixiviation. Rain-water is by some considered the very best drinking-water. It certainly answers the purpose perfectly well, and is probably neither better nor worse for the absence of the earthy salts usually found in river and spring water. When carefully collected, kept for a week or two in an iron or brickwork cistern, till its organic matters are decomposed and cooled to a proper temperature, there is probably no better drinking-water to be obtained.

Snow-water contains less oxygen than rain-water, but differs from it apparently in no other important particular.

(87.) *River-water* contains all the impurities of rain-water, with the addition of such matters as it may collect from the soil; except that in some instances it may lose more organic matters by decomposition than it receives in its course. The impurities of river-water are as various as the constituents of the soil through which it flows. A large portion of these are necessary constituents of our bodies, and we may actually receive them partly from this source; but that they may be derived from other sources, and are not essential to the character of good drinking-water, is sufficiently proved by the excellence of rain-water, which does not contain them.

River-water is often unpleasantly muddy, but this fault may be corrected by rest, with or without alum, or by filtering. Rivers flowing through flat countries are apt to have marshes and marshy pools in the hollows near their banks, and they are always in some degree contaminated by the unwholesome water of these marshes. The water of such rivers has occasionally been found very unwholesome, causing epidemics of malarial fever (intermittent and remittent) and dysentery. These bad qualities may be obviated in some degree by boiling and cooling, as with marsh-water. Rivers as they approach the ocean become brackish, especially where there is much rise and fall of the tide. This seriously injures the water, but the fault is in some degree corrected if the water be kept for some time in iron tanks before using; and even throwing a handful of nails into a cask of such water greatly improves its quality.

Rivers afford the only adequate supply of water for large cities. The Thames, besides serving as an outlet for the sewers, formerly supplied the whole city of London with drinking-water by the various water-works built along its banks. "The Thames water has a smell of excrement even after the application of all usual means of purification."—(*Normandy.*) This disgusting and unhealthy arrangement is being gradually corrected. The Schuylkill, supplying the city of Philadelphia, passes by the manufacturing town of Manaynnk, and is, probably, not as pure as it might be, though it contains but about one-eighth as much organic matter as the Croton, and less than one-tenth as much as the Thames. Detroit, Michigan, has probably purer water than any other city in the world. The following are about the proportions of mineral and organic matter per thousand in some of the waters which supply large cities, varying much, of course, with seasons and freshets.—(*Bell.*)

WATERS.	MINERAL MATTER.	ORGANIC MATTER.
Schuylkill, ...	3.508 to 5.5	.037
Croton, ...	4.998	.276
Cochituate, ...	1.220	.500
Thames, ...	10.925	.392
Seine, ...	10.662	traces.

(88.) *Spring-water* varies much in quality. It is rain-water filtered through the soil, in which process it loses a large portion of the organic matters which it had received from the air, and it dissolves various minerals which it meets in the earth. Hence its quality varies with the character of the soil through which it flows. When the spring comes from a sloping hill of primitive or transition rock, the water having lost its organic matter, and received nothing injurious, it affords probably the very best natural drinking-water. But spring-water, according to the situation, is liable to receive every soluble substance in nature; and hence, the great variety of saline, sulphur, and chalybeate springs. A spring may occasionally drain a marsh at no great distance, and be contaminated by the injurious decaying material which belongs to stagnant water.

(89.) *Well-water*, or pump-water, may be considered as identical with spring-water. If the well be in a well-drained slope, with a basis of primitive rock, there is no better water anywhere, but in limestone and marshy districts it is about the worst. Wells are much more liable than springs to dangerous contaminations from local causes, especially in and near cities. The following extract from a newspaper is a case in point:

"POISONOUS WELLS.—Any one passing Richmond Terrace, Clifton, during the last week or ten days, must have remarked the long string of doctors' carriages drawn up in the neighborhood. The reason for this formidable display was the existence of illness in almost every second house, the inhabitants of which were afflicted with gastric fever (typhoid). Nearly a whole school of young ladies were lying ill at the same time, and there was scarcely a family which had not some of its members sick. It was not, however, till one death had taken place, and several were in imminent danger, that the cause of this extensive illness was discovered. It turned out to be produced by the use of a spring which supplied the place, and whose waters had been imperceptibly poisoned by a sewer breaking into it, and so vitiating their character as to cause gastric fever in every family using it. On being found out, of course the evil was remedied, but not before much mischief had been done. The necessity of a pure water supply and an improved system of sewerage were shown."— *Bristol Times.*

(90.) The *water of marshes* and stagnant pools is contaminated by the decaying organic matters collected in such places. If men should be constrained by necessity to use such water, they may get rid of much of the poisonous quality by boiling and cooling it, by which they stop the decay for the time, and drive off the poisonous gases held in solution. The air is expelled at the same time, so as to render the water unpleasantly insipid; but this fault may be corrected by aeration, or infusing any pleasantly bitter or aromatic plant, making tea.

(91.) On foreign stations, it frequently becomes an important matter to select the best place for obtaining a supply of wholesome water. In mountainous countries there is, as a rule, no difficulty, for every spring, unless possessing some evident mineral quality, affords such water as we need; and if it flow for some distance in a brook, it is none the worse. Before receiving water from a brook, it is desirable to follow it up for some distance to its source, in order to see that there are no stagnant pools or other source of contamination along its banks. If the bed of the brook is of pebbles or sand, and the banks sloping or abrupt, and its course rapid, there need not be much further questioning about the good quality of the water. In fact, it may often be an advantage to have the water flow some distance in a brook of this kind, as it affords excellent aeration, by which the proportion of atmospheric air and carbonic anhydride are brought to the proper average, and any mineral matter in excess may be precipitated.

But we have not always the advantage of such a situation. The water of marshy places is to be avoided, as well as that of sluggish little streams flowing through a flat country. In case of necessity, water from the middle of a large river should be taken in preference, as from its longer course its organic matter has had more time for decomposition, and for the poisonous results of decay to be dissipated. Low sand islands, without much vegetation, in the immediate vicinity of the ocean, generally furnish an abundance of excellent water, especially in seasons of much rain. The rain displaces the sea-water, and remains nearer the surface, so that it may be obtained perfectly good by digging shallow wells. Good water is sometimes obtained from wells of this kind, even so near the ocean that the rise and fall of water in them correspond with the movements of the tide. But with much rise and fall of tide, the water is liable to become brackish by infiltration from the ocean. If this is merely perceptible to the taste, the water need not be absolutely rejected, especially if we have iron tanks in which to preserve it; for it quickly loses its salts without other inconvenience than rusting somewhat the tanks.

CHAPTER XI

PURIFYING AND PRESERVING WATER.

(92.) RIVER-WATER is generally charged with earthy impurities. These may be principally removed by allowing it to remain for a time at rest in a tank or reservoir, using the clear water from the top after the subsidence of the insoluble material. The organic matter is at the same time decomposed and removed by the atmosphere. This is the process most generally available for purification on a large scale, and is greatly accelerated by the addition of a very small quantity of alum, four or five grains to the barrel, not enough to be tasted or to injure the water in any way.

(93.) A much more expeditious process, and more effective on a small scale, is by filtration. There are several ways of effecting this, but the most generally applicable is to pass the water through alternate layers of sand and gravel, with sometimes an addition of charcoal. Filters of various sizes thus arranged may be obtained almost everywhere, and can certainly be made by any common mechanic with but very little special instruction or supervision. They are often a source of much comfort. In the margin we represent a sectional plan of a filter which

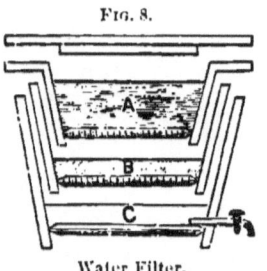

FIG. 8.

Water Filter.

may readily be made by a cooper. It consists of a vessel, A, to receive the muddy water, with gimlet-holes in the bottom which transmit it to B, the second compartment, packed with gravel, sand, and gravel in successive layers, through which the water filters to C, the third division, from which it may be drawn for use. The sand, thus situated, seems capable of arresting, not only mechanical impurities, but, in some degree, even soluble salts. This filter, being made up of separate pieces, may without trouble be taken apart, cleaned, and repaired. It has the disadvantage that being made of wood the water may be somewhat injured by the material. If made of iron or earthenware it would be nearly perfect. A very nice filter is made of soft sandstone by fashioning it into a vessel of conical form, about two inches thick, and mounting it in a frame, so that a vessel placed underneath may receive the water as it drips through. A dripstone of this kind may very well supply drinking-water for thirty or forty persons, and has the additional advantage, that it cools the water considerably in dry weather; but it has not sufficient capacity to filter water on a large scale.

(94.) Boiling and cooling some varieties of water may occasionally be advantageous. It precipitates the excess of carbonate of lime, and some other impurities. It expels the gaseous remains of decaying organic matter, and decomposes the poisons most likely to be present in marsh-water. The water by this process is deprived in some degree, if not entirely, of its poisonous properties; but by the loss of its carbonic acid and atmospheric air, it becomes so flat as to be quite unpleasant to the taste, and barely drinkable. By filtering and exposure to the air this may be corrected, and the water thus treated, *cocta et dein refrigerata*, becomes drinkable.

(95.) The distillation of sea-water is a means of obtaining good water on shipboard, which is likely to become of great importance. In sailing ships, on long voyages, it greatly economizes space, as it requires little more than a pound of coal to make a gallon of pure water, besides doing the cooking for the crew at the same time. In war steamers there is often much steam wasted by banked fires, etc., which might as well be condensed and used. Distilled water is deprived of air and salts, and is hence insipid, and is rendered further unpleasant by a disagreeable flavor, probably derived from the decomposition by heat of small quantities of organic matter. These disadvantages have in some degree been obviated by churning and other devices for exposing it to the action of the air; but the empyreumatic flavor is hard to get rid of without the intervention of considerable time. We are inclined to think that distilled water preserved in iron tanks about half full, long enough to lose its burnt flavor, perhaps a week, would likewise be sufficiently aerated, especially with the motion of the ship at sea. In this time it would further approximate to the characters of the best drinking-waters; it would receive its full portion of iron from the tank; it would certainly get all the chloride of sodium required without any special care; half an ounce of the carpenter's chalk to a hundred gallons would supply as much carbonate of lime as is usually present in the best drinking-water; and thus we may have about as good drinking-water as any in the world. If it be necessary to imitate more exactly any natural water, we have only to add, in proper proportions, a very small quantity of carbonate of potash, magnesia, and ammonia, and a few drops of sulphuric acid. The best waters vary greatly in the proportion of these salts; they are, however, always present in small quantities, and an excess of any of them beyond a grain or two to the gallon is enough to spoil the water. The ammonia, representing decaying organic matter, should be omitted altogether. Whatever is added in this way should be added as soon as possible, in order to allow time for thorough incorporation, in accordance with the natural affinities. The fresh water condensed to form the vacuum of the steam-engine is so highly charged with empyreumatic material, derived from the oil of the cylinders, that it is quite offensive, and useless even for washing clothes. We read somewhere of a crew being cast away on a desolate island without water. They had, however, the carpenter's pitch-kettle and a gun-barrel, which were arranged into an effective distilling apparatus of sufficient capacity to save their lives. The call for water was probably so urgent in this case that there was not much objection to the flavor.

At my suggestion, on board the flag-ship Lancaster, in 1870, the idea of aeration by a small pebbly brook was put in practice. A trough about ten feet long was arranged with transverse partitions to make little cascades, and half filled with pebbles. There was no filter about it, and no unpleasant flavor could be found in distilled water aerated in this way. It was worked on the spar-deck to insure pure air. The apparatus was afterwards changed to the form of a large funnel, as represented in the diagram (Fig. 9). A funnel of this kind, twenty inches square and twenty-five high, suffices for five thousand gallons in twenty-four hours.

(96.) The general use of iron tanks on shipboard, for preserving and purifying water, is one of the great improvements of modern times. The small amount of iron dissolved in the water does no harm, but probably assists in precipitating the organic matter which the water, as received, may happen to contain. The iron being acted on by the salts which may be in excess, they are decomposed, especially the sulphates and chlorides, and brackish water thus becomes good and wholesome. When the organic matters have once decayed, nothing susceptible of decay can be derived from the iron, and water thus preserved is no more subject to decay or change than rock crystal. Occasionally, in rough weather, some iron rust may make the water turbid; but this is no great disadvantage, and may readily be removed by a filter, or a provision of limpid water may easily be kept on hand by transferring limpid water from its sediment into clean tanks on proper occasions. Rain-water collected from roofs and kept in large iron or brickwork reservoirs is generally the best water obtainable in tropical seaports.

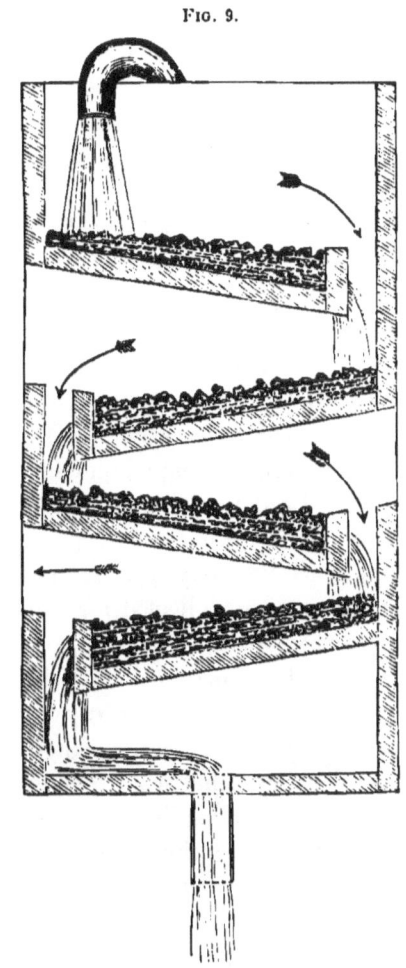

Fig. 9.

Aerator for Distilled Water.

(97.) Wooden casks were formerly in general use for keeping water on shipboard. But the wood is constantly decaying and supplying organic matter for offensive decomposition, as long as the water remains in contact with it. From this cause the water is always offensive, except during the first few hours after its introduction into the casks. The degree of offensiveness is much varied by circumstances. It is much mitigated by leaving the bung out of the cask for a day or two before using, so as to permit the escape of the offensive gases into the atmosphere. Scraps of iron, or a few nails, thrown into a cask, have great influence in preserving the water. The iron seems to prevent the solution of organic matter from the oaken casks, and, probably by combining with any sulphur present, prevents the decomposition from becoming of so offensive a character. Charring the interior of the casks and scrupulous cleanliness are measures which have their use; but wooden casks should never be used for preserving water, except for a very short time, as on boat excursions, or merely for transferring water from the beach to the ship. Custom can do much in the way of making this offensive water tolerable, and some seafaring men have pretended even to prefer water a little tainted in this way; but the number of them is very small, and such water is not wholesome.

(98.) Leaden reservoirs, tanks, and pipes were formerly much in use for collecting and keeping water; but lead has proved very dangerous, not only in this shape, but when used in roofs from which water is collected for domestic use. This material being much more expensive than iron, as well as unsafe, we suppose it will soon be superseded entirely for these purposes. The small leaden pipes, with their convenient flexibility, seem as yet to maintain a position among the water fixtures of large cities; the absurd maxim that what is most costly must necessarily be best, seeming to be the principal reason that this dangerous and expensive material continues to be used even to this limited extent. No serious accidents, that we are aware of, have ever occurred either in Philadelphia or New York from this cause. This exemption appears due to the salts and organic matter in the water, forming promptly a solid coating like paint on the interior surface of the leaden tube, in such a way as to prevent further corrosion. Another reason is, perhaps, the great abundance and consequent waste of water; so that a person drawing a vessel of water for use generally allows a quantity to run to waste first, thus unconsciously rejecting all the water which has remained any time in contact with the pipes.

Zinc and copper, it should not be forgotten, are likewise capable of poisoning the water which remains long in contact with them.

CHAPTER XII.

ALCOHOLIC AND VINOUS DRINKS—RUM—שׁכר.

The more carefully I have explored the question, the more I have become convinced that the undue use and uncontrolled employment of alcoholic drinks is an enemy which the physician and the philosopher ought most to fear in its opposition to the progress of humanity.—BOUCHARDAT.

(99.) WE treat of alcoholic and vinous drinks together, not because they are identical, absolutely, but because they are of so little use as mere drinks, and because they are all liable to abuse in the same way, with the same pitiable results. Alcohol separated by distillation from the vinous liquors in which it is formed acquires new properties, and can never, by mixing, be restored to the same intimate association with the other material of the wine as it previously possessed. Mixed alcoholic drinks appear, for some reason, much more injurious than wines containing an equal proportion of alcohol. "Alcohol by itself may be stated, in relation to the human economy, to be nothing but an irritant poison. It cannot enter the system except in small quantities associated with comparatively large quantities of water; and even then it produces poisonous effects, which are familiarly known from daily observation."—(Carpenter.)

(100.) Some of the principal alcoholic and vinous liquors contain alcohol or its elements in about the proportions indicated in the following table :

LIQUORS.	WATER.	ALCOHOL.
Rectified spirits of wine (s. g. 835), ...	50	50
Proof spirits (s. g. 935), ...	75	25
Brandy, whisky, and rum, ...	80	20
Port wine, Sherry, and Madeira, mixed with brandy, for the English and American markets, ...	90	10
Port, Sherry, and Madeira, prepared for use in the countries where produced, ...	95	5

Various other wines contain still less alcohol associated with the acids and other material of the fruits. Cider is a vinous liquor prepared from apples; perry, from pears; currant wine, from currants; beer, from barley, etc. They differ from wine only in containing the acids and salts of the fruits from which they are derived, instead of the acids of grapes.

These liquors may all have their use medicinally. "Give strong drink unto him that is ready to perish."—Prov. xxxi. "Use a little wine for thy stomach's sake and thine often infirmities."—1 Tim. v, 23. But medical prescription is not now our object. Some of them, doubtless, had their hygienic value, being capable of affording variety and a grateful change from mere water, when tea and coffee were unknown. They have always been liable to abuse, and we may quote the most important hygienic maxims in regard to them from literature almost as old as the flood. Thus we read in Proverbs xxiii:

20. Be not among wine-bibbers; among riotous eaters of flesh.

21. For the drunkard and the glutton shall come to poverty, and drowsiness shall clothe a man with rags.

29. Who hath woe? Who hath sorrow? Who hath contentions? Who hath babbling? Who hath wounds without cause? Who hath redness of eyes?

30. They that tarry long at the wine; they that go to seek mixed wine.

32. At the last it biteth like a serpent and stingeth like an adder.

(101.) Though very sure of the evils of any mere habit of drinking, we would not be understood to say that there is no good use for any of these liquors. Brandy, whisky, and rum are precious cordials and stimulants in many emergencies; they are capable of easy preservation, so that they can be carried, in good condition, to any part of the world. In pharmacy, alcohol is an important agent in obtaining the vegetable alkaloids, which are among the most powerful and convenient of all medicines; it is exceedingly useful in preserving the medicinal properties of many vegetable and mineral substances; and we need not omit that it is very useful in preserving anatomical preparations and natural history specimens. But for all this, the man is very unfortunate, a real object of pity, who has reduced his system to the necessity of receiving a cordial of this kind every day.

We are much accustomed to hear the ill effects of alcoholic

drinks attributed to their bad quality and adulteration.   But the sulphuric acid added to give a pleasant ethereal odor, and the various peppers and spices added to give pungency, are very innocent articles as compared with the intoxicating alcohol which is a necessary and constant constituent.   We do not entertain so good an opinion of strychnine, popularly known as an effective poison for dogs, or *Cocculus indicus;* and these are said to be occasionally added for the purpose of increasing the intoxicating power of these liquors.

(102.) Brandy and other alcoholic liquors lose much of their intoxicating property and improve in flavor with age.   When preserved in oaken casks, as is the rule, there is considerable loss of alcohol by evaporation, and a still larger proportional loss of various poisonous empyreumatic oils; and what is still more characteristic, there is dissolved tannin, coloring matter, and whatever else is soluble about the oak.   This gives to brandy the color which belongs to it, for it comes from the still limpid as water.   The dealers have a way of giving age without this tedious and expensive process.   They give the required color with a little burnt sugar.   They supply the tannin and other oak material with extract of bark or parings of leather from the shoemaker's shops, and they may get rid of the empyreumatic oils by filtering through charcoal.   So far we consider the adulterations comparatively innocent—only swindling.   Gross adulterations may be detected by chemical reagents, but the only test of genuine liquors is the aroma.

(103.) Since the general use of tea and coffee has superseded wine as the beverage of the morning and evening meals, it seems impossible, except where the grape culture forms a leading object of industry, to obtain wine of good quality without foreign admixture.   The best generally obtainable with us are port, Madeira, and sherry, as usually prepared for the English market. These are mixed with brandy to the extent of about twenty per cent., partly to give the degree of pungency which the palate of the liquor drinkers requires, and partly to preserve it from change. So that, as beverages, these wines are little better than brandy in disguise; but for medicinal purposes these brandied wines are well adapted, and have the great advantage that without any special care they are preserved in a pretty uniform condition for a long time. With genuine wines this is very far from being the case, for without special care the fermentation continues and breaks some of the bottles, and some of the wine is partially converted to vinegar. The wines are found in the market in various stages of progressive acidity, and this condition is apt to be disguised by acetate of lead and various other drugs which it is most important to avoid.

(104.) The first conspicuous result of alcoholic intoxication is feebleness of muscular power, a tendency to general paralysis. At first the ends of the fingers become enfeebled; the person can but imperfectly close the hand, and permits objects which he has grasped to fall. This weakness extends to the arm and shoulder. It soon appears in the legs; the gait is tottering and uncertain. In connection with this is a marked loss or diminution of sensation. This commences with a dulness of the sense of touch in the fingers and gradually extends over the whole body. The natural propensities are obliterated, but modesty and discretion being absent at the same time, the victims are frequently led to disgraceful acts which at other times they would avoid. Drunkards become subject to fits, generally epileptic. With respect to the intellectual faculties, a settled stupidity overwhelms them. The memory is weakened. The countenance indicates stupidity and sloth. The effects on the digestive system call for particular attention. The effect of drams, not very much diluted, is to stimulate and thicken the lining of the mouth and other surfaces with which the liquor comes in contact. A few drams may not produce any very appreciable effect in this way; but the person addicted to the habit of a morning dram, who never gets drunk, does suffer in this way. The mouth is commonly dry, especially in the morning; the tongue thick and cleft; there is uneasiness at the pit of the stomach, with distaste for solid food, and perhaps vomiting. Diluted alcohol is readily absorbed by the stomach in this condition, and promptly relieves the feeling for the moment. But this is not the case with solid food, which, not having a healthy stomach to digest it, putrefies, and the sufferer becomes saturated with the gases of putrefaction, readily perceived in his breath, and sometimes in his perspiration. He smells like carrion. The liver usually becomes diseased; at first enlarged by fatty degeneration, but later, the fat being absorbed,

induration is produced—*cirrhosis à petits grains*—the true drunkard's liver.   The consequence of this is incurable abdominal
dropsy, eventually fatal.   The course of nutrition under the use
of alcohol, however, may be stated to be, in the first place, exaggeration; the individual addicted to drink becomes fuller in
habit, with injection of the skin and redness of the face.   As the
organs become diseased with the deposit of fat in them, their
functional actions become embarrassed, and then, with depraved
digestion and the abstraction of the proper elements of repara-
tion, the blood becomes watery, and with impeded circulation in
the heart or liver, dropsical effusions, general or local, are inevit-
able.   The first augmentation of size is from the increase of fat
in all the tissues; the second is from serous effusions.   This
latter condition is known in common language as the " white
bloat."

The social use of alcoholic drinks, as a physiological question,
is still under discussion in England.   The consumption of these
articles is so enormous that many men do not easily submit to
Dr. Carpenter's opinions, and we have hence quite a number of
elaborate arguments in defence of the custom.   We quote from
the London *Lancet* part of the conclusion of one of these articles :

" Again, the teetotalers contend that in case of alcohol it is impossible to de-
fine moderation and excess; but this is equally true of tea, coffee, salt, sugar,
pepper, and many other things. . . . . The truth is, there is a certain recognized standard quantity of alcohol, salt, sugar, tea, coffee, etc., which all men
agree to call moderate, and the difficulty is not greater in the case of alcohol
than of any other article of daily consumption."

We are ready to admit the difficulty of defining with precision
the quantity of sugar and pepper which each person should use,
and even, for the sake of argument, that some persons use these
articles rather freely; but the journalist will hardly convince us
that such deplorable consequences as we have described as commonly resulting from indulgence in alcoholic intoxication ever
result from excess in the use of salt, pepper, tea, coffee, sugar,
etc.   We have never known the habit of using these things in
excess to grow irresistibly on the individual to such a degree as
to destroy or break up his family.

The rejoinder may as well be so stated, that even the drunk-ard will not be likely to misunderstand it. By the use of alco-holic drinks, men are so demented that it has been found neces-sary to establish special asylums and hospitals for their care—to restrain them in the use of liquor, to enforce bathing and clean clothes, with small hope of eventual cure. We know persons who use salt profusely, but they are not so demented as to need special asylums. They do not crowd the hospitals for insane, the jails, the almshouses.

CHAPTER XIII.

(105.) *Tea and coffee* are very rapidly superseding the dangerous vinous and alcoholic drinks as ordinary beverages at meals. There is nothing but advantage in this change. Other aromatic infusions may occasionally replace these advantageously. *Chocolate* requires to be associated with spice as a rule; it is otherwise too fat and heavy for most persons. The Paraguay tea and Carolina tea are probably just as good, hygienically, as the China tea, if they could only be collected and prepared for market with the same degree of neatness and precision. The imitations of coffee, made of parched corn, rye, beans, chiccory, etc., are not to be despised when the genuine article is not to be obtained; the parching being carried a little further than is proper with coffee, develops empyreumatic flavors which do not differ greatly from those found in the best coffee when parched too much. There must be something about these hot aromatic infusions very much in accordance with the wants of civilized man, which has caused the rapid spread of their use over the temperate regions of the globe in modern times. We have already alluded to the possible necessity of using the unwholesome water of marshes, and have recommended that it be boiled to deprive it of its poisonous properties. But mere boiling renders it insipid, and unwholesome from want of flavor. It hence becomes desirable to give such water flavor, and this may be done by infusing tea or any aromatic substance at hand which may be found agreeable. We would recommend the use of almost any aromatic or bitter weed of the forest, not actually poisonous, rather than the drinking of crude marsh-water. The infusion of sassafras, used in some parts of our country, furnishes, in some cases, no doubt, an agreeable variety; but it has not much to recommend it unless it be medicinally or in exceptional cases. Its flavor is rather unpleasant to most persons.

(106.) *The vegetable acids* form a constant and probably essential part in every good system of alimentation, especially in the tropics. We know so little of the manner of their action that we really have nothing to say on the subject, except that experience appears to have demonstrated their necessity, and that there are physiological necessities in the animal economy to which chemical analyses and formulæ afford us no clue. These acids are ordinarily supplied by the fruits and fresh vegetables which form part of our daily food; but at sea this is no longer the case, and the pickles and dried fruits of the ration seem not to be always a sufficient substitute. There is hence a necessity for these acids in some other shape, and we have some of them, in various forms, preserved for sea use, as vinegar, lemon-juice, citric acid, tartaric acid, bitartrate of potassa, and claret and other acid wines. These, besides their use as condiments, are variously mixed with water, sugar and aromatics to form drinks, which, used with moderation and discretion, are very advantageous in warm weather.

(107.) *Vinegar* is generally allowed at discretion for this purpose, and when mixed with a proper portion of water, sugar, or molasses and nutmeg, makes a very refreshing drink for a thirsty man, as he rests from active labor, in warm weather. Vinegar, besides acetic acid, contains a good portion of malic, tartaric, and other acids of the fruits from which it is derived, as well as some other material (nitrogenous?) of the fruit. It certainly serves an excellent purpose in the prevention of scorbutus, sea scurvy. But vinegar for this purpose should be made only from the juice of fruits.

(108.) *Lime or lemon juice* is perhaps even better than vinegar. It is not regularly furnished in our naval service, except medicinally; but with the English the greatest reliance is placed in it, and their comparative immunity from scorbutus in modern times is generally attributed to the use of this article. It is issued daily, after the first fourteen days at sea, in the quantity of half an ounce to each man. This is imbibed in the shape of lemonade at dinner, and adds prodigiously to the health and efficiency of the crew. The lime-juice for this purpose, after being pressed from the fruit, is simmered so as to coagulate most of the albumen, strained and mixed with a sufficient quantity of proof spirit to preserve it from fermentation, covered with olive oil, corked and sealed. Besides citric acid, it contains, especially when freshly prepared, other vegetable matter important to healthy nutrition. When long kept it undergoes further changes, and in the instances in which we have had occasion to use it after being thus kept, it appeared in no way superior to a solution of crystals of citric acid. It is common to attribute the disappearance of scorbutus in modern times to the use of this substance, but we must take into the account the general improvement of the seamen's rations in other respects, introduced at the same time. There is no more of this disease in our service or the French than in the English, though preserved lime-juice forms no part of the ration with us. The English have a great advantage in the systematic perseverance with which it is issued as soon as the prescribed fourteen days have elapsed. Citric acid dissolved in water in the proper proportion, with a little oil of lemon, makes a more pleasant lemonade and is perhaps nearly as useful as the lemon-juice, and it possesses one certain advantage, as its crystals may be preserved for any length of time without change. Tartaric acid may be used in the same way with the same beneficial results, and may be given advantageously in alternation with citric acid. Bitartrate of potassa, cream of tartar, is likewise useful on some occasions, but its sparing solubility is a decided inconvenience, and it probably possesses in a much less degree the useful properties which belong to all these substances.

Light acid wines, such as the wines of Bordeaux—vin de campagne of the French ration—must be classed here. They are saturated with the vegetable acids,—tartaric, citric, and malic, together with their salts, and they contain very little alcohol, just enough to preserve them from decomposition—about as much as is added in the English preparation of lime-juice. This wine is certainly an excellent antiscorbutic, not at all inferior to lime-juice. But I would not encourage its introduction into the ration, simply because it is wine, of an austere acid flavor, that our sailors do not like, and if we encourage among them the idea that there is any good property in wine, they will surely seek occasionally for wine more to their liking. The drunkard's craving "is not dead."

These acid drinks are liable to abuse. In warm weather there is such a pleasant feeling of refreshment as the immediate result

of a drink that the habit is readily formed of taking it too frequently. The result is pain and cramp of the bowels, with sometimes a little diarrhœa. These unpleasant symptoms promptly
disappear when the acid drinks are discontinued. It is in the
absence of fruits at sea that they are really useful.

(109.) *Farinaceous Drinks.*—On board steamships the firemen
employed about the furnaces are sometimes greatly exhausted by
heat. Their profuse perspiration renders a large quantity of water
necessary to supply the waste. The ingestion of clear water under
these circumstances appears to answer very imperfectly the wants
of the system. It seems to pass through the circulation to the
skin, percolate as through a sieve, and flow over the surface of
the body in streams. A large drink of cold or even cool water,
under these circumstances, on an empty stomach, is very dangerous, and liable to produce death with almost the suddenness of an
electric shock. Great practical advantage has been obtained by
mixing farinaceous substances, particularly oatmeal, with the
water to be used by the men employed at this kind of labor.

The oatmeal is mixed in the proportion of three or four ounces
to the gallon of water, and used according to inclination by the
firemen and coal-heavers. It might be difficult to determine why
oatmeal, for this purpose, should be better than cornmeal, or buck-
wheat, or rye, wheat, millet, etc., but the firemen themselves seem
to think it has the effect of making them as strong as horses. We
may safely allow something for this sort of prejudice, which we
know to be very potent among the influences on health and disease. The peculiar aroma of the oats is probably associated with
a pleasant degree of stimulation of the alimentary mucous surfaces
in such a way as to promote its complete digestion. It seems to
fill the bloodvessels without increasing the amount of cutaneous
exhalations. The men occasionally try acid, saccharine, and alcoholic drinks as substitutes for the oats, but always with unsatis-
factory results, except that they find molasses and water better
than clear water, and they who are disposed to insist on the excellence of rum and whisky, under all circumstances, petition for
these, and experience after each ingestion a momentary relief, followed by additional profuseness of perspiration and additional exhaustion.

The *attoley* of our Indians is a nutritive beverage of this kind, used principally at the South and throughout Mexico. It is made by parching their corn (maize) or other grain, pounding it to meal in a suitable cavity of a rock, with a smooth stone, and mixing it with a little sugar if they have it. About a tablespoonful of this is stirred with a pint of water from the spring, and swallowed at two or three drinks, according to inclination. An Indian, provided with about two pounds of attoley in a little bag, is prepared to perform the most fatiguing and dangerous journey of two or three weeks, without expecting any assistance or supplies by the way except water from the spring or brook twice a day. He appropriates, of course, any little food which comes in his way, but when this amounts to next to nothing he comes out of such an expedition without much apparent suffering or inconvenience. Nearly any other grain or grass seed seems to answer the purpose, though the Indian corn is generally preferred. The California Indians make a similar preparation by parching and pounding the seeds of a species of pine. This they call pinoley, and seem to think it nearly as good as the *atolè de mais*, Indian corn attoley. The parching has the effect of bursting the grains of starch and rendering the meal thus prepared more readily miscible with water; it likewise develops a peculiar aroma, due to resulting empyreumatic substances, which is probably advantageous, by affording a comfortable stimulus to the stomach and thus promoting digestion. The use of these preparations may be considered as demonstrating that a very small quantity of food, when fully digested and assimilated, is capable of supplying the waste of the system even through extraordinary labor and fatigue.

CHAPTER XIV.

THE PRESERVATION OF FOOD.

(110.) THE solid food required by the human organism is principally supplied by three or four species of animals, which, on account of their peculiar adaptation, have been domesticated for this special purpose, and by such fruits and vegetables as are neither poisonous nor inconveniently hard and fibrous. The preservation of these substances in such a way as to make them available as nutriment at sea, is of vast importance. The processes which are most effective in preventing ordinary decay or putrefaction, destroy, at the same time, in various degrees, the nutritive properties of the substance preserved.

(111.) *Salting*, packing in salt, seems with us to be the most generally available method of preserving the flesh of animals in a condition to be used for food. Muscular flesh, as beef, when fully subjected to the action of salt for a length of time, becomes unsuitably hard and probably undergoes other changes which render it nearly incapable of digestion by the human organism. The other animal tissues, especially fat, probably undergo less change. Hence fat beef, when salted, remains good much longer than lean, and the muscular tissue of pork, being much more thoroughly imbued with fat, is comparatively indestructible when packed in salt. Pork seems never to degenerate, as beef does, into a mahogany-like substance, beyond the powers of the teeth to masticate.

(112.) *Drying* seems to be the most generally available means of preserving alimentary substances. Nature furnishes us many dry vegetable substances, especially small seeds, capable in this state of almost indefinite preservation. If the seed be once broken, as grain is in the preparation of flour, and its vitality thus destroyed, its preservation is much more difficult and precarious. Very many fruits and vegetables—apples, pears, peaches, plums, cherries, etc.,—are capable of a useful degree of preservation by merely drying them in the open air. Meat in some countries is more generally preserved by drying than by any other process. The muscular flesh is cut from the bones in long thin strips, and these are hung in the open air to dry ; the drying is somewhat promoted and the flies kept off or annoyed in their operations by a very smoky fire. The flesh of the bullock, by this operation, is converted into hard strings and knots of no very pleasant fragrance, called jerked beef. It is so hard and intractable after this kind of preparation, that soaking, boiling, and stewing are scarcely sufficient to bring it within ordinary powers of mastication without a preliminary beating with a hammer, so as to separate somewhat the fibres. This kind of meat is the resort of hunters across the desert plains, and on all occasions when their hunting does not supply them sufficiently with fresh game. Likewise on the grazing farms of Spanish America it is the universal manner of curing meat for their own use during the season of poor cattle. As we have never tasted this meat and have had very little opportunity of observing its use, we may not be able to estimate its value correctly ; but we have never heard anything about it to induce us to believe that it can be advantageously used much more extensively than at present. Its comparatively small bulk, light weight, and easy transportation, render it valuable to the hunter as a precaution against starvation in the various emergencies of forest life.

Rapid desiccation, at a moderate temperature, as it may be effected in a vacuum, is one of the valuable processes of recent invention for the preservation of vegetable food. Almost every variety of vegetables may be preserved in this way with much of their original flavor. They are not injured by heat, as is apt to be the case with vegetables dried in an oven, or by decay, as occurs by drying by long exposure to the air. Vegetables dried in this way and packed in air-tight tin cans, are preserved in any climate for a very long time without much apparent change, and by immersion for an hour or two in fresh, cold water, before cooking, they acquire much of the bulk and fragrance which belong to them as fresh vegetables.

(113.) *Smoking* is, under certain circumstances, a valuable method, in conjunction with those already mentioned, of preserving meat. The smoke gives its antiseptic creasote to the meat, imparting a pleasant flavor at the same time that it assists in its preservation. It gives to the surface of the meat a crust so highly charged with creasote as to be very offensive, perhaps even destructive, to insects which might be otherwise injurious. But mere smoking is not sufficient to cure meat. Hams, moderately salted and considerably dried during the process of smoking, are well preserved and universally liked; and other parts of the hog treated in the same way are pretty generally appreciated. Some pieces of beef, particularly the rounds, are occasionally preserved in the same way, but it is liable to become mouldy in a short time unless pretty thoroughly dried, and if too much dried it is so hard as not to be of much use. Neither hams nor bacon seem to be generally available for long voyages, except as an occasional luxury or relief from the monotonous diet necessarily connected with them. In this limited degree they are very useful in improving the diet and thus preserving the health of those who go to sea.

(114.) *Immersion in oil*, so as to prevent the direct action of the atmosphere, is found greatly to retard though not altogether to prevent putrefaction. Sardines thus preserved are now common in most seaport towns. The oil and the necessary labor of packing them neatly for preservation, render them too expensive for very general use; but they are very useful occasionally to vary the monotony of sea diet. It is in connection with other preservative processes that immersion in fat or oil may become valuable, and is probably capable of great extension. The best preserved fish we have ever seen on shipboard were herrings, which had been salted a little, just as much as is required to give fresh fish a proper flavor; smoked a little, just enough to be perceptible; dried a little, probably in the process of smoking; trimmed of superfluous parts, heads, tails, and fins, and packed in small tin boxes, with oil, in the manner of sardines. We think this process of preserving herrings for use at sea should become common. Properly prepared lard-oil answers the purpose perfectly. Other species of fish and other meats may doubtless be preserved in the same way. It is a common thing in families to preserve sausages in this way. The sausages are seasoned as usual with salt, herbs, and spices, varying with the fancy of the different housekeepers, packed in earthenware, or preferably metallic vessels, and covered by pouring over them melted lard. They are preserved in this way for a very long time. We have eaten good sausages preserved in this way, which had crossed the equator and been carried more than half round the world. The Indians of the Northwest preserve the flesh of the bison somewhat in this way. In the season when the animals are in good order whole villages start on hunting expeditions. As soon as an animal is slain the muscles are cut into strips and hung up to dry as in preparing jerked beef; but before it is thoroughly hardened it is beaten into shreds, packed in suitable vessels, and the melted fat of the animal poured over it. Bison beef, thus prepared, is called pemmican, and is the winter food of several tribes. Of its properties as food we know little, except that these people are fond of it and enjoy health while using it.

(115.) *Immersion in vinegar* is a process occasionally available for the preservation of both animal and vegetable food. It deprives the food thus treated of all natural flavor, and substitutes its own, which is greatly esteemed in some of the articles thus preserved. They are exceedingly pleasant for occasional use. There is generally some spice added to improve the flavor. Pigs' feet and other parts of the animal rich in gelatin, boiled and pickled in this way, are an occasional luxury everywhere; and other meats are sometimes preserved in the same way. There is no valid objection, that we are aware of, against preserving meat in this way for the purpose of affording additional varieties of diet. It has never been tried to any extent on shipboard. From Dr. Beaumont's observations, we learn that meat thus prepared was the most rapidly digested of all the alimentary substances subjected to experiment. We feel confident that great advantage would result, in long voyages, from having a few jars of meat thus preserved, to issue to the seamen, as a relief from the monotony of the usual ration. Whether the nutritive properties of the meat are impaired by this process, as by salting, we believe has never been directly determined; but whatever the change, it is probably so different in character from the change produced by salt, that an occasional meal of it may reasonably be expected to correct, in some degree, the bad effects of a long-continued salt diet.   The vegetable substances preserved in vinegar are principally unripe cucumbers and cauliflowers.   They are now a regular and very important article of the seaman's ration.   It would seem that the refreshing properties of fresh vegetables are more perfectly preserved in this way than any other; hence the value of these pickles as antiscorbutics.   In case of deficiency of the regular pickles, any obtainable vegetable, not too ripe, or almost any herb, not too tough and fibrous, should be pickled for this purpose.

Immersion in molasses appears to be an available process for preserving potatoes, with a good portion of their antiscorbutic properties.   The potatoes are pared, sliced, and placed in a barrel, which is then filled with molasses.   They become quite black and pretty hard, but our whaling ships find advantage in the use of them.

(116.) *Heating and seclusion from the atmosphere* is another valuable device for preserving food for a time.   But there are some important prevalent errors on this subject.   We often see it stated that putrefaction cannot take place without the presence of the atmosphere, and it is hence inferred that animal food may be indefinitely preserved by perfectly excluding the atmosphere. This is a serious mistake.   A slow putrefaction goes on, as any one will discover who undertakes to eat meat preserved by this process, after it has been kept four or five months in the tropics. Roast beef, roast mutton, turkeys, fowls, venison, etc., undergo a degree of decomposition, become soft and flavorless or disgusting; not in the way of flesh freely exposed to the air, but in a way peculiar to themselves.   Soups, rich in gelatin, and seasoned with a fair portion of spice, retain their natural flavor and useful properties much longer.   We have seen some fruits and vegetables— peaches, pears, asparagus, and tomatoes, which had been preserved for years by this process.   They retained much of their natural flavor, and this we take to be the best available test of their useful properties.   On the whole this must be included among the useful means of preserving a variety of vegetables for a long time in a state fit for food.

We must guard against too strong a reaction against this method, and probably the best way to do this is to state freely its defects and difficulties as soon as they are recognized. It appears that the heat, in this case, acts by killing some organic germs, or changing the condition of some nitrogenous material, which, existing both in the meat and in the atmosphere, act the part of a ferment under ordinary circumstances. It would seem that the absolute exclusion of air is not necessary, but that any included air must be heated, for we have seen this process successfully conducted by persons who were so ignorant as to suppose the air all excluded, simply because no more would escape, with the boxes exposed to the heat of a water-bath, though there was considerable space in the vessels not occupied either by fruit or liquid. Fruits are constantly preserved in this way in glass, in which the liquid shaken up exhibits air-bubbles. It is necessary that the inclosed air, as well as the fruit, should be heated to about the temperature of boiling water; if the least portion of fresh air be admitted, ordinary putrefaction is established without delay.

(117.) *Constant cold* seems capable of preserving fresh meat for a very long time. A few years ago, in Siberia, a carcass of an elephant was found frozen in the ice, with wolves, foxes, and bears feeding on it, though there is no evidence of such an animal having lived anywhere since the invention of letters. It was common to preserve fresh fish for transportation to market, by packing them in ice, long before ice became a common summer luxury. It has become the custom to pack considerable quantities of fresh meat in the cargoes of ice which are shipped to tropical countries. The meat with the ice is transferred to ice-houses, and sold as called for, to persons who would otherwise be unable to appreciate the difference between Boston beef and the beef of tropical climates. Ocean steamers, by carrying large quantities of ice for the purpose, are enabled to supply their passengers, during a passage across the Atlantic, with all the luxuries in the way of fresh food which they can purchase in New York, and this without being incommoded by cages and pens of live stock. Unfortunately this method requires too much space and too many precautions to be generally available for the crew of a ship of war, which may be obliged to keep at sea constantly for months, and requires the space for other purposes.

(118.) Another important means of preserving fresh food on board ship is to *keep the object, animal or vegetable, alive*. Animals, such as beeves, pigs, sheep, and poultry, are often embarked alive with this view. But since it has become possible to obtain ice nearly everywhere, the live stock on shipboard has become of comparatively small importance. It is easy to preserve beef in ice much longer than any animal of this kind can be kept on board in condition fit to serve the purpose of food. Pigs and poultry stand rough usage better, and may accommodate themselves to the circumstances, but it is impossible to accommodate enough on board for general use. They are generally used by the officers on short passages, and a few are kept for the purpose of varying occasionally the monotonous diet of long passages, and to afford some savory food for the sick and convalescent.

In speaking of beans as an article of the ration, we have already suggested the importance of preserving them in such a way as not to destroy their vitality. This is effected by having them thoroughly dried in a dry atmosphere, and afterward protecting them from moisture and atmospheric vicissitudes. If a bean be once broken, and its vitality thus destroyed, its preservation is much more precarious; and for this, among other reasons, we object to the use of bean flour and such things. They undergo decay more or less rapidly, no matter how prepared or how well packed. Other small grains, wheat, oats, barley, etc., may be preserved as well as beans. Various nuts, as walnuts and almonds, are thus preserved in small quantities, as a dessert, and answer a useful purpose.

Many fresh fruits are preserved for a short time by processes which have their continued vitality in view. Thus oranges and lemons, from tropical countries, are abundantly supplied in all our large towns. They are picked before they are quite ripe, with as little bruising or other injury as possible, wrapped separately in paper, and packed in rough boxes. The fruit thus packed continues to ripen, if not to grow, not so rapidly or so well as on the tree; but by the time it reaches us it is nearly ripe; and as this is generally so arranged as to happen during the cold weather of winter, the fruit remains for some time in good condition. Apples are

sometimes packed in the same way and shipped to tropical climates. Cranberries are brought to us in barrels filled with
water, which prevents them from being injured by bruising or
the evaporation of their juices. While thus immersed in fresh
clean water, they keep a long time in cool weather, without apparent deterioration. Currants, gooseberries, and other small
fruits, not quite ripe, placed in a bottle of water and corked, are
often kept for a whole year in good condition. Their preservation seems to depend on the same circumstances, the continuance
of their vitality, though in a modified state, which may be compared to the winter torpor of the bear and the hibernation of
various other animals. The preservation of potatoes, yams, and
other tubers, is of the utmost importance to navigation. It is
effected by exposing them, with adherent earth, to a dry atmosphere, till their surface appears quite dry. They are afterward
guarded from injury, such as bruising, as well as from wet or a
too dry atmosphere. They are best preserved on shipboard
packed in old flour barrels with a little straw, some holes being
bored in different parts of the barrels, so as to afford the proper
degree of ventilation. The layer of dry earth attached to the
potatoes, answers the same purpose as the paper in the case of the
oranges; it guards them from bruising, and absorbs the moisture
which may result from any little speck of decay. The potatoes
kept in this way are found particularly advantageous by our
whalers on the Pacific. Yams, we are inclined to think, they
will find still more useful. They certainly keep much better
than potatoes, and the best varieties, properly cooked, are not to
be distinguished from them in flavor. The most fastidious con-
noisseurs in these matters may be easily deceived in them, if the
yams be mashed or cut up by the cook, so as to destroy the form;
and those who imagine the yam to be coarse and quite detestable,
are very easily fooled in this way. The people of Norfolk, Virginia, are very fond of yams; but their yams are not yams at all,
but a variety of sweet potato.

(119.) The idea of some sort of *small garden* for fresh vegetables on shipboard has not been altogether neglected. Thus we
read of a tank of water being advantageously kept on deck for
the cultivation of cresses. We would suggest something much
more productive of fresh vegetables, without so much interference

with the deck of the ship.   There are many small seeds—beans, peas, mustard, lettuce, parsley, horseradish, turnip, etc., which may be kept on board for a very long time, and by means of a suit-

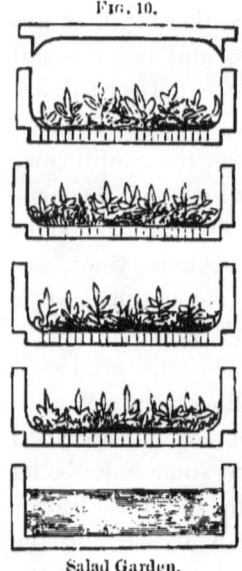

Fig. 10.

Salad Garden.

able apparatus they may readily be made to grow, till they develop two or three leaves to each seed.   They are thus capable of furnishing, in abundance, the fresh material for a nice salad, under circumstances which would otherwise render this quite impossible.

I have used the apparatus represented in the margin for this purpose.   It consists of a series of earthen vessels, fitting on top of each other, perforated like colanders, except the lower one, and provided with a loose lid.   Each of these vessels, except the lower one, is supplied with a layer of seeds, previously washed and soaked; the whole is adjusted in position, and a cupful of water poured into the upper part, whence gradually percolating it moistens the seeds in the whole series; any superfluity of water collecting in the lower jar.   Every two or three days, the water is poured from the bottom into the top of the series, and in the course of a week or more, varying with temperature, condition of the seed, etc., the whole apparatus is found to be packed full of tender sprouts.

CHAPTER XV.

(120.) September 10th.—We are approaching the coast of Mexico, about to enter a foreign port where nature furnishes many articles useful for food with which we are unacquainted. Nearly everything except the domestic animals being new to us, we may advantageously recall some of our zoological and botanical studies, for the purpose of a better appreciation of them. It is a good and safe rule to appropriate as food whatever we find the natives of a country to use habitually and safely.

CARNIVORANTS.

(121.) The flesh-eating animals, as a rule, are not good for food. We are quite unable to say why this should be so; but, like many other facts of nature, we are obliged to receive it as a fact—a conclusion of universal experience. Cats and other flesh-eating animals, even on the point of starvation, if offered flesh of this kind, will generally smell it and walk away in disgust. Though food of this kind is doubtless unwholesome, it is not directly poisonous, and might be used in small quantities as a resource against starvation. The repulsive flavor of the flesh of these animals seems due to the nature of their food, and under peculiar circumstances their flesh is esteemed as meat.

(122.) *The bear*, in the fall of the year, when nuts are abundant in the forest, ceases to be carnivorous; feeding and becoming fat on acorns, chestnuts, etc. He is then hunted for his flesh and fat, which form a principal winter supply of our frontier settlements, and of the inhabitants of the borders of forests nearly everywhere.—(*Godman.*)

(123.) *The dog.*—A variety of domestic dog, on some of the islands of the Pacific, before the general introduction of pigs, was raised for use as food, and fatted exclusively on vegetables.

Europeans, who have occasionally tasted the flesh of these dogs
at feasts, concur in the statement that this kind of meat is not
distinguishable by the flavor from pork.

(124.) *The northern lynx (Felis borealis.)*—"The flesh of this
lynx is considered good food by the hunters, being fat, white,
and flavored like the hare, on which it principally feeds."—
(*Godman.*)

(125.) The other orders of animals, nearly allied to the carnivorants by their predaceous habits, living principally on insects
and small animals, are almost universally rejected as food, partly,
no doubt, on account of their generally insignificant size. They
are capable of conversion into food in cases of emergency.

(126.) The amphibious carnivorants, the *seal* and the *walrus*,
are regarded as the very best of meat by the inhabitants of the
countries where they abound; though, with our habits, and in
our climate, such food would probably be absolutely disgusting.
The Arctic regions would perhaps be quite uninhabitable by man
without the flesh, the fat, and the hides of these creatures. The
men of Dr. Kane's party, with all the appliances which they
were able to carry from New York, found walrus flesh their only
effectual relief from *scorbutus*—sea-scurvy.

PACHYDERMS AND RUMINANTS.

(127.) The animals of these two orders, living almost exclusively on grass and seeds, supply the great bulk of animal food
to the inhabitants of the world. The flesh of any and all of
them forms good, wholesome food, generally esteemed; differing
much in delicacy of flavor, according to species, age, sex, climate,
soil, food, etc. The flesh of *the hog* rivals that of the ox in
general importance, though much less esteemed by us. Some of
the Asiatics who use the ox for agricultural labor, never think of
eating his flesh, and regard beef with the same sort of repugnance
as with us attaches to horseflesh; while they use pork to the
exclusion of nearly all other animal food. The domestic hog,
not being very fastidious in his diet, is liable to become unfit for
food if improperly fed. Many persons among us, besides a very
extensive religious sect, decline the use of pork altogether, probably for this reason. This, as well as the Asiatic prejudice against

beef, and our own against the use of horseflesh, may be very unreasonable and absurd; but we all have such prejudices, and perhaps would not be benefited by being reasoned out of them. In case of the real want of animal food we should not hesitate to recommend the slaughter of horse, if one in suitable condition be obtainable.

"Three disgusting and dangerous diseases in man owe their origin to the ingestion of the flesh of the pig,—tapeworm, hydatids, and trichinosis. Professor Leidy, of Philadelphia, was, I believe, the first who observed the *Trichina spiralis* in the pig, the meat of which animal has always been, so far as we know, the cause of this dangerous disease,—trichinosis. It ought always to be examined before being used as food, and in case it presents a suspicious appearance, it ought to be subjected to a microscopic examination. A thorough boiling or roasting, as also intense salting and smoking, will kill the trichina, though imperfect preparation by these methods will not."—(*Keller*.)

(128.) *Beef* is with us the most esteemed of all animal food. But in tropical countries we have always found this meat tough and tasteless, and not so good as mutton, or even goatflesh. The flesh and milk of these animals are liable to become poisonous by their feeding on poisonous weeds. Thus the cow and the deer have been known to feed on the *Rhus toxicodendron*, poison oak, their flesh and milk becoming poisonous, so as to give rise to a curious epidemic of the Western States, known by the name of staggers or milk sickness.—(*Chase*.)

The goat, likewise, when nearly starved, feeding on rubbish lots about our cities, has been known to eat the *Stramonium*, Jamestown weed, which generally grows in such places. The flesh and milk of the animal, in these cases, have in some degree the poisonous properties of the weed.

The flesh of diseased animals is generally poisonous. The following cases, from the London *Lancet*, February, 1864, are to the point, and show the danger of slaughtering such animals:

"On the 22d of October, 1863, a bull was taken ill on a farm and in a county which I decline to name. My reasons for not mentioning the place are, that every effort has been made to keep the secret, as in a host of similar cases, and it will serve no purpose whatever to expose those who, in ignorance, and in consequence of the lax state of the laws on the subject, acted as their neighbors would have done. A laborer on the farm, who had formerly been a butcher, volunteered to slaughter the sick bull, that its carcass might be saved for the butcher's stall. Unfortunately, the poor man had previously injured his hand with a spade. It was said that the bull was dying from pleuro-pneumonia, but others declare that the disease was of too rapid a type to be the very prevalent lung complaint. Certain it is that four pigs died after eating a part of the viscera of the bull, and two dogs nearly lost their lives in the same way. The bull was disposed of to a butcher for the sum of £5, and after this, not only was it seen that the pigs and dogs had been injured by eating the flesh, but the laborer suffered intense pain in his hand, was seized with severe symptoms, and died on the fourth day after dressing the bull.

"Many readers of the *Lancet* may suppose that this is a solitary case, or at all events a rare one. . . . . To my own knowledge, four other men have died, presenting symptoms such as the above, under similar circumstances, in the same county, during the last four years. Another man, a butcher, nearly lost his life, and the surgeon who attended him asked him what had been done with the diseased cattle he had dressed. This question was asked, as the surgeon feared that the carcasses were at that time being cut up in the town where they had been slaughtered; but he was somewhat consoled by the usual reply, 'They had been sent to London.'"

"A landed proprietor wrote me concerning an instance of serious illness in East Lothian. An animal was slaughtered and sent either to Edinburgh or London. After the carcass had been dispatched the pigs were taken ill, and several died; they had eaten of the animal's entrails. The man who dressed the bullock nearly lost his life, and only recovered after nearly losing his eyesight. His vision has only been restored in one eye.

"In the Edinburgh slaughter-houses similar accidents have been witnessed, though every effort is made to conceal the truth. During the outbreak of malignant anthrax in Lincolnshire last autumn, a shepherd scratched his arm while dressing a sheep, and he very nearly lost his life.

*   *   *   *   *   *   *   *

"My opinion, based on a careful consideration of the whole subject, is, that the public health is materially affected by the wholesale slaughter of diseased animals as human food. Several years ago I declared that it was impossible that human beings were not frequently injured by eating the flesh of cattle that had died of splenic apoplexy in the country; and the reason why cases have not been published, is that the carcasses have been sent to large cities, *where they would not be distinguished from the carcasses of perfectly healthy animals*, and the evil results of eating the poisonous flesh could not be distinguished from any ordinary case of dysentery or typhus."—(*Gamgee.*)

(129.) It would appear that the flesh of animals is desirable for food nearly in proportion as they are exclusively fed on vegetables. Thus the ruminants, the ox, the sheep and deer, which eat nothing but vegetables and a few grasshoppers and spiders to season their diet, are universally esteemed as food; or, if there is an exception, it is to be accounted for by the animal being es-

teemed as a laborer and companion. And the pachyderms, the
hog, elephant, camel, and horse, naturally using similar diet, are
similarly esteemed. The rodents, likewise, the hare, squirrel,
muskrat, etc., such of them as are taken wild in the fields and
forests, are often used as food. But there are animals of this
class which frequent human habitations, very indifferent what
they eat, and therefore very disgusting. Under peculiar circumstances perhaps even these animals might be eaten. The flesh of
animals varies much in flavor according to the quality of their
food, and acquires therefrom much of its peculiar flavor and
aroma.

CETACEANS.

(130.) Most of the cetaceous animals—whales, porpoises, etc.,
—feeding on fish, are rejected as food. They are, however, advantageously used sometimes on long voyages. But *the sirenians,*
herbivorous cetaceans,—siren, lamantin, dugong, and sea-cow—
feeding exclusively on sea-plants, are esteemed as most exquisite
meat, and being nearly enough allied to fish to be eaten on
fast days, they are pursued with a degree of active enterprise
which threatens their entire extinction.

BIRDS.

(131.) *The rapacious birds,* feeding almost exclusively on the
flesh of other animals, are nearly unfit for food, and are universally rejected ; in these respects resembling the carnivorous mammals. Their flesh is likewise greatly modified by the nature of
their food. The entire body of the vulture has in a strong degree the smell and doubtless the taste of the putrid flesh on which
it feeds. Some hawks are very nice about their food, living
mostly on small birds, and we have known the flesh of such
hawks, when fat and tender, to be eaten, and its flavor compared
to that of the chickens on which they were supposed to have fed.
But this is the rare exception.

The nearly allied orders, *passerines* and *scansores,* feeding to
some extent on animal food, principally insects with their grubs
and eggs, are of small account as food. But their food, being
less exclusively of the animal kind, and of lower animal or-

ganisms, they are undoubtedly better meat. Some of them fatten on particular kinds of grubs, as the woodcock, and withal being difficult to obtain in quantities, are esteemed as great delicacies. The robin (*Turdus migratorius*), in the autumn, feeding partly on berries, and migrating in large flocks, is greatly persecuted by idle boys, who seem delighted to eat almost any small bird which they can manage to shoot. With these insignificant exceptions, these birds are not used for food, but in case of great scarcity we should not hesitate to recommend almost any of them.

(132.) POULTRY.—The most extensive order of birds, the *gallinaceans*, subsist largely on vegetable seeds and fruits, especially during the autumn and early winter; and their flesh supplies a large amount of excellent meat. The *domestic fowl* is found throughout the habitable globe, civilized and savage. Even they who from religious feeling abstain from killing animals for their flesh, raise and keep these birds, in large numbers, for their eggs. *The turkey* of America was found by the early settlers in a state of domestication among the Indians. This magnificent bird has been transferred to nearly all parts of the civilized world; but it is not so prolific as the common domestic *poultry*, and as yet not very abundant beyond the limits of the United States. There are already several distinctly marked varieties of this bird as the consequences of its domestication.

(133.) The flesh of birds, as well as of mammals, is liable to become poisonous. From disease, no doubt, it may become poisonous, but of this we are unable to mention an instance. The pheasant, partridge-pheasant of Audubon, has occasionally been found poisonous. This has only been noticed in the winter season, with the earth generally covered with snow, so that the bird has been unable to get at his usual food. Under these circumstances, he eats both the leaves and the berries of the *Kalmia*, sheep-laurel. The flesh of any of the gallinaceous birds might possibly become poisonous under such influences.

(134.) DUCKS.—*The water birds*, waders and swimmers, vary much in their forms, habits, and food. Some of them, as the rails, snipes, and plovers, living principally on earthworms, which do not impart any unpleasant flavor, are very delicate food in their season. But they are so small and scarce as to be of little account. Most species of *ducks* and *geese* prefer grass and seeds to any other food, and when they are in good condition, feeding on their favorite food, their flesh is much esteemed. Several species have been domesticated and they are everywhere found in the markets. *The canvas-back duck* (*Fuligula valisneria*), is justly considered most exquisite meat. Its favorite food is the root of the *Valisneria spiralis*, a fresh-water grass, which it obtains by diving. The exquisite flavor of the bird is, no doubt, due to this grass, as when taken in other situations and out of season the meat is tough, fishy, and worthless. *The red-head* (*Fuligula erythrocephala*), sometimes accompanies the canvas-back, helping to eat the valisneria after he has pulled it. In this case, it is not easy to distinguish between the flavor of the two species. The ducks generally, if unable to get their favorite food, readily take to insects, worms, and small fish about the margins of streams; in which case their flesh is scarcely fit to be eaten, except by some unfortunate who may be as nearly starved as the poor ducks themselves.

(135.) The question has often been presented, in the course of long voyages, of the propriety of using various species of *sea-birds* for food. This question may readily be answered, in any special case, by reference to the following rule: All birds and mammals are wholesome for meat, except such as by their tough-ness defy the powers of mastication and digestion, and such as by their disgusting flavor or smell effectually repel the hungry. The flesh of the adult males, as a general rule, possesses more of these repulsive properties than the young and the females. Sea-birds feed almost exclusively on fish, and their flesh has a repulsive fishy flavor. By removing, with the skin, the layers of fat with which the bodies of these birds are loaded, and parboiling, this disgusting flavor may be in some degree removed. *The albatross* has been advantageously used (La Pérouse), and likewise *the penguin*. (Dumont d'Urville).

(136.) *The eggs* of all these birds seem to be edible; varying much in delicacy of flavor, but having none of the fishy flavor which sometimes belongs to their flesh. Some markets are regu-larly supplied, from neighboring islands, with the eggs of sea-birds, which are scarcely to be distinguished from the eggs of domestic fowls. The collectors are careful to procure fresh eggs of about the right size, with perfect indifference as to the species of bird which may have deposited them. A supply of fresh eggs, from a bird island, might frequently be of immense advantage to the crew of a ship.

REPTILIANS.

(137.) We have heretofore treated of animals whose flesh varies much in quality according to their species, age, sex, and condition; but there is not one of them which can be considered in any degree poisonous. As we descend in the scale of created beings, however, we find species which are more or less poisonous; and the further we descend in the scale, the greater the proportion of species which cannot be safely eaten.

(138.) *The sea-turtles*, which are by far the most important animals of this class, include some poisonous, or at least unwholesome species. The *hawks-bill* (*Chelonia imbricata*), the turtle which furnishes the tortoise-shell of commerce, is one of the poisonous species. It has caused dizziness, nausea, vomiting, and diarrhœa, with great prostration. But we are not aware that it has actually caused death.—(*Dampier.*) *The loggerhead* (*Chelonia caretta*) is the largest of these animals, sometimes weighing one thousand pounds. It is worthless, on account of its repulsive odor; the eggs even have a disagreeable musky smell. The same may be said of *the leathery turtle* (*Sphargis coreacea*), which is an enormous creature, nearly as large as the loggerhead.

(139.) *The green turtle* (*Chelonia midas*), the most abundant of all, is most excellent eating. In some seaports it is so abundant as to be constantly in the market like beef. At the Island of Ascension, ships regularly receive this turtle in lieu of beef. They are secured by turning them on their backs when they come in to deposit their eggs; and afterwards they are kept in a pen, sufficiently large to inclose a pool of sea-water for their use. By this arrangement they are supplied at all seasons. This is very advantageous, as a ship may embark a number of turtles, and keep them alive on board, months if necessary, till actually needed; whereas beef cannot be kept in a good condition on board but a few days. There are, doubtless, other species of sea-turtle which are good, and at various ports we chance to visit, we may safely adopt the experience and opinions of the natives in reference to their good or bad qualities.

(140.) The fresh-water chelonians, *terrapins*, are generally much esteemed, and are excellent food. *The snapping-turtle* (*Chelonia serpentina*), is much liked by some, though the old ones are sometimes rather musky. But the *Emys palustris, Emys terrapin, Emys rubriventris*, and probably twenty more, the most common species, are universally considered among the best of meats. The species which are not good are generally called *mud turtles*, and have a disgusting musky flavor.

(141.) There is one species of land tortoise, of great importance to navigators on the Pacific, *the Gallipagos turtle* (*Testudo planiceps*). This animal is found only on a small group of islands nearly under the equator. It thrives perfectly on shipboard, apparently requiring neither food nor water. A large one can carry a man on his back, and gives about two hundred pounds of meat, which makes a most excellent gelatinous soup. It is said that settlers there have lately introduced cattle, and that the tortoises are becoming scarce on account of the tramping down of their nests and consequent destruction of the eggs. If this be so, we hope that the mistake will be promptly corrected by destroying the cattle; for the tortoise being capable of long preservation, is infinitely more valuable than beef as a supply for ships. There is a still larger land tortoise, the *Testudo indica*, found in Asia, but it is so rare that we do not know much about it.

(142.) *The iguana* of tropical America feeds mostly on fruits and vegetables, and is considered by the Indians as a delicious morsel. Of the rest of the reptiles, *crocodiles, lizards, snakes, salamanders, etc.*, many are eaten by the inhabitants of various countries. But the poisonous character of some, with their repulsive forms and habits, and the fact that they are only procurable when things more to our liking may be had, renders it unnecessary for us to think of them as food.

Many of these reptiles are to be avoided on account of the poison infused into their bite. *Bibron's antidote*, composed of alcohol, bromine, and iodine, saves life in cases of wounds from these animals; and we should freely use, internally and externally, either of these substances, which first comes to hand. There are many ugly-looking *sea-serpents* floating on the surface of the China Sea. They are often caught by sailors in their draw buckets. They are said to be exceedingly venomous, and it is well to be shy of them; and if any accident should happen from them, it should be thoroughly published in the papers of the principal seaports, especially of China and India, for our sailors are somewhat incredulous about the venomous properties of these animals.

FISH.

(143.) A very large proportion of all created beings are fish. When we reflect that three-fourths of the earth's surface is covered by water, everywhere inhabited by them; each species adapted to some particular location—the river, the brook, the lake, the bay, and the ocean; the surface, the shoal, and the deep water; the sand-bank, the rocky reef, and the muddy bottom— we begin to comprehend something of this immensity. This vast number, probably millions of millions of objects, of thousands of species, are alike in so many respects that we need not say much about them except in common. They are all predaceous, the stronger feeding on the weaker throughout the whole class; but varying somewhat in the degree of their voracity. They all have a peculiar flavor, which is nearly the same in all of them, some being more delicate in flavor than others, and some so strong as to be considered unfit for use. It is curious that this fishy taste, so generally liked where it belongs, is exceedingly disgusting when by careless cookery it is imparted to other meat. Fish, though less substantial than most other meat, is an invaluable resource in varying the food, not only of sailors but of men everywhere.

The quality of fish seems to vary more with the condition of individual animals than with the species. Thus almost any fish is good in its best condition, when cooked and eaten soon after its removal from the water; and all of them, even the best, deteriorate very rapidly if kept a short time, and become even poisonous. This deterioration is progressive, and the shorter the interval of time between the water and the gridiron the better. In warm climates this deterioration is sometimes so rapid that fish is quite unfit for use, unless cooked within an hour or two after it is caught. For a time after depositing their spawn fish are unfit for use, disgusting in flavor, and unwholesome if not poisonous. This is the case with salmon, shad, herring, and all other fish which it has been possible to observe in this respect, and the inference seems reasonable that the rule is universal. This accounts for the fact that the same kind of fish, at the same place, is sometimes good during one week and poisonous the next. Some species of fish are, perhaps, always poisonous, independently of any peculiarity of condition.

(144.) Many accidents occur from fish-poisoning. One of our ships approaching the Straits of Gibraltar, the crew, in a calm, caught a great number of Spanish mackerel (*Scomber colias*), a much-esteemed and very common European fish ; and some thirty of the crew were poisoned, though none fatally, before the fish was suspected.—(*Horner.*)

During the first Japan expedition, our ships at Simoda were supplied with a very excellent small fish, the *Clupea thryssa*, which abounds there. After a week or so it was observed that the fish were not so good as usual, and several persons who ate them were attacked with fish-poisoning.

At Cape Town, South Africa, the authorities warn strangers against a poisonous fish, *Tetrodon capensis*, which abounds there. "A fatal accident from this fish occurred recently on board a Dutch ship at St. Simon's Bay. Her Britannic Majesty's ship Winchester being near, her surgeon, Mr. Jameson, was called to assist the sufferers. He found that the boatswain's mate and purser's steward had been suddenly taken ill after eating part of a well-known deleterious fish common there, called toad-fish, or bladder-fish, the *Tetrodon*. They had been warned that the fish was poisonous, but were resolved to try the experiment, the boatswain declaring that the liver was not poisonous, but a great delicacy. They had partaken of dinner at 12 o'clock ; immediately afterward they partook of the fish, and scarcely ten minutes had elapsed when the boatswain became so ill that he was unable to raise himself without the greatest difficulty ; his face was flushed, his eyes glistened, pupils rather contracted, his mouth was open, lips livid, somewhat blue ; his forehead covered with perspiration ; the pulse weak, quick, and intermittent. The patient was extremely uneasy and in great distress, but still conscious ; he complained of pain from constriction of the throat,

and appeared inclined to vomit. His state soon assumed a para-
lytic form; his eyes became fixed in one direction; his breathing
was difficult, and accompanied with dilatation of the nostrils;
his face was pale and covered with cold perspiration; his lips
livid, and in scarcely seventeen minutes after partaking of the
fish he was dead. The symptoms of the purser's steward were
similar. He died within twenty minutes after partaking of the fish.
The quantity eaten by the two men was the liver of one fish, which
might have weighed four drachms." [15.55 grams.]—(*Jameson.*)

A species of *Sparus*, porgie, has been noticed as poisonous at
the Hawaiian Islands. Several species of *Clupea*, herring, have
been observed to be poisonous: *Clupea thryssa*, of the China Sea
and Indian Ocean; *Clupea tropica*, of the West Indies; and
Clupea meletta, of the Pacific; so that every small herring or
sardine-like fish should be suspected, in fact avoided, till positive
information is gained of its properties. There is a large species
of perch in the West India waters (*Sphyræna becuna*), which has
often been the occasion of accidental poisoning.

(145.) Though it has not been certainly determined that any
species of fish is always or essentially poisonous, yet accidents
have so frequently occurred with some of them, that they should
always be rejected. The genera *Diodon* and *Tetrodon*—sea-
porcupine, toad-fish, blower, puffer, etc.—being puffed up with
air and covered with spines, are generally, if not always, poisonous, and their appearance one would think enough to excite disgust at the mere idea of eating them.

The only available means of testing the poisonous properties of
fish is to cause a small animal, as a cat, to eat some of it. Its
poor flavor may excite suspicion.

The following list comprises all the fish which have proved
poisonous of which I have been able to find an account:

Scomber cœruleus, Spanish mackerel.	*Tetrodon ocellatus*, spotted blower.
Scomber maximus, king-fish.	*Tetrodon sceleratus*, puffer.
Scomber thynnus, bonito.	*Tetrodon pennatii*, Pennant's toad-fish.
Clupea meletta, tropic sardine.	*Perca major*, baracuta.
Clupea thryssa, yellow-bill sprat.	*Perca venenata*, rock-fish.
Clupea tropica, tropic herring.	*Perca venenosa*, grooper.
Coracinus fuscus, gray snapper.	*Sphyræna pecuna*, Jamaica perch.
Coracinus minor, small snapper.	*Balistes monoceras*, old wife.
Coryphona splendens, sailor's dolphin.	*Sparus chrysops*, gilt-head.
Tetrodon capensis, cape toad-fish.	*Sparus pagrus*, porgie.
Murena minor, conger eel.	

MOLLUSKS.

(146.) This division of animals supplies comparatively very little food. Many species of squids form the principal food of whales, and, therefore, probably are not poisonous. Some of them are eaten by people where they abound, and are considered good meat, which has been compared in flavor to the claw of the lobster. At Simoda, Japan, during the first expedition, the common calamary (*Loligo vulgaris*) was noticed in considerable quantities, preserved by slightly salting and drying it. When broiled and eaten hot, the flavor was good.

But most of the mollusks are to be avoided rather than sought after. There is so little that is appetizing in the appearance of most of them, that comparatively few experiments have been made with a view to their conversion into food; so that here is a large field which may be cultivated when the human race increases so as to make the use of such food necessary. We do not know whether any of them are essentially poisonous, but it is believed that any and all of them are very liable to become so under very ordinary circumstances, as happens with fish.

(147.) *Snails*, which are eaten by some people, feed on plants and have appeared to be poisonous when collected from poisonous plants. The caution which this fact suggests cannot probably be of much value to any American.

(148.) The acephala, including oysters, clams, date-fish (*Pholas*), muscles, and cockles, are the most valuable of the mollusks. Nearly all of us appreciate the good varieties of the oyster in its season. The others are less savory, and some of them pretty tough; but good cooking and seasoning make good soup and other good dishes of almost any of them, if the animal itself be in good condition.

In temperate climates, during warm weather, these animals have an appearance of white opacity, and the liquid inclosed in the shell has the same appearance, indicated by the term milky. This condition continues four or five months. During this season they are ill-flavored and very unwholesome, a moderate meal of them frequently causing a severe attack of cholera morbus. In warm climates this condition continues much longer, and in such situations it is always dangerous to use them, except with the utmost caution in regard to quantity as well as quality.

The remaining mollusks are so little capable of conversion into food, and so likely to be poisonous in the localities where they are found, that we should deem it unnecessary to particularize, even if we possessed sufficient knowledge of their properties.

ARTICULATES.

(149.) In regard to the insects, spiders, and worms which form the bulk of the animals of this division, we have but little to say. They are eaten largely by birds. People in a low condition of civilization have eaten roasted grasshoppers, etc., mingled with other food, as a resource against starvation.

The bodies of many insects are imbued with acrid poison, sufficiently powerful to produce a blister if the animal be crushed and allowed to remain a certain time in contact with the skin. The *Cantharis vitatta* (potato fly), has such properties. Any insect of this kind would produce worse results if introduced into the stomach. They are probably rather peppery food even for birds. Other insects have poisonous fangs, which cause their bites to be dreaded; and some have a special sting in the tail no less terrible. The poison in these cases seems to be acid in its nature, and may be promptly neutralized by ammonia. Spirits or water of ammonia instantly applied is, therefore, the appropriate remedy. This remedy may cause as severe smarting as the sting for which it is applied, but this promptly subsides. It is doubtful whether a healthy adult man has ever been killed by the wound of one of these animals. There have been persons who have died of malignant erysipelas, excited by the bite of a spider; but we are not quite certain but that these were cases of ill-health, similar to those rare cases in which a like result has followed the scratch of a clean cambric needle.

(150.) The *scorpion*, often seen on board ship, in hot climates, is noted for the severity of the wound which he inflicts with the hook at the end of his tail; and the centipede, in similar localities, makes about as severe a wound with his jaws; but I have never known a serious accident from either of these animals. Men and even horses have been killed by the attack of an entire swarm of bees, though a single one of them makes a much less severe wound than some of the less gregarious insects. Their honey compensates us in some degree for this, as it is about the only generally esteemed article of food derived from the whole class of insects.

(151.) The principal *crustaceans*—lobsters, shrimps, and crabs—are generally used for food; but they have their times and seasons, like the mollusks and fish. They are never good or wholesome unless cooked while quite fresh, and, in fact, they are so tenacious of life that it is scarcely possible to kill them before they are spoiled by decay, except by casting the living animals into boiling water. It is probable that the flesh of these animals is sometimes poisonous on account of some peculiarity of their food. If stale they certainly are unwholesome. The sickness which they occasion is cholera, similar to that caused by poisonous oysters. There are other and rarer crustaceans, which in cases of emergency might be used with the same precautions required with crabs and lobsters.

RADIATES.

(152.) The whole radiate division, so far as known, scarcely affords either food or poison. Many of the animals are armed with long threads covered with an acrid secretion, with which they are able to inflict great pain and numbness if they come in contact with a pretty large surface of the body, and on this account they should be carefully avoided in bathing. Even the little floating bladder, Portuguese man-of-war (*Physalia atlantica*), makes a very sharp stinging, as of nettles, if one of its threads comes in contact with the hand. One species of sea-egg or sea-urchin has been named *Echinus esculentus*, from which we may infer that it has been eaten.

"These are distinguished into three sorts, the black, the gray, and the shooting sea-egg. . . . . The inside of the shell is lined with about five lobes of a granulated yellow substance resembling the roe of a fish. These lobes are in length about three inches; . . . . however, their bulk depends much on the time of their being taken, for these lobes are larger and even better tasted in the full than in the wane of the moon; but if not quickly eaten or put into strong vinegar to harden, they very soon dissolve into a reddish liquid."—(*Hughes.*)

As these animals feed on each other, the probabilities are that they are not essentially poisonous, but that they may become so from adventitious circumstances, as the ingestion of poisonous food, peculiar conditions of the animal at particular seasons, and various degrees of putrid decomposition.

It is pretty sure that some of the *Protozoa* influence our health, either beneficially or otherwise. It would seem that almost every drop of water in the world is inhabited by animals, mostly infusorians. With every glass of water we swallow hundreds, perhaps thousands, unconscious of harm; perhaps they are even necessary for our comfortable existence. Some of the parasites which infest the human body may be derived from this source. The Guinea worm (*Filaria guineensis*), the *Trichina spiralis, Lumbricus,* etc. These minute objects may be the eggs, chrysalids, or larvæ of unknown animals, capable of transformation into dangerous parasites in our bodies, and hence the propriety of the Japanese custom of boiling water, especially of doubtful character, before drinking it, and of thus avoiding the necessity of swallowing drugs to poison these creatures.

CHAPTER XVI.

(153.) VEGETABLES and fruits vary so much in their physiological effects, that a fair comprehension of the subject requires more detail than we have given to the subjects embraced in the preceding chapter. Besides considering the fitness of the various classes of plants for food, and their dangers as poisons, we feel called upon to notice their physiological action on the system in a general way, and in some instances their properties as medicines. This subject is not without its difficulties, which appear to have been nearly overlooked by one party, and needlessly exaggerated by another. By one party we are told that with a competent knowledge of botany we may, in a strange country, among plants which are new to us and unknown in the pharmacopœias, select with confidence appropriate remedies for diseases, point out the dangerous poisons, and select wholesome food. The other party tells us that plants very nearly allied botanically are quite different in properties, and that hence this sort of knowledge is of no use except as it enables us to recognize known species. The truth is found between these extremes of opinion. We find that the plants nearly enough allied to be included in the same genus, are almost universally so nearly identical in properties that they are used indiscriminately for the same purposes; and that the plants even of the larger subdivisions or orders, mostly have a general resemblance in properties. But we do occasionally find, on the other hand, that plants nearly allied are very different in their effects. Thus the plants producing the edible potato, tomato, and egg-plant, are nearly allied with those producing the deadly nightshade, the poisonous henbane, the fire-red pepper, and the disgusting tobacco; hence it is not always quite safe to infer that a strange plant has precisely the same properties as its botanical relation with which we may happen to be acquainted.

POLYPELATOUS EXOGENS.

(154.) RANUNCULACEÆ.—*The Buttercup Family of Plants.*— The plants of this family have a colorless acrid juice, generally more or less narcotic. Some of them are dangerous acro-narcotic poisons. Their active properties are mostly dissipated by drying, or the temperature of boiling water.

The numerous species of *ranunculus*, buttercups, which grow all over our country, are, so far as known, identical in their action on the system. These herbs bruised and applied to the skin are capable of raising a blister. Children have been killed by swallowing the flowers.

The *Clematis*, virgin's bower, in all its cultivated varieties, has irritating properties, not excelled in virulence by those of the buttercups themselves.

The various species of *Hepatica*, liverwort; *Coptis*, goldthread; *Helleborus; Aconitum*, wolfsbane; and *Cimicifuga*, bugbane, have well-known medical properties. Hellebore and aconite are dangerous poisons.

(155.) *Helleborus niger*, black hellebore, was much used by the ancient physicians, especially in the treatment of insanity. It is an active emeto-cathartic in appropriate doses, but in excessive doses, an acro-narcotic poison.

(156.) *Aconitum napellus*, wolfsbane, monkshood, is an active and dangerous acro-narcotic poison. It has no smell, but when chewed it occasions a strange tingling sensation about the mouth, particularly in the tongue and throat. In large doses it produces symptoms of gastric irritation, accompanied or followed by great muscular rigidity, convulsions, stupor, coma, and death. Dr. Mull, of Birmingham, England, took tincture of aconite for four days, beginning with five drops, two or three times a day, increasing the dose to six, eight, and ten drops, so that on the evening of the fourth day he took ten drops. On the morning of the fifth day the symptoms of nervous derangement attributed to the use of the medicine appeared, and he died on the morning of the seventh day.—(*Dunglison.*)

There are other species of aconite, of similar properties, from which the leaves in the shops are probably in part derived. It is remarkable that this poison, called wolfsbane, should produce symptoms somewhat resembling hydrophobia.

(157.) *Cimicifuga racemosa*, bugbane, blacksnake-root, appears to be a nervous sedative, without any very decided action on the secretions. In excessive doses it may possibly act as an acro-narcotic, but it certainly is not at all dangerous in this way. It would appear, from some of the cases cited, to have been used very advantageously in chorea and other diseases of irregular nervous action. There are several other species of cimicifuga, less common, but of similar properties.

Delphinium staphisagria, stavesacre of Southern Europe, is a dangerous acro-narcotic poison, used in ointments to destroy vermin. At least seven species of *Delphinium*, larkspur, are found in our country, and are probably as poisonous as the European species.

Coptis, goldthread, is a simple bitter, comparable to quassia.

(158.) MAGNOLIACEÆ.—*The Magnolia Family.*—This order comprises the most magnificent of our flowering forest trees. The bark, leaves, and fruit are more or less aromatic, and they are strongly bitter and tonic. There is no dangerous poisonous property in any tree of this order.

The fruit of the *Illicium anisatum*, star anise-seed, has, in a strong degree, the aromatic and pleasantly stimulating properties which belong to the spices generally.

(159.) The *Liriodendron tulipifera*, tulip poplar, is less aromatic than the preceding, though its flowers have a delightful fragrance, which perfumes the breeze. Its bark, being less unpleasantly bitter than cinchona, and an excellent tonic, was rapidly coming into general use in the treatment of intermittents, when the discovery of quinine superseded both.

(160.) ANONACEÆ.—*Custard Apples.*—This order of plants consists of small trees and shrubs, which produce some of the most delicious fruits known. All parts of these trees are somewhat aromatic and tonic, without any very decided properties worthy of notice, except in their delicious fruits. The rind of these fruits is of a dark-green color, rather thick and coarse, and marked off somewhat in the manner of the pineapple. There is no dangerous property in any fruit of this form that we are aware of, except in the pineapple itself, which belongs to a very different order.

(161.) The custard apples (*Anona squamosa*), and other species, are the most common of these fruits in the West Indies. We have never known any harm to result from eating these delicious fruits, even among men just in from long voyages, and

FIG. 11.

Anona Squamosa.

liable on this account greatly to exceed the bounds of prudence. There are many varieties, varying much in quality, but they are all good. The subdivisions of the rind of the custard apples are rounded and prominent, lying over each other in the manner of scales. Each fruit of the best varieties weighs about four ounces.

(162.) The sour sop (*Porcelia ?*) is abundant in the same localities. It is pleasantly acid, with a mixture of rather tough fibres in its pulp, but it is by no means to be despised in warm weather, especially if other fruit be scarce. It is quite wholesome. It is a much larger fruit than the custard apples, and not so regular in form. The subdivisions of the rind are not so distinctly marked, being merely indicated by little black spines.

(163.) The cherimoya of Peru (*Anona tripetala*, Tschudi), is perhaps the most delicious fruit known, rivalling the mangosteen of India. We have never heard of any one impairing his health, or subjecting himself to discomfort, by eating cherimoyas. This fruit is about as large as the preceding; it weighs one or two

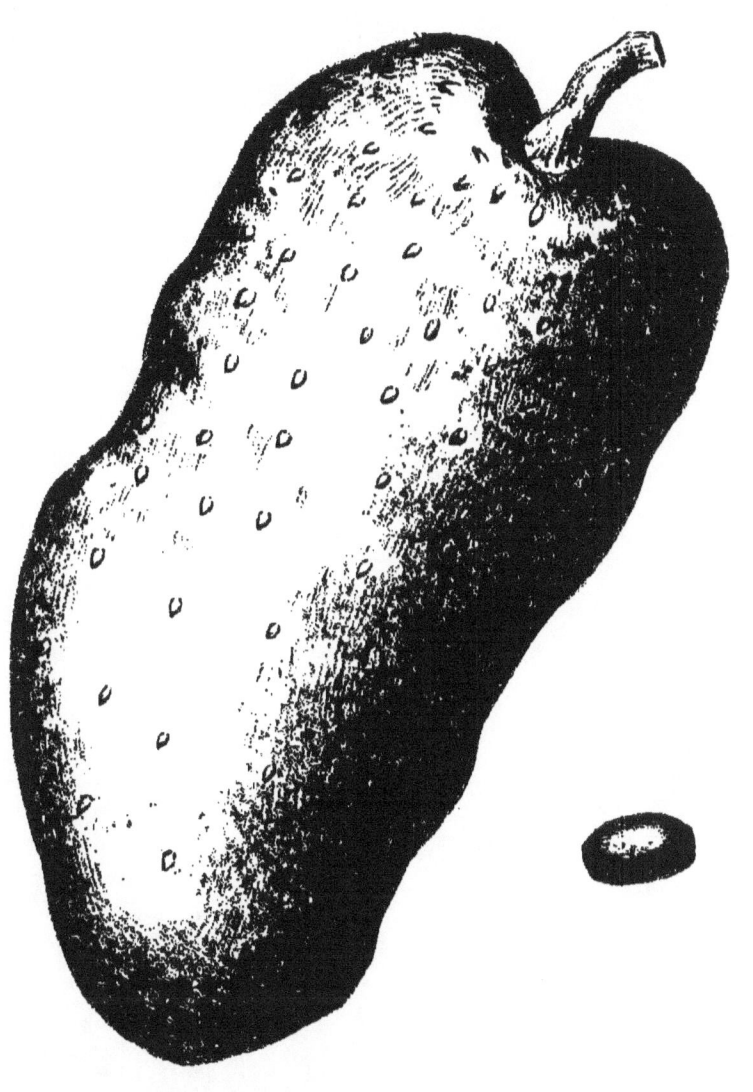

pounds. The subdivisions of the rind are distinctly marked, but in this fruit the dividing lines are ridges, the lobes of the fruit being indicated by shallow pits.

(164.) The Cincinnati custard apple (*Asimina triloba*, Dunal; *Uvaria*, Torrey and Gray; *Anona*, Linnæus), grows on a small and beautiful tree, fifteen or twenty feet high, in Pennsylvania, and the States south and west. The fruit is regularly sold in the

FIG. 12.

Anona Tripetala, Cherimoya.

Cincinnati market during its season, October. It is symmetrical in form, about the size of the custard apple, but more like the cherimoya in structure. This fruit is highly esteemed by some, its flavor being compared to that of ripe persimmons. When we reflect what cultivation and selection of varieties have done for the apple, the pear, the grape, the plum, and the peach, we may reasonably hope that by similar influences this may eventually become more delicious than any fruit which now exists in this part of the world, especially as it now has a regular market, so that such influences are at work. There are six other species in the United States, but they are all shrubs, and their fruits are not so large and are less pleasant to the taste.

(165.) SARRACENIACEÆ.—*American Pitcher Plants.*—These plants have no very active properties. One of them, the *Sarracenia purpurea*, has lately obtained a reputation as a prophylactic, and even cure, for small-pox. This credit, not being supported by any sufficient evidence, is probably without good foundation.

(166.) PAPAVERACEÆ.—*The Poppy Family.*—The plants of this order are partly characterized by a milky or opaque-colored juice. Among them is the most important known medicinal plant, the *Papaver somniferum*, the opium poppy. Most of the plants of this order, perhaps all of them, possess somewhat similar properties, and hence must be used with due caution.

Chelidonium majus, celandine, is said to possess cathartic properties, and its juice has been used to cure warts and other cutaneous diseases.

Sanguinaria canadensis, blood-root, is an acrid emetic, all parts of the plant possessing active properties. It is not much used. In large doses it is an acro-narcotic poison.

The other plants of this order, *Argemone, Glaucium, Meconopsis, Eschscholtzia*, etc., probably possess in a less degree the anodyne and soporific properties of opium, and require caution in their use.

(167.) CRUCIFERÆ.—*The Mustard Family.*—This extensive family of plants, containing about two hundred genera, and probably two thousand species, is one of exceeding importance; but, as there is a uniformity of properties throughout, we can afford to be brief. These plants contain an acrid oil, diffused through every part, which contains sulphur as one of its constituents. They are entirely devoid of starchy or saccharine matter. Though some of them, as mustard, are pretty active, and might be applied to the body in such a way as to do harm, there is not one which can be considered poisonous. They do no harm beyond the local irritation. We may likewise admit the possibility that a person might hurt himself by eating too many uncooked turnips or radishes. Some of the plants belonging to this extensive order are to be found in all parts of the world, and are very valuable to those persons whose long-continued sea diet has made a salad of such articles a great luxury. They are known as scurvy grass, cresses, etc. In our temperate climate some of them, as cabbages, turnips, horse-radishes, nasturtiums, etc., are preserved for use through the winter, and have caused *scorbutus*, the sea-scurvy, the old winter plague, to disappear.

(168.) CAPPARIDACEÆ.—*The Caper Family.*—These plants resemble very closely the cruciferous, both in form and properties. The leaves and bark are bitter and nauseous, some of them, perhaps, poisonous. One of them, the *Capparis spinosa*, supplies the essential ingredient of caper sauce, so much approved of with boiled mutton.

(169.) MALVACEÆ.—*The Mallow Family.*—The plants of this order abound in mucilage, and the softer parts, leaves, etc., form excellent emollient poultices. They possess no active properties.

The *Abelmoschus esculentus*, okra, affords the ugly-looking pods which enter extensively into the composition of gumbo soup. They are likewise used as pickles, and perhaps in other ways. The important plants of this order are two or three species of *Gossypium*, cotton.

(170.) AURANTIACEÆ.—*The Lemon Family.*—This order is composed of beautiful trees and shrubs. The flowers, leaves, and the rind of the fruits are abundantly charged with volatile oil, of delightful fragrance. These oils are much used in perfumery. The great importance of these plants is in their fruits, the pulp of which, containing much free citric acid, is much sought for in warm climates.

Some of them, as the orange, *Citrus aurantium*, abound so much in sugar, and are so moderately charged with acid, that we eat them as they come from the tree, without other preparation than the removal of the rind. Some varieties are so bitter as to be unfit for use, except medicinally, or as a prophylactic against malarial fevers.

Other species, *Citrus limonum, Citrus medica*, etc., are too acid to be eaten as fruits. But they are invaluable on account of their cooling acid juice; which, duly mixed with sugar and water, forms lemonade, which, when used in moderation in warm weather, is the most pleasant and most wholesome of drinks. Lemon-juice, derived from these fruits, and properly prepared, is the great dependence of the British navy against that terrific pestilence, the sea-scurvy.

(171.) GERANIACEÆ. — *Geraniums.*—The beautiful plants which constitute this order are cultivated for ornament throughout the civilized world. Their leaves are fragrant with volatile oil, varying in character with the species. The roots are simply astringent, without bitterness or other unpleasant flavor. One species, *Geranium maculatum*, is officinal.

(172.) ANACARDIACEÆ.—*Sumachs.*—This order of plants is composed of trees and shrubs, with a resinous or milky juice, very irritant, and even caustic, but of great value as a material for varnish. The celebrated Japan varnish, which becomes so exceedingly hard and durable, is composed largely of the juice of a species of *Rhus*. The exhalations of this varnish are so irritating as to produce a troublesome inflammation of any exposed surface of the skin. The workmen are obliged to apply it in the open air, and to keep themselves in such a position that the wind shall carry the exhalations away from them while the varnish is drying. The exhalations from the growing plants of this order produce a similar result; but we have observed in regard to this, that a young, vigorously growing poison vine, may be approached in any direction, and even handled with impunity; whereas an old plant, with a few withering, half-dead branches, is very apt to affect those who go anywhere near it. The young plants, when cut down and drying, are equally dangerous; and worst of all is the smoke of these weeds when burning.

Rhus toxicodendron, one of the plants of this order, has been used medicinally. It is a dangerous, acro-narcotic poison, similar in its operation to strychnine, and it was used in similar cases. This is the plant which has been recognized as producing staggers, the milk sickness of the Western country; the poison being transmitted through the cow to those using her milk or eating her flesh.—(*Chase.*)

(173.) The cashew of the tropics, *Cassuvium pomiferum* and *Cassuvium pyriferum*, is derived from a plant of this order, *Anacardium occidentale*, and is said to contain a delicious oily pulp; but its rind has a caustic juice, which blisters the skin and cures warts. This fruit is often seen in the markets, but it requires care in handling.

(174.) The celebrated mangosteen of Southern Asia, *Garcenia mangostana*, is said to belong to this order, all parts of the plant except its fruit being poisonous. In this case it would seem that the most delicious fruit is associated in the same plant with the most deadly poison.

(175.) VITACEÆ.—*Grapevines.*—These plants mostly produce grapes, generally delicious acid fruits; some of them, too

Fig. 13.

Cassuvium pomiferum.

acid to be eaten without sugar and cooking. The leaves are likewise acid. The juice of grapes, more or less fermented, had been the ordinary drink at meals till tea and coffee took its place. The ill-effects of excess in wine were about as well understood anciently as at present. "Wine is a mocker, strong drink is raging; and whosoever is deceived thereby is not wise."—(Prov. xx, 1.)

(176.) LEGUMINOSÆ.—*Beans.*—This very extensive order of plants possesses considerable variety of properties, perhaps without embracing a single poisonous plant. But the calabar bean, one of the most virulent of known poisons, is referred by our authorities to this order (*v. Loganiaceæ*, § 192). The seeds of most of them are beans and peas, which are edible and of great value for food.

(177.) Some species afford gummy or mucilaginous extracts or exudations, which are merely nutritive or demulcent. Such are the *Acacia vera*, *Acacia arabica*, etc., which supply the gum arabic of commerce; and the *Glycyrrhiza glabra*, the source of licorice.

Many species afford simple astringent extracts. The *Ptero-carpus erinaceus* is said to be the source of kino; and *Hematoxylum campeachianum*, logwood, furnishes a similar extract.

Other species afford balsamic exudations. The *Myroxylon peruiferum*, is the source of balsam of Peru; *Myroxylon toluiferum*, of balsam of tolu; and *Copaifer officinalis*, of balsam of copaiva.

(178.) Still other species are among the most valuable of ca-thartic medicines. *Cassia senna* and several other species supply the senna leaves of the shops. *Cassia marilandica* has similar properties, but is less active. The *Cassia fistula* and other species are likewise cultivated and used for this purpose.

(179.) The pods of one species, *Mucuna pruriens*, cowhage, are covered with prickly down, easily detached, which, coming into contact with the face or hands, causes a most intolerable itching. The plant is on this account to be avoided. This prickly mate-rial, mixed with molasses, is administered as a vermifuge; and without appearing to injure the stomach or bowels, it is very effective in stinging the worms to death.

Mucuna tuberosa bears tubers in some respects comparable to the potato; its starch-granules are very large and symmetrical.

(180.) *Indigo*, a product of the *Indigofera tinctoria* and other species, has been said, I do not know on what evidence, to be a "violent poison." This is probably a mistake. A few years ago I was called to see immediately a child poisoned with indigo. The child, about a year old, while his mother was too busy wash-ing clothes to see what he was about, got possession of a new blue-bag and did as children are apt to do with such things. When the blue-bag was wanted it was found with the baby, but its con-tents had mostly disappeared. I found the child apparently quite well, only wondering a little, perhaps, at the unusual hubbub. A moderate dose of ipecacuanha caused the ejection of a large quan-

tity of blue matter from the stomach; but I was unable to perceive any symptom of pain, or distress, or derangement of health
about the child, except what was fairly referable to the operation
of the emetic. This child had at least one-fourth of an ounce of
indigo in his stomach for more than an hour.

(181.) ROSACEÆ.—This extensive order supplies many of our
most delicious fruits and most beautiful flowers, and not one dangerous poison.

It is not necessary to particularize the properties of apples,
pears, and quinces; plums, peaches, and almonds; cherries,
apricots and nectarines; dewberries, raspberries, and strawberries.
The bark and roots of many of the plants furnishing these fruits
are bitter astringents, more or less used in medicine.

The kernels of the bitter almond, *Amygdalus amara*, and other
fruits of this form, are capable of furnishing prussic acid, a deadly
poison. The taste of these kernels, however, is such as to obviate
all danger from them.

(182.) Indian physic, *Gillenia trifoliata* and *Gillenia stipulacea*,
appears to be a safe and efficient emetic, which may be substituted,
without much inconvenience, for ipecacuanha.

(183.) MYRTACEÆ.—Nearly if not quite all the thirteen hundred plants belonging to the myrtle family are supplied with an
aromatic volatile oil, chiefly residing in the pellucid dotting of
the leaves. They furnish many of the common spices. These
plants, as well as the *Rosaceæ*, belong to the class *Icosandria* of
Linnæus, and are not poisonous. The fruits belonging here are
the *Punica granatum*, pomegranate; *Psidium pyriferum*, white
guava; and *Psidium pomiferum*, red guava. A curious property
of the guavas is that the green fruit is astringent, causing constipation, while the ripe fruit has an opposite effect. The most important spices of this order are the *Caryophyllus aromaticus*,
cloves: and *Myrtus pimenta*, allspice.

(184.) CACTACEÆ—*Prickly Pears.*—These curious plants are
found to possess very valuable properties in the dry deserts, where
they mostly grow. They are in no way poisonous, and their
slightly acid, watery juice is available for drink in situations where
water is not obtainable. It is said that asses and mules can very
well manage to remove the prickles, and possess themselves of

this precious material. They produce fruits which vary much in size, form, and flavor, according to the species.

(185.) The *Opuntia vulgaris* bears a beautiful, smooth, scarlet, pear-shaped fruit.

Other species bear a green and prickly fruit.

(186.) There is a climbing triangular vine of this family, which bears a very fine red fruit, weighing about a pound. In Mexico this fruit is called pitaya.

(187.) PASSIFLORACEÆ—*Passion Flowers.*—There are several species of passion flower which bear edible fruits, called granadillas, maypops, etc. These fruits are not generally very attractive; but there is a delicious fruit of this kind, which flourishes at the Island of St. Thomas, and doubtless elsewhere.

(188.) CUCURBITACEÆ—*The Melon Family.*—This order of plants contains some delicious fruits; but it is necessary to remem-

FIG. 14.

Citrullus colocynthis.

ber that they are nearly allied to colocynth, briony, and elaterium, dangerously active cathartics. The poisonous principle of these fruits is generally associated with bitterness, so that there is not much danger of poisoning except from the more familiar of them.

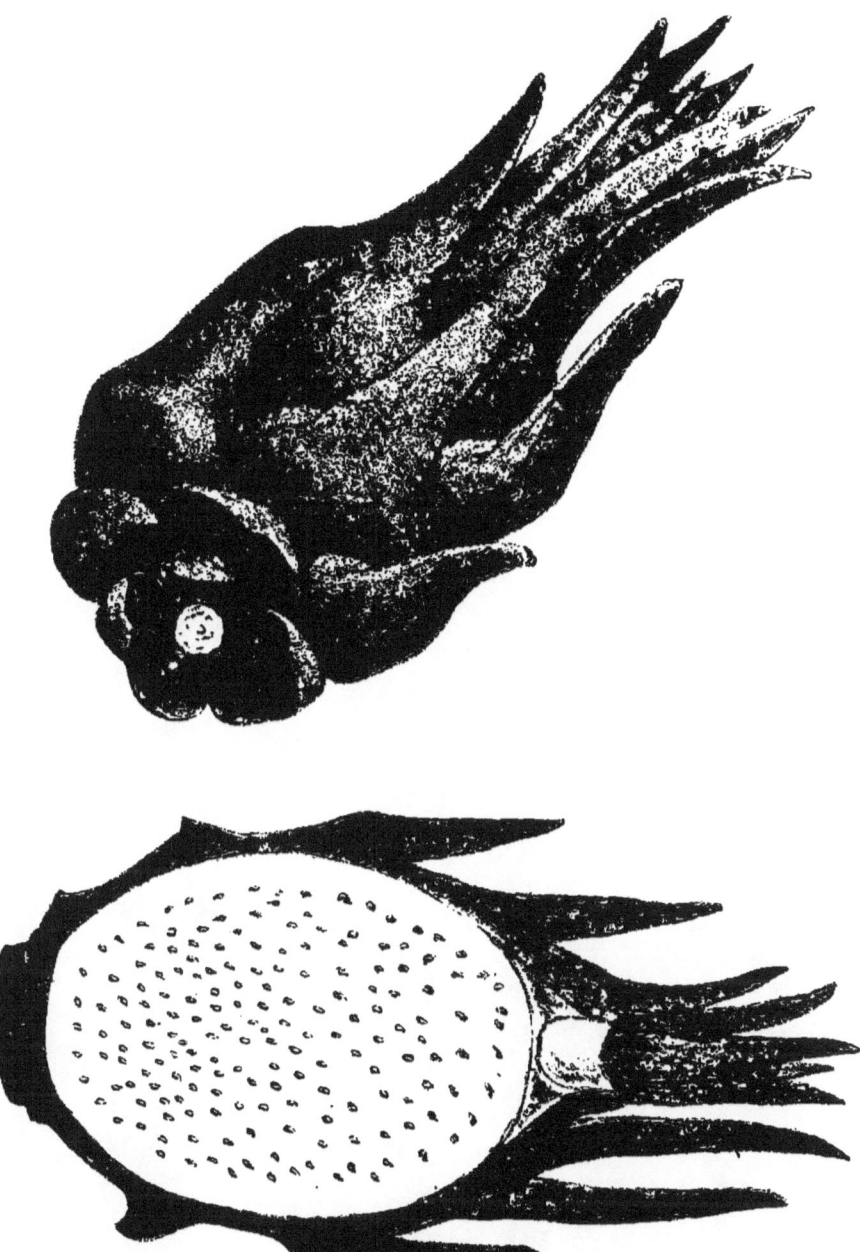

These, when unripe or badly prepared, may be poisonous. All of these fruits should be used with great moderation.

The common cucumber, *Cucumis sativus*, sliced thin, with salt and vinegar, quickly loses all deleterious properties, and is a delicious and wholesome salad.

The watermelon, *Citrullus vulgaris*, is a very dangerous fruit. Where it has been long and carefully cultivated, varieties have been produced which when ripe are delicious and wholesome. There have been occasions of men eating watermelons unripe and of inferior quality, from which serious accidents have occurred. They generally produce an attack of cholera morbus, which may prove fatal. We have seen in the market at Mazatlan, Mexico, watermelons capable of producing this result. The French army in Egypt suffered much from watermelons of bad quality.

Pumpkins and squashes, the various species of *Cucurbita*, are eaten only when cooked, and in this condition they are good food.

(189.) *The pawpaw* of the tropics, tree melon, *Carica papaya*, is a tree sometimes attaining the height of twenty feet. The fruit is about the size and form of the common muskmelon. The pulp is rather insipid, but the seeds, some of which should be eaten with the fruit, have a pleasant pungent flavor, curiously like the flavor of watercresses. This fruit is very common and much eaten by sailors, and we have never known harm to result. When eaten freely it produces a moderately laxative effect.

(190.) UMBELLIFERÆ—*The Parsley Family.*—This extensive order embraces plants which vary exceedingly in their properties. They are generally merely aromatic and carminative; as fennel, anise, dill, carui, etc. Some of them by cultivation lose their aromatic and stimulant properties in some degree, as carrots, parsnips, celery, etc.

Some of these plants supply exudations of unpleasant fragrance, which are used as antispasmodic medicines. The *Ferula asafœtida*, and *Dorema ammoniacum*, furnish products of this kind.

Conium maculatum, poison-hemlock, and *Cicuta virosa*, water-hemlock, are powerful acro-narcotic poisons.

MONOPETALOUS EXOGENS.

(191.) RUBIACEÆ.—The plants of this order possess various and active properties. Not one of them, however, is dangerously poisonous. *Rubia tinctorum* furnishes the madder of commerce, a valuable dyestuff.

FIG. 15.

Apocynum cannabinum.

The ipecacuanha of the shops is the root of the *Cephaelis ipecacuanha* of Brazil. It is the most gentle and efficient emetic substance known, causing the evacuation of the stomach with the least possible amount of distress or pain. It is said that other species and allied genera possess similar properties.

Various species of *Cinchona*, growing in the elevated mountain regions of tropical America, supply us with quinine, the most important article of the Materia Medica except opium.

Coffee is the fruit of the *Caffea arabica*, the great benefits of which will probably never be estimated as highly as they deserve.

(192.) LOGANIACEÆ, *Poison Beans;* APOCYNEÆ, *Dogbanes;*
ASCLEPIADACEÆ, *Milkweeds.*—All the plants of these three orders
are poisonous. Some of them produce the most deadly poisons
known. Strychnine, the active principle of *Strychnos nux vomica*
and other species, is among the most active. It is already obtaining a place by the side of arsenic in the annals of secret
murder. The *Strychnos toxifera* and *Strychnos cogens* are the

FIG. 16.

Apocynum androsæmifolium.

source of the terrific woorari with which the Indians of Central
America poison their arrows. The *Strychnos tieute,* of Java, is
the celebrated upas tree. The *Cerbera tanghin,* of Madagascar,
is said to be so poisonous that a single seed, the size of an almond,
is sufficient to poison twenty men. This is the celebrated ordeal
nut of the east coast of Africa. The ordeal nut of the west coast,
Physostigma, the Calabar bean, is referred to the order *Leguminosæ,* though represented as precisely as bad as the other; one
bean the size of an almond being sufficient to kill twenty men.

One of the Asclepiadaceæ, in 1871, was introduced to the
medical profession under the name of *Cundurango,* as an effective

cure for cancer. It was found to be a new plant—a new genus was suggested to hold it; and it received the appropriate name of *Pseusmagennetes*, father of lies.—(*San. Rep.*, 1873.)

(193.) Pink root, *Spigelia marilandica*, is probably the least dangerous plant of its order. It is one of our most esteemed vermifuge medicines, and has never been known to do harm when administered with due caution. I recollect meeting, a few years since, a much-esteemed friend in the course of his morning round, who expressed himself somewhat as follows : " I have just witnessed one of the most distressing scenes which it has ever fallen to my lot to encounter. Yesterday a fine healthy child of Mr. G., our apothecary, was a little cross, so far as I can understand, and perhaps picked his nose, from which the nurse concluding he had worms, applied to the clerk in the store for medicine, and received a package of the last puffed quackery. The infusion was prepared and administered in accordance with the directions, and the consequence was the convulsions and death which I witnessed. I had not the heart to hint it to the family, already sufficiently distressed, but it must be done. The

FIG. 17.

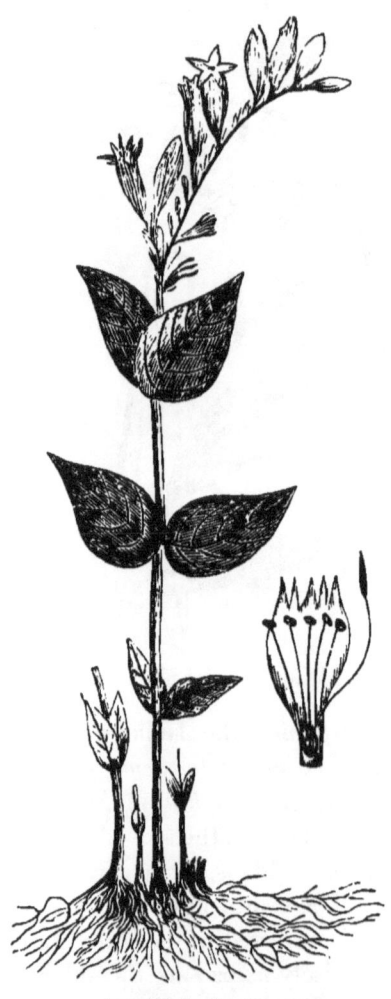

Spigelia marilandica.

same murderous trick was enacted here about six years ago; the same sort of almanac was gratuitously distributed, and I traced to this cause the death of twelve children, which occurred with similar symptoms at that time. I examined a package of the medicine, and it contained nothing but clear leaves of spigelia, the stems and roots being removed." Dr. Chalmers (*History of South Carolina*) gives an account of the death of two children, caused by pink root. The symptoms produced by a poisonous dose of this plant are giddiness, dimness of vision with dilated pupils, convulsions of the muscles of the eyes, general convulsions, and death. On the whole, I am inclined to the opinion that a large proportion of the deaths of children by convulsions are deaths from carelessly administered worm tea.

Two other species of spigelia, *Spigelia anthelmia* and *Spigelia glabrata*, are mentioned as active poisons known in the West India Islands.

(194.) COMPOSITÆ—*Sunflowers; Asters.*—This immense order of plants, including at least one thousand genera and ten thousand species, is remarkable for containing a great many medicinal plants, none of which has any dangerous activity.

Lactuca sativa, garden lettuce, the young leaves of which make a pleasant salad, becomes pretty strongly narcotic as the season advances, and the inspissated juice, called lactucarium, though much less active, is comparable in some respects to opium.

Chamomile, *Anthemis nobilis*, and other species, are simple bitter tonics, sometimes proving emetic and diaphoretic, if taken infused in large quantities of warm water. The same may be said of *Eupatorium*, boneset, and most of the other ten thousand plants of this order.

(195.) LOBELIACEÆ.—The few plants constituting this order have acro-narcotic properties very similar to those of ordinary tobacco. Like other plants with such properties, they are medicinal, but require to be used with great caution.

Lobelia inflata, Indian tobacco, was the principal medicine of the celebrated Samuel Thomson. He attributed to it almost miraculous powers. It was said to evacuate bile and other crudities from the stomach without causing nausea or disturbing wholesome food, or interfering in any way with healthy digestion. But since the decease of this celebrated individual, and his equally celebrated botanic system of medicine, this plant has fallen into disuse. It is occasionally recommended to be smoked in a pipe in cases of asthma.

(196.) ERICACEÆ—*Heaths.*—This extensive family of plants furnishes a great variety of edible berries—cranberries, whortleberries, blueberries, bilberries, deerberries, bearberries, etc. Some of the berries and plants are not much esteemed, except as flavoring ingredients. Such are the *Gaultheria procumbens,* partridgeberry, and *Pyrola umbellata.* The plants of this family have generally diuretic and astringent properties. Two genera, the rhododendrons and the kalmias, have narcotic poisonous properties. The *Kalmia angustifolia,* and other species, have proved fatal to sheep, and they appear not to have any instinctive disposition to shun this poison. The berries are sometimes eaten by the ruffed grouse, partridge pheasant, when the ground is covered with snow, and the flesh of the birds is thus rendered poisonous.

(197.) The *Oxycoccus macrocarpa,* cranberry, as it is capable of easy preservation through the winter, is, perhaps, the most important of our small fruits.

(198.) SCROPHULARIACEÆ—*Mullein Family.*—This important family produces some ornamental flowers, without fragrance. They are bitter and disgusting to the taste, many of them are narcotic poisons, and all suspicious. Some of them turn black in drying.

The *Digitalis purpurea,* foxglove, the most important plant of the order, is a valuable medicine. But it possesses dangerous properties, on account of which it must be used with great caution. The other species of digitalis possess similar properties. The same may be said of most of the plants of the order, though they are generally less active. They should be avoided.

The mullein, *Verbascum thapsus,* has the narcotic and sedative properties in so moderate a degree that the leaves are safely applied to painful tumors as a poultice.

(199.) LABIATÆ — *Mints.* — This striking family of plants, embracing more than two thousand species, has many properties in common with the Cruciferæ. They are all pervaded by a pleasant, aromatic, volatile oil, which differs somewhat in each plant, and gives to them their characteristic properties. There is not one plant of this extensive order which is in any way poisonous.

(200.) CONVOLVULACEÆ — *Morning-glories.* — The various plants of this order are pervaded by an acrid juice, which, in many instances, renders them very actively cathartic. This property depends on a resinous material, which appears to be peculiar in each species. The farinaceous matter of the root of one or more species, sweet potato, is so little infected with this active material as to be excellent food. Dangerously active properties are to be suspected in any unknown plant of this order.

The *Convolvulus scammonium* supplies the dangerously active scammony of the shops. *Ipomœa jalapa* produces the well-known jalap. *Ipomœa pandurata*, wild sweet potato, has similar properties. *Ipomœa batatas, Batata edulis*, is the cultivated sweet potato, of which there are about twenty good varieties cultivated, and many more bad ones.

(201.) SOLANACEÆ— *The Potato Family.*—This order, containing more than one thousand species, is one of the greatest importance, as it contains some species which produce a large portion of our best food ; others supplying important medicines, and still others which are most deadly poisons. The close resemblance of plants possessing such various properties has led to frequent fatal accidents. The poisonous properties depend on the presence of vegetable alkaloids, each peculiar to its particular class of plants, *Solania, Atropia, Daturia, Hyoscyamia, Nicotina*, etc. These alkaloids are of such delicate organization that they are readily destroyed by warmth, moisture, light, etc. It seems impossible to prepare extracts of hyoscyamus, belladonna, or stramonium of any reliable strength, because the active principle is mostly destroyed by the necessary application of heat. In the same way these plants lose much of their activity by mere drying, and nearly all of it by being kept long in a dry state. Some of the fruits, when green, are deadly poison, which, when fully ripened in the sun or cooked, are wholesome and pleasant food.

These plants are so dangerously poisonous that any unknown plant with the leading characters of the order—monopetalous, pentandrous, light blue, white and blue, or lurid flowers—should be avoided with the greatest degree of suspicious caution.

(202.) The common tomato, *Lycopersicum esculentum*, is a valuable fruit, in no way poisonous or injurious to health, even when eaten green or in almost any possible degree of excess. Preserved in air-tight cans, it forms one of our most valuable resources for vegetable food through long winters and during long voyages. There are numerous other species and varieties growing in various parts of the world, with similar properties. They may any of them be appropriated for food with confidence.

Red pepper, *Capsicum annuum*, possesses simply stimulant properties, void of serious harm.

The egg plant, *Melongena esculenta, Solanum esculentum*, is a popular vegetable, never eaten except when cooked, from which, so far as we know, no harm has ever resulted.

The common potato, *Solanum tuberosum*, in its abundant supply of farinaceous food, comes next in importance to rice and wheat. The plant and even the tubers contain a portion of the poisonous solania; but not enough to do harm in any quantity which could possibly be eaten. By cooking this is effectually destroyed. Practically, raw potatoes have been found the most effectual remedy for scorbutus.

Bittersweet, woody nightshade, *Solanum dulcamara*, is doubtless poisonous, though not very actively so. Professor Dunglison, says: " He has seen it chewed by boys in large quantities, and has chewed it himself when a boy, without observing any effect from it, except what was caused by its saccharine and gummy matter. The decoction, extract, and fruit have all been given in large quantities, with no effect." We remember to have read the account of a very different case which occurred to Dr. Isaac Parrish : " The little patient died with symptoms of narcotic poisoning, which it was impossible to account for till an examination discovered the stomach full of the berries of this plant."

(203.) Black nightshade, *Solanum nigrum*, has a bad reputation, which it probably deserves. It is an ugly weed, with a repulsive smell, which probably prevents accidents, for otherwise its black berries might thoughtlessly be eaten. The *Solanum pseudocapsicum*, Jerusalem cherry, has similar and more active properties. It has a scarlet berry.

(204.) *Atropa belladonna*, deadly nightshade, is one of the most active of acro-narcotic poisons, but, like the rest, its suspicious appearance and bad smell are such that we rarely hear of any accident from it.

The same remarks are applicable to henbane, *Hyoscyamus niger*, and thornapple, or Jamestown weed, *Datura stramonium*. This last is, however, a very common weed, and accidental poisoning sometimes occurs from children swallowing the seeds.

FIG. 18.

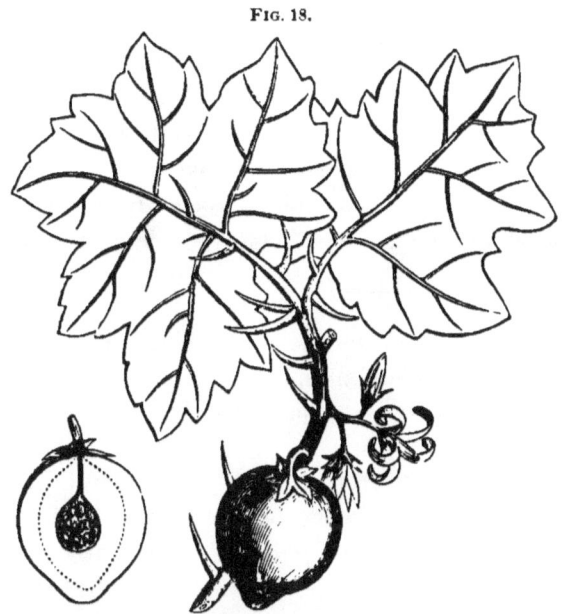

Solanum, Bachelor's Pear.

Tobacco, *Nicotiana tabacum*, *Nicotiana rustica*, and other species, is poisonous like the others, its repulsive flavor preventing its use except by those who have other inducements besides their own senses. It is curious that the system becomes rapidly accustomed to this plant, so that it may be used in large quantities, without injury so far as concerns acute poisoning, whatever may ultimately be its effects, moral or physical, on the individual.

The ground cherry, *Physalis viscosa*, is occasionally eaten, and so far as we know without harm. The various species of physalis, called pops, winter cherries, alkekengis, etc., have yellow flowers, and thus want one of the suspicious characters which we have mentioned as belonging to most of the poisonous plants of this order.

There are numerous other species of solanaceous plants, which, from the tempting appearance of their fruit when separated from the plant, have been the cause of serious accidents. Some of them are named morellos from their resemblance to dark-colored cherries. It is well to be very shy of these morellos. One of them, called bachelor's pear, a dangerous poison, has somewhat the form and size of a pear, attached to the stem by the larger end. But we have neither the space, inclination, nor means of enumerating all the Solanaceæ. They are to be treated with suspicion and avoided till we receive positive evidence of their innocence. And we are even to receive the evidence in their favor with the caution, that some of them are eatable when well cooked, which are dangerous otherwise.

APETALOUS EXOGENS.

(205.) LAURACEÆ—*Laurels.*—The plants of this order are pervaded by a stimulant aromatic oil. They furnish us with cinnamon and camphor, and our own *Laurus sassafras* has the same general properties.

A delicious fruit, avigato, avocado, avicato, or alligator pear, is the fruit of the *Persea gratissima, Laurus persea,* of the West Indies.

(206.) EUPHORBIACEÆ—*Spurges.*—This family of plants, embracing about twenty-five hundred species, requires special attention on account of the serious accidents constantly occurring with them. They are pervaded by an acrid poisonous matter, which resides principally in the milky juice and about the seeds. The fresh seeds mostly have a pleasant flavor, not unlike the flavor of walnuts. The consequences, however, of eating them are terrifically different. The poisonous property appears to be easily destroyed by heat, in some instances, or it may even be washed away in water, as in the processes of preparing farina and tapioca.

(207.) Castor oil is a product of the *Ricinus communis*, and when properly prepared is one of the mildest of the medicines of the class to which it belongs. It is even used in small quantities as a salad oil, without unpleasant results, its flavor not differing materially from that of olive oil.

(208.) Croton oil is derived from *Croton tiglium, Croton pa-*

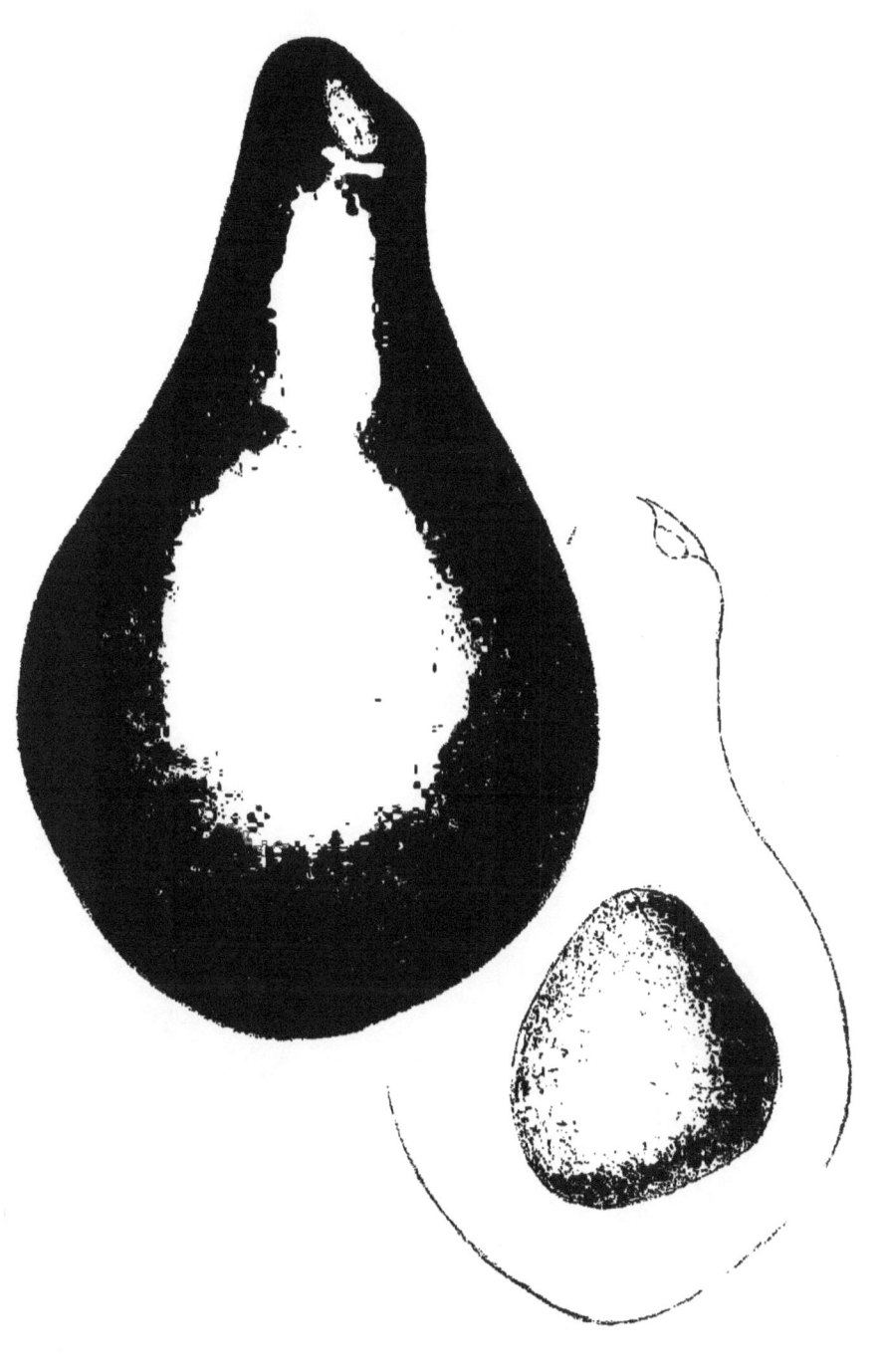

rana, and perhaps other species. It possesses a dangerous degree of activity, and requires to be used with great care to avoid bad consequences.

(209.) *Jatropha curcas* and some other species are cultivated for their oil, which is burned in lamps. The following accident with this plant has been recorded: "Two men of the United States schooner Taney, being on shore at Porto Praya, Cape de

FIG. 19.

Ricinus communis.

Verde Islands, tasted the seeds of the *Jatropha curcas,* which grows abundantly on these islands, and finding them pleasant, ate of them: one to the extent of a handful, the other being satisfied with three or four seeds. In both cases vomiting and purging of a violent character came on in the course of an hour, and in the case of the man who ate but few the effect went no further. In the other case alarming symptoms supervened; the muscles of the extremities were contracted by violent spasms; the patient was affected with dizziness, vertigo, and great restlessness; the respiration was quick and panting; the skin became cold and moist; and the pulse small, thready, and intermittent. The heart's action was very irregular, and so weak that its impulse could with great difficulty be perceived. These alarming symptoms continued for several hours. After about five hours of assiduous attention, reaction occurred and he fell asleep. The next morning he was nearly well. The seeds were ripe and of the kind used by the inhabitants as an active purgative."—(*Farquharson.*)

There are probably twenty other species of physic nut equally dangerous.

The *Jatropha manihot*, manioca, cassava plant, has a large, starchy root, which is variously manufactured into food by grating, washing in water, and parching, the product being variously

Fig. 20.

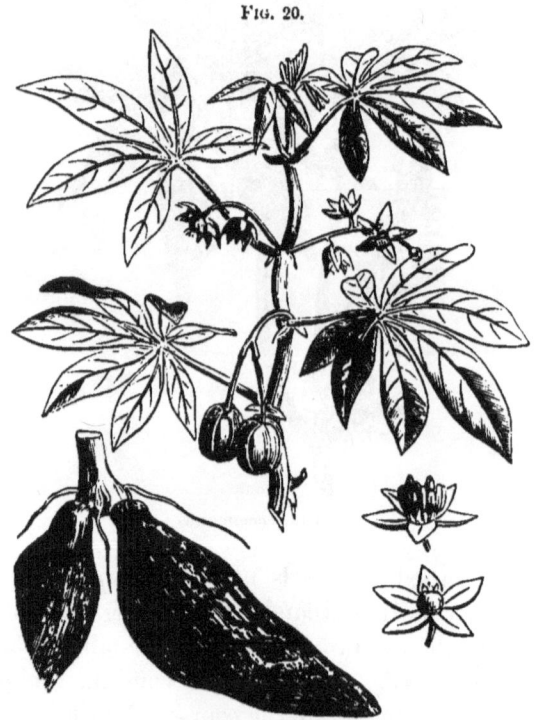

Jatropha manihot.

named tapioca, cassava, or farina, according to the form produced by variations in the process. The juice of this root, which exudes in the process of grating, is a very active irritant poison, but with a very small amount of careless washing the resulting farina is quite harmless. It is easy to see how the sad accidents are constantly happening with this root. A cook unacquainted with its poisonous properties, and seeing it eaten, is tempted, in the absence of potatoes, to put some of this nice-looking farinaceous root into his soup, and the result is that his whole mess of soup is rendered more or less poisonous.

(210.) The celebrated *mançanilla* of Spanish America, *Hippomane mancinella*, is perhaps the most poisonous tree of this order.

FIG. 21.

Hippomane mancinella.

The juice is used by savages to poison their arrows. "If some of the crude milky juice falls upon even a horse, the hair of the part soon falls off and the skin rises up in blisters, which will require a long time to heal. It has been observed that fish, the barracuta and others, which eat the fruit dropped casually into the sea, are often found dead in the swash water, and if taken alive and eaten they often prove poisonous. Even the large white crab that burrows in the sand, if near these trees, is not to be made use of as food. Formerly no one dared to cut down one of those trees without having first made a large fire round them in order to burn the bark and dry up the juice, which flies from them in cutting; but now naked negroes venture to cut them down green, only using the caution of first rubbing their bodies with lime-juice, which prevents the juice from corroding or ulcerating the skin.   Bruising the tender leaves and boughs in fish-ponds has often been a roguish practice of taking and destroying fish, for the fish very soon after become stupid and float with their bellies upward.   The pulp of the manchineel fruit does not exceed the seventh of an inch thick, inclosing a hard strong shell, which contains the seeds.   The juice of the fruit is poisonous like that of the leaves."—(*Hughes.*)

The term mançanilla, diminutive of mançana, an apple, is probably applied to various trees bearing small poisonous fruits of similar appearance.

Fig. 22.

Hura crepitans.

The sand-box tree (*Hura brasiliensis*) is quite a large tree of this family, the leaves and other parts of which exude, when wounded, a very poisonous milky juice, of which various stories are told, rivalling those we hear of the mançanilla itself.

"These trees are called sand-boxes, from the use that is made of their fruit to that purpose."—(*Hughes.*)

GYMNOSPERM EXOGENS.

(211.) CONIFERÆ.—The pines, cedars, junipers, etc., are charged with resinous juice. They supply an immense amount of valuable timber, but nothing more poisonous than turpentine and juniper berries.

(212.) CYCADACEÆ—*Sago Plants.*—The *Cycas revoluta* and other species supply in their stalks a large quantity of starchy material devoid of any active property.

"*Zamia integrifolia* and other species are the source of the Florida arrowroot."—(*Carson.*)

SPADICEOUS ENDOGENS.

(213.) PALMACEÆ.—The family of palms are replete with useful properties. They afford abundant food and shelter to man in all tropical climates. Some of them afford astringent extracts, but there is not one of them possessed of any dangerous property.

Fig. 23.

Ceroxylon andicola.

ARACEÆ—*Indian Turnips.*—The plants of this family are important on account of their large starchy roots, corms. The few species which grow in temperate climates are of little account, but in tropical regions they form a large portion of the farinaceous food of the inhabitants. In the islands of the Pacific Ocean they are extensively cultivated, supplying there the place of rice, wheat, and potatoes. They are all pervaded by an acrid juice, which in many cases is found so concentrated as to act as an irritant poison. This irritating or poisonous property is readily destroyed by drying or cooking. They

are usually cooked by boiling, and the water thrown away contains much of the poisonous matter in solution.   Dreadful accidents have happened by putting this vegetable into soup.   Every
strange plant with acrid taste, which bears its flowers on a simple
spadix, should be avoided as a poison; and such plants as are
known should be cooked with proper care, keeping in view these
dangerous properties.   Several genera, many species, and innumerable varieties are cultivated for food.   In Oceanica they are

FIG. 24.

Arum triphyllum.

called taro, kalo, alo, etc., and in the West Indies, eddos or eddas;
in Brazil they are called ynhamès and taiovos.   The great danger from them is, that a cook, not understanding their properties,
may put really good vegetables, which should not be so cooked,
into his soup.

PETALOID ENDOGENS.

(214.) BROMELIACEÆ— *Pineapple Family.*—The pineapple, which is the important plant of this family, is, in places where it abounds, generally regarded with disfavor; and strangers are generally cautioned against its use.   We think it is merely excess that is to be guarded against.   Seamen arriving in a port where this fruit is abundant, after perhaps thirty days' privation of everything like fresh fruit, have doubtless often injured themselves very much by eating too many pineapples; and hence we infer a good reason for this caution.

(215.) DIOSCOREACEÆ— *Yams.*—Several species and numerous varieties of yams are cultivated in different countries.   They

FIG. 25.

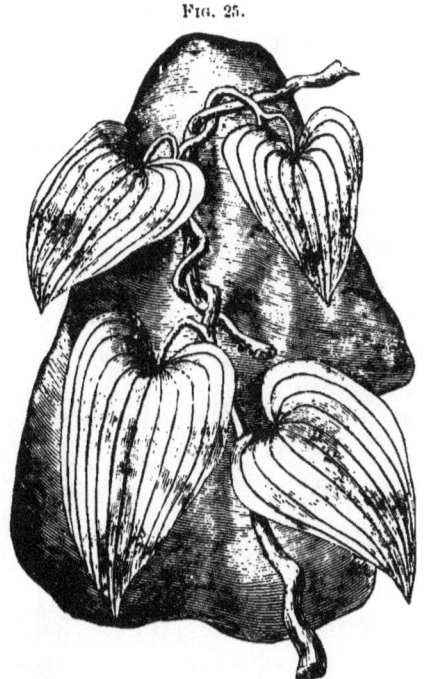

Dioscorea alata—Yam.

are probably capable of as extensive use as the common potato. The good varieties are as good as potatoes, and the poor varieties are no worse than poor potatoes.   There is a good deal of popular misapprehension in regard to the properties of this vegetable.

Some persons having eaten poor varieties, badly cooked, have propagated the notion that none of them are good. Some inferior varieties of sweet potato have been cultivated and used under this name, and have thus assisted in spreading the prejudice. They have one great advantage over potatoes, as they are easily preserved for a long time on shipboard in tropical climates.

There is some confusion in the use of the name of this valuable vegetable. The *ynhamè* of Rio de Janeiro is not a yam at all, but the enormous corm of a caladium. The proper yam at this place is called *carai*. Some varieties of sweet potato, and even common potato, and probably other tubers, have been sold for yams. So far as we know, all the *Dioscoreaceæ* are without active properties, though one of them is named *Dioscorea demona*, from which we infer that there is something unpleasant about it. I once attempted to cultivate the yam in our climate, but probably the summer is too short to ripen the tubers till suitable varieties are produced.

(216.) LILIACEÆ.—The lilies are more noted for their beautiful flowers than for any other property. Some of them, as asparagus and onions, afford nutritious articles of diet.

The squill, *Scilla maritima*, has more active properties than any other species, and this can hardly be considered dangerous.

There is on record a curious case of poisoning from the pollen of a common tiger lily. A little girl, four years old, picked an anther from a tiger lily and placed it in her nose. The consequences were great irritation of the part, with profuse discharge of yellow mucus, followed by vomiting, first, of the ordinary contents of the stomach, and afterward of mucus, colored the same as that from the nose. Drowsiness and other symptoms followed, with death in about sixty hours from the time of the accident.—(*Am. Jour. Med. Sci.*, vol. xlv, 271.)

(217.) MELANTHACEÆ.—This family is characterized by possessing powerful narcotic and poisonous properties. This is, perhaps, intended to be expressed by the names, *μελας*, black, *rere atrum*, truly black. These poisonous properties are partly due to the vegetable alkaloids, veratria and colchicia.

Colchicum autumnale, meadow saffron, is an acro-narcotic poison, which requires to be handled with care. It is observed, together with other plants of this family, to lessen greatly the action of the heart and circulation, and it was thought that it might be advantageously used in many cases of inflammatory disease, where bloodletting would otherwise be called for. More recently, *Veratrum album*, white hellebore of Europe, and *Veratrum viride*, American white hellebore, have been very earnestly recommended with the same views. A curious and disagreeable property of veratrum is the violent sneezing which its powder causes.

GLUMACEOUS ENDOGENS.

(218.) GRASSES.—This family of plants, containing nearly four thousand known species, furnishes more food to men and beasts than all the rest of the vegetable world combined. Its nutritive properties exist, in greater or less degrees, both in the herbage and in the farinaceous seed. Sugar is a frequent constituent, and is particularly abundant in sugar cane, sorghum, and Indian corn. There is, probably, no poisonous plant in this entire family; though common rye, *Secale cereale*, is subject to a disease which renders the infected seed poisonous. And the *Lolium temulentum*, darnel, has occasionally been injurious to cattle, probably from a similar cause. Possibly these cases of poisoning may have been caused by other weeds mingled with the grass.

CRYPTOGAMIA.

(219.) Nearly all the innumerable plants belonging to the grand division of flowerless plants are without active or otherwise important properties. A few of the ferns have anthelmintic properties.

The *fungi*, mushrooms, and toadstools, however, are dangerous substances, of which it is necessary to be suspicious. The only species that we know of which can always be trusted are the truffle of the Old World, and the common white mushroom with pink gills, when growing in open fields. All others, and especially such as grow in shady places, are to be carefully avoided.

(220.) In conclusion we may state, as the rule, that the actively poisonous plants have (usually) repulsive properties about them, so that there is very little danger from them. There are, however, four families of plants from which accidents have occurred and are likely hereafter to occur, either from poisonous matter naturally belonging to plants actually in use as food, but from which the poison is usually removed or destroyed by cooking; or from poisonous plants bearing fruit with a close resemblance to ordinary good esculent vegetables; or from the pleasant taste of the poisonous seeds of one family. Plants of the following four families have proved fatal from these causes. Their properties should, therefore, be understood, and enough of their general appearance and botanical characters to recognize them:

Cucurbitaceæ, the melon family, § 188.

Solanaceæ, the potato family, § 201.

Euphorbiaceæ, spurge family, § 206.

Araceæ, Indian turnip family, § 213.

CHAPTER XVII.

VERA CRUZ—LIBERTY ON SHORE—HABITS.

The words of King Lemuel, the prophecy that his mother taught him:
Give not thy strength unto women, nor thy ways to that which destroyeth kings.

It is not for kings, O Lemuel, it is not for kings to drink wine, nor for princes strong drink.—PROVERBS xxxi, 1, 3, 4.

(221.) SEPTEMBER 17TH, 1860.—We arrived at Vera Cruz, Mexico, early in the autumn, the season of fevers and other sickness. The ship was accordingly anchored at the Island of Sacrificios, three or four miles distant from the town, a situation sufficiently remote from the marshy land of the country, and with all its prevalent breezes from the ocean. By this arrangement we expected, with good reason, to escape from all serious disease, though there were a number of foreign ships at the same anchorage with cases of yellow fever on board.

The bumboats were soon alongside prepared to sell fruits, vegetables, etc., of the country, everything that they imagined the sailors wanted, and would be permitted to purchase. Nobody seemed inclined to buy cucumbers, from a well-founded apprehension that under the circumstances they were unwholesome. It was only necessary to suggest a little caution about eating too many oranges the first day, and as there were very few in the boats, and very dear, there was no difficulty in carrying out the suggestion. Free trade was therefore permitted. No harm whatever, so far as known, resulted from this permission, and the arrangement continued during our stay in port.

(222.) The seamen were frequently indulged with liberty on shore, mostly in the daytime. Much good and some harm resulted from this.

LIBERTY ON SHORE.

The bad habits of the sailor are doubtless those about which

King Lemuel's mother admonished him. Some came on board in various degrees intoxicated; some were infected with dangerous diseases; and some had to be carried on board. The great majority, however, escaped these mishaps, conducted themselves properly, came on board at the expiration of their liberty, and received nothing but advantage from their visit. The cheerful influences of these visits to the shore are exceedingly beneficial to health, lasting for weeks, and even months. We must here remark the strong contrast between this picture and such as would have been presented only a few years sooner when flogging was a recognized punishment. Nearly all would have been drunk, many diseased, most of them ragged and dirty, some nearly naked by swapping their clothes for rum; the whole ship a sort of pandemonium for several days in succession. Officers would have been sent to wander about the worst places in search of liberty men to be carried on board drunk; instances occurring of officers assaulted, beaten, and perhaps murdered while employed in this duty. The whole business was so hateful to the officers that they would not approve of liberty for the crew more than once in six months, and even contrived excuses, emergencies of service, etc., to protract the interval to a whole year; so that two occasions of general liberty would generally suffice for a cruise of three years. What a splendid chance to see foreign countries ! This has gradually changed, and is still changing more rapidly for the better. It is no longer considered particularly heroic to get drunk and use disgraceful language, to assault an officer, and perhaps try to murder him, and to stand up " like a man " when tied up to settle the account.

The men of their own accord return to the ship at the proper time, and the few who fail to return are arrested and brought on board by the local police. Many of them visit the shore about once a week, permission depending very much on the conduct of the individual during previous visits. It occasionally becomes a question whether the surgeon will recommend certain men to go on shore, and he is particularly hard to convince that getting drunk or other bad conduct is in any way beneficial to health. The constant pressure of these influences is rapidly bringing our sailors to conduct themselves much more like gentlemen during their visits to the shore in foreign countries. Very much remains to be done. Officers do not always fully appreciate these influences; the record of conduct may be written by an unfaithful person, and very gross faults overlooked. These difficulties must always exist in some degree.

There are other influences at work beneficially influencing the character of the sailor. The most important of these is the " honorable discharge," which is given at the expiration of the enlistment. It confers such advantages that all desire to possess it, and it cannot be given at any time or withheld capriciously, but the propriety of its being given to each particular man is a question open for decision till the termination of the cruise. The few who are so indifferent as to fail to obtain it have great difficulty in re-enlisting, as the rendezvous is often closed against all who do not possess it, and a nearly insuperable obstacle is raised against their obtaining petty officers' positions.

(223.) But the sailor is not altogether bad. If we expose his faults, which indeed are apparent enough, let us consider the circumstances of his life, which have deprived him in some degree of the habit of self-control, and give him some credit for such virtues as he actually possesses. His life is a life of contrasts. His intemperance is partly the consequence of long periods of enforced abstinence. His life of privation seems to relieve him so much from the necessity of self-control that he loses all power to resist temptation. After long periods of monotonous and unsavory food, he suddenly has spread before him a profuse feast. There is so little pleasure in his way that he denies himself no indulgence. His life brings all the passions into vivid contrast; hope immediately succeeding to despair; excessive labor to idleness; sadness to joy; in fact, pleasure to pain, and pain to pleasure, in every imaginable form. His impious swearing conceals a religious sentiment not much removed from superstition. He is unstable as the sea. He is the creature of impulse, and habitually of generous impulses. He is occasionally entirely forgetful of self in his generous impulses to serve others. We may relate a characteristic incident. Shortly after the Mexican war, 1848, one of our men, crossing the Rocky Mountains from California, separated somewhat from his party. Suddenly a stranger running came up and begged to be taken on his horse, as he was out of breath, and the Indians after him but a short distance behind the hill, and they would kill him. Ned suggested that the horse

could not carry them both very fast; the Indians might catch
them both. He begged for the sake of his wife and children;
for himself he did not much care, but his poor wife! his helpless
children! " Well, I have no wife or children, and am not out of
breath," says he, and dismounting he induced the stranger to
save himself with the horse. Meanwhile Ned, quietly concealed
among the bushes, had the satisfaction of seeing the Indians fully
occupied with their vexation as the horse travelled off. He
watched his opportunity and made his way to the camp by a cir-
cuitous route, and had the satisfaction as he came in on foot to
hear that the stranger had arrived an hour previously on horseback. With most men such forgetfulness of self to serve others
could only be inspired by the most earnest sentiment of duty,
and would be admired as an act of exalted heroism; with the
sailor it is a mere matter of generous impulse, nothing more.

CHAPTER XVIII.

VENTILATION—CLEANING.

(224.) Though the anchorage at Sacrificios is fully exposed to a breeze from the ocean, in nearly every direction, the calm and warm weather had such influence that the subject of ventilation had to be much and seriously thought of.

We need not much insist on the general importance of ventilation, as this is generally conceded; but there are some parts of its mechanism which we may advantageously study. If we notice the process of vitiation of the atmosphere in a close apartment, by a person breathing, we observe the air expired from the lungs deprived of a portion of its oxygen and charged with carbonic acid, which, being warmer than the rest of the atmosphere, ascends to the ceiling; another expiration sends another portion of impure air in the same direction; and thus the process goes on, continuously increasing the volume of contaminated air from the ceiling downward.

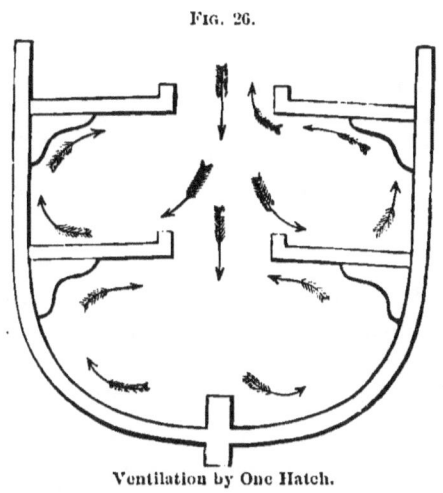

Fig. 26.

Ventilation by One Hatch.

Gradually a portion of this impure air, in contact with the walls and ceiling, is cooled, and, being charged with carbonic acid, a heavy gas, it descends to the floor; and thus we have two reservoirs of impure air, one above and the other below. The atmosphere is likewise deteriorated by exhalations from the surface of the body, which, being warmed, as

well as rendered impure, ascends in like manner to the upper
part of the room. This process continued would soon result in
such deterioration as would be fatal to life.

We have a very simple modification of this in the ordinary
railway carriage. The windows are of plate glass, closely fitted;
the doors nearly all the time closed; there are merely openings
in the elevated ridge of the roof. These are the only effective
ventilation openings. The atmosphere as used—heated and fouled
by respiration and perspiration, carbonic anhydride and all—ascends to the roof, to the projection upwards in the roof, and is
freely exchanged with the external atmosphere. Pure air from
without enters, and in accordance with its greater specific gravity
descends for the use of the passengers, without much mingling
with the air already used and escaping. These cars for each
passenger have about six square feet floor-space, and fifty feet
cubic capacity or air-space, as tight as plate glass and polished
wood can make them, except the openings in the roof; and they
are well ventilated. We start in the palace car, limited express,
at New York, in the morning; we ride nearly all day, with
double plate glass windows to keep out heat and dust and noise,
a door hardly opened more than three or four times in the whole
journey, and we feel no want of ventilation. Or we enter a
smoking car, full of men, all smoking like chimneys; the smoke
enters the air-passages and lungs of the smokers, to be brought
to about the same temperature of other respired air, and to be
charged with usual impurities besides the smoke; but it still
ascends to the openings in the roof, to be exchanged for pure air.
There is generally some smell of tobacco in the car, but no smoke
except the small spires from individual smokers. Nearly all our
arrangements for artificial ventilation are contrived under the
impression that there must be a nearly uniform diffusion of the
contaminated air through the apartment; but this of the railway
cars is based on the reasonable presumption that pure air and
foul air each follows its appropriate course, under the impelling
force of gravitation. If the foul air were heavier than pure air,
it would be necessary to have the openings in the floor, as in getting rid of water or other heavy fluid.

The atmosphere has the same properties on board ship as in a railway car, and some small vessels are ventilated by precisely the mechanism that we have described. The hatchway of entrance with its continuation, the trunk, corresponds exactly in position and function with the ventilation ridge of the car. These small vessels with but one deck are very perfectly ventilated : they only require the side openings of the trunk to be partially closed so as not to get too much ventilation. In larger vessels the same forces operate, but apartments are divided and subdivided as the vessel increases in size, till sometimes the matter becomes a little complicated. An air-port at the side is a great improvement, admitting pure air directly into the apartment without bringing it so much in contact with the impure, which still continues to ascend by the hatchway. With these arrangements, there is little danger of the air becoming seriously impure in cool weather, except from perverseness in closing hatches, or putting decaying material in close store-rooms, or chests, or closets.

(225.) But in very warm weather the atmosphere may be about as warm as the human body, so that it cannot be made much warmer by being breathed, and no such movement of ventilation is established. We then must have another force. Wind, the atmosphere naturally in motion, is the great force for this purpose, effecting ventilation, mostly, without either care or consciousness on our part. A scarcely perceptible breeze of one mile an hour, entering an air-port of eight inches diameter, supplies more than eighteen hundred cubic feet of air per hour. Now, it appears that a man, in ordinary health and exercise, breathes about fifteen cubic feet in the same time.—(*Dalton.*) His daily supply would come through the aperture in less than twelve minutes. Hence we see that want of air in this sense is scarcely possible. But probably a hundred times more air is needed for healthy ventilation than is required to supply oxygen for the respiratory process. The air has other objects besides supplying oxygen for respiration and removing carbonic acid. The surface of the body requires air in motion to remove its heat and exhalations, which are otherwise retained in the system, and become directly and promptly poisonous. This action of the air on the skin seems hardly less important than that on the lungs. The exhalations must have sufficient motion in the air to remove them promptly from the apartment altogether, or they undergo changes which render them dangerously poisonous. They adhere to clothing, bedding, and furniture, and in this situation become the poisonous germs which result in epidemics of typhus, and probably of nearly all the terrible epidemics which have from time to time devastated the world, including plague, measles, small-pox, dysentery, erysipelas, etc. It is on this account, as well as our instinctive consciousness of its comfort, that we need efficient ventilation.

(226.) Wind being the efficient force of ventilation, let us see how it may be made more useful. With a single hatchway above, the air propelled into an apartment has constantly to encounter the opposite current, which must simultaneously escape. As a general rule, there will be found some irregular obstacle to the motion of the wind in a direct line, so that it is reflected in such a way that fresh air enters by one side or corner of the hatch, while the impure air escapes by another. Thus, if the hatch be relatively large, and the breeze fresh, this ventilation is sufficient. An air-port in the side of the vessel is of course a prodigious advantage. It is still better if there be two pretty large hatches at some distance from each other. The pressure of the wind can rarely

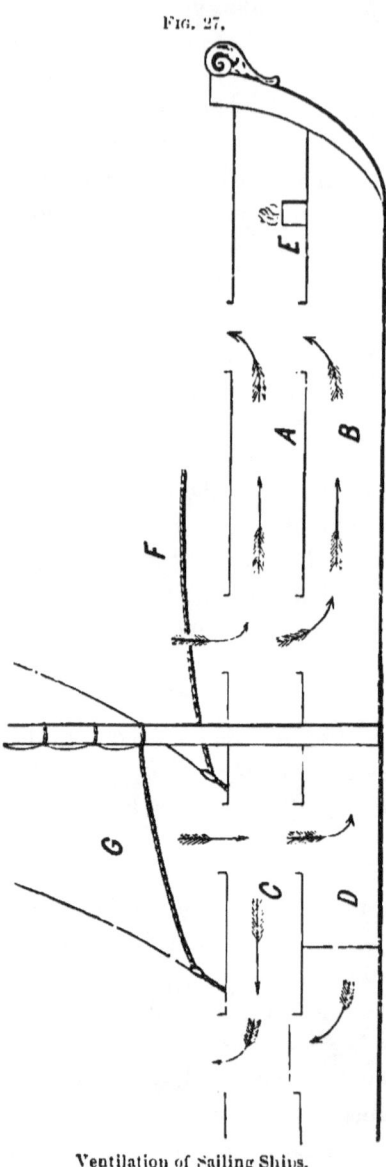

Fig. 27.

Ventilation of Sailing Ships.

be equal at both of them, so that if there be anything of a breeze, the air enters at one hatch and escapes at the other, thus flushing the apartment from end to end by a very efficient ventilation. This is greatly aided by the sails. In sailing ships, the mainsail is generally so situated with reference to the main-hatch, that there is a torrent of air driven down this hatch and up forward, so long as the mainsail is set. This leaves nothing to be desired for this part of the ship, at sea, with a fair breeze. In a gale of wind, the main-spencer, sometimes called the coffee-cooler, gives more ventilation than is desired by those whose apartments are below this part of the ship. In the annexed diagram the arrows are designed to indicate the direction of ventilation currents. *A*, refers to the berth-deck; *B*, fore- and main-hold; *C*, steerage ventilated by main-spencer; *D*, after-hold or spirit-room; *E*, situation of the galley; *F*, mainsail; *G*, main-spencer.

(227.) When the ship is at anchor, an important part of this machinery, the sails, does us no good, and it is necessary to use machinery specially designed for the purpose. When there is a fair breeze a good portion of every day, the ordinary wind-sails are sufficient. If the executive officer of the ship and the surgeon make frequent inspections, and make the condition of various parts of the ship a frequent subject of conversation, as directed by general orders, there are very few occasions when this amount of machinery is insufficient. The sense of smell affords us the best test of the sufficiency of the ventilation of any particular apartment. This sense, however, becomes readily blunted to habitual impressions, and the next evidence of defective ventilation is the headache, languor, and nausea.

In calm, warm weather, if long continued, the means already indicated are quite insufficient, especially for the lower decks of large ships. It has hence been found that these parts of the ship are not to be inhabited in warm climates; and it has even been noted that the larger the ship the greater the average mortality from ordinary diseases, and the greater the liability to suffer from epidemics. In such situations we are obliged to use additional means of ventilation or suffer distressing consequences.

(228.) Heat or fires may be used in various ways to create ventilating currents. The situation of the galley in ships-of-war, near the fore-hatch, is an excellent arrangement of this kind; since the air which it heats immediately ascends and escapes, so as to create a current coinciding in direction with that produced by the force of the wind. When the galley is placed below in a steamer it should be in the after-part of the same deck, so that its ventilating current may correspond in direction with that produced by the heat of the engine, rather than forward, where it would oppose or counteract it. The heat of the engine-room is, in fact, the great ventilating force of steamers, so long as there is fire in the furnaces. The entire atmosphere about the engine, being warmed and consequently expanded, ascends in obedience to its diminished specific gravity, follows the smoke-stack upward, and produces ventilating currents from all parts to fill the vacuum. This force is so efficient that ordinarily the course of the ventilating currents, even at the ends of these vessels, is towards the furnaces, near the centre; the reverse of

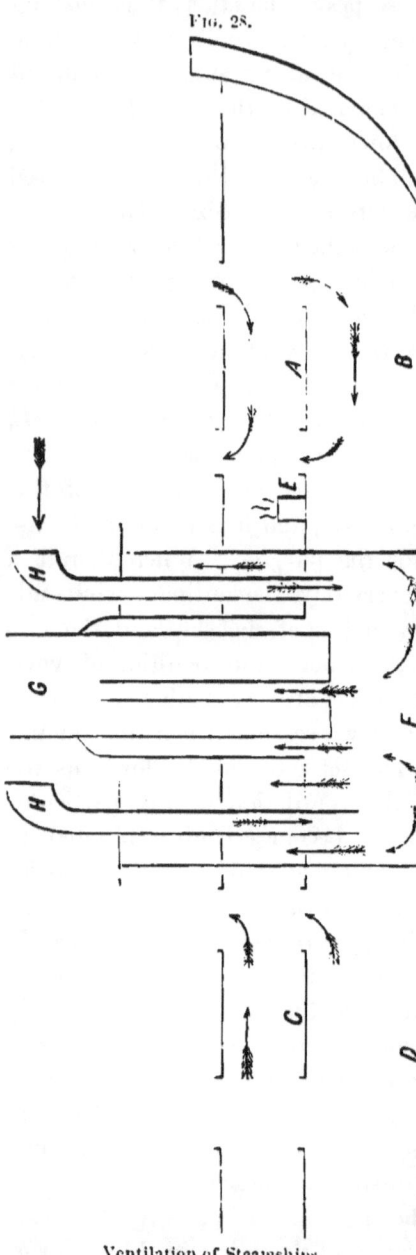

Fig. 28.

Ventilation of Steamships.

the direction in sailing vessels. The diagram is designed to indi-

cate, by its arrows, the direction of the various ventilating currents in a steamer. *A*, berth-deck; *B*, main- and fore-hold; *C*,
officers' apartments; *D*, after-hold; *E*, situation of the galley;
G, smoke-stack; *H*, ventilator. We would suggest that the ventilation of steamers might be greatly improved by attention to
this circumstance. Especially the ventilation of the orlop and
hold, by making vertical ventilating flues of light boiler-iron,
near enough the engine to be warmed by its furnaces, and com-
municating below with the orlop wings or other apartment to be
ventilated. Such flues might constitute a part of the thickness
of the bulkheads, and thus contribute to prevent the heat of the
engine from being so much diffused through the ship, as is the
case at present. Steamers at anchorage require the same ventilation machinery as sailing vessels do.

(229.) The importance of this subject is so universally conceded among reflecting men, that it has formed a favorite subject
of discussion and essays by practical writers. They have suggested a great variety of devices, some of which are effective and
useful, and it is very hard to imagine the reason of the total
neglect with which most of them have been treated. One set of
these plans proposes heat as the force to set the air in motion. The
Wittig ventilator, the most effective of these, will scarcely propel
air with sufficient force to blow out a candle.—(*Fonssagrieves.*)

It has often been suggested to associate ventilation-tubes with
the cooking galley, to act in the manner of the Wittig ventilator.
This is practicable, and might be useful, but it would be a labor
for Hercules to overcome the objections which it would encounter
in its initiation. It has likewise been proposed that the air necessary for the combustion of fuel in the galley might be drawn
through ventilation-tubes from the hold or other part of the ship
to be ventilated. This plan is open to all the objections of the
preceding, with the additional one of the supposed increase of
danger from fire; and, besides, any height which it would be
convenient to give the galley chimney gives only sufficient draft
for the combustion of the fuel, without any force to spare for
other purposes. Heat, the most efficient motor under ordinary
circumstances, is really inapplicable on shipboard, from the inconvenience of giving the flues sufficient height, unless we could
make the masts hollow for that express purpose. It has been

proposed to use bellows to pump fresh air into various parts of the ship, or, what amounts to nearly the same thing, to pump the foul air out. The only objections to these contrivances are the labor of working them and the space they occupy.

(230.) The most efficient and convenient contrivance for mechanical ventilation is the rotary fan, as much as may be like the farmer's winnowing fan for cleaning grain. We do not know of any other contrivance with which the light labor of one boy is sufficient to propel a column of air a yard in diameter, with sufficient force to blow out an ordinary candle; but the winnowing fan does this readily enough. In some vessels, the monitor class, for instance, it may be advisable to ventilate inhabited apartments in this way. The opening at the axis of the fan can be connected with an external air opening, so as to draw in pure air, and it may be propelled in any direction by the labor of a boy. And still better, when the engine is in motion, the fan may be worked by a small shaft or pulley.

(231.) It is, however, the hold, and other uninhabited parts, which occasionally demand mechanical ventilation imperatively. In windy regions and at sea this is easily enough accomplished by wind-sails, and only requires a little attention; but during calm weather, in tropical climates, something more is required. During our stay at Vera Cruz, the spirit-room and after-hold were so defectively ventilated and so offensive as to create some uneasiness; and the fan represented in the margin was designed, to be made by the carpenter of such materials as are always to be found on shipboard. But before this fan was completed we received a similar machine from another ship about leaving for home. This fan was very useful. It only required one hour of light work for a boy, in the cool of the evening, to change the entire atmosphere of the spirit-room or after-hold. The machine was worked on deck, and the air first drawn up was exceedingly offensive. The suction opening of the fan has a canvas hose attached, with wooden hoops at short intervals to prevent its collapse. This ventilator, or something like it, should be on board every ship that visits the tropics, or any calm warm region; even our own southern coast in summer. It has been stated in general terms to matter little whether fresh air is driven into the vessel, or the vitiated air drawn out, as a complete renovation of the atmos-

phere results in either case.   To this statement we may state an
exception : in ventilating the hold in the manner just mentioned,
the suction hose drawing air from the bottom of the hold, the
fresh air to supply its place must necessarily pass downward
through the other apartments ; but if we had attached the hose
to the propulsion opening of the machine, we should indeed have

FIG. 29.

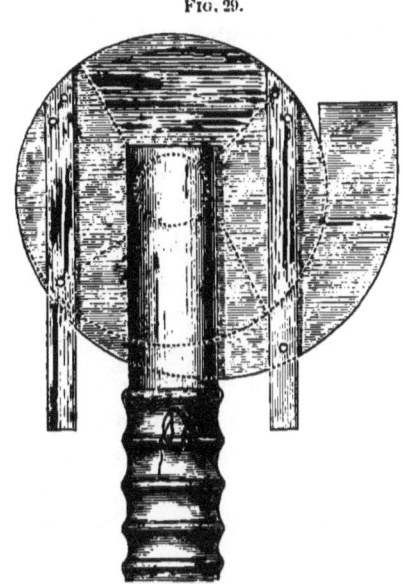

Fan for Ventilation.

propelled fresh air into the hold, but the vitiated and offensive
air expelled must have diffused itself more or less through these
apartments before its final escape.   We are wholly at a loss to
comprehend the usual indifference shown about these simple contrivances, which everybody understands, which add so greatly to
the comfort of all, and which save many valuable lives.   It seems
necessary to give the wings of the fan a velocity of about 2500
feet per minute.   It is sometimes more advantageous to drive the
fresh air down, as thus the foul air, smelled as it comes up, makes
known to the dullest apprehension that some good is being done,
and thus contributes to produce more zealous work.

(232.) The cleaning of the decks and other visible parts of a
ship, for the sake of neatness and good order, is generally quite

sufficient for all hygienic demands in this respect. The manner
in which it is done, however, is not altogether a matter of indifference. In dry, pleasant weather, nothing can be better than
holystoning with a profusion of water and sand, as the decks
promptly dry, leaving a bright, clean surface. But in warm,
calm weather, and the atmosphere saturated with moisture, it is
far otherwise. The decks, except the spar-deck, may be several
days in drying; and the atmosphere of the vessel, in the mean time,
is oppressive with the offensive effluvia of wet wood. This offensiveness of wet decks is something very different from mere dampness
of the atmosphere; for the atmosphere may be saturated with moisture even to the degree of precipitation, without any such feeling
of oppressiveness. During such weather, the berth-deck and
other covered parts of a ship should not be saturated with water.
It has been attempted to obviate this difficulty by dry holystoning. As usually practiced, this proceeding is very objectionable.
Dry sand is sprinkled on the deck, and ground in great measure
into dust, which fills the atmosphere and is inhaled by the men
employed at the work. These particles of sand, lodged in the
lungs, cannot fail to be a very serious cause of injury to these
delicate organs, and we may reasonably attribute a large part of
the consumption, which has been very prevalent in the navies
of the world, to this cause. Whether this may be obviated by
merely moistening the sand, so as to prevent the formation of
dust, we do not know. The only satisfactory way, which we
have seen, of cleaning the berth-deck in damp weather is to scrub
it with hot water, wetting but a small portion at a time, scraping
as much as necessary to remove spots, and wiping each portion
dry as the work proceeds; thus the water does not remain on any
part of the deck long enough to soak much into the wood.

Drying stoves, little movable sheet-iron stoves, with charcoal,
are a capital device for drying the berth-deck and purifying its
atmosphere. The floor oil-cloth, now commonly used in officers'
apartments, is greatly to be commended, as it can be washed clean
and wiped dry without inconvenience of any sort. Similar advantages may probably be obtained for the berth-deck by painting or varnishing, as is sometimes done with the floors of houses.

(233.) While lying at Sacrificios Island, a case occurred which renders it convenient to discuss briefly the subject of quarantines. A vessel joined the squadron from New York, and a few days after her arrival one of the crew was attacked with well-marked small-pox. The vessel was about twenty-five days from New York; the man had been some weeks on board the receiving ship there without visiting the shore, so that it is impossible to say how the disease was contracted. About two weeks before arriving at this port one of the men had an eruptive fever, resembling measles: this is supposed to have been a case of varioloid, the source of the small-pox contagion on board; but this man had returned from a cruise of more than a year on the West India station, without hearing anything about small-pox; was transferred on his return directly to the receiving ship, and remained there for three weeks, till his transfer for the present cruise, without ever having visited the shore. Do these cases prove the spontaneous origin of small-pox?

As both these men had freely mingled with the crew, being a part of it, and reports of the case might reach the authorities on shore, it was recommended that a quarantine flag should be worn for a few days, lest the market-boats should be interrupted. At the same time, no absurd restrictions were imposed on intercourse between the ships of the squadron, or the ships and town.

(234.) After the small-pox patient first mentioned was well, and the quarantine flag removed, another man of the same vessel was attacked. It was now concluded that quarantining enough had been done; the sick man was merely confined to a separate apartment with his nurse, none else being allowed to enter it, except under the direction of the medical officer. This case progressed favorably for a week after the appearance of the eruption ; but a sudden change of weather occurred, with a cool breeze, a norther; the pustules shrank ; he was attacked with lethargy, and died There was no other case of this disease in the squadron, or neighboring town.

(235.) The legislation on the subject of quarantine, much of it founded on the ignorant prejudices of persons who imagine epidemic diseases to originate and to be propagated by contagion only, has inflicted a great deal of mischief and cruel suffering. Every large city has interments every week, nearly every day, of persons dying of small-pox, typhus fever, and other contagious diseases. How nonsensical, then, the law which would confine a man merely because he has been on board a ship in which such a disease has existed, or, still worse, because he comes from a town in which such diseases exist. The notions on which these laws are founded, rigidly carried out, would not permit a man to come from the city of New York at any time whatever, without undergoing quarantine confinement.

The city of London has escaped great epidemics of the plague for two centuries, not through the influence of quarantines, but of a great fire, which destroyed a large portion of the city, and enabled the authorities to have it rebuilt in a more healthy style. The plague has likewise nearly disappeared from the island of Malta, not through the influence of quarantines, but, on the contrary, by being made the stopping-place for steamers on long voyages, which communicate at once or not at all. The places where the old system of quarantining prevails continue to suffer nearly as badly as ever. The city of New Orleans has nearly escaped the yellow fever since occupied by our troops, because the intelligent military authorities carried out rational sanitary measures. Baltimore, and the cities north of it, have escaped the same disease for half a century, because they are so abundantly supplied with river-water that streams of it are constantly running to waste through all the drains and sewers. Small-pox has ceased to be a terrific pestilence, sweeping a third of the population from the face of the earth about once in ten years, and has become a comparatively small affair, since the great discovery of Jenner has been generally practiced. We would not do away with all sanitary measures in reference to a vessel entering a port, but there should be abundant discretion allowed to intelligent, well-educated officers, in order that passengers need not be subjected to disease and death by senseless cruelty, or commerce to absurd and destructive restrictions. Persons, whether from distant cities or not, who have recently recovered from contagious diseases, should not enter a house occupied by other persons without due precaution. Their clothing and bedding should be thoroughly disinfected, not under the direction of ignorant prejudice, but of intelligent, well-educated persons. No punishment is too severe for the convalescent from small-pox, or the nurse who has recently been exposed to it, who would take a seat in a public conveyance with strangers, as has occasionally been done in our city passenger railway cars.

(236.) *February.* — The order was passed, "Up anchor for home." But the cruise had been so short that the seamen did not generally expect their discharge, and the order excited but little of the enthusiasm which we expect to see on such occasions.

A few days in Havana afforded an opportunity for a few little expeditions around the neighborhood and some social visits, to be remembered with satisfaction. The medical topography of this place may be explained in a few words. Havana is a walled city in a warm climate. A walled city is necessarily very compactly built, so as to include the largest possible number of people, with the smallest possible amount of walls to build and defend. The best part of the city, the vicinage of the governor's palace, is scrupulously neat and beautiful, with gardens of flowers and ornamental shrubbery. The good order of this part is such that the governor's family, and a few others as favorably situated for health, generally escape the yellow fever even in the worst epidemics. Cases of this disease, however, constantly exist in the city, and it is mostly a fearful epidemic during the latter part of summer. This epidemic is not hard to account for on our theory of the cause of this disease. Many of the back streets, crowded with population, are not paved or drained, so that pools of stagnant water receive all sorts of animal exuviæ, excrements, and remains, to putrefy among these crowds of human beings,—Spanish, negro, and mixed. Outside of the walls, too, especially in the immediate vicinity, even in some of the principal thoroughfares, the same nuisances may be seen. We do not wonder that

cases of yellow fever constantly exist in Havana, and an epidemic
occurs every summer.

(237.) *March 16th.*—The passage from Havana to New York
carried us in four days from tropical heats to severe winter; we arrived in a terrific snow-storm. Such sudden changes of temperature we have always found among the most trying incidents of sea
life; but it is really astonishing with how little of real suffering we
go through such a change if it is properly anticipated. It was
curious from the first moment of leaving Vera Cruz to see the
sailors examining their flannels and winter clothing, from day to
day. The woollen socks were examined and darned; the flannel
drawers patched and quilted; the pea-coats made all right, and
those who had no such garments made something still better, by
quilting two or three flannel shirts together, or one new one with
all available old ones. Mittens, too, of no matter how many
thicknesses, and caps with ears, to tie under the chin, were made.
The instant we crossed the Gulf Stream all these devices and a
good many more came into use. Fire was kept in the galley
night and day, so that men who were cold had an opportunity to
warm themselves and to make coffee. With these arrangements
it is astonishing with how little appearance of injury the transition
was borne—from summer to winter in one day. Men got cold,
shivered, and warmed themselves; they had catarrhs, pleurisies,
pneumonias, and frosted fingers; but with good appetites, and
hopes of soon reaching comfortable quarters, of serious sickness
there was but little.

(238.) The men on arriving at New York were somewhat dis-
appointed in their expectation of being made comfortable. The
ship was required to lie several days off the Battery, in a snow-
storm, before proceeding to the navy yard. Plenty of coal stoves,
however, properly disposed, with awnings and hoods over the
hatches, and other sailor devices, made warm and dry corners for
such as needed them when off watch. As soon as the ship was
moved up to the yard, a fine sunny day affording the opportunity,
all the men on the sick list were transferred to the naval hospital.
In a few days more there was an order to transfer the stores to
the warehouses of the navy yard and the men to the receiving
ship. Our ship was laid up " in ordinary," and the officers, in
the evening, were on the road to their various homes.

The ship went out of commission on the 1st of April, and before midnight the order arrived to refit immediately with the same officers and crew. The men were at hand and telegraphic despatches brought back the officers. We passed Sandy Hook, April 6th, outward bound, but no one knew whither. A few days, and we were in sight of Fort Pickens, at the entrance of Pensacola Bay. The fort was promptly relieved, and an effective force of the Second Artillery landed.

(239.) *April 12th.*—In the course of a month we have just passed from the tropical weather of Havana to a New York winter, with its succession of snow-storms and cold, and after remaining there nearly three weeks, have returned to the region of warm weather. These sudden transitions do not seem to have affected health very seriously; on entering the region of cold weather, there was much discomfort certainly,—some frosted fingers, some cases of pneumonia, many catarrhs, but not one death. The change in the opposite direction was still more satisfactory: in leaving New York we escaped from its cold, and the catarrhs disappeared gradually as the weather became warm. In the month of April there is no discomfort from either heat or cold at Fort Pickens.

CHAPTER XX.

PREPARATIONS FOR BATTLE—TRANSPORTATION OF WOUNDED —ACCIDENTS FROM FIREARMS — MOUTHS OF THE MISSIS-SIPPI—FRESH PROVISIONS—CURAÇOA.

(240.) THE passage to Pensacola included the probability of a hostile engagement on our arrival there, so that it was necessary to be prepared. Among the first necessities of wounded men are water and stimulants, as well as bandages, lint, and tourniquets. It would appear advantageous that, instead of a musket, about one man to every fifty should carry a satchel moderately filled with these things for the wounded. The tourniquet, however, in igno-rant hands, seems likely to do more harm than good, especially after great battles, where proper at-tention cannot always promptly reach the wounded. The general theory of the use of this instrument is so simple that every one imagines he knows all about the matter in an instant, and the moment he sees a wounded man he is for applying the instrument, and immoderately tight, with the effect of destroying the circulation of the limb. If the wounded man remains in this condition without proper attention for some hours, mortification of the limb and death of the sufferer is the probable consequence. This has, doubtless, been the case very often when the bleeding was quite inconsiderable, and when the patient would have recovered if his friends had not possessed this dangerous contrivance. If a large artery of one of the extremities be wounded, whether by ball or by sabre, the tourniquet is appropriate, and not otherwise; but a very small proportion of the wounds in battle are of this char-acter. As a rule, the application of lint and bandage, with mod-erate firmness, is more appropriate and more likely to save life.

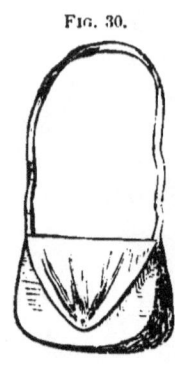

FIG. 30.

Surgeon's Haversack.

(241.) The transportation of the wounded is variously managed according to emergencies. When the wounded are merely to be taken below from the deck, the best arrangement is to have a stout man lift the wounded, by placing one arm back of the shoulders and the other under the knees. Holding him in this way he can carry him up or down stairs, or a short distance anywhere, with as little jostling or injury as by any available contrivance. If a wounded man be too heavy to be carried in this way he may be placed in an arm-chair and carried by two or three men. If too severely injured to be handled in a chair, he may be transported on a sick-bay cot, a cord of sufficient length being attached, if it be desired to lower the cot to the berth-deck. If men are to be carried any distance by hand, stretchers, wooden frames, with canvas (Fig. 32), should be provided, or the cots may be used with loops attached to the sides, so that muskets can be attached as bearing-poles. Pikes, oars, and boat-hooks are occasionally found useful for this purpose. The arrangement with muskets has the advantage that it transports so many muskets to the hospital. Two muskets, tied together by their bayonets, form a good bearing-staff, on which a man, not so badly wounded, may be carried in a hammock.

It appears that each wounded man on the average requires two comrades to assist him to the rear, and that they very rarely again reach the front, so that if a battle should continue till one-third were wounded, the other two-thirds would be away taking care of them. Hence the persistence of an army depends in battle greatly on the existence of a really efficient ambulance corps to attend to the removal of the wounded.

In an appendix to the first edition of this work there is described an ingenious and very convenient contrivance for removing the wounded on board ship, as arranged by Medical Inspector A. C. Gorgas. It consists essentially of a common cot, which, for this purpose, is made considerably smaller than usual; two pieces of board are joined at a right angle to make inclined planes under the knees; and there is a pillow and a band at the upper part to hold the patient securely in position. When it is necessary to lower the foot of the cot, as in descending a hatchway, the inclined planes hold the lower part of the body securely and com-

fortably. This *ambulance cot*, suspended by the cords at the ends,
makes a very good *invalid's chair*.

FIG. 31.

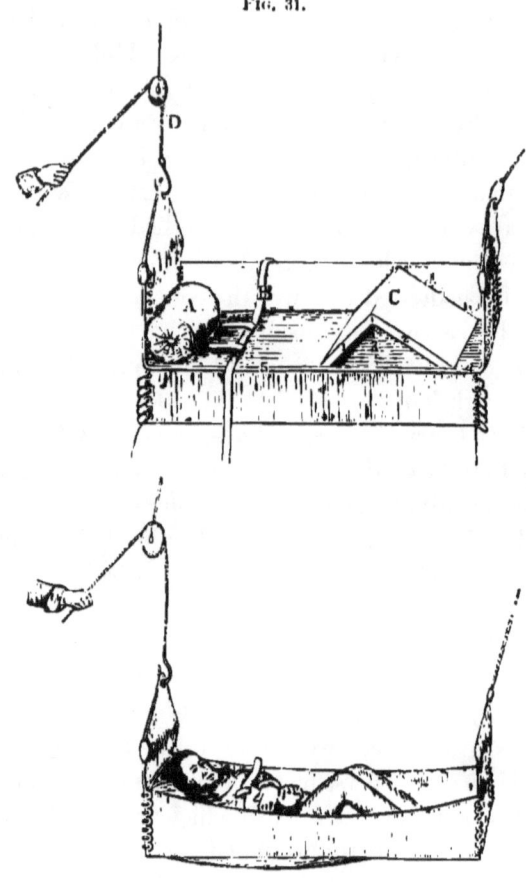

Ambulance Cot.

A stout arm-chair is sometimes securely slung, so that by means
of a whip on the mainyard a wounded man, an invalid, or even

FIG. 32.

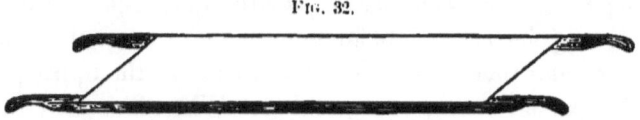

Hand-litter for carrying the Wounded beyond Musket range.

a lady or child, securely tied in the machine by shawls, flags,
cords, etc., may be safely hoisted or lowered from a boat, even

when the weather is too rough to come very close to the side of the ship. This is rather better than the cot, unless the patient is too weak to sit up.

(242.) But, in the course of our blockading service at Fort Pickens, an accident occurred which calls for a few remarks. On the return of the first armed boat expedition of the cruise the men commenced passing Minie rifles from the boat, and one of these guns was accidentally discharged, shooting a man through the thigh. Such accidents to boat expeditions are so common that it may be well to describe the manner in which they occur. When a boat expedition is to be fitted out a quarter gunner loads a dozen or two rifles, not omitting percussion primers, and lays them in an irregular heap. Another man transfers them to another part of the ship by taking them in his arms, as many as he can lift at a time, as if he were handling hoop-poles, carries them across the deck or up a ladder, and lays them down again in a heap. The guns do not always go off by this sort of handling ; in fact, I have never known a man to be shot by this part of the manœuvre, but I have noticed that most persons about observe the direction of the muzzles and stand clear. When the boat is brought alongside the guns are generally passed into it by men standing in a row, nearly the length of a gun apart, so that the muzzle is pretty sure to point toward some one. On the return of the expedition the guns are passed from the boat in the same manner. It is not very astonishing that frequent accidents occur from this manner of handling firearms. As far as my observation has gone, the first armed boat expedition of every cruise has always produced an accident in this way. In California, during the Mexican war, there was perhaps more preparation than fighting, and it was computed at the time that about one-third of the wounds and deaths from firearms were accidents from the manner of handling arms.

In the last edition of the *Ordnance Manual*, this subject is attended to. Percussion caps are not to be placed on the rifles in fitting out boat expeditions, and before passing the guns from the boat the primers are to be removed. Instructions to men in the use of arms are directed with some urgency.

(243.) The low sand islands of the coast, such as Santa Rosa, on which Fort Pickens is located, afford an abundant supply of

good water without further trouble than digging shallow wells in
the sand. They likewise have wholesome breezes from the ocean,
and are much less affected by annoying insects than the neighboring main land. With good sanitary police we shall be able to
maintain garrisons in good health on any of these islands which
it may become necessary to occupy.

(244.) From Pensacola we passed to Mobile Bar, and had a
good view of Fort Morgan in the distance. Two or three days
later we established the blockade at the Southwest Pass of the

Fig. 33.

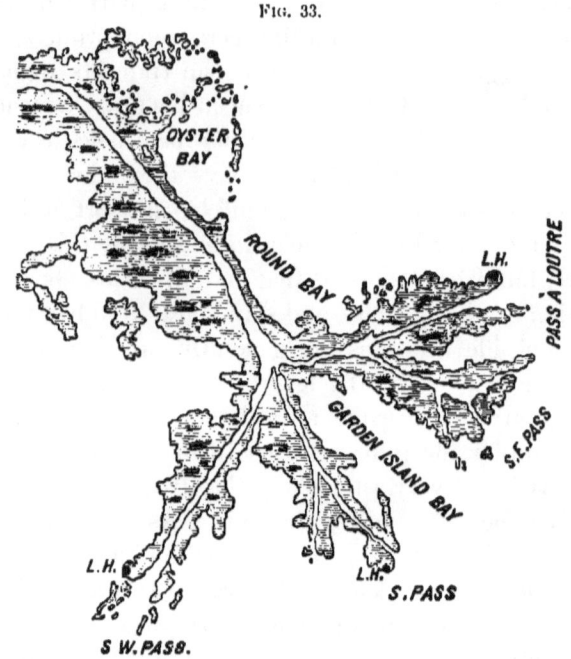

Mouths of the Mississippi.

Mississippi. At first there were vessels passing in and out every
day, presenting new objects of interest constantly. There is not
much swell here, and the ship lies very comfortably, just outside
the bar. The volume of fresh water is so great and remains so
distinct from the water of the ocean, that by watching opportunities we were able to draw from the surface alongside all the fresh
water required for use on board. This water was very muddy,
but by merely settling, it became sufficiently clear and palatable.

We had no occasion to seek better water. The depth of water on the bar is about fifteen feet, but the mud is so soft, that the vessels drawing eighteen feet, or even more, work their way through it. The steam-tugs bring them down till they stick fast in the mud and there leave them to the winds and currents. The small vessels generally get through in three or four days, but large vessels remain as many weeks or even months, so that the crossing of this bar is apt to cost as much as all the rest of the passage to Europe. It is really astonishing that no attempt has been made to carry the larger vessels over this point by camels or similar contrivance.

The situation here is quite healthy, and even at the lighthouse, six or seven miles above, among reedy islands, they never have intermittent fever. Everything seems to be so much submerged and so thoroughly washed by currents that the malarial miasm has no abiding-place. The Balize—the pilot station further up the river—seems to enjoy a similar exemption.

(245.) While at the Southwest Pass we had some experience of the considerate forethought and intelligent energy of the administration at home, in the extraordinary arrangements for the preservation of health. The most important of these was an abundant supply of ice and fresh provisions to the squadrons. A cargo sailed once a month from New York for the supply of the blockading vessels. The arrival of these supply vessels was very welcome, and a place for the storage of a few tons of ice was quickly arranged and quickly filled; and between the layers of ice were snugly deposited quarters of beef and saddles of mutton, enough to supply in profusion the whole crew for a week or ten days. The supply ship was then ready to go on her round to the coast of Texas, treating the other blockading vessels on her route in the same way. The benefits of this arrangement, affording salutary changes from salt diet, with the cheering influences of news from home, cannot be overestimated. The health and strength of the men, and consequently the efficiency of the blockade, have been greatly due to these beef-boats.

During the early part of the blockade, we drew a tolerable supply of fresh fruits from a very different source. Small cargoes of fruit from Cuba and Mexico came in occasionally, with intention of running the blockade, and fell into our power. They were permitted to sell out to our men at a good price and go on their way rejoicing, probably to reappear in a few days to go again through the same ceremony. The people engaged in this business always left us in doubt whether they were more desirous of supplying us or our enemies. Some of them doubtless acted the part of spies.

(246.) We had a cruise in the Caribbean Sea, and to the coast of Brazil beyond the mouths of the Amazon. We stopped at Kingston, Jamaica, and received a supply of coal. Some of the men behaved badly and got drunk. In consequence of this visit, in the course of a month, we had several cases of remittent fever, of no great severity, none of the cases proving fatal. The Island of Curaçoa at the time of our visit was quite healthy, and from an inspection of the locality, with its good pavements, its good sanitary police, and its sea-breezes, it may be expected to remain so as long as the inhabitants retain a personal recollection of the sufferings of the past. The Island of St. Thomas we found the centre of supplies and intelligence; it has an excellent harbor in a mountainous island of well-drained slopes. We passed south of the Island of Barbadoes, and with the island in sight had an epidemic catarrh, *influenza ;* and probably every person on board suffered from the disease.

CHAPTER XXI.

(247.) THERE are many causes of disease of which we know very little, and some of which we know absolutely nothing at all. The occasional prevalence of influenza, epidemic catarrh, may be mentioned as a case of disease in which no person of common honesty and common sense pretends to know the cause. Those who are unwilling to acknowledge this degree of ignorance may make guesses, and suggest some distemperature of air or earth, or some error of diet, or they may put down some of the symptoms for the cause, and say it is caused by fever, or irritation, or inflammation of the air-passages. They might as well suggest at once that influenza is caused by influenza. The only fair way to get over the difficulty is to say that the cause is in some epidemic influence, and to explain further that there certainly must be some influence, and epidemic is the single word in common use to indicate that we know little or nothing about it, except that it affects or falls upon the people (ἐπι, upon ; δῆμος, people), and causes many of them to suffer from disease in the same way at the same time.

But influenza is by no means the only disease which occurs epidemically. There have been epidemics of cholera, dysentery, typhus, etc., in fact nearly all the diseases which afflict humanity seem occasionally to prevail more extensively than usual on account of some epidemic influence. Sydenham was probably the first to fully appreciate the constant presence of some epidemic influence, or epidemic constitution of disease, as he called it. He describes several epidemic constitutions, running into and blending with each other, the constitutions constantly changing, in fact. These occurred in the following order :

I. Epidemic constitution of 1661, '62, '63, and '64 : Continual

12

fever, autumnal remittent; agues, intermittent fever; small-pox.

II. Epidemic constitution of 1665, '66: Pneumonia, pleurisy, and quinsy, in the spring of 1665; pestilential fever, a continual fever, very different from that of the previous constitution; plague, with carbuncles and bubos, at its height about September 10th, 1665, when eight thousand died in one week.

III. Epidemic constitution of 1667–'68, and a part of '69: Continual fever, variolous fever; regular small-pox.

IV. Epidemic constitution of 1669, '70, '71, and '72: Cholera, epidemic cholera of 1669; continual fever, a dysenteric fever; dysentery; measles, 1670; irregular small-pox, a black small-pox in 1670, '71, and 72; bilious colic 1670, '71, '72.

V. Epidemic constitution of part of 1673, '74, and '75: Continual fever, a comatose fever; measles, 1674; irregular small-pox, a malignant black small-pox, 1674, '75; cough, pleurisy, and peripneumony, 1675.

VI. Epidemic diseases from 1675 to 1680: Measles, 1676; cholera, epidemic, 1676; intermittent, 1677, '78, and '79; continual fever, comatose fever, like that of 1675 in 1679; cough, like children's cough, pertussis, 1679; intermittents, 1680, '81, '82, '83, '84, and '85.

(248.) Professor George B. Wood mentions similar epidemic influences prevailing over somewhat similar periods in Philadelphia, and more or less extensively over the United States. He gives accounts of the following, arranged somewhat differently:

An epidemic of malarial fevers commenced in 1795, and lasted ten or twelve years; another, commencing in 1822, lasted ten years.

An epidemic of yellow fever commenced in 1792, and lasted two or three years; another, commencing in 1820, lasted one year.

An epidemic of typhus commenced in 1812, and lasted six or eight years; another, commencing in 1836, lasted two years; and another, commencing in 1851, lasted five years.

An epidemic cholera commenced in 1832, and lasted two years.

An epidemic influenza, producing neuralgia, commencing in 1838, lasted five years.

There are here mentioned two epidemics of yellow fever, last-

ing a year or two, with an interval of twenty-eight years; three
epidemics of typhus, lasting from two to eight years, with intervals of sixteen and twenty-four years, the most severe epidemic
being succeeded by the longer period of exemption. The cholera epidemic lasted two years, travelling very irregularly over
the country. Malarial fevers prevail more or less in certain localities near Philadelphia every year, the years indicated being
years of unusual prevalence; but these fevers never occur in
densely built portions of the city. All countries and all places
have, in this way, their epidemic influences, and Philadelphia,
with this frightful array of " the pestilence that walketh in darkness," seems, by the published statistical tables, to be about the
healthiest city in the healthiest country in the world.

(249.) The word plague (*plaga*, a blow), in ancient writings,
seems generally to mean about the same as epidemic with us. It
certainly meant very various diseases and afflictions; thus there
was a plague of frogs, of lice, and of grasshoppers, as well as the
plague of leprosy, of boils, and of hæmorrhoids. But why the
terms plague and pestilence, of similar import, should be so frequently associated, is not apparent unless they were occasionally
appropriated to specific diseases.

The cause and nature of this epidemic influence we have said
is quite unknown. The most ancient theory is as true as any:
God so ordained it; has thus organized his creatures. Anciently
these diseases were mostly attributed to His wrath; and certainly
they mostly result more or less directly from violations of His
known laws. When we seek for the instruments of His will in
this matter, we get into a labyrinth of guesses, and ingenious and
plausible theories, in which hydrocarbons, fermentations, organic
germs, microscopic animalcules, and cryptogamic vegetations are
made prominently to figure. They nearly all refer to impurities
or distemperatures of the atmosphere.

(250.) But this want of knowledge does not extend to the consequences of epidemic influence; and from the observed course
of diseases we are enabled to announce as established the following laws of epidemics:

I. *The epidemic influence is sufficient to produce specific diseases,*
in some rare cases, without the intervention of any other cause.
We may instance as examples of this, the prevalence of influ-

enza in the summer season, without any peculiarity of weather
to account for it. In the commencement of epidemics of small-
pox there are generally three or four cases of the disease occurring nearly at the same moment in different distant parts of a
city, without any communication, direct or indirect, having occurred, and without the possibility of tracing the disease to direct
contagion.

II. *The epidemic influence is much more frequently merely a
cause of aggravation* in diseases which at the same time are propagated by well-known though possibly obscure causes. Thus
small-pox and measles, typhus and scarlet fever, are much more
prevalent and much more fatal during certain seasons when they
prevail epidemically, though propagated by contagion as they are
at all seasons, every season. Intermittents and other malarial
fevers during seasons of epidemic prevalence are much more fatal
than usual, though exhibiting their common forms and prevailing
principally in their usual localities.

III. *The epidemic influence sets in very violently at first*, and
gradually abates as the season advances. In evidence of this we
may state that the first few cases of diseases in all epidemics
mostly prove fatal (in regard to the epidemic cholera it is noticed
that the first few cases nearly all prove fatal), but the disease
gradually becoming more manageable, towards the close of the
season, it is scarcely more dangerous than ordinary catarrh. In
regard to small-pox, it is stated that as many as three in five
cases, sixty per hundred, prove fatal during the first few weeks
of an epidemic; and but very rarely is the proportion of deaths
more than two in five, forty per hundred, the whole epidemic
through, and very rarely is the proportion of deaths in this disease more than one in twenty cases, five per hundred. This law
holds good in all epidemics, so that if we lose all our first patients
in a disease thus prevailing, and none later in the season, we may
not, merely from this fact, infer that we have obtained any great
additional skill in the management.

IV. *The epidemic influence is frequently felt in slighter affections*
of similar character, before the disease is established in full force.
Thus mild cases of diarrhœa are very numerous for a week or
two before the first cases of epidemic cholera make their appearance.

V. *The epidemic influence is very generally felt by the lower animals,* and in some cases before any such influence is observed on the human race. Rush observes that cats, dogs, and birds died in great numbers, both before and during the yellow fever of 1793. And in the Grecian host before Troy—

> "On dogs and cats the infection first began,
> And next the fatal arrows fixed on man."—POPE.

(251.) Sydenham informs us that "the plague rarely rages violently in England oftener than once in the space of thirty or forty years." We have histories, however, of the following epidemics in London, which had an average interval of but eighteen years:

In 1593, there died 11,106 during the season of ten months.

In 1603, there died 29,992.

In 1625, there died 34,754.

In 1636, there died 11,000; this, however, was called the great plague, as it lasted twelve years, till 1647.

In 1665, there died 69,602 in nine months. This was the last great plague, described by Defoe.

But perhaps we are to come to the conclusion that this idea of epidemic constitutions is a delusion after all. The plague has been traced to the crowding, privation, and want of cleanliness in the old fortified cities. Hence after a sweeping pestilence, there is comparative health until the place becomes again crowded and dirty, with a new generation of subjects for the disease. Similar reasoning is applicable to small-pox: fortunately since the discovery of Jenner, we have the means of destroying individual susceptibility to this disease; but human nature is so perverse that every few years there grows up a new generation who will not believe in vaccination, till the community is startled by a few deaths from small-pox. The epidemic influence is a new generation of unvaccinated people; the vaccinators get to work and the deadly pestilence is avoided. And again, malarial fevers are occasionally epidemic—very prevalent and very fatal; such epidemics have been traced to derangement of the watercourses of the country by public works. Quite recently, in India, a terrible destruction of life was traced to the building of canals for internal navigation; and in our own country these epidemics are found to have coincided with similar public works. The damming of small streams for mill-ponds, has occasioned many such epidemics on a small scale. An epidemic pestilence has generally been noticed among the consequences of war; the destruction of property and the resulting derangement of industries, must necessarily entail subsequent privations, which can only be mitigated by all the alleviations which social science is able to suggest; but we have advanced so far in the right direction, that hereafter, instead of the terrific pestilence, perhaps the crisis of suffering may be passed without anything worse than an epidemic of vagabondism and beggary,—the tramp nuisance. Thus one after another, we trace the terrific epidemics to a manageable cause, and the epidemic constitutions vanish.

CHAPTER XXII

ENDEMICS—MALARIAL FEVERS.

(252.) THE diseases of whose causes we know but little are of the very highest importance, and require from us the most careful study. Some diseases occur principally in particular localities, and are hence called endemic (εν, among; δεμος, the people), as coming among the people. This term seems not very different, etymologically, from epidemic; and these words have occasionally been used in a confused manner; but their proper application is very distinct. Thus, there is a curious disease of the hair, *Plica polonica*, thought to be peculiar to Poland, and hence said to be endemic in that country. Intermittents, as they prevail principally in level marshy districts, are said to be endemic to marshy lands. The yellow fever, prevailing more or less constantly in all the cities of tropical America, is endemic in those cities. When unusually prevalent and exceedingly fatal, without apparent reason for this change of character, yellow fever is said to prevail epidemically, or to have become epidemic. In this case an epidemic influence is supposed to be superadded to the ordinary causes of the disease. We must pass in review the most important and most curious endemic diseases.

(253.) The malarial fevers, intermittents, remittents, etc.,—the periodic fevers—are endemic to marshy localities. Their obscure cause is supposed to be some emanation from the soil itself, contaminating the atmosphere. This supposed emanation is called malaria or malarial miasm. It is too subtle to be discovered by the senses, or any sort of chemical analysis yet devised, and is only known by its effects in causing disease. It has been supposed to be some one of the poisonous carbohydrogens; but none of these has been found capable of producing any such disease; and coal mines known to abound in these substances appear not to injure health in this way. Sulphide of hydrogen, too, has been suspected; but with some observation of men, in an atmosphere contaminated by this substance, I have never seen any evidence of its contributing to produce this form of disease. When we inquire into the circumstances of the origin of this malaria, although its essential nature eludes us, we arrive at facts of the greatest practical importance. No more important subject of study can occupy the human intellect; and the little that is already known is of the utmost importance to all those who would enjoy exemption from these destructive diseases.

The circumstances which are considered necessary for the development of the malarial miasm, marsh-fever poison, are a quantity of decaying vegetable matter, with an appropriate degree of warmth and moisture. The vegetable matter is subject to some doubt; it certainly exists in all marshes in sufficient abundance, but the diseases under consideration have been observed in situations where decaying vegetable matter is rather scarce; however, it is not perhaps absent anywhere except in the burning craters of volcanoes. And again, immense masses of vegetable matter decay without producing any disease.

(254.) Intermittents, remittents, pernicious fevers, and congestive fevers, all occur in the same place, at the same time; the cases of mild intermittent, by aggravation, becoming remittent in their progress; and the congestive and remittent frequently become intermittent in their course of melioration. We will mention in succession the most important circumstances connected with the origin of these diseases.

I. *The malarial miasm requires for its development an appropriate degree of moisture.* The soil may be too dry to produce it; as the deserts of Arabia and Africa, and elevated slopes of land nearly everywhere. And again, the soil may be too wet to produce it; hence we notice in very wet seasons the overflown marshes, where it usually prevails, are healthy, and the higher lands become infected. The lighthouse keepers about the mouths of the Mississippi are exempt from these diseases, probably because their marshes are mostly submerged.

II. *A rather high summer temperature, of at least one month's duration, seems necessary to produce this miasm,* in any degree of strength likely to impair health. Hence these diseases are nearly unknown in elevated mountains where the temperature is uniformly cool, as well as in countries like New England, Canada, and Labrador, where the summer, though sufficiently warm, is very short. The necessity of long-continued heat for the production of this poison is further illustrated by the occurrence of the diseases progressively worse, both in the severity of the disease and the greater number of cases, as the summer advances. They are diseases of the fall rather than of the spring or summer.

III. *The darkness of night is necessary for the development of the miasm,* or at all events for its action. The most deadly spots in the world with reference to these diseases are visited with perfect impunity in the daytime; though to remain a single night would be nearly certain death. Thus the citizens of Charleston, South Carolina, have been accustomed to visit their plantations in the daytime, whenever they feel an inclination to do so, but they are very sure of a dangerous attack of country fever if they remain over night, except in the winter season. Our squadron on the African station enjoys complete exemption from this pest, since the regulation is uniformly enforced which prohibits any officer or man from being on shore after sunset. The country prejudice against night air is well founded.

IV. *The miasm seems incapable of being transmitted any great distance from its source,* though it must reach the body principally through the atmosphere. It is either diluted in the atmosphere to such a degree as to be harmless, or it is rapidly decomposed. I can find no sufficient evidence of its ever having been wafted, under any circumstances, to a ship anchored as much as a mile from the shore. But there are abundant instances of perfect immunity where vessels have been anchored in the midst of infected marshes, for months together, near the middle of a river about a mile wide.

V. *The malarial miasm never affects the well-built parts of a city.* We cannot say whether this immunity is due to drainage and pavements, or whether the pulmonary and cutaneous exhalations of congregated people are incompatible with it, or whether the smoke and gases from the numerous culinary and other fires in some way destroy it, or whether each of these exerts a salutary influence. But the fact as stated appears to admit of no reasonable doubt.

VI. *Very slight obstacles have been known to interrupt the diffu-*

sion of the miasm, such as groves of trees, the destruction of which has rendered uninhabitable places previously healthy.—(*Rush.*)

VII. *After exposure to the miasm, several, but an uncertain number, of days elapse before any symptoms of the disease are noticed.* While the system is thus charged with the poison, slight causes of excitement, severe labor, exposure to cold or to the heat of the sun will immediately produce an attack.

The malarial miasm produces various forms of disease, so various that it is very hard to comprehend that they all are due to the same cause, and they have hence been called by many different names. People of quiet habits, long exposed to the moderate action of a malarious atmosphere, lose flesh and become impoverished in blood; they are weak, but are not considered sick; they are suffering from malarial anæmia. This is likely to change any day, in consequence of unnoticed irregularities, and most probably to a simple intermittent, with its chill and fever, and sweat, every second day, the patient being quite well during the interval; or it may be every day, or every third or fourth day; and the disease receiving new names according to the interval becomes a quotidian, tertian, quartan, septan, etc. But, instead of this simple intermittent, with leisure to count the days, we may have a pernicious fever, an intermittent with violent and dangerous brain symptoms; the patient becoming delirious during the paroxysm, and lethargic, even to death, perhaps in the second paroxysm, or even the first. The sudden, more concentrated action of the poison, is much more likely to produce other forms of disease; the paroxysm comes every day, and the patient is not nearly well during the interval; he has a remission: this is a simple remittent; it may vary greatly in severity, or it may be complicated with the brain symptoms, violent delirium, with danger of lethargic death: it is then a malignant remittent. These peculiarities appear to result from the peculiarities of constitution of each individual patient, and from the degree of concentration or manner of application of the miasm; but there are other complications: the patient may have been defectively nourished, and we shall have malarial fever with scorbutic complications; he may have some of the characteristic symptoms of typhoid fever, malarial fever with typhoid complication; if patients be crowded, as has often been the case, we are pretty sure of typhus fever com-

plication, a terrific contagious pestilence breaking out in the midst
of the patients. The foregoing are the principal circumstances
which vary the character of malarial fevers, and, as these few
elements admit of almost infinite variations, it is not strange that
many kinds of malarial fever are described under different names.
Nearly every unhealthy place in the world has a name for its
fever: hence African fever, Bengal, Bulam, Carthagena, Madras,
Walcheren, Whampoa fever, etc. In our army reports the complicated types, typhus, typhoid, adynamic, scorbutic, and malignant, are blended together under the simple designation, camp
fever. Sometimes very intractable malarial diarrhœa seems to
result from the action of this poison, more especially from the
use of bad water in malarious districts.

The following figures from reports in the Surgeon-General's
office, showing the number of cases of malarial fevers, and gun-
shot wounds and other injuries, and deaths from these diseases
and wounds in the United States army during the first two years
of the war, indicate sufficiently the importance of the study of
these diseases :

	Cases.	Deaths.
There were reported during the year ending June 30, 1862 :		
Malarial fevers, ...	146,605	6,554
Gunshot wounds, ...	17,496	4,421
Total wounds and accidents, ...	44,886	4,857
Total diseases and wounds, ...	878,918	19,040
During the year ending June 30, 1863 :		
Malarial fevers, ...	327,739	14,121
Gunshot wounds, ...	55,974	8,775
Total wounds and injuries, ...	98,475	10,142
Total diseases and wounds, ...	1,171,803	52,152

(255.) In discussing somewhat fully the phenomena and causes
of malarial fevers, we have suggested the most important measures of prevention. We should never spend the night, or even
a part of the night, unnecessarily, in the infectious locality. In
the central parts of a city, or on board of ship anchored a mile
from the shore, we are certainly safe from these destructive

fevers.   At Whampoa, near Canton, China, there are a number of ship-chandlers and others, who, with their families, are quite healthy living on board hulks anchored in the stream, though a single night on shore would be nearly certain death to them.   In anchoring in a river it is desirable to anchor near the middle of

FIG. 34.

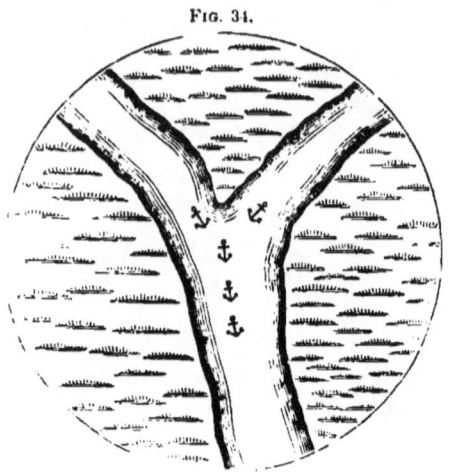

Anchorage in a river.

the stream, and, if possible, opposite a fork ; for, besides the additional breadth of water at such points, the breeze conforming in its direction with one or another of the branches, more constantly reaches the ship thus situated.   Persons obliged to spend the night in an infectious district should use such screens as they can procure against night-air, even a mosquito-curtain ; and they should avoid much exertion, or exposure to the sun.   It is advisable, under such circumstances, to take a small dose of quinine every day as a preventive.   Quinine, in pretty large doses, frequently repeated, has enabled recent African explorers to pass through terrific localities.

In most European countries, the peasants who cultivate land thus unhealthy live in villages in selected healthy spots, and walk to their labors in the field every morning to return to their villages before night.   Some such arrangement must be adopted by our own people before Florida or even Eastern Virginia can be fairly settled up.   This plan has social advantages over the usual one, which isolates the farmer's family among his fields.

It appears that the malarial poison is soluble in water, and it is thus carried into the soil; at any rate it often exists in the soil to a dangerous degree. Thus the turning up of new soil for cultivation has proved very fatal to residents of the neighborhood. I remember to have visited a small, steep, rocky island, in the Bay of Panama, otherwise quite healthy, which was very quickly fatal to every one of the few workmen who first attempted to remain on it at night, after there was a portion of its surface levelled for a coal heap; and a few months subsequently the island was occupied with difficulty. Fatal casualties of this kind may always be avoided, if the workmen will merely spend their nights in a healthy place.

We have now pretty well determined the means of avoiding malarial miasm and its consequences; but human nature interposes obstacles. We see men going to nearly certain death; we reason, we explain, we argue; and a man who has never studied the subject suggests his "I should think" in opposition to us. The ignorant man's "I should think" may carry the day against us, and our hygienic precautions go for nothing, except that we can sometimes use the privilege of saving ourselves. We see this in every city over the land; this ignorant "I should think" controls legislation and is slaying its myriads. We have the same difficulty in the military service. Expeditions are planned, topographical engineers are consulted about visible obstacles, but no reasonable calculations are made for the diseases, which even in campaigns of hard-fought battles will destroy three times as many men as all the bullets. The medical man is not consulted till after the mischief is done, the men sick and dying. The surgeon by his reports then suggests that the force is being weakened, and may hint at the cause. The subject is discussed by those in authority, who knowing very little about the subject, their discussion is apt to end in something very like the old-fashioned "I should think." I have always found the most effective way to manage this business is, to set up prejudices in the right direction, by discreet social conversation, and when this produces nothing, to follow it up by a report if necessary, the occasion for which may be explained, by stating the propriety of putting certain views *formally* on record before going into such risks as are contemplated. Such reports should state the case in good

terse language, and conclude with a recommendation too pointed
to be evaded.   If this do not succeed, it is understood that a copy
may go with comments to the files of the department; and the
responsibility of a sweeping pestilence is in the right place as
nearly as we can make it so.   Sometimes our recommendations
may involve alterations in the plans of a department, and then
commanding officers feel that they must have such reports before
they are safe in acting—even ask for them.   The best illustration
which I remember of the manner in which this has to be done
occurred in China some years ago.   We were anchored in the
Pearl River, above Canton, opposite Macao Pass, and the captain, whom I had pretty well indoctrinated previously on the
subject of rice swamps, sunset boats, and night air, mentioned
that he had orders to observe the tides in this part of the river,
and hinted at the difficulty of finding a suitable place for a tide-
staff, the edge of a rice-field appearing to be the only available
place.

"We are healthy here; cannot we get a post or two down
somewhere on a bar, at a distance from the shore?"

"The current is strong; it would be in the way; boats would
run against it and tear it up."

"Perhaps you might get observations enough in the daytime?"

"Hardly; we may not be here long, and the work should not
be half done."

"Leaving all risk of sickness out of the question, how would
you arrange it?"

"Place a tide-gauge at the nearest point to the ship, with two
men, and relieve them by other two at mealtimes."

"A month of such observations would cost us about eight
lives."

"Oh, no."

"Yes; the first set, six men, down in one week, and others at
the same rate; twenty-six down in a month, one-third to die—
eight and two-thirds; the calculation a little strong, perhaps, so
we will throw off the fraction—eight deaths a month."

"Well; but we must do something."

"Men should not spend a night in that swamp; they can pull
up to the staff at the right moment, which surely can be antici-

pated, make their observations, and pull out into the river again, back to the ship if they have time."

" The current is very strong; hard work, and no rest."

" They had better spend the night, if need be, pulling against the current in the middle of the river."

" Well; we will try it so."

The plan was tried and I soon heard that it only required fifteen to twenty minutes to pull ashore on slack water, make the observations, and return. There was no difficulty about it. The observations were continued for several months; as long as there was any motive for continuing them, and the results are recorded in the history of the Japan expedition. This little conversation doubtlessly saved several lives, for without it the men would have been spending nights in the rice-field before I should have heard anything about the tidal observations. This kind of sociability must be discreet; the most important of all the official duties of the medical officer must be performed by stealth; to attempt it otherwise is to excite such opposition that it cannot be performed at all. On the African station we are greatly assisted by the following—

GENERAL ORDER.

Sanitary Regulations for the United States Squadron on the Coast of Africa.

1. No officer or man will be permitted to be on shore before sunrise or after sunset, or to sleep there at night. This rule applies not only to the continental coast but to the Cape de Verde Islands.

2. No United States vessel will ascend or anchor in any of the African rivers, except upon imperative public service.

3. Boat excursions up rivers and hunting parties on shore are forbidden.

4. Vessels, when possible, will anchor at a reasonable distance from shore, far enough not to be influenced by the malaria floated off by the land breeze.

5. Convalescents from fever and other diseases (when condemned by medical survey) are to be sent to the United States with the least possible delay.

6. When the general health of a ship's company shall be reported as impaired by cruising on the southern or equatorial portion of the coast, the earliest possible opportunity will be given them to recruit, by transferring the ship for a time to the Canaries or other windward islands of the station.

7. Boat and shore duty, involving exposure to sun and rain, is to be performed, so far as the exigencies of the service will admit, by " Kroomen " employed for that purpose.

8. All possible protection from like exposure is to be afforded to the ship's company on board, and the proper clothing and diet of the crew, as well as the

ventilation and care of the decks, will be made a frequent subject for the inspection and advice of medical officers.

9. These regulations are to be considered as permanent, and each commanding officer of the squadron, on retiring from the station, will transfer them to his successor.

(256.) In order to enforce our hygienic precepts and to prove that we are teaching no new doctrines on this subject, the following quotations from an excellent old book are introduced :

Another evil, less known and less suspected, but not less dangerous, is the sending of Europeans in open boats, after sunset, where the soil is swampy, or where there are great night-fogs. The duty alone of fetching fresh-killed butcher's meat at night for the use of the ship's companies in the East and West Indies has destroyed every year several hundred seamen. In those parts of the world, butcher's meat must be brought on board at night, immediately after it is killed, otherwise it will not be fit for use next day. But surely a contract for sending it on board . . . . might be made with the natives, ... and it ought to be considered that this trifling sum is advanced for the preservation of many lives. During the sickly season at Batavia, a boat belonging to the Medway, which attended shore every night, was manned three times successively, not one having survived that service, ... so that at length the officers were obliged to employ none but natives of the country on that business. Great numbers of men have perished from being employed in this manner at Bengal, where European ships often anchor in the most unhealthy parts of the river, and even after the rainy season the men are often obliged to perform such service in boats.

In a voyage to the coast of Guinea, performed in the year 1766, by the Phœnix, ship of war, the officers and ship's company were perfectly healthy till, on their return home, they touched at the Island of St. Thomas, in the Gulf of Guinea. Here the captain unfortunately went on shore to spend a few days. In the same house were lodged the captain's brother, the surgeon, some midshipmen, and the captain's servants. But in the course of a few days every one, to the number of seven, who had slept in the house were taken ill, and all of them died except one, who returned to England in a very ill state of health. The ship lay at anchor there twenty-seven days, during which time three midshipmen, five men and a boy remained on shore for twelve nights to guard water-casks, under pretence that the islanders would steal them; all of these were likewise taken ill, and two only escaped with life. At that island only those who slept on shore were taken ill; no other man of the ship's company was seized with any distemper during their stay. Even during the whole voyage, except these, only one man died, and he was killed by accident. None of those who slept on shore escaped the sickness, and of them only three survived it. While the Phœnix continued at this place, twenty or thirty of her men went daily on shore, rambling, hunting, shooting, fishing, bartering for provisions, washing linen, and otherwise employed, so that almost the whole ship's company of two hundred and eighty men were, in their turns, on shore upon the island in the daytime, not one of whom who returned at night was taken ill or suffered even the slightest indisposition.

In the year following, the Phœnix made another voyage, and happened again to touch at this island, where she lost eight men out of ten who had imprudently remained all night on shore. At the same time the rest of the ship's company continued in perfect health, who, after spending the day on shore, always returned to their ship before night. On board the Hound, sloop, then in company, only one man died during the whole voyage, the officers having been particularly careful not to permit any of the people to continue all night on shore.

If ships on their passage to India touch at the Islands of St. Iago (Cabo Verde Islands), Madagascar, Johannes, Mohilla; at Culpee in the River Hoogly, Batavia, or Beneoolen, those persons who go on shore should always return before night. These places have proved particularly fatal to Europeans who sleep on shore.

It may at first sight appear almost impracticable to find a convenient and safe retreat from sickness which rages at times in many foreign climates. Mankind are more ready to start difficulties on this subject than desirous to remedy them. Where can that safe retreat be found on the coast of Guinea? The answer is, that all places on that coast are not equally unhealthy. The English have found the Island of Goree much more healthy than their settlements on the Senegal and Gambia.

When a mortal sickness, in the year 1765, prevailed at Pensacola, by which a regiment newly arrived there lost one hundred and twenty men, and eleven out of twelve of the officers' ladies are said to have died, the companies of the men-of-war, lying at a mile distant from the shore, enjoyed the most perfect health. It is likewise remarkable that such gentlemen as were seized with this fever at Pensacola and carried on board quickly recovered, or, at least, the fever, being divested of its most mortal symptoms, soon assumed the form of an intermittent.

The just inference is that if a ship was fitted as a floating factory, and secured at a due distance from the shore, at all places where it may be found necessary and safe, it would be the means of preserving every year a multitude of lives. The idea of a floating factory is not new; ships, so called, have been securely moored in different parts for the advantage of trade; they are here proposed for the benefit of health. A floating factory, store, or residence, may be fitted up in any taste whatever, either for convenience or pleasure.—(*Lind.*)

CHAPTER XXIII.

YELLOW FEVER.

(257.) ANOTHER most important endemic disease is yellow fever, black vomit, *typhus icterodes*, *nova pestis*. This disease seems to prevail in every tropical city, occasionally extending its ravages in warm weather to some of the cities of temperate climates. It never occurs in the fields except as persons escaping from an infectious city carry with them the seeds of disease, and sicken and die anywhere. It is therefore an endemic of cities in warm countries. This disease has perhaps sometimes been confounded with the malarial fevers; but that it has a specifically different cause, we think fully established by the following considerations. All the acknowledged forms of malarial fever are occasionally present at the same time and in the same place, and frequently change from one type to the other in their course, conveying irresistibly to the observer the impression that the difference is due to the greater or less violent action of the same cause, and to peculiarities in the constitution of individual patients. With yellow fever nothing of this kind is observed; but there are cases of every degree of severity, some proving fatal in a few hours, while others are scarcely sufficient to interrupt attention to business; but none of them exhibit anything like the intermittent character. The fact appears to be that occasionally the morbific poison, no matter which, malarial, yellow fever, small-pox, typhus, or cholera, assaults and overcomes the powers of life with such suddenness that there is actually no development of the characteristic symptoms of any of these diseases; they all act alike. The patient becomes faint, falls, has some black evacuations; he is pulseless, the skin bloodless, dusky, and shrunken to the bones; he expires in a few minutes, or perhaps an hour after the first appearance of disease. These are the cases which, individually, it may be impossible to discriminate,

and we may not be able to say whether the patient dying thus
suddenly has died of small-pox, yellow fever, or cholera. And
it does not seem very important, for the sufferer is beyond all
chance of assistance from us from the very beginning. The
following may be stated as laws of development of the endemic
of tropical cities :

I. *Somewhat protracted warm summer weather is necessary for
the development of the yellow fever poison.*—Thus, at Havana,
where there are cases the year round, the number of sick rapidly
increases with the warm weather, and in the latter part of summer. At New Orleans, where the disease appears regularly every
summer, it always declines with cool weather and disappears with
the first frost.

II. *The yellow fever miasm is only active during the night.*—
This seems to follow from the immunity enjoyed by fishermen
and truck farmers, who merely visit the city during the day to
attend the markets. Instances having been reported of strangers
passing through an infected city, without remaining over night, in
all cases, so far as we have heard, with impunity. During the epidemic at Norfolk, Virginia, in 1855, many persons went to farm-
houses in the neighborhood to reside during the continuance of
the disease, and visited the city nearly every day throughout the
season with perfect impunity, only being careful to leave before
sunset. More evidence is needed on this point.

III. *Yellow fever is by no means a contagious disease.*—This
is sufficiently proved by the custom, general since the epidemic of
1793, and probably before, of whole families, even after some of
them are fatally infected, removing to houses of friends in the
country. The infected in this way occupy the same room with
members of the farmer's family, are nursed by them, and die
under their care; and no instance can be found of the disease
communicated in this way. Volumes have been written to prove
the yellow fever to be contagious, and other volumes to prove the
contrary; but it is not necessary for our purpose further to refer
to them. During the epidemic at Norfolk, steamboats plied
regularly every day, except Sundays, to Baltimore, merely avoiding their old wharf, which was in the midst of the disease; they
landed about a mile down the river, at a place without population, and open to the air of the country. Hundreds of families

left by these boats, carrying with them as much clothing as they pleased, and even bedding. They remained for the season at Baltimore, Washington, Richmond, Carlisle, Chambersburg, York, Bedford, Gettysburg, and other places, many carrying in their bodies the germs of the fatal disease by which they perished among their hospitable entertainers; but they did not in a single instance communicate the disease to the families among whom they sojourned.

His Majesty's ship-of-war Tweed being at that time (during the yellow fever of 1764) in Cadiz Bay, several of her men were taken ill on shore, but by being carried on board all of them recovered. Neither did the black vomit or any other deadly symptom of that fever make its appearance in any of the ships. The dread of this distemper forced many people of fashion to retire into the country, where they remained in perfect safety from it.— (*Lind.*)

IV. *The yellow fever poison may originate on shipboard independently of any communication with an infectious city.*—Many instances might be mentioned where no possible communication could have existed, as some of the vessels had not approached within several miles of any land whatever. They had merely sailed from Europe, not perhaps in the best condition of stowage or cleanliness, and the disease broke out as the vessels experienced the high temperature of the tropics.—(*La Roche.*)

The ships which principally suffered were either defective in arrangements for cleanliness, or had been long in commission without opportunity for thorough cleansing. The last case is that of the United States steamship Susquehanna, which, after a full cruise in the Mediterranean, show-ship, well holystoned, a pattern of neatness as far as visible, attempted, in 1858, to continue her cruise in the West Indies; but nearly as soon as she encountered hot weather, the yellow fever made its appearance on board and was terribly fatal. In some steamships the disease has appeared to depend on the faulty manner of placing the machinery, so that the floor beneath the engines was not sufficiently accessible for the purpose of cleaning. Under these circumstances a pool of offensive mud is formed, principally of worn-out oil, and it cannot be removed without removing the engines entirely.

V. *The yellow fever infection sometimes originates in the decay of accumulations of human excrements and exuviæ.*—The city of Canton, China, which is in precisely the climate for the disease, and is said to be very filthy, probably never suffers from it, and the following circumstances may have something to do with its immunity. The surface of the ground is pretty well covered with buildings, and paved; and the site is so low and level that the rise and fall of the tide washes out the sewers every day; the excrements are assiduously collected in buckets and carried off to manure the fields, so that though these buckets frequently offend the nostrils of the pedestrians, there are no accumulations of such material in the city. The town of Key West, Florida (Cayo Hueso), was formerly a pestilential place; and a few years ago a board of navy surgeons were sent there in the midst of an epidemic, to investigate the matter. Some pictures were made of these doctors approaching the wharf warily, cocked hats on their heads and boat-hooks in their hands, with which to feel pulses without undue personal risk. They, however, probably learned in reference to the place about what every navy surgeon who had ever been there knew before. But they made a report, together with a recommendation that a few ditches should be dug, certain accumulations of filth removed, and that a general cleaning up, draining, and whitewashing should be practiced. From that time to the present, Key West has been a comparatively healthy place. New York, Philadelphia, and Baltimore, which formerly suffered occasionally from this disease, have been entirely clear of it, since they have been abundantly and conveniently supplied with water from the rivers, so that constant streams flow through all the streets and sewers.

(258.) If we would prevent the yellow fever, or check its ravages, we must reflect upon the circumstances under which it usually occurs, and note what has been done in Canton, Baltimore, Philadelphia, and New York. Such measures, more thoroughly carried out, are necessary at New Orleans, Key West, and Havana. In regard to the question of quarantine in this disease, we may safely say, that all restraints which prevent the sick from reaching a healthy locality are absurd, and with our present knowledge on the subject, outrageously cruel, little better than deliberate murder. A yellow fever patient, even carrying his

clothing and bedding with him, has never been known to communicate the disease to another person in a healthy locality, and
the experiment has been tried thousands of times. But in regard
to a ship, it may be full of poison; and in such a case it should
not be moored in a close dock, with dwelling-houses about it, nor
should the cargo be discharged in such a situation. Families
living near vessels in this condition, and especially workmen employed on board, have frequently lost their lives by such reck-
lessness. There seems, however, to be no great risk in discharging such a ship, under the direction of competent inspectors,
away from populous places; for systematic ventilation, chlorine
fumigations, and the light of day have been found capable of
rapidly decomposing or dissipating the poison. The safest and
most economical way in our climate is to wait for hard frost.

(259.) To prevent yellow fever on board ship, we must practice those measures which are required to prevent diseases generally; cleanliness, purity, ventilation, good food, and cheerful
social influences, are the necessary means. The cleanliness must
not be of that kind which we sometimes describe as being "skin-
deep." It is of no avail to scour and scrub while the debris of
decaying cargo is accumulating in the hold. When a ship is
newly fitted, it is pure in this respect, but it cannot possibly remain so. The deterioration is steadily progressive from day to
day, though it may be greatly retarded by assiduous care. Whenever it is necessary to remove articles from the hold, there is an
opportunity to collect and remove more or less of exposed fragments and dirt. When arrangements are being made to receive
new stores, or new cargo, it is convenient to break out and rear-
range the old, collecting dirt and fragments, using very freely
chloride of lime and whitewash, particularly about secret recesses.
It seems impossible to avoid tedious repetitions when we under-
take to indicate the means of preserving health, as we are often
permitted merely to vary the form of expression, no matter what
the disease. The universal prophylactic is purity, material and
moral purity, personal and social purity, at home and abroad, by
night and by day, of air and of water, in all places and at all
times, *purity*.

(260.) If circumstances prevent a person from leaving a place
where the yellow fever prevails, he should select his residence in

the highest and healthiest available spot; should sleep preferably
in the highest part of the house, avoid the night air, using mos-
quito bars rather than nothing for its exclusion; use nutritious
and wholesome food, avoid fatiguing exercise, exposure to the
sun, and excesses of all kinds; maintain a cheerful, confident
temper, for which a clear conscience and earnest Christian feeling,
the baptism of the Holy Spirit, appear to be the most essential
circumstances.   If it be necessary to enter an infected spot, go in
the daytime and do not stay long.   Attempts to guard against
the disease by low diet and physic are worse than useless, as they
enfeeble the system and render it less able to resist the action of
the poison.—(§ 277.)

CHAPTER XXIV.

(261.) SCORBUTUS, sea-scurvy, having been a most terrible endemic disease on shipboard, during the last and preceding centuries, comes naturally to be noticed here. The common English name, scurvy, is rather objectionable, as it is not necessarily a scurfy or scabby disease; and the translators of the Bible (Leviticus xxi, 20, and xxii, 22) appear to use the word scurvy as synonymous with scabies or itch, to which scorbutus, the true sea-scurvy, has no sort of resemblance. We greatly prefer the term scorbutus, though it may be a barbarous Scandinavian word with a Latin termination. It is the name of this specific disease and of no other.

(262.) Scorbutus was formerly the endemic of cold climates, as it prevailed extensively in all cold countries during the winter. But now that its cause is known and understood, it has ceased to belong to the class of endemic diseases altogether. The cause of this disease, undoubtedly, is deficiency of food, either in quantity, quality, or variety, so that the digestive organs are incapable of appropriating sufficient nutriment. It hence prevailed terribly in protracted sieges, where poor food was necessarily used, because better than none, and variety was limited to the small number of articles within reach. It was the winter endemic of cold countries, till civilization and agriculture furnished a varied supply of vegetables and fruits for the winter season. It must have been pretty common in England when the Queen had to send a special messenger to Holland before she could obtain the necessary material for a salad.

Cold with moisture is likewise an exciting cause, by rendering a larger amount of food necessary. Hence when seamen have been but indifferently nourished by all that their digestive organs could appropriate in mild weather, they have generally suffered severely by running into cold and stormy regions on the same diet ; the cold and additional exertion rendering a greater amount of nutriment necessary. Other causes have been suggested and disproved, some of which it may be well to mention. Sir Gilbert Blane, as late as 1785, thought it might be contagious. The old navigators, many of them, supposed it a terrific pestilence of the climate in which they happened to be. Salt and salt food have been assigned as the cause ; but Lord Anson's crew suffered on the west coast of Mexico, when living on fresh meat ; the Russian army, at the siege of Azof, suffered when they had no salt meat ; and besides, salt-makers are not peculiarly subject to the disease. Salt meat, especially if long kept, on account of its progressively increasing hardness, and consequent defective digestion not affording due nutriment of itself, may thus be a cause. Within a few years, it has appeared to some, reflecting that the sailor's beef is all salted with soda salts, in the midst of an ocean of soda salts, the need of sufficient potash for the healthy constitution of the tissues might be the cause of this disease; and they suggested starch, containing the needed element, as the appropriate remedy. This has been used with great alleged benefit. This is a satisfactory report so far as it goes, but we are unable to understand why starch on this theory should be much better than bread and beans, usual articles of food when the disease made such havoc.

(263.) *Of the symptoms*, the phenomena of this disease, we need not say much, as nobody has really seen them during the present century, and it is not likely that they will ever be seen again. A full account of them in their varied forms is given by Lind, the last and best authority on this subject. When after a deficiency, somewhat protracted, of nutritive and varied diet, with total absence of fresh food, we notice a dark discoloration of the more transparent parts of the skin, the lips, gums, tongue, and eyelids, with purplish or yellow spots on various parts of the body, we are pretty sure of the establishment of the scorbutic tendency; and if, in addition, we notice fetid ulceration of the gums, with bending up and stiffening of the knees or elbows, we need not hesitate to say that the patient is suffering from scorbutus, however much these symptoms fall short of the awful pestilence, the ravages of which are so terrifically portrayed in Hackluyt's *Col-*

lection of Voyages. When the disease has proceeded so far there is no time to be lost.

(264.) The only real antiscorbutic remedies which we are disposed to acknowledge are good, varied, fresh food, and cheerful influences, cleanliness, neatness, and order.

The necessity for *variety of food* seems to be very imperfectly understood. During the early part of this century experiments were performed with the object of determining the comparative nutritive value of the various proximate elements of meat. A dog was fed with pure gelatine and water, and he soon became disgusted with his food and died; it was hence inferred that gelatine was not nutritive. A similar experiment was tried with albumen, and with like result, and with fat and the other constituents of meat in succession. No one of the constituents, singly, being capable of nourishing the animal, the inference followed that the entire flesh is necessary for nutrition. An unfortunate canary bird was fed exclusively on sugar and water, and he soon became blind and fell dead from his perch. A poor bird fed exclusively on rice did no better. It would seem that many persons greatly injure their health by attempting to live on a few articles of food which they deem wholesome, instead of using the variety in the midst of which we are placed, and for which our organization appears to be adapted. The changing seasons of the year, with their peculiar fruits for each month, if not for each day of the month, seem to supply just such a variety as is required for healthy nutrition.

(265.) *Freshness of food* is a quality on which more depends than could readily be imagined. The earlier voyagers to Canada found great advantage in using the fresh foliage of the spruce pine, *Abies canadensis*, which they chewed, infused, made into beer, etc. Captain Cook found equal advantage from the foliage of a similar tree growing on the island of New Zealand. Equal advantages have resulted in time of need from the use of some cruciferous plants found growing about Hudson's Bay and elsewhere, which on this account have received the name of scurvy grass. When Lord Anson arrived at Juan Fernandez, Crusoe Island, a boat's crew, who went on shore for the purpose, loaded their boat with any grass which came in their way, not caring

about the kind, but only that it was green. This mixture of weeds
was found as effectual as spruce boughs and spinach.

During an experience of twenty years in the navy I have seen
the scorbutic tendency developed twice on shipboard. On the
first occasion the ship, the frigate Savannah, was on her return
from California, during the Mexican war. The crew had had
very few fresh vegetables, not even good beans, for nine months;
and the salted and dried provisions had mostly been on board
nearly the same time; some of it had been packed three or four
years previously. As soon as we reached the cold and stormy
weather of the South Pacific, the symptoms began to appear;
brown spots, big and little, about the arms and legs, ulcerated,
fetid, bleeding gums, rheumatic pains with rigidity and contrac-
tion of the flexor muscles. The preserved lemon-juice, citric acid,
wine, etc., in various mixtures, had a pretty extensive trial and
with great benefit. These articles had been long kept, though
probably not so long as the beef and pork. The relief was but
partial, and a day's duty in the cold on deck was sufficient to
renew or aggravate the symptoms in some of the cases. It was
even noticed that many were relieved by merely being excused
from duty; their ordinary diet was sufficient while they were quiet
and warm, but not enough for the wants of nutrition when they
were exposed to cold and labor. This scorbutic disposition continued, though without much actual suffering, for two or three
weeks, when we met a whaling ship, from which we obtained a
basket of potatoes. These were distributed, a potato to each, on
condition that they were to be eaten raw. The jack-knives were
soon busy scraping them to pulp, which seemed to possess a delicious flavor. The sore gums healed, the blotches disappeared,
the legs and arms became flexible and free from pain, and no
more was heard of the scurvy.

The second occasion was on board one of the vessels of the
Japan expedition. We sailed from New York direct for the
Straits of Sunda. The passage exceeded four months, during
which we did not see land except a distant island. The latter
part of the passage was stormy and cold. When about ninety
days out, and beyond the Cape of Good Hope, the scorbutic
tendency became apparent. All our remedies only mitigated the
disease and kept it in check. We could not see that the pre-

served lime-juice was any better than a solution of crystals of
citric acid, with a little wine or ale. And our canned meats,
oxtail soup, boiled beef, roast beef, and roast mutton, did not
afford effectual relief; but there remained a number of men who
had to be excused from duty till we arrived at the Straits of
Sunda, when a boat-load of oranges and cocoanuts, with a few
chickens, brought perfect relief.

(266.) This mere freshness of food has an importance which
we find it difficult to comprehend. The proximate principles of
vegetable food, so far as we know them—sugar, starch, and gum;
the vegetable acids, alkalies, salts, and oils—seem capable of perfect preservation for very long periods; but it is found that after
such preservation they are incapable of affording proper nutriment without something fresh—some animal or vegetable substance but recently deprived of life. This important quality
probably resides in the nitrogenous, the azotized material, held
in solution in the juices or sap of vegetables. This nitrogenous
material, which appears to be a principal agent in the decay of
all organic tissues, seems likewise necessary to their proper digestion as food.

Nitrogen, in fact, seems as interesting in its relations as any
other of the recognized elementary substances, though the chemists do characterize it mostly by negative properties,—without
affinities or repulsions—may be mechanically mixed but not
chemically combined with anything by any known process. It
constitutes nearly four-fifths of the atmosphere, where it is in the
condition of mechanical mixture or diffusion. The only known
power in nature by which it is brought extensively into combinations is the influence of organic life. Vegetables pretty certainly
and animals probably appropriate it directly from the atmosphere,
as well as from the remains of preceding organisms. Very few
vegetables, if any, can exist or grow without the nitrogenous
compounds which they receive from their predecessors in life,
and certainly no animal can exist without them. It hence appears that nitrogen is found in nature only in the atmosphere, its
great natural reservoir; in the tissues and fluids of organic beings;
and in various states of chemical combination which result from
the decay of these tissues and fluids.

The multitude of organic beings on the earth, by their excretions and bodily decay, furnish an immense quantity and untold variety of these combinations, the importance of which it is impossible fully to appreciate. Some of the best understood, though perhaps not the most important of these combinations of nitrogen, are the following: Ammonia, of nitrogen and hydrogen; nitric acid, of nitrogen and oxygen; cyanogen, of nitrogen and carbon; and ferro-cyanogen, of nitrogen, carbon, and iron. By chemical manipulations with these four an endless variety of substances is obtained, having nitrogen as one of their constituents. The vegetable alkaloids—quinine, cinchonine, morphine, meconine, atropine, daturine, etc.—universally have nitrogen as one of their constituents. There are a vast number of other nitrogenous substances, the result of vital actions of the innumerable beings which inhabit the earth. Some of these we have been enabled to study and comprehend in some degree; others essential to our existence will, doubtless, elude human comprehension forever. It is probably to some of these, so delicate in their chemical affinities as to be incapable of protracted preservation, that we are to look for the necessity of fresh food. Or is it that some spark of molecular life still adheres, for a time, to dead organisms, and that this is a necessary element of nutriment?

However this may be, or whatever may be the cause, a small quantity of fresh food, some animal or vegetable substance recently removed from the domain of life, seems absolutely necessary for the preservation of health. And it is not by the amount of nutriment that it furnishes, but by some peculiar stimulus which it supplies to the powers of assimilation, enabling them to appropriate other food; for a potato, an onion, or a handful of weeds, no matter what, so that it is fresh and not really poisonous, answers the purpose.

The universal use of potatoes and other fresh vegetables, furnishes the needful amount of fresh material for the most part. The preserved lemon-juice, so much used in the British naval service, no doubt has its use, and when freshly prepared is fully as good as any common grass, but we have no doubt that its useful properties are lost or greatly impaired by long keeping. The various processes for preserving food with as much as possible of the condition of fresh vegetables and meats have much utility, as they afford means of warding off disease. These we have described elsewhere, together with a contrivance for supplying fresh vegetables for a salad at sea.

(267.) Cheerfulness, cleanliness, neatness, and good order are of the first importance to health on shipboard and everywhere else, but here we find it necessary to suggest a caution. One of the symptoms of scorbutus is an indisposition, almost an inability, to move: this has been mistaken for laziness, moroseness, and skulking; and death has occurred suddenly from driving the sufferer on deck with the view of promoting cheerfulness and activity. Laziness is a consequence not the cause of this disease.

CHAPTER XXV.

(268.) THE other endemic diseases, having little reference to our subject, may be noticed briefly.

Plica polonica is a curious disease of the hair, which occurs principally in Poland, though it is occasionally met with in other countries. It is hence considered the endemic of Poland. The roots of the hair are enlarged and become very sensitive, so much so that occasionally the hair is painful to the touch. The hair at the same time grows very rapidly and is glued together by a viscid, fetid secretion, so that combing is quite out of the question. It hence becomes the habitation of crowds of vermin, and the sufferer is a most disgusting and repulsive object. This disease, like other peculiarities of physical organization, is, perhaps, in some degree, hereditary, but it seems that the principal cause is to be found in national habits,—long hair and the want of cleanliness. It would appear that the disease may be prevented and even cured by the cautious and systematic use of scissors, soap, combs, brushes, etc., not forgetting to use a little mercurial ointment occasionally for the insects.

(269.) *Bronchocele*, goitre, is a disease which is seen in all parts of the world, but it is very common in Switzerland. It is a tumor in front of the neck, an enlargement of the thyroid gland. The disease occasions but little pain or uneasiness, except when the tumor becomes very large, and then it may seriously impede respiration. The cause of this disease is quite unknown; we only know that it is endemic in Switzerland, prevailing more in some valleys than others, but without anything peculiar about them which can be indicated as the cause. The snow-water theory and such like conjectures have been disproved by further

observation.   This disease is certainly and promptly removed in
most conditions by the cautious use of iodine, and by this means
may be prevented from attaining a troublesome size and figure.
But as we know nothing of the cause, we are not able to suggest
any means of preventing this disease.   We certainly should not
recommend to persons in health the habitual use of iodine or any
other medicine, which might produce worse consequences than
bronchocele.

(270.) *Cretinism* is another and more terrible endemic of Switzerland, prevailing principally in some of the valleys of the
Upper Rhone, inclosed by high mountains.   Nearly the only
thing certainly determined about the cause of this terrible disease is that it occurs in some of these beautiful and fertile valleys.   This disease is characterized by the small size and deformity of the sufferers, with crooked limbs, comparatively large
heads, and weakness of intellect, bordering on idiocy.   Poverty,
with wretched and filthy habitations, has been suggested as the
cause, especially as persons in more comfortable circumstances,
even in the same villages, are much less subject to the disease.   It
is certainly hard to exaggerate the morbific effects of such causes,
but they ordinarily produce very different diseases from this.
We are more inclined to the opinion that the disease, with its intellectual and bodily weakness, prevents its subjects from acquir-
ing comfortable habitations and other comfortable and healthful
appliances.   The only circumstance which seems common to the
localities is that they are all deep valleys inclosed by high mountains, such as we may suppose to prevent the free circulation of
air, and this, we are inclined to believe, is in some way the cause.
We know so little of the cause of this disease that we have not
much to say about the means of avoiding it.   We may safely recommend to the people cultivating these valleys to select healthy
localities in the neighboring mountains for their villages, near
enough to enable them to walk to their fields for necessary labor.

(271.) *Elephantiasis arabum* is a curious endemic disease in
many tropical countries.   It is characterized by a thickening of
the skin, particularly about the ankles.   This thickening extends
so much about the limbs and becomes so enormous that the legs
are in some instances fairly comparable to those of an elephant,
and hence the name of the disease.   It prevails in particular

localities, all of which I believe are within the tropics, but there are many tropical countries in which no such disease is known. As we know nothing of the cause of this disease, except its endemic character, we are unable to suggest any means of avoiding it in the localities where it prevails. We have known persons who had observed the commencement of this disease to leave the island of Barbadoes, and thus avoid any troublesome increase of this affliction, so long as this exile from their native country continued.

(272.) *Cholera infantum*, the summer endemic of children in large cities, appears to be caused by various circumstances unfavorable to health, acting on the impressible organization of children. Deficiency of daylight, produced by high buildings crowded together, an atmosphere contaminated by decaying human exuviæ and excrement, the consequence of crowding and defective ventilation and unwholesome food, particularly factitious milk and the milk of diseased animals, appear to be the principal causes of this scourge of civilization. The only means of avoiding it is to escape from its causes, by placing children, during the prevalence of this disease, in the country, in the midst of healthful food, light, and air.

Verugas.—The Spanish conquerors of Peru found a curious endemic of warts (verruca, a wart), and even suffered from it in one of the upper valleys of the Rimac, about (20) twenty leagues from Lima. The disease is there yet; it affects particularly the nose, the eyelids, the ears, the hands. It is a fever, with an eruption of vascular tumors or bloody vesicles, the size of a pea, or even an inch in diameter. These tumors are not painful, dry up into hard scabs and drop off; but if roughly handled or cut they bleed profusely. The suspected spring-water is found to be very pure, and a party who went to assist in getting the iron railroad bridge in position, and took water with them, brought back the infection, and in about a month had verugas.—(*San. Rep.*, 72.)

Stricture of Œsophagus—mal de engasco—exists endemically in Southern Brazil, district Limeïras, province San Paulo. The disease comes on gradually and ends in death by starvation in about a year (λιμος, hunger). Can it be that the Brazilians thus name the district because people there sometimes die of starvation?—(*San. Rep.*, 74.)

14

(273.) *Milk sickness, Staggers*, is the name of a disease formerly endemic in some portions of our Western country.   It was acute poisoning, caused by eating the flesh, butter, or milk of cattle which had fed on a particular poisonous weed, *Rhus toxicodendron*, poison oak.   It appears that under certain circumstances, when the pasturage is very bare, the cattle eat grass more or less mixed with this weed, and as they are by no means fond of it, they eat but little at a time, till gradually the entire flesh of the animal is imbued with poison, without any symptoms of poisoning being observed.   This was formerly a very serious affair, but the disease has disappeared with the cultivation of the land, and a general understanding of the cause of the mischief.   The flesh of the deer has been found poisonous occasionally from the same cause. The disease was endemic in localities where sprouts of poison oak grew so mingled with the grass that the cattle were unable to obtain their food separate from the poisonous weed.

(274.) The *Guinea-worm* is a peculiar, long, threadlike worm, found in the bodies of persons living on some parts of the African coast and in the West Indies.   Its presence is indicated under the skin by a little red, itching spot.   This ulcerates or is opened artificially, and the head of the worm is found.   The whole animal requires to be removed very carefully to avoid a very troublesome sore.   There has been a great deal of speculation and doubt about the source of this worm and how it could insinuate itself into such a situation.   It was observed that persons using water from a particular well suffered, while their neighbors escaped.   A microscopic examination of the water resulted in the discovery of many peculiar organic objects supposed to be the organic germs of this worm.   These are swallowed with the water, and probably insinuate themselves into the tissues from the bowels, growing in their progress.   In places where this disease is a serious annoyance it may be obviated by the Japanese custom of always boiling water before drinking it, using tea, etc., and being careful never to drink fresh water directly from the well.

(275.) *Trichinosis.*—Germany, the land of sausages and hams, has suffered from an endemic disease, the cause of which has but recently been discovered.   This disease is by no means confined to Germany, as numerous cases have already been reported in our own country.   Two or three deaths occur in a family, of typhoid

fever, with some anomalous symptoms; suspicion is aroused, and
a microscopic examination of the remains of the ham or sausage
proves the existence of the newly recognized cause of ham-poi-
soning. The following case, which is going the rounds of the
medical journals, led to the discovery of the cause, and places the
whole subject in its proper light :

(276.) "About the middle of October, 1863, there was a festive
celebration at Hettstädt, a small country town near the Hartz
Mountains, in Germany. Upwards of one hundred persons sat
down to an excellent dinner, and having enjoyed themselves *more
majorum*, separated and went to their several homes.

"Of these one hundred and three persons, mostly in the prime
of life, eighty-three are now in their graves; the majority of the
twenty survivors linger with a fearful malady, and a few only
walk apparently unscathed among the living, but in hourly fear
of the disease which has carried away their fellow-diners. They
had all eaten of poison at that festive board. It was not administered by design or negligence, but was unknown to all concerned.

"When the festival had been finally determined upon and the
dinner ordered at the hotel, the keeper arranged his bill of fare.
The *Rothwürste*, smoked sausage, was therefore ordered at the
butcher's, the necessary number of days beforehand, in order to
allow of its being properly smoked. The butcher went expressly
to a neighboring proprietor and bought one of two pigs from the
steward, who had been commissioned with the transaction by his
master. It appears, however, that the steward unfortunately sold
the pig which the master had intended not to sell, as he did not
deem it sufficiently fat or well-conditioned. Thus the wrong pig
was sold, carried on a barrow to the butcher, and worked into sausages, which were duly smoked, delivered at the hotel and served
to the guests at dinner.

"On the day after the festival, several persons who had par-
ticipated in the dinner were attacked with irritation of the intestines and fever, loss of appetite, and great prostration. An active
inquiry was made into all the circumstances of the dinner. Every
article of food and material was subjected to a most rigid examination, without any result in the first instance, but when the
symptoms in some of the cases invaded the muscles of the legs,

particularly the calves of some of the sufferers, the description
which Zenker had given of a case of fatal trichinous disease was
remembered. The remnants of sausage and pork were examined
with the microscope and found to be swarming with incapsuled
trichinæ. From the suffering muscles of several of the victims
small pieces were excised, and, under the microscope, found
charged with trichinæ in all stages of development. It could
not be doubted any longer that as many of the hundred and three
as had partaken of the *Rothwürste* had been infected with trichinous disease by eating of trichinous pork, the parasites of which
had, at least in part, escaped the effects of smoking and frying.

"Almost everywhere the commonest rules of cleanliness are
disregarded in the rearing of pigs, yet pigs are naturally clean
animals. A due regard to cleanliness will prevent trichinæ in
the pig. In wild boars, of which many are eaten in the country
around the Hartz Mountains, the trichinæ have never been found,
neither has it been met with in sheep, oxen, or horses. Beef is
the safest of all descriptions of meat, as no parasite has ever been
discovered in it."

(277.) *Tarantismus.*—An endemic under this name was formerly described as occurring in some parts of Italy. It was
caused by the bite of a big spider, and cured by liquor and dancing. The fact is that the bite of the tarantula is pretty severe,
nearly as bad as the sting of a hornet, and, like the wounds of
other poisonous insects, it is relieved by alcohol or ammonia. We
might about as well consider hornet-stinging an endemic disease,
especially in places where the insects are made cross by throwing
sticks at their nest.

Acclimation.—There seems to be a very general impression,
almost universal, that the human constitution may accommodate
itself to almost any climate ; and especially to any malarial condition of climate, so as to enjoy health in almost any locality. So
far as mere *temperature* goes, the accommodation only requires a
proper change of habits, in regard to food, clothing, and exercise. If the Esquimaux should be transferred to a hot climate,
they could not continue to eat ten pounds of blubber a day,
clothe in heavy suits of peltry, and run about hunting bears and
walrus. Nor could the Chinaman—in his summer dress of solid
shoes, loose drawers, and light shirt overall, shading and fanning

the whole surface of his body—enjoy an Arctic winter. We
have a climate with a winter and a summer temperature somewhat resembling these extremes; and we probably suffer in health
occasionally, from our slowness in accommodating our dress to
the changes of temperature; for the warmer the summer weather
the greater the number of deaths, is the report of the students of
mortuary statistics. It has struck me that in hot climates we really
need heavier clothing than is usually worn by the natives; the two
garments of shirt and drawers arranged for decency, for shade,
for fans, and to protect from insects, is not dress enough for the
European newly arrived at Canton; some of the older residents,
however, do occasionally wear pan-ja-mas, for an hour in the
morning, and they enjoy it like taking a cold bath.

But it is mostly in reference to *malaria* that acclimation has been
most discussed, generally assuming that the natives of malarious
countries are quite healthy. This is a great fallacy to begin with:
the people of Lincolnshire, England, never became healthy, with
their centuries of acclimation, and acclimatation, and acclimatization, till the draining of their fens. The Italian Maremma, near
Rome, was drained under the emperors, was healthy, was covered with villas and gardens. The drains have been gradually
destroyed by mere neglect, and the Maremma is malarious. Some
of the descendants of the owners of the villas are still there,
living in thatched huts among the ruins, supported partly by
rearing cattle, but principally devoted to stealing from each
other and robbing an occasional stranger. They are lanky, or
more politely, they are spare in form, of dark complexions, and
mostly they suffer from painful splenic tumors. This is the result of fifty generations of acclimatization on these beautiful and
fertile fields. It is the same story everywhere. I have never seen
a healthy people or well-cultivated fields on malarious ground.
But men are in some degree acclimated? Certainly they are.
Schweinfurth, in beginning his African explorations, had an attack of remittent fever; he took care of himself till he recovered,
and then he congratulated himself that his liver was so hardened
that malaria could not kill him. However, there are those
among us who think the African explorations too expensive,
seeing that they cost the liver and eventually the lives of such

accomplished and painstaking votaries of scientific and benevolent enterprise. But mere high temperature is a very different thing from malaria; and Lind has truly informed us, that there are healthy spots in all unhealthy countries, as well as malarious spots in healthy countries; and some of the African explorers by using the healthy spots for recruiting stations, and by keeping their ears buzzing with quinine, have kept on their feet long enough to do some good work. I have spent several months in succession, in various parts of the Gulf of Guinea, and with care to avoid malaria, without a single case of fever among the crew, till two perverse fellows, regardless of orders, remained all night on shore; and they both suffered.

Yellow fever is the disease in which acclimation is most important and most readily appreciated: this is the endemic of cities in warm climates. It resembles small-pox and measles, in the fact that it rarely affects the same person more than once. Children are not so severely affected and rarely die. Hence, the adult natives are usually exempt; they do not suffer except in great epidemics; they consider the place quite healthy when strangers are dying in large numbers or flying for their lives; they call it *stranger's fever*. This character of the disease unfortunately is often lost sight of, as in the epidemic at Norfolk, in 1855, when medical students and nurses, quite unprotected, were encouraged to go to the afflicted city, to do the work of nurses, and the consequence was just what should have been expected: they quickly sickened and died, thus making more work for the nurses and gravediggers, instead of helping. The same blunder, on a small scale, was repeated at Pensacola, in 1874. There is no scarcity of acclimated persons in the southern cities, and they should do this duty.

In regard to most of the endemics we have mentioned, acclimatization has just the opposite effect to that usually claimed for it. *Plica polonica* does not affect strangers, but only Polanders. *Elephantiasis arabum*, at Barbadoes, does not affect new comers, but only natives. And referring to tarantismus, probably the tarantula, centipede and scorpion would bite natives and strangers alike.

CHAPTER XXVI.

(278.) In several of the preceding chapters we have been considering certain diseases, the causes of which being wholly unknown, they are called epidemics; and certain other diseases, the causes of which are but little known, except the fact of their prevalence in special localities, hence called endemics. It is perceived that the list of these dreadful epidemics and endemics is constantly being diminished with our advance in knowledge. We have learned something of the causes of some of the formerly dreadful epidemics, and how to avoid them.

(279.) We come next to the consideration of contagious diseases, those which are communicated from one person to another by contagion or personal infection. There are many dreadful diseases, of the causes of which we scarcely know anything, except that the diseases are contracted by being near or in contact with an individual already affected, as small-pox, measles, and mumps, hydrophobia, typhus, and syphilis. A person receives into a small wound a little of the saliva of a hydrophobic dog, and the chances are at least nineteen in twenty that he receives no very material harm, but there is about one chance in thirty that he will be afflicted with perhaps the most terrific malady known to humanity. We hence learn that hydrophobia is contagious, but we are wholly ignorant why this poison, so terrifically fatal in the one case, is altogether without appreciable action in all the others. We are not able even to indicate any chemical or mechanical difference between the saliva of the hydrophobic dog and that of a perfectly healthy animal.

Similarly in reference to *small-pox*, a person unprotected enters the room of a patient, the atmosphere of which does not greatly differ, either chemically or mechanically, from that of an adjoining room, but the person so entering is pretty sure of suffering in about a fortnight from the same terrible disease. The blood and the various excretions of the small-pox patient, though they may not differ apparently from those of people in health, or people suffering from other diseases, will produce the disease with certainty in persons exposed to their action. Probably the only reliable test of the presence of small-pox infection, except the presence of a patient, is the peculiar smell of the disease, and this is believed to be quite characteristic. This disease may not only be communicated by contact, but its poison is capable of diffusion in the atmosphere to a certain distance, and the very interesting and important question, to what distance, does not admit of any precise answer. It may be stated as the rule, that it cannot be communicated through the atmosphere beyond the room in which the patient and his clothing are. It has been stated that this disease may be taken as far as it can be smelled, and this is probably as precise an answer as the question admits of, and suggests the caution in approaching a patient of this sort to keep to windward if practicable, so as not to smell it very much. Since the introduction of vaccination by Jenner this disease has lost most of its terrors. It no longer sweeps off one-fourth of the population of all the cities every fifteen or twenty years.

(280.) *Measles*, like small-pox, is propagated by contagion through the atmosphere, but it has never been such a terrifically fatal disease. The popular impression is that these and various other diseases can originate only by contagion, but this is probably a mistake, and the opinion is steadily gaining ground that any and all of them do occasionally originate from some epidemic influence. Something very like measles has been produced by the ordinary mould which grows on damp straw.—(*Salisbury.*)

(281.) *Scabies*, itch, a disease of careless dirtiness, is a contagious disease, which depends mainly on the irritation caused by the presence of microscopic insects. These, on favorable occasions, crawl from one person to another, and thus propagate the disease. Some of the older authors, under the name *morbus pediculosus*, describe a wretched state of things, caused in part by the presence of larger insects. These cases were occasionally seen when combs, brushes, and soap were not such common articles as at present. The free use of soap and water is sufficient to prevent the propagation of scabies, even in the extreme cases of shaking hands with a person subject to the disease.

(282.) *Syphilis* is another contagious disease, caused by uncleanness, moral and physical. It so deeply impairs the constitution of the sufferer that its painful consequences are frequently transmitted, hereditarily, to the children of the third and fourth generation, extirpating whole families, root and branch. Indeed, the opinion appears to be gaining ground that pulmonary consumption and all the forms of scrofula are mainly consequences of this disease, transmitted hereditarily to the unfortunate progeny of the impure. This disease is accurately described in the book of Leviticus, xiii, 2, 3, 4: "When a man shall have in the skin of his flesh a [rising] *swelling*, a sore, or a [bright] *raw* spot, and it shall be in the skin of his flesh like the [plague of leprosy] *ulcer of syphilis*, then he shall be brought unto one of the priests. And the priest shall look on the [plague] *sore* in the skin of the flesh; and when the [hair]* *raised margin* in the sore is [turned white] *inverted and white*, and the *sore* [in sight] *apparently* deeper than the skin of his flesh; it is a [plague of leprosy] *syphilitic ulcer* (*a Hunterian chancre*); and the priest shall look on him and pronounce him [unclean] *infectious*. If the raw spot be white in the skin of his flesh, and apparently not deeper than the skin, and the *margin* thereof be not *inverted* or white, then the priest shall shut him up that hath the *sore* seven days." By the same authority we learn that secondary syphilis is not contagious in the ordinary acceptation of the term (Lev. xiii, 12, 13). A still older authority alludes to the disease of the bones, which some of the moderns have foolishly attributed to the use of mercury. (Job xx, 11): "His bones are full of [the sin of his youth] *his secret diseases*." Again (Prov. xii, 4), "She that maketh ashamed is as rottenness in his bones." We know not how, either in fact or fancy, she can either be or cause such rottenness without the intervention of this disease; but with it she certainly does cause absolute material rottenness of the bones. It is vulgar language to-day to describe them as rotten with this disease. *Blennorrhœa virulenta*, the running described in Leviticus xv, is a contagious disease. Though not so terrible in character as the disease above

---

* The part of the body referred to is naturally without hair.

described, it is caused by the same habits and acts, and it has been described by many authors as the initial state of that disease.

(283.) The only known means of avoiding these diseases is purity, moral and material purity. But other devices have been tried. In Leviticus xiii, seclusion of the patient seems to be relied on to prevent the spread of the disease, and this is certainly a step in the right direction. The seekers after information in regard to the means of avoiding these diseases will hardly be satisfied merely to be told that they are to be escaped with certainty only by avoiding the well-known cause. It may, therefore, be suggested that if they cannot be pure, it is well to be as cleanly as they can, and there is much virtue in soap and water. It has been noticed that these diseases are generally contracted during a drunken frolic, so that the avoidance of drunkenness and drunken associates will very often prevent the disease. Seamen in the navy suffer much less than formerly, probably on account of the temperance reform. In Paris, and some other of the European capitals, it is attempted to prevent these diseases by police regulations. Certain persons are regularly licensed and subjected to a most rigid and careful inspection about once a month. The insufficiency of this is demonstrated by the enormous amount of disease found in the Parisian hospitals. About the end of the fifteenth century prodigious havoc was created by a battery of lewd women in the Austrian army, at that time engaged in the siege of Naples, and a remnant of the army was saved only by raising the siege. [General Butler, at New Orleans, in 1862, did better. The police regulation was that this sort of artillery should be kept in jail; but this being found insufficient, he ordered that pretended ladies, no matter what their apparent rank, who approached his men with insulting (?) language or gestures, should be treated in the same way.] In the Book of Numbers there is suggested a prophylactic which was once found effective. (Num. xxx, 1.) "The people began to commit whoredom with the daughters of Moab. And behold one of the children of Israel came, and brought unto his brethren a Midianitish woman, in the sight of Moses, and in sight of all the congregation of the children of Israel, who were weeping before the door of the tabernacle of the congregation. And when Phinehas, the son of Eleazar, the son of Aaron the priest, saw it, he arose up from among the congregation, and took a javelin in his hand. And he went after the man of Israel into the tent, and thrust both of them through, the man of Israel and the woman, so the plague was stayed from the children of Israel. And they that died of that plague were twenty-four thousand."

A curious part of the history of this plague is, that at one time it was generally supposed to have been carried to Europe by the companions of Columbus. Sydenham, a most respectable authority, tells us that "it first came from the West Indies, in the year 1493, for before that time the name of it was not so much as known among us." Now the most common name of the most common form of the disease, which occurs upward of twenty times in Sydenham's description, occurs at least nine times in the Septuagint translation of the fifteenth chapter of Leviticus. So we think he was mistaken. He is correct in the following quotation: "But when, by reason of the continuance of the disease in the said parts, the contagion is carried up, and by degrees infects the blood, all the symptoms increase by degrees, especially the pain; so that the sick cannot keep his bed, but is forced in a restless manner to walk about his chamber till morning. Moreover, by reason of the violence of the pain, the skull, and bones of the legs and arms, grow up in hard nodes, called exostoses, like the spavin in horses; which bones, that have nodes on them, by reason of continual pain and inflammation, become at length carious and putrefied. Phagedenic ulcers also seize various parts of the body, and most commonly begin in the throat, and are propagated by degrees to the cartilage of the nose, through the palate, and soon consume it, so that wanting its support it falls. The ulcers and pain increasing daily, the sick is devoured by ulcers and putrefaction, so that he lives a grievous life, by reason of the pain, stink, and scandal, which is worse than any death; but at length, one member rotting after another, the torn carcass is hid under ground, being very odious before to all above." To avoid these terrible consequences, it is important to avoid the advertising quacks, who only know enough to frighten out of their money those who have not the disease, but merely deserve to be swindled.

I had hoped by examining such official reports as came in my

way, to demonstrate very great improvement in the character of
the navy with reference to this matter; but I have been disap-
pointed. For several years after the close of the war, the number of admissions was very regularly between (59 and 60) fifty-
nine and sixty per thousand mean force for all enthetic diseases;
for ten years (1866 to 1875) the average is (58.4) fifty-eight and
four-tenths; in the year 1876, the admissions were (56.8) fifty-
six and eight-tenths per thousand. Hence, the diminution in
five years appears to be about (3) three per cent., or (.6) six-
tenths of one per cent. per annum,—at which rate these diseases
would diminish about one-half in a century.

In the last reports of the Navy Department, the tables are so
arranged that the degree of prevalence of syphilis primitiva may
be studied separately; in 1876 (mean force, 12,307; syph. prim.,
271), the admissions were (22) twenty-two per thousand mean
force. This is not very encouraging; but if the young men of
our cities can be kept as continent as the average sailor, we need
not despair. Let us not weaken by crude experiments the restraints now existing, which every middle-aged man must understand pretty well, from recollections of personal experience.
Something like the following has been proposed: have handsome
gilt signs attached to the fronts of houses, so that the old stager
may suggest to go in and take "something," while the shy boy
who hesitates is to be laughed at as a "chicken-hearted baby."
Boards of health perhaps might do more than at present: they
have charge of hospitals for patients suffering under "contagious
diseases;" a reasonable amount of confinement in the hospital
might do the patients good, without serious harm to the community.

CHAPTER XXVII.

TYPHUS FEVER.

(284.) TYPHUS is a contagious disease originating from a species of impurity not readily appreciated by the poor and the ignorant. There is a general unconsciousness that anything capable of exerting a pernicious influence can emanate from the body of a healthy person. It is very important that the community should be taught their error in this respect; and that there are aeriform excretions, both from the skin and the lungs, capable of rendering a confined atmosphere exceedingly poisonous in a short time. We have sometimes been taught to look upon the consumption of oxygen and substitution of carbonic acid as the only or principal contaminating influence, but this is very far from being true. The small amount of carbonic acid found in an atmosphere thus contaminated is not sufficient seriously to impair health, and is probably fully compensated by slightly fuller respirations, as is necessary in the attenuated atmosphere of high mountains. Neither are we authorized to attribute the deleterious properties to watery vapor, the other bulky material of cutaneous and pulmonary exhalations. The little animal matter, which eludes all ordinary observation, contains the pestilence that walketh in darkness. This animal matter varies for each animal species, and perhaps for each individual on the earth; for animals are recognized by a smell peculiar to each; and we know that a dog is generally able to follow his own master through crowds by the smell alone. This can only be accounted for by supposing the exhalations from the master to differ from those of all other men. The animal matter exhaled must vary almost infinitely from disease, for many diseases are recognized by the smell. The exhalation from a small-pox patient causes small-pox; that from a person infected with measles causes measles; and the same may be said of scarlet fever, whooping-cough, typhus, etc.

But it is necessary to bear in mind that the exhalations from perfectly healthy people are poisonous, except when very rapidly diluted by mingling with the atmosphere. Under all ordinary circumstances this dilution is so rapid and complete that no harm results, and it is in fact accomplished without our consciousness. On various occasions, however, numbers of persons have been forced into small rooms deficient of ventilation to such a degree as to occasion great discomfort, and even almost instant death. In some of these cases the consumption of oxygen and substitution of carbonic acid may have proceeded to such a degree as to cause death by suffocation; perhaps generally the deaths among persons suddenly thrust into such places may have been from this cause; but the long-continued ill-health of those escaping immediate death, is certainly not owing to the inhalation of carbonic acid.

(285.) The exhalations from healthy persons, when fresh, are but moderately poisonous, but after they have undergone in some degree the process of decay common to all animal matter, they are terrifically poisonous. The exhalations of persons quite healthy, but merely wretched and negligent of cleanliness, as those in prison or in very crowded poor tenements, produce typhus fever. The exhalations of persons merely wounded, produce erysipelas and hospital gangrene. The exhalations of puerperal women produce puerperal fever, so frequently and so terrifically fatal, that a lying-in hospital is nearly an impossibility. The exhalations of starving animals are particularly offensive and poisonous.

The exhalations of the sick are much more dangerous than those of the healthy. Those of persons suffering under some of the contagious diseases produce those diseases; and it is well to note that they become much more virulent by partial decay, and hence the great importance of removing promptly the remains of persons dying of contagious diseases.

(286.) *Typhus* appears mostly to originate in this way. The poor and wretched are not sufficiently aware of the importance of frequent changes of clothing and bedding, especially in cold weather. Their bedding, by being used too long without cleaning or airing, becomes saturated with their cutaneous exhalations, which by the warmth of their bodies undergo decay, rendering

them poisonous to such a degree and in such a way that they
produce typhus fever. One case originated in this way, the disease spreads rapidly by contagion. If a number of individuals
occupy the same small apartment or same bed, we may easily
comprehend that their bedding will the more rapidly be charged
with this poisonous material. Hence we see that violations of
the tonnage laws of emigrant ships, so that they are much
crowded, usually produce this terrifically destructive disease;
which is so contagious that on these occasions it is pretty sure to
destroy the lives of a number of physicians and nurses at the
quarantine hospitals. If apartments are much closed, so as not
to be freely ventilated, the exhalations are much more liable to be
concentrated to a dangerous extent; and hence typhus and other
contagious diseases prevail much more in winter than in summer,
much more in cold and temperate climates than in the tropics.
The mere airing of bedding and clothing has great power in removing and dissipating the poisonous material.

(287.) Deficient nourishment may contribute to produce, or it
may greatly aggravate, an epidemic of typhus fever. Hence
pestilence and famine are usually associated. The population of
the Cape de Verde Islands is generally in great part destroyed
about once in ten years; the destruction being sometimes attributed to pestilence derived from the neighboring coast of
Africa, and sometimes to famine. Both pestilence and famine
probably take part on every occasion, sometimes the one and
sometimes the other predominating. Formerly the occupants of
prisons were defectively nourished, partly with a view to economy,
and occasionally for the purpose of aggravating punishment.
Under these circumstances, typhus, aggravated more or less by
the scorbutic condition, prevailed terrifically in prisons; hence
called jail fever or spotted fever. The bringing of prisoners
into court for trial from these places, used to kill judges, jurymen,
and sheriffs by the dozen.

(288.) Bearing in mind these causes of the disease, we have no
difficulty in pointing out the means of prevention. Personal
cleanliness, in reference particularly to clothing and bedding, is
necessary; the beds should be separated and aired as much as
possible during the day, and only made up at night. Too many
persons should not be kept in small or defectively ventilated

apartments; and to accomplish this object it may be necessary to enact laws and enforce scrutinizing police regulations. So far as ships are concerned, the present tonnage laws, imposing severe penalties for carrying more than a prescribed number of passengers for each hundred tons capacity, if rigidly enforced, are sufficient for all ordinary voyages. But if the number of passengers be a little exceeded in the voyage from Europe, and the passage protracted a few days beyond the average, this terrific scourge is pretty sure to have its victims. On the California steamers the authorized number of passengers is habitually exceeded, without other harm than the temporary discomfort; but the time occupied in the passage is short, and all hygienic influences compatible with such crowding are assiduously used. In the city of Philadelphia, the census officers of 1860 found a district in which there were many tenements so small, so crowded, so filthy, so dark, and so poorly ventilated, that they felt it their duty to report the neighborhood as likely to become the focus of infectious disease. The Board of Health, on examination, coincided with them in this opinion, and required the houses to be closed as tenements; such of the occupants as had no better provision were transferred to the almshouse. It has since been made the duty of the police officers of each precinct to report every tenement which they may find deficient in certain specified conveniences and accommodations deemed necessary for the preservation of health. Eventually competent sanitary inspectors must relieve the police from this duty.

(289.) The present building laws of Philadelphia are doing much good by preventing the building of such places. The city of London was swept every few years by a great plague, till the immense conflagration generally referred to as the Great Fire. In 1665 occurred the last great plague, during which in nine months 69,602 persons perished of the disease; the conflagration following swept the vacant houses in the worst part of the city; and thus the authorities were enabled to lay out broader and better streets, and to have the burnt district built up in a better and more healthy shape. London has had no great epidemic of this disease since the great fire.

(290.) Quarantine regulations have probably done much more harm than good in this disease. Not that we would have persons suffering under this or any other contagious disease mingling indiscriminately with the community, but these regulations directed exclusively to one point have tended much to distract attention from much more important measures. So long as in every large city there are localities in which typhus constantly prevails, and the weekly reports of interments show deaths from it constantly, no amount of arbitrary cruelty practiced against strangers arriving in ships can possibly eradicate the disease. Let us not be misunderstood : the weekly reports of interments prove the constant prevalence of both small-pox and typhus in New York city, and yet we do not think that every person, sick or well, who attempts to pass from New York into any other city, whether by ship or by railroad, should be immediately hanged ; but this the rigid quarantine notions require.

Attention must be directed to home causes, and if this be done everywhere, the disease will be reduced to its minimum.   It may be observed that the more energetic the quarantine, and the more reliance is placed on it as a means of security, the more other and more important means are neglected, and the more constantly and more terribly do epidemics of this and other contagious diseases prevail. Some ports of the Levant are nearly without commerce on account of the excessive rigor of their quarantine regulations, and the plague continues to prevail among them almost as badly as ever. Other ports under more enlightened views have removed these absurd impediments to commerce, have become prosperous, and the plague has ceased to appear.

What is really required is, that when a person affected with dangerous contagious disease arrives, whether in a ship or in a wagon, he should be treated in the same way as a person found similarly suffering at home ; he is to be placed in a healthy place suitable for his recovery, where none will have any inducement to approach him, except such as are needed to take care of him, and where none can approach him without being warned of their danger.   His clothing and everything else likely to have been contaminated by the disease must be burnt or thoroughly disinfected.   All other disinfectants sink into insignificance in comparison with free ventilation, soap and water.   Heat, chlorine, ozone, permanganate of potassa, carbolic acid, etc., are all of them occasionally useful.

CHAPTER XXVIII.

(291.) *Typhoid fever*, the common winter fever of our country, appears to be produced in nearly the same way as typhus, and has been called *typhus mitior*, the milder typhus. It is altogether a less formidable disease, and is so little contagious that it is doubted by many whether it should be ranked with the contagious fevers at all. Certainly the contagion of typhus is not capable of producing typhoid fever, or the typhoid contagion of producing typhus. It seems curious that the same cause should produce two perfectly distinct diseases, sometimes the one and sometimes the other; but this instance is not a singular one, as we are familiar with the fact that a severe fall may cause either a broken bone or only a simple contusion. The typhoid fever is to be avoided in the same way as the typhus, except that here there is less danger of contagion to guard against. The typhoid contagion is supposed to attach particularly to fecal evacuations, and hence particular care should be exercised in regard to them.

(292.) *Erysipelas—Dissection Wounds—Hospital Gangrene—Puerperal Fever.*—Probably several distinct and rather rare diseases have been described under the name of erysipelas, or St. Anthony's fire. When in a hospital there are too many patients, it is observed that all the wounds are apt to put on an unfavorable appearance, and instead of healing they are apt to become flabby and pale or purple and to mortify; the mortification spreads rapidly up the limb and speedily terminates in the death of the patient. At the same time the most insignificant scratch will put on a serious appearance, red lines running up the limb, and redness or inflammation, with strong tendency to mortify, rapidly spreading from the seat of the injury. When this tendency is fully established the same symptoms occur without even a scratch. This is hospital gangrene and malignant erysipelas.

Dissection wounds, which arise sometimes from incautiously
handling the remains of the dead, are attended by similar symptoms. Nearly the same thing has happened from wounding the
finger with a perfectly clean cambric needle, in persons peculiarly
disposed to this kind of disease, either constitutionally or through
the influence of surrounding morbific causes.

Erysipelas sometimes prevails epidemically, in situations far
removed from hospitals and crowds of sick and wounded, and
even varies so much in symptoms as to authorize the belief that
distinct diseases are confounded under this name. In one variety
the local disease is merely redness and swelling, with some itching
or smarting of a more or less extensive surface of the skin : this is
erysipelas simplex. In another variety, with perhaps less irritation of the skin, there is a disposition to serous effusion in the
subcutaneous cellular tissue, giving rise to swelling, which readily
pits on pressure with the end of the finger : *erysipelas œdematosa.*
In a third variety the peculiarity is a strong tendency to mortification of small patches of cellular tissue, while the skin remains
comparatively sound ; each mortified spot forms an abscess, which
discharges its matter and slough through the skin : this is *erysipelas phlegmonoides.* In another variety the cuticle is raised in
little blisters, and the skin beneath rapidly mortifies : this is *malignant pustule,* or *erysipelas gangrenosa.* Like other serious diseases,
erysipelas may be accompanied by typhous prostration : it is then
erysipelas typhosa. The redness of the skin and irritation, caused
by the direct action of the sun's rays or other simple irritant, un-
attended by fever or serious constitutional derangement, is not
usually considered as erysipelas at all : it is a *simple erythema,* but
has been described as *erysipelas erythematosa.* Different from all
these is *erysipelas vera,* true erysipelas, which is a rare febrile disease, with some blended red and yellow discolorations of various
portions of the skin.

(293.) The question of *contagion,* in these forms of disease, is
of immense importance, and it is a question in which the doctors
do not always agree. We think ourselves pretty safe in the
opinion that simple erythema is not usually contagious. *Hospital gangrene* and the erysipelas usually prevailing with it are not
very contagious through the atmosphere. Attending physicians
and other persons in good health, merely visiting the sick and

spending much of the time in the open air, are in no great danger of suffering from the disease; but wounded patients are in great danger—sure to suffer—and nurses and other constant attendants are far from safe, with all the precautions possible in their case. This narrows down the question without determining positively whether the disease is contagious through the atmosphere, or endemic, attaching itself to the hospital and its accumulation of decaying morbid exhalations. The morbific power of discharges from the wounds of patients suffering under this disease is peculiarly persistent. A sponge or piece of muslin which has been used in dressing them seems never to be thoroughly disinfected till it is reduced to ashes. But as the disease is not very contagious, with reference to patients not wounded, in healthy, well-ventilated places, we may recommend that the patients be distributed, but with the utmost care that they be not brought too nearly in contact with wounded persons.

(294.) Some epidemics of erysipelas are undoubtedly contagious. We may instance the epidemic of 1842-'45, which in some parts of the country was called *black tongue;* in other parts, *big head,* etc. The disease was plainly communicated from the patient to his family and visitors, and persons infected communicated the disease to families whom they visited. Individual cases occurred in which no connection could be traced, as occurs in small-pox and all other contagious diseases.—(*Peebles.*)

(295.) *Puerperal fever,* a very fatal contagious disease, is so very intimately connected with some forms of erysipelas as to possess a fair title to be considered the same disease, merely modified by the peculiar condition of the patient. It is so exceedingly fatal and contagious that the obstetrician, having attended a patient with this disease, is obliged to abandon practice and seclude himself for a month or more; or, if he have the hardihood to continue practice, he will have his conscience burdened by the reflection that most of his patients in the puerperal condition die through his fault.—(*Holmes.*)

There is something very curious in the persistent power of this contagion as regards its capability of affecting women in the puerperal condition. The obstetrician, with all possible appliances in the way of soap and water, and changes of clothing and ventilation, is unable to rid his person of its dangerous power. The late

Prof. Chapman used to teach its indestructibility in nearly the following language :

"Some years ago it was attempted to attach a lying-in ward to the Pennsylvania Hospital, but the building was hardly occupied before the puerperal fever made its appearance, and the project was reluctantly abandoned. Some years after, when soap and water, chloride of lime, ventilation, and whitewash had done all they could do to destroy and remove the poison, it was thought safe to reoccupy the ward. But the very first woman who came there to be confined died of puerperal fever, and all further attempts to use the building for this purpose were abandoned."

(296.) The most reliable means of preventing these diseases must be inferred from the foregoing description of the circumstances under which they mostly appear. Too many patients, especially wounded, should not be permitted to occupy one hospital. In very large hospitals the wards should be considerably separated from each other, so as to admit of independent, efficient ventilation. On the first appearance of any symptom of these diseases, the patients should be separated as much as possible, and no more should be admittted. Physicians, nurses, and other attendants of such hospitals, or attending private patients with puerperal fever, especially in seasons of epidemic prevalence, should be very cautious in their visits to other persons, and especially they should not enter the house of any family in which there may reasonably be expected any special liability to any of these diseases.

Great improvements have recently been made in arrangements to prevent these diseases. Hospitals are not permitted to be crowded, but tents or sheds are scattered about the grounds. New hospitals are arranged in separate pavilions, even with single rooms independently ventilated. Even cottage hospitals, of five or six beds, have been organized in some villages, for the reception and care, at moderate cost, of strangers and the poor without proper home accommodations.

CHAPTER XXIX

"Rerum causus cognoscere."

(297.) MANY theories have been suggested to account for various epidemic, endemic, and contagious diseases, each of which appears to be correct as regards particular instances; the error common to most of them is their exclusiveness. The only common cause of all, or nearly all these diseases, is impurity, of one kind or another, operating in various ways.

(298.) The *animalcular theory* is certainly true in reference to scabies and some other diseases, but this does not prove that animalcules are the cause of all diseases, though it may afford ground for suspicion in many cases. Several instances, somewhat resembling the following, might be stated: "A short time ago, in a country district near Dresden, several persons were taken ill with rheumatic and typhoid symptoms, and one woman became gradually worse and worse, more emaciated and weaker, and at length was removed to Dresden, and placed under the care of Professor Zencker. There she died. No apparent cause was present to account for her muscular weakness and pain, her emaciation and death. But her body was dissected, and it was noticed, on examination with a microscope, that the muscular tissue, which was everywhere atrophied, was covered with minute spots. These spots were separated, and their anatomical structure proved that each spot was an encysted entozoon, known to naturalists as the *trichina spiralis*. The woman's body was full of them. Did these cause her death? How were the entozoa introduced? Virchow took a piece of the muscle, and mixing it with other food, fed rabbits with it. In five or six weeks the animals died emaciated, and on examination their muscular system was found to swarm with the same parasites. The source of the mischief was eventually traced to the flesh of a pig, which had been killed, cured, and eaten. The hams and sausage contained a large number of *trichinæ*. These experiments not only proved the animalcular origin of the disease, but that the entozoon was introduced from without; that it was introduced, like many other *helminthæ*, through the medium of meat containing living organisms, and it pointed with numerous facts of the same kind, to the necessity of exposing animal and vegetable substances to a sufficient degree of heat to destroy any organic germs which they may contain, before they are used as human food."—(*Medical and Surgical Rep.*, 1862.)

(299.) *The Cryptogamic Theory.*—It has been suggested from time to time, that many diseases are due in one way or another to cryptogamic vegetation, microscopic mushrooms, etc. Some cutaneous diseases have been found to consist, in part, of cryptogamic vegetation; but whether as a cause of the disease, or only one of the symptoms, is not determined. It may be merely a symptom of weakness and decay, like moss on the bark of old trees. The great epidemics and miasmatic fevers have been attributed to microscopic vegetation of this kind floating in the atmosphere, and insinuating itself into our organs. This, for all we know, may be true in some cases; but up to the present time no particular disease has been definitely connected with any particular species of organism in the atmosphere, except possibly, the case of measles caused by musty straw; though the microscope has revealed that the atmosphere, at all times and in all places, is filled with various species of organic germs, which, under favorable circumstances, may be developed into distinct vegetation. It is impossible, in the present state of our knowledge, to determine to what extent variations in the character of this organic dust may be the cause of disease; but we should certainly make a great mistake if we should consider them as the only or even the principal cause.—(*Mitchell.*)

(300.) There is another way in which cryptogamic vegetation has caused epidemics. Various plants, cryptogamic and others, are poisonous; and if these from any cause should enter largely into the food of people at any particular time, they will probably cause an epidemic disease. The grain of rye is subject to a curious fungous growth, called ergot, which, entering largely into food, has caused, in Europe, terrible epidemics of dry gangrene. Persons inhaling the dust of musty straw have been affected with a disease resembling measles.—(*Salisbury.*)

The endemic called milk sickness, staggers, in some of the new settlements, is caused by the cow, deer, and perhaps other animals eating the leaves of *Rhus toxicodendron*, for want of better food.

(301.) *The zymotic theory* ($\zeta v \mu o \omega$, to ferment), like the preceding, has two branches. It has been suggested that many of the contagious and epidemic diseases occurring but once to the same individual, they might be explained by supposing that in our organization we have among our fluids some material capable of change in the presence of its appropriate ferment, as sugar is changed by fermentation in the juice of fruits; and this material having once undergone the fermentative process, we are necessarily exempt from a second action of the same kind. This at present is a mere hypothesis, explaining nothing, and with all probability against it. There is not a particle of evidence of the existence of any such element in all the anatomical and chemical examinations to which our solids and fluids have been subjected; but, on the contrary, it seems that all the material of our bodies is being removed and replaced through the agency of nutrition, so that such fermentative process once set up, with the constant renewal of material, could only cease with the life of the individual.

There is another zymotic theory, more important to our present purpose, and which, whether true or false, requires our attentive consideration. The earth, the air, and the water of densely inhabited places are charged with human and animal excrements and remains, and vegetable matter in process of decay. This decay is influenced by various circumstances of heat, moisture, electricity, ferments, etc., and gives rise to various poisonous materials, gaseous, liquid, and solid. When these things are allowed to accumulate to a great degree under certain conditions of warmth and moisture, disease certainly results quite independently of any imported contagion, or any foreign source of evil. But may not a vessel, arriving with yellow fever, bring into the locality its peculiar ferment, capable of starting a fermentation which shall result in the establishment of yellow fever, rather than some other disease which would otherwise result? There are many facts which would lead us to adopt the affirmative side of this question, though none of them are absolutely conclusive. Epidemics of this disease have generally been attributed to the arrival of a particular ship, though it is certain that this disease is not contagious. This we say is not conclusive, for ships arrive every day ; and we may generally have our choice of half a dozen vessels which have arrived on any day which may be found to coincide with the first appearance of the epidemic.

Just now this subject is being studied with great earnestness, and every *amœba* and amœboid, monad, bacterium, and vibrion, micrococcus, cryptococcus, and sporangium, is having a thousand microscopes pointed at his suspicious little body, and a thousand critic's eyes ; and even in the navy, every ship is supplied with a microscope and other appliances to hunt out the little mischiefs—*omnibus ab oris maribusque.* This earnestness is really called for by the great importance of the subject, and by the important results already realized. A few years ago measly pork was supposed to be unhealthy, but how or why nobody knew ; it is now well known, by the study of natural history under the microscope, that each of the specks is a young tapeworm, ready to punish the man, or dog, or cat, that ventures to eat pork. More recently Professor Leidy saw under the microscope some curious unknown objects in human muscles : the microscopes were pointed at the unknown ; they were found in various animals ; the natural history of *trichina spiralis* was studied ; the Hetstädt tragedy (§ 276), made known the cause and the ready means of preventing the awful sausage poison, which had been the terror of Germany and one of the pests of the world for centuries. The workers in this business are driven by an irresistible impulse to see and to know : besides their time, they spend their hardearned money for microscopes and expensive accessories : they do all this without expectation of other reward than the consciousness of helping in the work, and they are well paid. There have been counted a hundred and sixty-one (161) trichinæ in one grain of pig's flesh, so that a person eating an ounce of sausage might swallow 70,437 of them. In searching for the cause of typhoid fever, objects have been seen estimated to measure the fifty-thousandth ($\frac{1}{50000}$) of an inch ; whether this is the cause, or this its measurement, we do not know, but probably we shall know. The outbreak at Lausen, Switzerland (*Nature*, Apl. 6, 1876), requires that the infective germs be as small as this. Three cases of typhoid occur at a farmhouse, a mile distant, on the opposite side of a mountain ridge; the dejections of the patients are thrown into a brook, which irrigates a meadow and flows off in another direction. The inhabitants of Lausen, using the water of a certain spring, suffer in large proportion (130 cases, 170 per 1000); those having private wells escape entirely. Two thousand (2000) pounds of salt thrown into the brook produce a rapid increase of chlorine in the spring, thus proving the connection. Fifty-six hundred (5600) pounds of flour are mixed with the water of the brook, and no trace of it can be found in the spring. This spring must have an underground channel from the field. The salt filters through the porous soil into the channel. The soil is close enough to stop the starch-granules of wheat, but it is not close enough to stop the typhoid infection. Hence the fair inference that typhoid germs are smaller than starch-granules. But we need not be very positive that there are any germs in the case. There are soluble poisons in existence, and they cause some diseases, and there are living organisms that cause others.

(302.) We find by observation, not only among animals, but even in the inorganic world, the tendency is for things to produce their own likeness. Thus fire in contact with suitable material produces fire, and there are many other well-known though less familiar changes which take place in the chemical constitution of bodies indicated by the term *catalysis*. We classify many facts and lose nothing by allowing that epidemics may sometimes originate in this way. The accumulation of excretions and filth to be converted into pestilence having been allowed to occur, we infer the probability of an epidemic, whether typhus or dysentery, cholera or measles, small-pox or diphtheria, is not determined. But, as a spark starts the conflagration, some apparently trivial circumstance determines this matter. Whether this comes about by animalcular generation, or cryptogamic vegetation, or by some sort of catalysis more or less analogous to combustion, we do not know in all cases, and perhaps we shall never be allowed to know. We do know, however, what is infinitely more important to us, that it could not have occurred in either way, if the dirt had not been allowed to accumulate.

(303.) These considerations enable us to form a proper estimate of some of the police regulations for the preservation of health. The most important of all is the seasonable removal of dangerous dirt, decomposing organic material. But as purity in this respect is not absolute, something more is occasionally necessary. In the latter part of summer, when domestic filth is particularly prone to decomposition, a vessel with yellow fever cases on board should not be brought to a wharf in the midst of a dense population; but it is in every way advantageous to remove the passengers and the sick from the vessel, subjecting them to such restraints as are necessary for their comfort and care. There appears to be no harm in discharging the vessel into warehouses at some distance from the city, under the direction of competent inspectors. With typhus, small-pox, and syphilis, the practice should be different. We must not countenance the notion that these diseases can be absolutely excluded from a city by any regulation, however strict. People are constantly dying of these diseases in every large city, so that the contagious germ is always near—always present. But the sufferers, whether arriving on a railroad or found in a secluded alley, should be promptly removed to healthy situations, and the community should be protected from too near individual contact with them. I have known a person to lose his life by going into a barber shop to have his hair trimmed and meeting there a person who had recently recovered from small-pox. We want protection from contagious diseases in barber shops, in hackney coaches, and in railway carriages.

CHAPTER XXX.

(304.) SEPTEMBER 21ST.—We arrived on the coast of Suri-
nam, Dutch Guiana, and had a view of the trees at the distance
of a mile for a few hours, till a boat visited the shore and returned. We made a similar visit to French Guiana. Our next
stopping-place was south of the equator,—Maranham, Brazil.
The principal, perhaps the only white people, were a retired slave-
trader from Kentucky and his family. The rest of the inhabitants are a mongrel set of Indians, Negroes, and Portuguese. If
Maranham is not subject to severe epidemics of yellow fever, it
must be for want of material,—white people and unacclimated
strangers; for, though well situated on a handsome bluff, it is a
badly policed, unclean town, in a tropical climate. It is a small
place, almost rural.

(305.) On the homeward passage we spent a week on the direct
line between Fernando Noronha and Bermuda, and although
this is the great route for vessels homeward bound from nearly
all parts of the world, except Europe and North Africa, we did
not see a single vessel of any description; there was only sky
and sea.

(306.) In the latitude of Cape Hatteras, in a storm, we had a
startling accident: the outboard ejection was broken off. This
is a cast-iron tube, leading to an opening, 18 inches by 30, in the
outside planking below the water. Two minutes lost and the
ship would have gone down in mid-ocean. The firemen seem to
be always ready; boards, blocks, ropes, and wedges were in place
as if by enchantment, so that this part of the machinery was
effectually kept in place. As many men as could get into the
narrow space were stationed there during the rest of the passage,

one or two to hold blocks and wedges, while another was busy
with a sledge, driving them back into their places as fast as they
worked loose. One man lay on the top of the boiler, invisible
except his hands and wedges, and could not be coaxed out till
our arrival in New York.

(307.) The medical history of this cruise was not eventful; as
dull as the history of a country without either war or famine:

Average number of men,	. .	. . 299
Number of days in commission, .	.	. 438
Whole number of patients treated,	.	. 582

Or 1.622 per thousand per annum; so that on the average each
man was on the sick-list once in (7½) seven and a half months.

Returned to duty, ...	573
Transferred to hospitals, 7; sent home, invalids, 2; total, 9;	
equal to 25.1 per thousand sent to hospitals.	
Deaths, ...	none.

The only remarkable thing about these figures is the large
number of admissions to the sick-list without any serious disease.

(308.) In conclusion, we must discuss the subject of *discipline*,
not with any idea of exhausting our subject, but because this is
one of the constantly present forces whose influence on health is
often little thought of. It is difficult to estimate it at its proper
value; it has never been overestimated. Correct discipline, enforced by constant attention to faults, so that they rarely escape
notice, and such reproof and moderate punishments as do not
greatly degrade or reduce to despair, together with a consistent
example of Christian kindness and forbearance, with such as are
reasonably conscious of their faults, are the principal means of
doing good in this direction. Mr. Dana, author of *Three Years
before the Mast*, is one of the principal benefactors of seamen.
Congress, by abolishing the punishment of flogging, has done
more to improve the health and character of seamen than by any
other act of legislation. The enormity of this outrageous bar-
barity, which continued in considerable vigor up to the middle
of the nineteenth century, could hardly be believed without the

evidence of official records; but this evidence exists in the returns of punishments on file in the Navy Department and in the old log-books. This barbarism was swept away by act of Congress in 1850, and the transition to a better system has been more rapid and attended with less confusion than could readily have been imagined. Some officers seemed to think that all lawful means of discipline were done away with among these degraded men, and in their efforts to discover punishments, according to the usages of the sea-service, not prohibited by law, and in some degree corresponding to their notions of necessary severity, they reinvented some of the obsolete tortures of the Middle Ages,—the drunkard's jacket, the wooden horse, etc. But these things were never common, and have nearly passed into oblivion.

In the Blue Book of 1876, we find the following order: "Cells for the confinement of prisoners, are not to be less than $6\frac{1}{2}$ feet long and $3\frac{1}{2}$ feet broad, with full height [seven feet] between decks, and are to be properly ventilated." This is 22.75 square feet ($2m^2$, 1044) of floor surface, and 160 cubic feet ($4m^3$, 48) of air space. It would not seem proper to appropriate more space for this exclusive purpose aboard ships in regular commission; it is about four times the size of the previously authorized cells, which were not much used except for ornament or for the wardrobe of the master-at-arms. These cells are to be "*properly ventilated.*" I have had some opportunities of observing what was considered proper ventilation; and I will relate a case, omitting names and dates merely to avoid suspicion of willingness to indulge in personal criticism. One fine morning I received at the hospital a patient who came in charge of a strong guard, with the usual hospital ticket, and a private message, intimating that the man was serving out a court-martial sentence, and it was important that he should not be allowed to escape; he was anæmic, bleached nearly to death, could scarcely stand up a moment without fainting. He rapidly recovered, declaring his three hours a day running in the garden, the very best medicine he had ever heard of. But the man is a convict, and something else must be done, or he goes back to serve out the rest of his sentence. My first visit was to the surgeon, under whose care the patient first came, to see how the land lay without exciting attention. The prison is a hulk, not fit to confine prisoners for any long period; but there are prisoners sentenced to various terms, one of them as much as five years. About a year ago a commission found it unfit for a prison and recommended it to be broken up. Everything about it is neatly kept by a colonel of marines in command, a courteous gentleman, but it is killing the men— *delenda est.* A copy of the report of the commission was found; it merely stated that the hulk is unsuitable for a prison, and recommended that it be discontinued. A visit to the commandant of the station supplied important information. The care of such prisoners is troublesome; they were transferred to the ship from a worse place. A commission had recommended a change, but nothing better was suggested, and nothing came of it. A visit to the colonel in command was satisfactory. It included an invitation to inspect the cells. Immediately below the spar-deck are the cells; a corridor (5) five feet wide runs lengthways through the centre; on each side are the cells, about ten on each side, (12) twelve feet square and (8) eight feet high. There is a narrow passageway between the back of the cells and the side of the ship. The door of each cell has a grated opening for ventilation (24 by 18 inches), three square feet area, and there is a similar ventilation aperture back of the cell, just opposite a circular air-port (7) seven inches in diameter. There are about six prisoners, and the place is scrupulously neat. It would not do to stop here, or the abomination would stand forever. Prisoners are perverse fellows, and have confederates outside. To prevent improper communications, it was necessary to obstruct entrances to the side passages. The openings opposite the air-ports were occasionally closed to prevent communication by boats. Some of the grated openings in the doors had to be made closer, especially for prisoners sentenced to a diet of bread and water. Two or three of the doors had boards nailed tight over the ventilation apertures, and auger-holes bored for ventilation; in one of the doors, probably the worst one, I counted (17) seventeen auger-holes, ($\frac{3}{8}$) three-eighths of an inch in diameter. This was inspection enough. A commission had already recommended the discontinuance of this prison, in language so tame that the report rested quietly in its pigeon-hole. Another style of report must be written. The general good order is commended without superfluous words. The gradual obstruction of ventilation, with its causes, was alluded to, on the berth-deck of a ship—about as well ventilated as a good cellar at best; the aggregate area of the 17 holes, $\frac{3}{8}$ inch, was carefully computed, and found to equal one hole of (2.38) two inches and thirty-eight hundredths, about the ordinary size of the bung-hole of a barrel. The idea of a man in a barrel, and receiving his allowance of air and light through the bung-hole, carried the day. The prison was discontinued in the course of a week, preliminary orders having arrived by return of mail. So far as the navy is concerned, where these sentences are very few, and can only be adjudged for offences punishable with death, this incident is not worth recording; but in the United States there are more than (1000) one thousand county prisons, some of them no better than they should be. This incident shows to what the best of them tend, even when managed by courteous and estimable gentlemen, when there is no efficient system of independent inspection. *Proper ventilation* is apt to mean a hole in the door or in the wall, without reference to the fact that the whole arrangement is in a poorly ventilated building.

With a very full share of sea-service, it is curious that I have never seen any of the horrible tortures that have been described as the necessary consequence of the abolition of flogging. The difficulty seemed absolutely irremediable to an officer who had grown up under the notion that disorders are to be suppressed only by punishment. As for imprisonment, the ship at sea is a close enough prison. Additional pain might be inflicted by flogging; confinement in a cell was only a relief from rough hard labor, unless smothering or starvation could be added; confinement in irons was no punishment at all, unless so arranged as to impose a painful attitude—it was only punishing the other men who had to do the work. On rare occasions these tortures have been inflicted; and I accidentally learned of a characteristic series of them. A number of men were to be tried for desertion, and some annoying busybody put it into their heads to ask me to defend them. I learned from the commandant that the men had been punished about enough already, but if I would accede to their wishes, they would probably go into the trial more cheerfully, do better, and give less trouble. The private statements of these men coincide in all important particulars. The following is selected as being the most graphic.

" You left the boat, of course, and they will be likely to prove it, but you have an excuse; tell me all about it."

" I did leave; I have done wrong, try to do right, and hope that I have succeeded so far as to have the good opinion of the officers and men that know me.   I left on account of the terrible system of punishment; have no fault to find with my own treatment, but could not help seeing terrible punishments inflicted, not for crimes only, but for all sorts of petty offences. Solitary confinement on bread and water was a common punishment; it meant being locked up in a dark closet with a bucket.   This unpainted wooden bucket is emptied every evening when hammocks are piped, and it smells in hot weather like anything.   It is a nuisance, not only to the prisoner, but to all the men sleeping near the cells.   The cells are thirty inches square, the door without any opening for ventilation except a crack at the top.   A man fainted in one of these cells, and they had to carry him to the windsail and sprinkle him with water before he revived.   The punishment of ' confinement in double irons,' is to have regular irons on the legs, and the hands ironed behind, and fastened to a chain three feet long hanging from a beam above; this chain is long enough for a man to stand at ease, and when he gets tired of that he can turn around till his chain gets twisted, and then he can go around the other way; but the men get too tired of it for anything, and so they lean forward and hang by the hands. They sometimes go to sleep hanging in this way.   Sometimes the irons make the wrists a little sore, but they are pretty smooth, and do not fit so close but that the prisoners get bits of rag between, and thus save their arms a little.   Sometimes they try to stand up so long that they get to sleep standing, and then they are liable to fall suddenly, so as to hurt themselves by coming up with a jerk on the chain.   Tricing up was a lighter punishment, in which men were tied up alongside of the reel.   These punishments, though terrible to look at, need not frighten a correct man if they were only inflicted for serious offences.   The terrible thing is, that they are inflicted for the smallest breach of discipline,— occasional awkwardness at work, want of smartness at learning, and such other things as no man whatever can be sure of escaping. I have known a man to be confined in a cell on bread and water for awkwardness and stupidity in handling his musket.   But the worst things are not called punishment at all. Early in the cruise the men were dissatisfied and tried to run (desert). After they were punished for attempts of this kind, they were secured every evening for safe-keeping. They were ironed in a row by the feet to eye-bolts and shot-racks. The most celebrated of these runners was a chap I think his name was Humphreys. One evening at chaining-up time he could not be found; no matter how much they called he did not come. He was found and secured on the spot, not a pleasant place, and left there for five days. The next time Colty was missed he was not so easily found. The boatswain's mates had a noisy time, whistling and calling, ' Colty Matthews! Do you hear, there, Colty Matthews?' This lasted till near midnight, and the men in their hammocks wished all the colts and all the boatswains in the warm place. Matthews had found a box in a dark corner under the heel of the bowsprit, filled with wash-deck gear, and when the concert came off he was sleeping so soundly that he did not hear it at all, or more likely he was peeping behind the squilgees and laughing all the time. Towards morning a noise was heard like the grating of holy-stones, and he was found sleeping very comfortably. I never heard that anybody had the heart to wake him. But in the morning he was reported, the squilgees were cleared out, he was put back in the box and a lid was nailed on. The lid had a round hole near the corner, large enough to pass a tin-cup. When he got out he was as much inclined to run as ever; he left and returned no more. Alas, poor Colty! I have told this in a laughing way, but it was no joke for the man nailed up in the box. The officers never spoke of the men as horses or colts, and the boatswains did not sing out for Colty Matthews, but I suppose used his first name; do not remember his name; do not know whether the captain ever knew of the man being nailed up in the box; do not know whether the executive officer ever saw it; do not know who nailed on the lid. The box was four or five feet long, nearly two feet high. Do not know who ordered it nailed down, or who nailed it down; but I saw the man in it. I think there was something wrong in the way of examining offences. Punishment was common enough, but it was not common to see the captain examining cases at the mast, the accused facing the witnesses; have seen it, but it was not the common way.

Things were reported by the master-at-arms or the ship's corporal and nobody else called; and maybe they suggested the punishments, particularly those with a spice of wit or nastiness. They must have thought it a good joke when Matthews was nailed up in his box. The ship has always been a hard ship. In the beginning we had a good crew: there were 1500 men on the receiving-ship when we fitted out, so that there were plenty to choose from. If they could not choose they had to take them as they came, so that there must have been a pretty fair average. There were some very good men, and some very bad. Yes, I must tell about myself. Was never much punished; was captain of the mizzen-top; something went wrong, and we were called lubbers; the men did not like it and found fault with me, so I went down and asked to be disrated; did not know how soon my time might come to be punished for some fault that I could not possibly avoid, and I felt very badly. So when the ship was going to sail, I staid ashore and hid till I had a chance to go aboard the other ship; was kept in double irons about a week; have been on duty ever since, mostly in a boat; have never been punished since. I hope the court will be lenient with me."

The reader who has become interested in the above narrative should know some additional particulars. The narrator was aided and encouraged by a steady fire of leading questions. On his trial he received an excellent character; no one was able to specify an offence for which he had been punished; he was the smartest man they had ever seen aloft. He was defended in a two-minute speech showing how he hated to be called a lubber, and ignoring conclusive evidence of guilt, the court acquitted him. The other men were found guilty and sentenced, but the revising officer, keeping his word to consider them punished enough, the findings and sentences were formally approved, but in consideration of previous good character, or subsequent good conduct, or that they had already been punished—in consideration of something good or something bad, the punishment was remitted. John Matthews, Colty, was nailed up for five days in a box, four feet long, three feet wide, and two feet high, notched on one side to fit under the heel of the bowsprit. One man lived fifteen consecutive days in a sweat-box. The officers principally responsible for these outrages were eventually tried by court-martial, convicted, sentenced, and punished, and one of them is believed to have ended his unhappy career by suicide.

It has been asked, What has this matter of discipline and punishments to do with your business of care for the sick? There really are men so constituted that it appears necessary to answer very plainly this question.

(309.) Clergymen, lawyers and physicians, judges, juries and magistrates, philanthropists, philosophers and essayists, the thinking part of mankind, are now divided into two great parties by their differences of opinion as to the best way to treat the degraded, the imbecile, and the criminal. These parties may be called the reward party and the punishment party. The *punishment party* should come first, being the most ancient. It cites Divine authority; offences must be adequately punished. If you reward the criminal and the worthless, you compel the poor man to become criminal, so that by hypocrisy he may come in for some of the good things going. The *reward party*, which probably includes nearly all the physicians, take a different view of the matter. The poor man, whether criminal or not, whether aboard ship or in prison, when obliged to do the roughest and hardest work, and to live on the cheapest food capable of maintaining health and strength, is in a position where not much more in the way of punishment can be inflicted without impairing his strength to labor; you may flog him, but this degradation impresses him in such a way that he rarely gets over the vilification so far as to be of any value for labor; you may confine him in a painful position, but his limbs so stiffen under this treatment that his labor is very much lessened in value; you may starve or smother him, but this does not mend the matter; you may hang him, and if a constitutional murderer, this is perhaps the very best thing to do with him, for otherwise he is likely to be pardoned and permitted to commit more murders. When a man is in prison on prison fare, there is not much more of physical punishment available without destroying his health and ability to labor; and when we consider the facility of the step of petty larceny, for instance, or shipping to relieve pressing want, the strength of these young men may be worth preserving. The undertaking is by no means a desperate one. All men, and some beasts, are greatly influenced by their consciousness of what is thought of them, their love of approbation. We have seen on a previous page that men were vexed and punished by being called lubbers. This is a good and legitimate punishment, but it should not be spoiled by being made too common, and, applied to a large party of men, may reach some one who does not deserve it ; " Very well done on the main-yard," might have done as well, particularly if the men on the main-yard deserved it, for men will really work harder to gain praise than they will to avoid censure, but the officer in charge of the work is the proper judge of this, and perhaps he could not see any work deserving praise at that particular time.

In the navy, the reward party is likely to carry the day. Formerly by law all serious offences were punishable with " death, or such other punishment as a court-martial shall adjudge," but in practice nearly everything, from spitting on the deck to murder, was punished by flogging ; more anciently it was keel-hauling, throwing the man overboard and pulling him up again before he was quite drowned. We now have a Blue Book of regulations, in which the section on rewards is half as long as the section on punishments, and better still, while the punishments are awarded for specific offences, some of the rewards accrue from the mere absence of punishment or of black-mark reports. It is a rather elaborate system, requiring some keeping of books, but it embraces every enlisted man, and is producing most admirable results.

There is no occasion to misunderstand this matter. The rewards, in the ordinary sense, are not rewards at all. When a man does his work well it is hardly a reward to tell him so. When he receives better pay for better work, it is only fair compensation. When honorably discharged, a bargain is made with him that he may reship on better terms than a stranger just from the penitentiary. When he is allowed a portion of his pay at stated periods to meet his little wants, he is treated with some little show of decency and justice. When a fair record of his conduct is kept, so as to distinguish the good man from the indifferent and bad, we are only making a decent effort to give him reasonable credit for what he is worth. But these are the rewards of which we think so much ; for they produce good order, good health, and good work. The punishments are mostly of a very different character, such as death, imprisonment for life, or for a

term of years at hard labor, fine and imprisonment, imprisonment with or without irons, solitary confinement on bread and
water.   We have, however, advanced so far in the right direction, that some of the punishments are merely withdrawing or
withholding of the rewards, reduction to the next inferior rating
with corresponding loss of pay, deprivation of liberty on shore,
the withholding of liberty-money, praising the other fellows.

One thing more is needed : the statistics of punishment should
be studied where the records are kept; and annually there
should be published, for the information of Congress, a statistical
report showing the number of punishments in each squadron,
for each description of offence, the number per thousand of mean
force, etc.   Such reports would surely show us the effect of each
act of legislation, and of each description of reward and punishment; and they would thus greatly aid in removing disorders of
the criminal character.   Both offences and punishments would
diminish still more rapidly.

APPENDIX.

(310.) THE confusion that exists on this subject is curious. Anciently every city had its own *yardstick*, differing somewhat from the yardstick of its neighbors; in modern times one of them was selected to be *the yardstick*, and an exact copy of it was made and deposited in the Tower of London: this curious piece of platinum is the standard of reference for all our weights and measures. The carpenter's measuring-rule, about as long as his foot, is the third of the yard; it is divided into twelve inches, and these are our measures of length. To avoid the confusion that must occur if the standard measure be lost, a pendulum beating seconds, mean time, in the latitude of London, in a vacuum, at the level of the sea, was measured and found to be 39.1393 inches, or 1.087175 yards.

MEASURES OF LENGTH AND SURFACE.

I. *Cloth Measure.*

One yard, yard = 36 inches, is simply divided into halves, quarters, and eighths. Formerly the arrangement was:

2¼ inches make . .	.	. 1 nail,
4 nails, . . .	.	. 1 quarter,
4 quarters, . . .	.	. 1 yard,
3 quarters, . . .	.	. 1 ell Flemish.
5 quarters, . . .	.	. 1 ell English.

II. *Timber Measure.*

1 foot = 12 inches = 144 lines = 1728 seconds. The duo-decimal subdivision continuing indefinitely is used for surface and cubic measurements and computations. Formerly 3 barley-corns made 1 inch, etc.

III. Road Measure.

1 mile = 8 furlongs = 320 rods = 1760 yards.
1 furlong 　　　　　 = 40 rods = 220 yards.
1 rod, pole, or perch = 5.5 yards = 16.5 feet.

IV. Land Measure.

1 acre 　 = 4 roods = 160 perches = 4840 square yards.
1 perch = 　　　　 30.25 sq. yd. = 272.25 square feet.

MEASURES OF WEIGHT.

(311.) In this work several kinds of weight are used, and occasionally in such a way as to leave the careful reader in doubt as to the particular weight intended. For instance (§ 144), we read that two seamen, being informed that the Cape toad-fish is poisonous, determined to try the experiment on themselves, and ate part of one fish, weighing four drachms. 4 drachms avoirdupois is = $109\frac{3}{4}$ troy grains, and 4 drachms troy is = 240 grains; in strictness we should conclude that the quantity was $109\frac{3}{4}$ grains, though the writer probably meant 240 grains; but in this case the confusion of weights is not important, as the fools were both dead in less than twenty minutes.

Our standard of weight is a *troy pound*, deposited with the yardstick in the Tower of London. One cubic inch of distilled water, at 62° F., and 30 inches bar., weighs 252.458 grains.

V. Avoirdupois Weight.

1 pound, 1 ℔ = 16 ounces 　= 7000 grains.
1 ounce, 1 oz. = 16 drachms = $437\frac{1}{2}$ grains.

VI. Apothecaries Weight.

1 pound, 　　℔j = 12 troy ounces = 5760 grains.
1 troy ounce, ℥j = 8 drachms 　　 = 480 grains.
1 drachm, 　　ʒj = 3 scruples 　　 = 60 grains.
1 scruple, 　　℈j = 　　　　　　 = 20 grains.
1 grain, 　　gr. j = 　　　　　 = $\frac{1}{5760}$ pound.

The United States Pharmacopœia uses the troy ounce, 480 grains to the ounce; the British Pharmacopœia uses avoirdupois pounds and ounces, $437\frac{1}{2}$ grains to the ounce.

MEASURES OF CAPACITY.

VII. Liquid Measures of the United States Pharmacopœia.

One minim,	♏j = .9369 grains.
One fluid drachm,	f℥j = 60 minims.
One fluid ounce,	f℥j = 8 fluid drachms.
One pint (octans),	Oj = 16 fluid ounces.
One gallon (congius),	Congi = 8 pints.

One pint of distilled water at 60° F., 30 in. bar., weighs 7291.1109 grains.

VIII. Liquid Measure of the British Pharmacopœia.

1 minim	= .91146 grain.
1 fluid drachm = 60 minims	= 54.6875 grains.
1 fluid ounce = 8 fluid drachms	= 437.5 grains.
1 pint = 20 fluid ounces	= 8750 grains.
1 gallon = 8 pints	= 70,000 grains.

One gallon of distilled water at 62° F., 30 inches barometer, weighs 70,000 grains.

IX. Liquid Measures of the U. S. P., compared with other measures of capacity, and the weight in grains of water at 60° F.

United States Pharmacopœia.	Cubic inches.	Cubic foot = 1728 cubic inches.	Fluid ounces, B.P. = 1.73296 cubic inches.	Pints, B.P. = 34.6592 cubic inches.	Gallons, B. P. = 277.27384 cubic inches.	Weight of water in grains.
Gallon, . . .	231	0.1337	133.2980	6.6649	0.83311	58,328.8872
Pint, . . .	28.875	0.0167	16.66225	0.8331	0.10414	7,291.1109
Fluid ounce, .	1.80469	0.00104	1.04146	0.0521	0.00651	455.6944
Fluid drachm,	0.22559	0.00013	0.13016	0.0065	0.00081	56.2118
Minim, . . .	0.00375	0.00002	0.00217	0.0001	0.00014	0.9369

1 cubic foot = 7.4805 gallons = 59.6442 pints.
1 gallon B. P. = 1.20328 gallon.
1 fluid ounce B. P. = .96025 fluid ounce.

The foregoing are some of the weights and measures in common use in the United States and in Great Britain. It is necessary to understand all of them if we would read intelligently common books of science in our own language. To understand common market reports of the prices, etc., of commodities, we must understand some more. They are gradually undergoing modification; the unreasonable subdivisions are omitted, and in

the market-place binary fractions—halves, fourths, and eighths—
are substituted. In works of science the decimal fractions are
used, as being more in accordance with our system of decimal
arithmetic. But this is a slow process, that brings us no nearer
to any international standard, and it does not satisfy men conscious that much valuable time is wasted over the needless complications. In France, during the first republic, an effort was
made to correct this, together with all other absurdities, as they
were supposed, of the social condition. It was not thought
philosophical to take for the standard of measures either the
length of the cloth-merchant's arms or his measuring-stick, or
the length of the carpenter's foot or of his foot-rule; but the
forty-millionth part of the circumference of the earth, measured
over the poles, might answer; to be consistent, it should be the
hundred-millionth. This starting-point is called a meter (μετρον,
a measure, a meter); and it is found to be a little longer than
the English yardstick, or even the seconds pendulum. It had
been observed that the Chinese use a system of decimal subdivisions in their weights and measures, corresponding with the
system of decimal arithmetic, and it was thought right to learn
reason and common sense even from the heathen; hence we have
the French metrical system.

(312.) It seems quite impossible for us to realize the immense
advantages we enjoy from the fact that, in every known country
of the world, the system of numeration is the same. This system
happens to be decimal. Whatever is written or spoken in any
language in reference to numbers is decimal. As far as history
goes no other system is known, except as a matter of philosophical
speculation. The ethnological inference, however, is that other
systems have been in use. The inhabitants of Northwest Mexico,
according to Clavigero, counted regularly up to four, the number
of fingers on one hand, and then they counted four and one, four
and two, etc. The islanders of the Pacific counted up to five, and
then said five and one, five and two, etc., including the thumb,
to make their full number; or, possibly, they counted by the toes.
The people of Central and Southern Asia must have counted all
the fingers of both hands, including the thumbs, to get their complete number, and then they counted ten and one, ten and two,
etc.: this is the decimal system that colonists carried to Greece,

and Italy, and Spain. The emigrants from Central Asia, moving north and west, perhaps had frequent occasion to place their fingers and toes near together to keep them warm, and they counted them all up to twenty for a complete number, and then went on counting twenty and one, twenty and two, etc.; and we find a remnant of this vigesimal system in the present French four-twenties, four twenties and one, etc.; and in English literature, two scores and five, three scores, etc., now about obsolete. But this is a very primitive condition of the science of numbers, which even the crow is imagined in some degree to possess, when it is insisted that he can count as high as three, the number of toes on the front of his foot.

The decimal system of numbering has become universal, probably from the habits of the Arabs sitting on the floor and counting their toes when they invented arithmetic and algebra. If they had worn shoes and counted on their fingers, we might have had an octaval system of numerals, corresponding with the halves, quarters, and eighths, into which the trader naturally arranges his merchandise. I would favor in any rational way the reformation of this whole subject, so as to have an octaval system of numbers, octaval subdivisions of weights and measures. It might be a good thing to start the matter by an octaval system of weights and measures and coinage, leaving the arithmetic to follow. But we need not seriously object to the rising of the sun, and so we proceed to accommodate our work to coming events. To facilitate necessary computations the following tables are added.

X. *Metrical Measures of Length, compared with the Measures in most Common Use in the United States.*

Metrical.	Inches.	Feet of 12 inches.	Yards of 36 inches.	Miles of 1760 yards.
Millimeter, . .	0.03937	0.0032809	0.0010936	0.0000006
Centimeter, . .	0.39371	0.0328090	0.0109363	0.0000062
Decimeter, . .	3.93708	0.3280899	0.1093633	0.0000621
Meter, ...	39.37079	3.2808992	1.0936331	0.0006214
Kilometer, . .	39,370.790	3,280.89920	1093.63310	0.6213824

1 inch = 2 centimeters .539954.   1 yard = 0 meter .914384.
1 foot = 3 decimeters .047945.   1 mile = 1 kilometer .609315.

XI. *Measures of Surface.*

Metrical.	Square feet of 144 sq. inches.	Square yards of 9 sq. feet.	Acres of 4840 sq. yds.
Centiare, square meter, ...	10.76423	1.1960	0.000247
Are, 100 square meters, . . .	1076.4299	11.9603	0.024711
Hectare. 100 are, ...	107,642.99	1,196.033	2.471143

1 sq. inch = 6 centimeters .451367.   1 sq. yard = 0 meter .836097.
1 sq. foot = 9 decimeters .289968.   1 acre = 0 hectare .404671.

XII. Measures of Capacity.

METRICAL.	Cubic inches.	Cubic feet of 1728 cubic inches.	Fluid ounces of 1.80469 cubic inches.	Pints, U.S.P., of 28.875 cubic inches.	Gallons, U.S.P., of 231 cubic inches.	Bushels of 2218.19 cubic inches.	Pints, dry measure, = 7.64 bushel.
Milliliter, cubic centimeter,	0.06103	0.000035	0.0339	0.0021	0.00026	0.0000275	0.00176
Centiliter,	0.61027	0.000353	0.3390	0.0212	0.00265	0.0002751	0.01761
Deciliter,	6.10271	0.003532	3.3899	0.2119	0.02648	0.0027512	0.17608
Liter, cubic decimeter,	61.02705	0.035317	33.8992	2.1187	0.26484	0.0275121	1.76077
Kiloliter, stere, cubic meter,	61027.052	35.316581	33899.20	2118.720	264.840	27.12846	1760.77341

1 minim = 0 milliliter .062.
16.231 minims = 1 milliliter.
1 fluid drachm = 3 milliliters .697.
2.705 fluid drachms = 1 centiliter.

1 fluid ounce = 2 centiliters .957.
1 pint = 4 deciliters .732.
1 gallon = 3 liters .785.
1 pint dry measure = 5 deciliters .679.

1 cubic inch = 16 milliliters .3862.
1 cubic foot = 28 liters .3153.
1 bushel = 5 deciliters .6791.

XIII. Measures of Weight.

Metrical.	Grains.	Troy ounces of 480 grains.	Avoirdupois ounces of 437½ grains.	Avoirdupois pounds of 7000 grains.
Milligram, ...	0.01543	0.000032	0.000035	0.000002
Centigram, ...	0.15432	0.000322	0.000353	0.000022
Decigram, ...	1.54323	0.003215	0.003527	0.000221
Gram, ...	15.43235	0.032151	0.035274	0.002205
Kilogram, ...	15432.3488	32.150727	35.273941	2.204621

1 grain = 0 gram .064799.

1 ounce avoirdupois = 28 grams .3496.

1 troy ounce = 31 grams .103496.

1 pound avoirdupois = 0 kilogram .453593.

1 ton of coal = 2240 pounds = 1016 kilograms .475.

We sometimes find quantities stated in weights and measures that we are not used to, and we find it convenient to reduce them to others by these tables. For instance, the exhibit of the navy ration (§ 61) begins with fourteen ounces of biscuit, and if we want to know what it would be in metrical weight, we turn to Table XIII and find that one ounce avoirdupois equals 28 grams .35, which multiplied by fourteen gives 396 grams .9 (397 grams); and proceeding similarly with the other articles of the ration the table stands as follows :

Exhibit of the Navy Ration, for Each Day of the Week, in Metrical Weights and Measures.

Articles.	Quantity.	Sunday.	Monday.	Tuesday.	Wednesday.	Thursday.	Friday.	Saturday.	Weekly quantity.
Biscuit,	grams.	397	397	397	397	397	397	397	2779
Beef,	"			453.6			453.6		907.2
Pork,	"		453.6		453.6			453.6	1360.8
Preserved meat,	"	340				340			680
Flour,	"			226.8			226.8		453.6
Rice,	"	226.8							226.8
Dried fruit,	"			56.7			56.7		113.4
Pickles,	"				113.4			113.4	226.8
Sugar,	"	56.7	56.7	56.7	56.7	56.7	56.7	56.7	397
Tea, or	"	7.1	7.1	7.1	7.1	7.1	7.1	7.1	49.7
Coffee, or	"	28.35	28.35	28.35	28.35	28.35	28.35	28.35	198.45
Cocoa,	"	28.35	28.35	28.35	28.35	28.35	28.35	28.35	198.45
Butter,	"	56.7				56.7			113.4
Desiccated potato,	"					56.7			56.7
Desiccated mixed vegetables,	"					28.35			28.35
Beans,	deciliter.		2.84		2.84			2.84	7.52
Molasses,	"					2.37			2.37
Vinegar,	"							2.37	2.37

The usual manner of stating the chemical impurities of water is a little confusing, unless the relative value of these weights is kept in mind. In the Report of the Massachusetts State Board of Health for 1874, there are tabular statements of the results of analysis of the water of the various lakes and rivers of the State, and the proportions are given in parts per 100,000, and in grains per United States gallon, on consecutive pages ; but the books on this subject are not always so accommodating. In *Parke's Manual of Hygiene* (edition 1878, p. 61), the amount of certain impurities sufficient to impart taste, is given in grains per imperial gallon ; we give these quantities in tabular form, with the corresponding number of grains per United States gallon, as likewise the parts per thousand. We recommend the uniform practice of writing such numerical statements in parts per thousand, and then by reading more or less of the figures beyond the decimal point as whole numbers, we will say parts in ten thousand, parts in a hundred thousand, or parts in a million :

MAY BE TASTED IN WATER.	Grains per imperial gallon = 70,000 grains.	Grains per U. S. gallon = 58328.887 grs.	Parts per 1000 or grains per liter.
Sodium chloride, . . .	75	62.5	1.07143
Potassium chloride, . .	20	16.7	0.28571
Magnesium chloride, . .	55	45.8	0.78571
Calcium sulphate, . . .	30	25.	0.42857
" carbonate, . . .	12	10.	0.17143
" nitrate, ...	20	16.7	0.28571
Sodium carbonate, . . .	65	54.2	0.92857
Iron, ...	02	.017	0.00028

This may be read,—Sodium chloride is tasted in water, when in the proportion of one part per thousand, or one gram per liter ; potassium chloride, when about three parts in ten thousand ; magnesium chloride, when seventy-eight parts in one hundred thousand ; iron, when three parts in ten millions, or twenty-eight parts in a hundred millions, if we wish to be so exact.

The physician of the future, even the physician of the present, will write prescriptions in grams and centigrams; he will neglect and eventually forget the grains and scruples, and these in another generation will become matters of history or tradition, like groats, four-pence-ha'-pennies, and eleven-penny-bits; the decigram, the milligram, the dekagram, and the hectogram, though occasionally referred to, will not fare much better. But for the present we need simple formulæ for reducing weights of one standard to the other.

We have but to remember that the gram nearly equals (15.4) fifteen and four-tenths grains, and to compute all the rest by simple processes of mental arithmetic :

1 gram	= 15.4 grains.
10 centigrams	= 1.54 grains.
1 centigram	= 0.154 grain.
1 kilogram	= 15,400 grains, = 2.2 pounds.
100 grains	= 6 grm. .4, six grams, four-tenths.
10 grains	= 0 grm. .64, sixty-four centigrams.
1 grain	= 0 grm. .064, six centigrams, four tenths.

Instead of writing the abbreviation grm. between the whole number and the decimal, it has been proposed to draw a line from the top to the bottom of the paper, as the accountant rules his books for dollars and cents; and if we choose we may write grams over the column for grams, and centigrams over the centigrams; just as you would distinguish the different parts of a knife by writing " this is the blade " on one part and " this is the handle " on another part.

This all looks like plain sailing, but there are (50,000) fifty thousand physicians in the United States, and they will need fifty thousand lead-pencils to blacken up the margins of their books with the new weights till the printers have time to print them new books; the fifty thousand apothecaries will need fifty thousand sets of new weights; and this will encourage the mining of copper, and zinc, and tin. Who is to pay for all this? In the first place the physician and the apothecary must pay ; the sick will pay the physician and the apothecary with interest. Some of those supporting the sick earn their livelihood by making lead-pencils, some by printing, and some by mining, so that the matter moves in a circle ; with some individual inconvenience, the result is convenience and comfort; more precision, more safety ; just weights, just measures; more charity, less alms-giving ; partial evil, universal good.

AUTHORITIES.

AMERICAN JOURNAL MEDICAL SCIENCE.—American Journal of Medical Science, new series, 1841 to 1864. Philadelphia, Blanchard & Lea.

BELL.—Dietetic and Medical Hydrology. Philadelphia.

BOUCHARDAT.—Annuaire de Thérapeutique, etc. 22ème année. Paris, 1862.

BOUDIN.—Etude sur le Recrutement, etc. Annales d'Hygiene, xl, 268. Paris, 1849.

CARPENTER.—Use and Abuse of Alcohol.

CHASE.—Cincinnati Lancet and Observer. June, 1861.

CONDIE.—American Journal of Medical Science, iv, 410. Transactions of the College of Physicians.

DUNGLISON.—Human Health.

DUNGLISON.—Therapeutics.

DUNON.—Etudes sur la Verruga. Paris, 1871.

FARQUHARSON.—Poisoning by seeds of *Jatropha curcas*, by R. J. Farquharson, M.D., United States Navy. American Journal of Medical Science, xx, 102. July, 1850.

FONSSAGRIVES.—Traité d'Hygiene Navale, par le Docteur J. B. Fonssagrives, professeur, etc. Paris, 1877.

FORGET.—Naval Medicine, from the French of Forget. London, 1835.

FOURCAULT.—Comptes-Rendus. Mars, 1844.

GAMGEE.—Dangers of Slaughtering Diseased Cattle. London Lancet, February, 1864.

GODMAN.—American Natural History, by John B. Godman, M.D. Philadelphia, 1828.

HACKLUYT.—Collection of Voyages.

HAMMOND.—A Treatise on Hygiene, with Special Reference to the Military Service, by William A. Hammond, M.D. Philadelphia, J. B. Lippincott & Co., 1863.

HOLMES.—Puerperal Fever as a Private Pestilence, by Oliver Wendell Holmes, M.D. A pamphlet. Boston, 1855.

HORNER.—A Cruise in the Mediterranean.

HUGHES.—The Natural History of the Island of Barbadoes, by the Rev. Griffith Hughes, A.M. London, 1750.

JAMESON.—Linnæan Transactions. November, 1860.

KELLER.—Trichinosis. American Journal of Medical Science, xlvii, 352, April, 1864.

KNEELAND.—On the Contagiousness of Puerperal Fever, by Samuel Kneeland, Jr., M.D., of Boston. American Journal of Medical Science, xi, 45.

LA ROCHE.—Yellow Fever, Considered in its Historical, Pathological, Etiological, and Therapeutical Relations, by R. La Roche, M.D., etc. Philadelphia.

LALLAIGNE.—L'Air à Différente Hauteur, où ont respiré un grand nombre d'hommes. Annales d'Hygiene, xxxvi. Paris, 1846.

LARREY.—Surgical Memoirs.

LIND.—On Scurvy. London, 1757.

LIND.—On Hot Climates: An Essay on the Diseases Incident to Europeans in Hot Climates, with the Method of Preventing their Fatal Consequences, by James Lind, M.D., etc. Philadelphia, 1811.

MAGENDIE.—Gazette Médicale. Décembre, 1843.

MEDICAL AND SURGICAL REPORTER.—Buffalo Medical and Surgical Reporter, edited by Julius F. Miner, M.D. 1862.

MITCHELL.—Cryptogamic Vegetation the Cause of Disease, by J. K. Mitchell, M.D. Philadelphia, 1847.

PARKES.—Manual of Practical Hygiene, 1878.

PEEBLES.—Facts in Relation to Epidemic Erysipelas, by J. F. Peebles, M.D. American Journal of Medical Science, xi, 23. 1846.

QUETELET.—Expériences sur la Force Musculaire. Annales d'Hygiène, xii, 204. 1834.

SANITARY REPORTS.—Sanitary and Medical Reports, published by authority of the Navy Department.

SALISBURY.—Remarks on Fungi, with Experiments, etc., by J. H. Salisbury, M.D. Newark, Ohio. American Journal of Medical Science, xlvi, 17. July, 1863.

UNITED STATES PHARMACOPŒIA.

WOOD.—A Treatise on the Practice of Medicine, by George B. Wood, M.D., Professor, etc. Philadelphia, Lippincott, Grambo & Co. 1855.

VOCABULARY.

(The most important technical words are explained in the body of the work, and may be found by reference to the Index.)

ACRO-NARCOTIC.—Acrid narcotic; causing excitement and stupor, or coma.

ANÆMIA.—Poverty of blood.

ANÆSTHETIC.—Privative of sensation, either of the sense of touch or of the sensation of pain.

ANTHRAX.—Carbuncle. A dangerous and painful mortifying sore.

APETALA.—A subdivision of exogenous plants, characterized as being without petals. Their flower-leaves, no matter how brilliantly colored, are considered as constituting the calyx merely. Section 205.

APOPLEXY.—A sudden failure of the powers of life, partly characterized by effused blood, or great congestion in the brain. An epidemic among cattle, in which the spleen, or melt, is somewhat similarly affected, has been called splenic apoplexy.

AROMATIC.—Possessing fragrance, as the spices.

BANKED FIRES.—The slow fires kept under the boilers of steam-engines when the machinery is not in motion.

CATALYSIS.—The breaking up of the chemical constitution of a body by external force, as fire, produced in various ways.

CHOREA.—A convulsive disease, generally called St. Vitus's dance.

CINCHONA.—The Peruvian bark.

COMA.—An appearance of profound sleep from disease, so that the patient cannot be aroused.

CONTAGION.—The propagation of disease by contact, either direct or indirect, with an individual already affected by the same disease. In some cases this occurs from direct bodily contact; in others by contact with solid or liquid excretions of the sick, or by emanations from the sick carried by the atmosphere. Contagion, infection, malaria, and miasm, are often improperly used synonymously.

CRYPTOGAMIA.—The grand division of flowerless plants—ferns, mosses, and mushrooms.

DESICCATED.—Thoroughly dried.

DIAPHORETIC.—Producing cutaneous perspiration.

EMETO-CATHARTIC.—Producing or causing vomiting and purging.

EMPYREUMATIC.—Caused by the action of fire. Organic matter burned in closed vessels produces many unpleasant empyreumatic substances.

ENDOGENS.—Endogenous plants are characterized by having the wood of their stems irregularly disposed, without pith in the centre, or concentric layers of growth; leaves mostly parallel-veined, but in three or four orders a little netted; young plants with but one seed-leaf, and the leaves arranged alternately; the parts of the flower mostly in threes, never in fives.

ENTHETIC.—Inoculated diseases—those diseases caused by morbid matter applied directly to a sore, or abrasions of surface; the word is commonly applied to contagious sexual diseases.

ENTOZOON.—A parasite living within the body.

EPILEPTIC.—Belonging to epilepsy.

EXOGENS.—Exogenous plants are characterized by having stems of bark, wood, and pith; the wood growing by additions to its surface, so as to form concentric annual layers; the leaves net-veined; the young plants with two opposite seed-leaves; the parts of the flower mostly in fours or fives.

FRACTURE.—A broken bone.

GALLEY.—The cooking-stove on shipboard.

GANGRENE.—Mortification.

GASTRIC.—Having reference to the stomach.

GLUMACEA.—A subdivision of endogenous plants, with flowers destitute of any proper flower-leaves, except small scales or bristles—chaff.

GLUMES.—The husky scales which form the chaff of the grain-bearing plants and grasses.

HELMINTHA.—Worms.

HYDROPATHS.—Hydropathists. Persons who profess to believe that all diseases are best cured by the use of water without any other medicine.

ICOSANDRIA.—Of twenty anthers. This class is distinguished from polyandria (many anthers) not so much by the number of anthers as their mode of attachment. In the first, the anthers being attached to the petals, mostly five in number, are generally a regular multiple of five; while in the second class, being attached to the receptacle, they are much more irregular in number, though not necessarily more numerous.

INFECTION.—The influence on living beings of material capable of producing specific disease, whether the infecting poison be solid, liquid, or aeriform, and whether emanating from diseased individuals or from other sources. This term differs from contagion, as it includes the action of poisons emanating from other sources than from diseased individuals; thus we have yellow fever infection and malarial infection, though neither yellow fever nor the malarial fevers are believed to be contagious diseases.

LETHARGY.—Drowsiness gradually becoming more heavy, to coma and death.

MALARIA.—Malarial miasm. The poisonous emanations of marshy places, which cause the intermittent and other periodic fevers.

MIASM.—Miasma. A poison of unknown composition infecting the living body through the atmosphere; as small-pox miasm, yellow fever miasm, marsh miasm.

MONOPETALA.—A subdivision of exogenous plants, with flowers of both calyx and corolla, the corolla being all united into one petal.

NARCOTIC.—Causing sleep or stupor.

NERVOUS.—Referring to the nerves or brain.

OFFICINAL.—Kept in the shops as medicine.

PETALOIDEA.—A subdivision of endogenous plants, with flowers not collected on a spadix, but with floral envelopes answering to the calyx, or both calyx and corolla, either green or colored.

PHAGEDENIC.—Eating, wearing away.

PLANTAR ARCH.—The arch formed by the bones of the foot.

PLEUROPNEUMONIA.—An inflammatory disease of the lungs and side. A contagious cattle disease of this kind occasionally prevails.

POLYPETALA.—A subdivision of exogenous plants with both a calyx and a corolla of several petals.

PROPHYLACTIC.—Protecting against disease.

PUERPERAL FEVER, *puerperal peritonitis.* The fatal contagious fever of lying-in women.

PURULENT.—Of pus, the matter of an abscess.

SACCHARINE.—Of sugar.

SATCHEL.—Haversack, a small sack to be carried by a strap over the shoulder.

SEDATIVE.—Tending to allay irritation.

SPADICIFLORA.—A subdivision of endogenous plants with flowers on a spadix fleshy axis; mostly without calyx, or corolla, or glumes; leaves sometimes net-veined.

STERNUM.—The breast-bone.

STUPOR.—Drowsiness less profound than lethargy or coma.

SULKS.—Nostalgia; homesickness. This term is principally used with reference to African slaves.

VARIOLA. Small-pox.

VERMIFUGE.—Worm-destroying.

INDEX.

www.ingramcontent.com/pod-product-compliance
Lightning Source LLC
Chambersburg PA
CBHW060607030726
47498CB00005B/1573